WRESTLING
with JESUS

D. K. MAYLOR

ISBN: 1461087481
ISBN-13: 9781461087489

Please direct inquiries to www.WrestlingWithJesus.net

WRESTLING *with* JESUS

A candid dialogue with the Master on what Christians *must* know about their religion—but will never hear in church

D. K. MAYLOR

PROLOGUE

Looking back, I can see that his plan made sense. The tantalizing mix of secrecy and symbol, the lighthearted intrigue—the gradual circumventing of my resistance. It must have been clear that I wasn't quite ready for a head-on revelation. The *spirit* was willing, but the imagination was still far too weak.

So even as the watershed moment grew near, I could never have envisioned the astonishing events that awaited nor the grave danger they would pose to the Christian empire. Luckily, the hours ahead were still wrapped in mystery as I pulled off the interstate and made my way into the country just after dawn.

A clear spring morning was unfolding across the Old South, and the rising sun thawed the lingering night chill as I drove to a secluded area near a quiet river, not far from a lush section of foothills. With the first rays of light sneaking over the summits, I was struck by the resulting silhouette—a near-perfect rendering of a dove in flight. But while Mother Nature's shadow art was unexpected, the overall setting was not. This was definitely the place I'd been seeing in my dreams.

The dreams weren't prophetic, though; I wasn't having visions of some mystical, unknown locale. I had traveled this part of the country thirty years earlier while taking a break from college. Not sure of my life's direction after emerging from my sophomore year, I had decided just to drift awhile. And even though the trip during my youth had been routine and uneventful, somehow the place stuck with me.

Driving along in the dim early morning light, I hadn't seen another car for at least ten minutes. Nearing my destination, I pulled off the road and maneuvered my old GMC truck through an opening in the dense forest. I drove maybe two hundred yards, weaved my way back to sunlight and parked in a clearing just beyond the trees.

Alone amidst the woods, I felt I had entered my own Shangri-La, an electrically luxuriant spread of open fields that spanned about fifty acres along both sides of the river. I recognized it immediately as the location I had once visited and had recently seen in dreams. The place was deserted except for a few deer across the river and the birds chirping, chattering and squawking among the trees.

Seeing no man-made structures or any sign of a resident landowner—I was surely trespassing—I climbed out of the truck, popped the rear hatch, grabbed two folding wooden chairs and positioned them beneath some majestic oaks, brilliantly green from recent springtime rains. Forty feet away, the unruffled river flowed through from the nearby hills, and small, thriving clusters of water lilies nestled in a few inlets along the banks.

Here, near the water's edge, I began arranging my bare-bones "field office." Between the two chairs with their slightly worn seat cushions I placed a small, round patio table, about two feet high, onto which I laid some ballpoint pens, a clipboard, bottled water, and a new 500-sheet box of my preferred writing paper. Beside one chair I laid a leather satchel containing personal items and a few books, including several versions of the Bible and a pocket dictionary.

The scene now looked almost exactly the way it had appeared in my strange, recurrent dreams.

∽

The morning breeze was cold and brisk, but the sun was brilliant, warm and comforting—even healing. The country air was clean and crisp, reflecting my own growing sense of inner clarity. I grew philosophical: have we missed something? Have we spent our lives reaching and straining, bartering away the vast majority of our limited breaths and heartbeats, scraping tooth-and-nail for baskets of junk while the precious gems of creation lay strewn everywhere at our feet?

I had known for many years that by American standards I had basically missed the boat. I owned almost nothing and had never even mortgaged a house. Divorced many years and still without a life companion, I had no family of my own and made my way by doing freelance journalism and occasional odd jobs. Apart from my university days away from home, I had lived nearly five decades in the city of my birth in the Sun Belt, just a few hours' drive from the Mexican border.

Admittedly, my eccentric lifestyle had taken its toll on the psyche over the years—but on this particular day I was surprisingly free from any sense of lack and was immersed in a joyfully liberating awareness of simple, timeless existence. I felt no need to peer into the future nor any desire to swim reminiscently in that proverbial water under the bridge. My world, though outwardly Spartan, suddenly felt complete. Such breakthrough moments had been rare in my life, and I couldn't remember the last time I'd felt that kind of peace. I was blissful in a way I'd forgotten was possible. At one point I thought, "I couldn't be more content if God Himself were right here with me."

∽

In the unusual dreams that prompted me to make this trip, I was seated in one of the chairs on this very spot under the oaks next to the river. I didn't know why, but the second chair had always remained empty. As a rule, I never assigned much meaning to dreams and rarely remembered them when I awoke. I certainly felt no compulsion to analyze them. But this single, persistent dream was different, and I always recalled it with photo-like detail on the mornings after it came upon me in my sleep. This wasn't difficult, however, since the dream was always a repetition of the same basic scenario. Aside from its peculiarity, it was consistently pedestrian and nondescript.

Except for one odd thing…

In each dream, as I was calmly sitting in my chair next to the river, enjoying the view and not thinking of anything in particular, there on the ground around me, as conspicuous as a nun at a heavy metal concert, lay several brightly colored Easter eggs.

After a few weeks, the dreams subsided as abruptly as they had begun. But though short on content, they were nonetheless gripping. I simply *had* to re-visit the place—a two-day drive eastward near one of the huge forest preserves on the far side of the great Mississippi. (To satisfy the curious, let us simply call it "somewhere in Dixie.")

Heeding the apparent dream symbolism of the eggs, I had planned my arrival for a specific Sunday in April: the Christian holy day of Easter. I felt instinctively that something important might occur, but beyond that I hadn't a clue.

For many months preceding the dreams, I had pondered writing a book based on some spiritual ideas I'd been exploring. It occurred to me that, subconsciously, this might explain the reason for the dreams. Were they a sign that my inspiration for the book would finally crystallize, there in the serenity of the isolated river valley?

With everything in place, I sat down. Still wearing a light jacket to fend off the fading chill, I drew several long, deep breaths while the fast-awakening sun enveloped me in the warmth of its primeval womb. Trusting and childlike, I surrendered to its selfless nurturing and wondered how many wayfaring souls throughout history must have taken comfort from the profound glory of a simple sunrise. For several minutes I sat with eyes closed, absorbing its life-giving radiance into every cell. It was Easter morning, and my soul felt resurrected.

❧

What happened next I still cannot explain. Having lived quite some time under intense emotional strain due to my uncertain life situation, perhaps I simply fell into a sort of half-sleep and had what's known as a lucid dream, in which one plays director of his own slumber time wanderings from somewhere in consciousness limbo. Some have suggested that I merely imagined it all, suffering as I had from long periods of chronic stress.

In the end, the mechanics of the process are probably unimportant. After all, what does it matter how a man like Jesus shows up at your door? No one's going to believe it anyway. The point is, when a guy like that wants to talk, you *talk*.

In retrospect, the strangest thing about the encounter wasn't that I was interacting with one of the most revered and influential figures in history, or even that the man had overcome the generally restraining handicap of having been two millennia dead.

No, the most peculiar aspect of my meeting with Jesus was that I felt absolutely no sense of marvel while it was happening. I was exhilarated, but there were no feelings of wonderment or awe because of *him*. Not once during our momentous meeting did I question the bizarre reality of it. Yet that is precisely the thing: I did not *perceive* it as bizarre. It felt as natural as running into a good friend at the grocery or shooting the bull with the guys at the car wash.

I should note, however, that when the gathering ended I experienced a weird sense of time warp and was somewhat disoriented, unsure of the typically clear boundary between experience and imagination. The feeling reminded me of creepy testimonials I had read regarding alien abductions. I couldn't decide whether I had temporarily *entered* reality—or temporarily *left* it. Either way, what occurred during those remarkable hours remains seared in my memory and was, for me, as real as a rainstorm and as solid as a nickel-plated axe.

Due to the far-fetched nature of this account, the reader may rightfully wonder about my religious background. Reared in various Protestant churches from early childhood, I abandoned Christianity around age thirty-eight and have since gone well over a decade without the least desire to return to those roots. For me, the church had become irrelevant. I wanted neither its cloudy, futuristic comforts nor its immediate, uneasy challenges. As the years passed, Jesus had become—in my world, at least— hardly more than a name. Not just *any* name, of course, for his is a name charged with emotion, mystery and perplexity—a name with nearly unmatched historical sway, even after centuries of his absence.

Jesus Christ. Powerful. And yet so utterly defenseless, too. Indeed, what outlandish thing has not been claimed, performed or attempted in his name? And all the while, silence. Not a single response from this allegedly resurrected savior-god since his ignoble death twenty centuries past. Still, his influence remains nearly undiluted. For many, the mere mention of the man evokes a deep and visceral response. Jesus: the most loaded word of God.

Suddenly the word became flesh! Without annunciation or the slightest fanfare, one of history's most commanding figures— the man known as Jesus of Nazareth, nearly two thousand years deceased—had instantly appeared from the forest like a laid-back camper on a day hike. He walked casually out of the woods to my right and strolled easily into the clearing toward my humble bivouac by the water.

Yes, it all happened just that quickly. Jesus had come as he once warned he might—quietly, like a thief in the dark. Without speaking, he gave a friendly, relaxed nod as he took in the view, clearly appreciating the beauty of the countryside. I was so instantly comfortable in his presence that I barely gave it a second thought. Though very attentive, he too was quite cavalier.

Although I recognized Jesus immediately, to this day I cannot say why. Having been suckered by the arts, I had always envisioned him resembling Da Vinci's or Bassano's depictions in their famous portrayals of the Last Supper. But aside from his clothes, Jesus looked nothing like his traditional Western stereotype. No classic Hollywood jaw line, hazel eyes or long, flowing chestnut hair. So how had I realized it was Jesus? I simply don't know. I can only say that even though his *features* were unexpected, his identity—his *presence*—was as familiar as that of a brother.

He was, I would say, a somewhat handsome man, though certainly not a likely candidate for a celebrity magazine spread. Fit and slightly muscular, he appeared to be in his mid- to late forties. About five-ten, he weighed perhaps a hundred seventy pounds and was dressed in a long, off-white robe with a braided leather strip around the waist. He had well-worn desert sandals strapped to his feet and, except for the biblical garb, for the most part looked average Middle Eastern. His complexion was darker than usually imagined, and he had thick, slightly curly black hair with occasional woven strands of gray; dark, penetrating eyes and a short, scruffy black beard. No one going by any of the usual pictures would ever recognize him, not even at a small backyard cookout.

When our eyes finally locked, his gaze was compelling and I could hardly look away. He had a kindly, almost mischievous smile, and he behaved as though we'd known each other forever.

Without shaking hands (I realized the following day that we never actually touched) he sat down in the chair opposite me. Trying to conceal embarrassment at my curiosity, I stole a glance at his hands and feet. He responded as if my thoughts were freshly cleaned laundry hanging on a line for all the neighbors to see. "No scars," he said. "That was never the point."

We both knew why we were there: I had yearned for answers, and he was obliging me with an interview.

With this brief recounting of conditions and events, I will dispense with further details and henceforth let the following dialogue speak for itself. Here, then, is the conversation that ensued on that extraordinary day by the river…

CHAPTER ONE

DK: Well, I should've known. Just when a fella thinks he's found a quiet refuge from the storm, in walks some hippie forest hermit to break the solitude.

J: Show a little gratitude, pilgrim. That Milky Way traffic was a *nightmare*…

DK: *Heh heh.* You know, I thought this trip might hold a few surprises. Pretty clever how you laid the groundwork, what with the dreams and all. You do this on a regular basis?

J: Just when it's appropriate. I generally work best at the level of consciousness. I find it's safer that way.

DK: Yeah, I would imagine so. Your biblical life wasn't exactly a summer vacation.

J: No, I meant that it's safer for *you*. Once word gets out that I popped in on someone, they tend to be worshipped, vilified, hounded, or hauled off to a nuthouse.

DK: Oh, I see. Well, in my case that shouldn't be a problem. My résumé's not that impressive, so I don't have any reputation to defend. Besides, I don't much care anymore what people think.

J: Seems you've attained quite a level of detachment.

DK: It's the blessing of the underachiever. Believe me, what I lack in ambition I make up in apathy.

J: I can see right away that I've chosen the right guy…

DK: Say, I'm surprised you don't have an accent. Except for the outfit, you could easily pass for a guy from D.C., L.A. or Chicago. No, wait—I take that back. You'd be just fine in L.A.

J: I chose the *clothes* for *my* comfort and a *voice* for *yours*. Only a matter of convenience. I could speak full Aramaic if you'd prefer. Or even Swahili.

DK: No, no... English'll be just fine. Lately I've gotten really bored conversing in obscure African dialects.

J: Of course...

DK: Gosh, I hardly know where to begin.

J: Relax and say whatever comes to mind.

DK: It's just that you've been hallowed for so long, I wonder if I need to show some kind of special reverence.

J: Yes, you may address me with the terms "thee" and "thou."

DK: Uh... well, okay. It might be a little awkward, but I'm sure I can adju—

J: Chill out, old buddy, that was a joke. Who do I look like— Queen Elizabeth? Listen, do me a favor. Take me down from the crucifix and talk to me like you'd talk to anyone else. I don't want this meeting coming off like a re-hash of the King James Bible. Treating me special only separates us and stifles communication.

DK: Alright, what do you suggest?

J: Let's just talk like a couple of buddies down at the pool hall. No pretension, no formality, no sucking up. Is it a deal?

DK: You got it.

J: Good, now tell me whatever you'd tell your best friend.

DK: You still owe me money from last weekend.

J: Cute...

DK: Wow. A face-to-face meeting with history's most famous carpenter. I guess I should start by saying thank you. By the way—why me?

J: The network guys were booked.

DK: Serves me right, fishing for a compliment.

J: Incidentally—just for the record, I wasn't a carpenter.

DK: You weren't?

J: Nope. Wouldn't know a sawhorse from a cow pony.

DK: I'm a little confused. The sixth chapter of Mark's gospel says—

J: I know, I know—it says I was a carpenter. It's hard to get past a couple thousand years of humbug. You may not realize it, but that passage from Mark is the only one in the entire New Testament referring to me as a carpenter. The story says that people were astonished by my teachings and the miracles I was performing. They asked, "Is not this the carpenter, the son of Mary…?"

DK: Right. Seems pretty clear to me.

J: But there's a problem. Although the original word was translated as "carpenter," it's also used to describe a very scholarly person or a teacher—even a great builder. It implies someone who's a master of his trade. In the gospels, at least seven different groups called me "rabbi," which means "teacher," and various passages have people referring to my "authority" and to my "teachings." Carpenters didn't have authority, they weren't called "teacher," and they didn't have teachings. So, considering the fact there's not another scrap of evidence that I was a woodworker, which definition makes more sense—carpenter or teacher?

DK: Okay, let's go with teacher. But why the confusion?

J: Translators blew it, that's all. Probably just an honest mistake. Happens a lot, actually. To convey just a hint about the tremendous challenges of Bible translation, consider the beautiful prologue to the gospel of John. The passage famously opens, "In the beginning was the Word…" Now, the actual Greek text says that in the beginning was the LOGOS—a concept so theologically and cosmologically significant to the ancient Greek world that it merits a separate discussion of its own. To make a point, however, the term LOGOS has more than half a dozen different and complexly interrelated meanings, not one of which would even casually be translated as "Word."

DK: So like the LOGOS translation, Mark's "carpenter" bit was just a scholarly screwup.

J: As simple as that. The story is also recorded in the thirteenth chapter of Matthew. But in *that* account the people asked, "Is not this the carpenter's *son*?" Now they've got my *father* doing the hammering. The Bible has lots of discrepancies like that. Some people resolve this one by concluding that my father and I *both* were carpenters.

DK: I suppose that wouldn't be likely if your family truly descended from the royal lineage of David.

J: Actually, that "throne of David" stuff is just some dramatic New Testament spin. My family and I were never members of the dynastic hierarchy; but neither were we the common laborers most people envision. Anyway, I didn't mean to start off with a lecture. I just wanted to set things straight on a few basics. It could be awhile before my next interview.

DK: That raises an important point: Humanity's been waiting *twenty centuries* for this. What the heck took you so long?

J: Once martyred, twice shy.

DK: Seriously… after you disappeared, you just clammed up. What happened?

J: Oh, I've never stopped communicating—but the interactions are rarely physical. Problem is, most folks want *substance*. Once the body drops off, you become a "no-body." People assume that only bodies can communicate and that death renders communication impossible. So they lose interest.

DK: Well, they sure didn't lose interest in *you*.

J: That's true. With me it went the *other* way. After I left, folks started referring to me in lofty, reverent tones… like the phony way they talk about a guy at his funeral. I was idolized and deified—made into some kind of superhero.

DK: Evidently you *are* a superhero.

J: In what way?

DK: Oh, c'mon. You must know that countless millions think of you as God's only son.

J: Sure, I'm aware of that. The concept is that the great life-energy of the cosmos has a single child—*male*, naturally—whom he mysteriously conceived within Mary's womb without human intervention. I'm surprised more people haven't wondered why God didn't require this surrogate mother process when He created Adam. For him, God needed only a handful of dirt.

DK: What's that got to do with you?

J: Well, if God had *really* wanted to make an impression and prove my divinity, why not just gather a few thousand people down at the beach and have me descend from the sky, right before their eyes? Wouldn't that type of miraculous advent generate a lot more clout? Why mess with the drawn-out drama connected with a controversial pregnancy?

DK: The church says that your *humanity* is a crucial part of your makeup—so skydiving wouldn't have done the trick. Anyhow, it's not just the story of your birth that makes you different. Scripture contains lots of other assertions about your specially divine nature. For example, at your baptism a voice from heaven proclaims, "This is my beloved son, in whom I am well pleased."

J: Even if you accept that celestial voiceover bit, it certainly wasn't original. About two thousand years before my birth, pyramid texts reported the coronation ceremony of a Pharaoh. In those writings God declares, "He is my beloved son in whom I am well pleased." So there's nothing new or exclusive in the heavenly blessing story. Besides, the vaporous voice didn't say, "This is my *only* beloved son."

DK: Well, I think we just assu—

J: Not so fast with your assumptions. I never claimed to be unique or special. Not once did I refer to myself as God's only son.

DK: What about your declaration, "I and my Father are one"?

J: I was just stating the obvious. The Father and I *are* one—just as the Father and *you* are one. I never said, "*Only* I and my Father are one." Had I believed I was God's sole child or that I was the only person capable of God-consciousness, I never would have instructed my disciples, "Be ye perfect as your heavenly Father is perfect." And again, notice that I referred to God as *their* heavenly Father too. Even my famous prayer begins with the words "*Our* Father."

DK: What about this one: after your arrest in the gospel of Mark, the high priest asked you pointedly, "Are you the Christ, the Son of the Blessed?" Your answer was, "I am."

J: That encounter is described in each of the four gospels—and all four writers tell it differently. Matthew says that Caiaphas demanded, "…tell us if you are the Christ, the Son of God." In that version my response was, "*You* have said so." The gospel of Luke has another variation which reads, "…and they said, 'If you are the Christ, tell us.'" In that story I'm said to have replied, "If I tell you, you will not believe; and if I ask you, you will not answer."

DK: Sounds like double-talk from an indicted congressman.

J: In the gospel of John, there's no mention of Caiaphas even *asking* about my divinity. As for the passage you quoted from Mark, the response "I am" has been terribly misconstrued. I wasn't answering Caiaphas' question in the affirmative—otherwise I would've just said "Yes." Instead, I was making a simple but profound existential declaration: "I am." It has far more significance than you might think.

DK: What does it mean?

J: It's a statement of pure being and refers to the indefinable, unfathomable, universal Self. It's the most fundamental expression of the Great Mystery. You'll find it's pretty common among the spiritually enlightened. The words "I am" reflect an understanding of the timeless, spaceless nature of the Absolute, or what most people refer to as God.

DK: Not exactly a *Christian* concept.

J: I beg to differ. One of the most respected early Christian patriarchs, Saint Clement of Alexandria, expounded on this very idea when he described God, or what Greek cosmology refers to as "First Cause." For Clement, God was beyond space, time, name and conception.

DK: Alright, but it's certainly not a *biblical* thing.

J: Are you sure about that? In Exodus 3, Moses informs God that the Israelites are pressing him to determine God's name. But God tells Moses only this: "I AM THAT I AM." When Moses returns to his people, he announces: "I AM hath sent me unto you." I talked about essentially the same thing in John 8:58 when I explained that the eternal "I AM" existed even before Abraham.

What's wrong? You look confused.

DK: I *am*.

J: Ah well, don't stress. "I am" is just an assertion of unchangeable *beingness*. It's got nothing to do with identity, credentials or qualifications. Even in the New Testament, whenever I'm quoted making an "I am" statement, the phrase is usually followed by a sweeping metaphor: "I am the vine; you are the branches..." Things like that. Identifying with *personal* traits is extremely self-deceiving, and lots of great spiritual teachers have warned against it. So when a master proclaims, "I am," he's merely conveying that his reality is far beyond names and attributes of any kind—earthly *or* heavenly.

DK: And I thought my college philosophy final was tricky.

J: The first few eons are the toughest...

DK: So getting back to that meeting with the high priest: the gospel writer says you told Caiaphas that he would personally witness your earthly return and see you assume a leadership role at "the right hand" of God.

J: It would've been a highly arrogant prediction, to say the least. And Caiaphas obviously didn't live to see anything of the kind.

DK: In answering Caiaphas' question about your divinity, the scripture writer has you calling yourself not the "Son of God" but the "Son of *man*." And it wasn't the first time you referred to yourself that way.

J: It was an ancient title symbolizing someone who represents all mankind. Scripture writers were just using a little creative license. Surely you don't believe I went around referring to myself as "the Son of man." Would've been a little weird, don't you think?

DK: So there were others with that title?

J: Oh, lots of 'em—even in pre-Christian writings. One work, called Books of Enoch, predates Christianity and has Enoch as a kind of Messiah character who ascends to heaven and is welcomed as the

"Son of Man." He's a divine "messenger of God" who's called "the Christ" and even "a light to the Gentiles." Sound familiar?

DK: Sure. But then what's all this business about you being "God's Son"? It's caused a helluva lot of controversy.

J: Don't be too hard on my disciples. It's not unusual for students to venerate the teacher, and I certainly wasn't the first in history to be called divine. That's been going on almost since man conceived of a supreme being. Even now, you've got folks on the planet who are said to be direct incarnations of God.

DK: True, but the church bills *you* as a one-and-only. The real McCoy. A one-of-a-kind blend of God and man. I've never really understood it, but that's how you're packaged.

J: The idea that the great Superforce has only one child is ridiculous. God's offspring—or his "son," to use the obvious earthly analogy—is his entire creation. It's just a simple metaphor, for heaven's sake. Even a public school graduate oughta see *that*.

DK: Well, I can tell you one thing: the church sure doesn't view it that way.

J: I'm not responsible for anyone's interpretations. Once a myth takes hold, it's pretty tough to bring down.

DK: But even myths tend to have *some* factual basis.

J: The "son of God" idea took root in astro-theology. Like some of its predecessors, the Christian religion is *full* of links to ancient sun worship.

DK: *This* I gotta hear…

J: Well, it's no secret that earliest man revered the sun as the giver and sustainer of life. It was the most prominent thing in the sky, so it was the obvious focal point. The sun was held sacred and was worshipped for bringing the world light, warmth and a feeling of safety. Every morning was a new creation, and with each new dawn a universe of possibility sprang forth. Nighttime, on the other hand, was relatively cold, ominous and frightening. It exposed man's fear of the unknown. So it wasn't much of a stretch for ancient cultures to assume that night was ruled by an invisible "Prince of Darkness."

DK: Then it was only natural to associate light with goodness and life while connecting darkness with evil, fear and death.

J: Right. The sun alleviated man's physical and mental insecurities and was seen as the source of all cosmic benevolence. As time progressed, humans shifted their focus from the heavens to the earth and began attributing divinity to specific individuals. At first, these characters were only mythological; but eventually they included actual *historical* figures, some of whom came to be called sons or daughters of God. Like me, they were considered a mystical mix of divinity and flesh. But it all began with the celebrated daily birth of "God's sun" which, in English, also turned out to be a nice play on words.

DK: Some cultures believed the sun actually *was* God.

J: Yes, and even the Bible contains remnants of that belief. In the King James Version, Deuteronomy and Hebrews both refer to God as "a consuming fire." Now you know why.

DK: So the sun played a key role in the development of religion.

J: Absolutely. In early civilizations, each rising of the fiery orb was seen as God's re-entry into the world of darkness, and every morning the divine was literally "born again." Celestial bodies in general have historically been highly revered, and even the English words for the days of the week are reminders of the fact. The first, of course, is Sunday, which is obvious. Next is Monday, or moon-day. Then Tuesday, named after the god Tiu and connected with Mars. Wednesday is associated with the god Woden and with Mercury. Thursday, for Thor, the god of thunder, is also connected with the planet Jupiter. Friday, named after the goddess Freya, is linked with planet Venus. And finally Saturday, the day of Saturn.

DK: I'm ashamed to say it, but until this moment I never knew…

J: In the same vein, most Christians would be startled to hear that several major aspects of the gospel stories of my birth, my life and my death also have very specific astronomical and astrological corollaries.

DK: Yeah, the movie "Zeitgeist" covered that in quite some detail. I was shocked at what I learned.

J: Even some popular Christian phraseology about me can be traced back to ancient religions' humanizing of the sun—it comes walking on clouds, brings life to the world, and so forth. The sun was quite aptly viewed as a "savior from heaven" and is literally "the light that shines in darkness." In John 8:12, the writer has me claiming two very specific titles: "light of the world" and "light of life." Christians generally assume that these names originated with *me*. But they were actually ancient solar titles of the Greek god Helios, a divine personification of the sun.

DK: *Good heavens*, you might say.

J: A few more tidbits…

The ancient Egyptians knew the sun was at its highest point, or nearest zenith, when there was little or no shadow cast by the pyramid. It was then that they offered prayers to the "most high" God in his "heavenly temple," phrases you've probably heard used in church. As it set, the sun displayed a kind of corona, shooting out rays of light from its perimeter; so it went to its "death" each evening wearing a visible "crown of thorns." Even today, earthly kings are sometimes "coronated" with a crown of spikes, symbolizing the piercing rays of the sun. I could go on, but you get the idea: the oldest religions and their various gods—including ol' Sandal Straps here—have quite a bit in common with your nearest star.

DK: I think I hear thunder in the distance…

CHAPTER TWO

J: I'm glad you've developed a sense of humor about religion and its stern view of God. For millions of others, though, it's no joking matter. They envision a humorless, rigidly demanding deity who's dangerously intolerant of backtalk or scrutiny. As a result, most believers never really examine their views about the God of their religion. They may not be quite so juvenile as to see Him with a long, white beard and sitting on a throne in heaven. But they *do* generally perceive Him to be just a larger, more powerful version of their own egos.

DK: I'd say that's roughly how some folks see it.

J: It's the kind of thinking you'd expect from a third-grader, maybe—but not from educated adults. The Bible says that man was made in the image and likeness of God. But it's been observed that man continuously returns the favor by creating God in *his* image. Too many go from cradle to grave without ever questioning their spiritual foundation. As mere products of their environment, they rarely arrive at their convictions through any kind of soul-wrenching search for meaning or prolonged existential suffering. They mostly just lock onto the ideas they inherited from others and then tuck 'em away, out of sight—sort of like the letter you've got stashed in your satchel.

DK: Hey, how the heck did you kn– Oh…right. Sorry, I'm not used to dealing with omniscience. But yeah, for some reason I decided to pack that letter and bring it along. Obviously I hadn't expected to be sharing it with anyone—least of all with *you*.

J: Well, who better to hear it than its intended recipient?

DK: True, but under the circumsta—

J: C'mon, pilgrim, you were brave enough composing it in the sanctuary of your office. Show a little confidence and lay your cards on the table.

DK: Sure… ummm... I mean absolutely. Of course. Lemme see now… I suppose I could start with…. uh… well, as you obviously know, over the last few years I've grown pretty cynical about my faith, and I began having more questions than answers. I saw so much hypocrisy, even within *myself*, that I was forced to question the real benefit of Christianity—and even of religion in general. As a result, I developed serious misgivings about the Bible. Instead of ignoring passages that seemed inaccurate, conflicting or outlandish—as I had done for years—I stopped repressing and denying my doubts and began voicing my concerns to various friends and clergy.

J: But you didn't find them too helpful.

DK: Oh, they generally *meant* well. But they usually just talked around the core issues and didn't seem very willing to get their hands dirty or entertain any meaningful dissent. They always commenced with the assumption that the Bible was incontestable and that my questions must therefore have been misguided or based on gaps in my knowledge, even though they themselves couldn't fill in the gaps. Finally, just to work out a little angst and frustration, I sat down a couple of years ago and recorded my thoughts in a letter directed specifically to you. After that, I just tossed it in a drawer. I mean what else could I do? It's not like you've got mail delivery in heaven.

J: Well, we do—but it costs like hell.

DK: Oh, I get it: you're one of those *comedian* messiahs.

J: Gotta bust that media stereotype *somehow*, right? So c'mon, out with the damning epistle.

DK: Well, alright, here you go. I'll just take a walk along the river while you look it over.

J: You don't understand, comrade. I don't wanna *read* the letter. I'd like *you* to read it *to* me.

DK: What!?? Look, I know I'm responsible for my actions and all, but I honestly never imagined that I'd have to—

J: You're waffling, pilgrim. If you're gonna talk tough and issue challenges, you gotta be willing to back 'em up.

[Jesus was only playfully prodding here, but I was growing genuinely nervous. The letter was extremely hard-hitting, as he surely realized. A few moments of awkward silence followed while I stalled and fidgeted.]

J: You're apprehensive. What's the problem?

DK: Guess I'm a little embarrassed. I mean let's be frank: the letter is fairly harsh, and I was pretty darned angry when I wrote it. By the time I decided to vent, I'd begun to feel as if I'd wasted nearly thirty years of my life. Anyhow, what's the point of me reading it if you already know what it says?

J: C'mon, humor me. It'll prime the pump and give us things to talk about. Besides, you've been dying to get it off your chest. Consider it cheap therapy.

DK: Are you sure? I really hit below the belt with this one.

J: Don't worry, I never take things personally. And compared with my visit to ancient Palestine, listening to a little honest grousing is a piece of cake. Just lie down and I'll start my session timer.

DK: Well, alright… I guess there's no time like the present.

J: Actually, there's no time *but* the present.

DK: No, I suppose not… Well, okay then, here goes. But don't forget when I'm reading that you're dealing with a mere mortal—in fact, one of the *merest*.

J: Fear thee not, thou humble hack. I've got more patience than a cable guy at the Playboy Mansion.

DK: Ah, what the hell. I mean if I haven't been stricken dead *by now*… By the way, it's a little long, this thing. More like a novelette, actually. You'd better settle in awhile. And I'll have to read it straight from the paper, so it might sound a little stiff.

J: Whatever's comfortable…

[Not sure how this is going to be received, I nervously clear my throat and begin reading.]

DK: *Dear Jesus,*

> *I am writing today to announce that I have reached a critical juncture in my lifelong spiritual journey. Having been many years a zealous adherent of the Christian religion, I regret that I can no longer remain innocently trusting and compliant in my faith, nor can I timidly continue accepting the accounts of your life as presented in the four New Testament gospels. Naturally, I am forced to question as well your widely supported status as God.*
> *I fear I have reached the limits of my credulity in this matter and, unless you are willing to address my concerns, I can no more defer to the supposed authority of the Holy Bible or to any organization that endorses it.*
> *While it is not my intention to be unkind, I must convey my growing uncertainty about Christianity along with my mounting distrust of its sacred*

foundational writings. In so doing, I rely on your
purportedly benevolent and forgiving nature should I
overstep the bounds of propriety.

It is written that God once told the prophet
Jeremiah, "Before I formed you in the womb, I knew
you." I will infer that, as eternal joint-partners, you
and your Father also knew *me* in this same pre-
existential manner. As a member of the omniscient
Holy Trinity, then, you must surely have known this
letter was coming, and therefore nothing I say herein
should surprise you."

J: Pretty ceremonial so far. Sounds like a dispatch from the House
of Lords.

DK: I prefer an air of formality when corresponding with God's
direct relatives.

J: You never know who's listening in, eh?

DK: My thought exactly…

Speaking of the Trinity, allow me to begin my
process of inquiry with this, one of the great mysteries
in all religion. According to the Christian church, you
are the second component of the sacred Trinity, the
Father being the first and the Holy Spirit the third.
As I understand it, all three of you are God, each
indistinguishable and inseparable from the other two.
By simple force of logic, then, you are your own Father
and your Father is his own Son.

Regarding the Holy Trinity, therefore, we find
that the Father is God, the Son is God, and the Holy
Spirit is God—each member seemingly comprising
himself, his two colleagues, and the combination of
all three at once.

Is it possible here that Christendom is demanding
too much of its disciples? For it has bequeathed us
a holy triad consisting of an eternal Father who is
without beginning or end; a Son who, against all
earthly precedent, was inexplicably with his Father
from the beginning; and a nebulous spirit (also
referred to exclusively in the masculine) who emerged

mysteriously from the previous two but is, like them, devoid of any obvious temporal beginnings. Certainly this is all quite astounding. But just as astoundingly, the creation of this all-male deity trio was wholly accomplished with nary a female involved!

As you know, I am a man of at least average intelligence. I must confess my difficulty, however, in comprehending the existence of beings who are simultaneously separate and connected, different but identical, and partial yet complete. It is incomprehensible that three entities of different kind and quality could be merged into one, each representing a distinct and discernable *part* of God, yet ever equating to *all* of Him as well.

While this arrangement challenges every shred of instinct and sensibility, the church insists that we regard the Holy Trinity as a single unit. "After all," your clergy is quick to remind us, "there is but *one* God."

The official position is that understanding the Trinity is not essential to our salvation. For this most welcome consolation, I offer a joyous and grateful "Hallelujah!" To the church's further assertion that such things are simply unfathomable to human intellect, I wearily and wholeheartedly reply, "Amen."

J: Wow. I haven't been needled like this since Calvary.

DK: Believe me, there's a pincushion full of needling where that came from…

Please understand that this thorny proposition of three-gods-in-one has apparently not been a major barrier for most believers. But I did want to provide example of the peculiar and sometimes distressing concepts advanced by your church to its constituents.

Notwithstanding that you have been with your father from the beginning, the Trinity was not a part of ancient Judaism, which is, of course, Christianity's very foundation. Biblically the term "Trinity" is never used, nor is the concept ever really explained. Perhaps scripture writers simply found it too difficult to manage in the limited span of only sixty-six books.

But now, on to more serious matters…

As you must know, there exist gaping holes and critical discrepancies in the records your followers provided us after your death. Not least among these is the glaring disagreement between the gospels of Matthew and Luke regarding your genealogy. Although both writers claim that you descended directly from the throne of King David, Matthew records only twenty-eight generations involved while Luke lists a full forty-three. Disturbingly, this biblical "generation gap" implies a time differential of two or three hundred years at the very least.

To cite just one incongruity, Matthew says that your paternal grandfather was a man named Jacob. Luke, however, declares that the fellow's name was Heli. Given the supposed infallibility of Christian scripture, such striking irregularities may hardly be considered trivial. Scholars and laymen alike have found it highly troublesome that, apart from identifying your father as Joseph, the authors of Luke and Matthew cannot agree on even a single name in the entire messianic lineage.

Still more confusing is why these gentlemen even *bothered* delineating Joseph's prestigious bloodline, when both writers go great lengths, by way of the virgin birth report, to explain that Joseph played no part whatsoever in your creation and that he was not your father in the first place!

In theory, all Christian scripture was inspired directly by the Holy Spirit (who via the mystical Trinity is also you). Apparently you engaged in a kind of virtual dictation to the authors of the holy canon. I suggest, however, that you might have gained far more credence amongst doubters by supplying the four gospel writers with substantially more history of your life. We know so little of your infancy, your childhood and your development as a young adult.

Our greatest interest, naturally, would lie in having a thorough description of the details surrounding your conception and your birth. Was your mother truly a virgin impregnated by God—inseminated, as it were, by the Holy Spirit? If so, why were we given so little information on this most remarkable historic event?

Certainly you are aware that, aside from grocery store tabloids, reports of such strange affairs are exceedingly unusual. As skeptics are quick to point out, the validity of the virgin birth account hinges entirely on a dream by your father. (Or did you consider Joseph your stepfather?) Further weakening the story's credibility, the content of the alleged dream is, suspiciously, relayed to us by a third person who was not an eyewitness or even personally familiar with any of the key figures involved.

Frankly, good sir, this seems precarious stuff on which to build a major world religion. One must be impressed, however, by Christianity's establishment of such widespread, unquestioning acceptance of the virgin birth story, even well into the age of modern science. For if a woman nowadays were to announce she had become pregnant by the Holy Spirit, she would not likely find many believers, regardless of any revelatory dreams to which her husband might make claim.

Can we in the present age safely rest our faith on such scant evidence concerning your special conception? Is it possible that a few of your passionate supporters simply embellished the story in their zeal to advance the Christian cause?

I wonder: did news of your mother's divinely inceptive pregnancy cause any scandal? Were the townsfolk aware of the details behind her impressive claim? Did they express concern that the entire scenario depended wholly upon scientifically unverifiable events such as personal dreams and private angelic visitations?

I do not mean to—excuse the pun—belabor the virgin birth. But I feel the subject should be broached, as it contains crucial implications for all subsequent assertions about your life.

Also regarding your advent: how are we to reconcile the statement that a star led the wise men to your birthing place? Although I am no astronomer, as far as I can determine stars do not normally change *course. Was it a special kind of star worked up just for that exceptional occasion—or was it the common variety we have today?*

No doubt your heavenly Father could have easily synchronized your birth with the normal path of a star already existing. But that could indicate, as some have proposed, that the "wise" ones who initially found you were actually astrologers, since few others routinely pay much attention to the stars. It is well known that the Bible contains scores of important astrological allusions and related symbology. Why, then, does it also carry so many warnings and injunctions concerning the practice of such ancient arts?

Here is yet another puzzle: The church declares that you existed before time. Did you, therefore, retain self-conscious awareness during your nine months' gestation? Did you possess God-consciousness from the very beginning of your human existence? Did you, as a young boy, realize that you were the ruler of the universe and the Lord of all creation?

CHAPTER THREE

J: Say, you sure you're not holding back?

DK: Pretty raw stuff, eh?

J: *Sheesh.* There's more sugar coating on the average cold tablet.

DK: Sorry if it comes across sounding a little crass. I'm afraid tact was never one of my virtues.

J: Don't fret, pilgrim. I didn't show up expecting diplomacy: I know you too well. Just throw the old 'dozer back in gear and plow ahead.

DK: That's the way to take it like a man! Okay, back to business…

I'm afraid you must forgive me, dear Jesus, for my crude impertinence. But what thinking person could read the astonishing content of Christian scripture and fail to raise an eyebrow of suspicion? Thus do I merely seek rational explanation for that which appears, from this end, both dubious and impractical.

For instance, if you were born into this world fully-God, did you have to study in school—or did you know all things right from the start? Were the other kids jealous? Were the instructors resentful? Did they all know that you were God?

And what of your romantic life? Most Christians assume that you lived a monk-like existence even from early adulthood. As a young man, did you never kiss a woman? Did you never spend time with girls or have the feeling that you were falling in love?

As you may know, there has been much speculation over the centuries about your relationships with various women of the gospels, especially Mary Magdalene. Yet there is scarcely a biblical hint that you possessed any ordinary manly desires for the gentler sex.

If you were in fact amorous with women, however, I believe Christendom would be much better off knowing it. Have you observed the unnatural and puritanical sexual eccentricities that have long afflicted earthly societies? Is it possible that religion is largely responsible for much of the perverse obsession, fear and inhibition that humans have developed around sex and the physical body?

Even today, the Roman Catholic Church upholds that your mother remained a virgin to her death. This doctrine is perpetuated despite scriptural passages—Matthew 13:55, for example—which clearly indicate you had several brothers and sisters.

By defending the principle of your mother's uninterrupted virginity, the church implies that sex is somehow unclean—perhaps even spiritually impoverishing. It insinuates that Mary's image would in some way be tarnished had she indulged sexually with her own husband, even if she had done so *after* her "miraculous" initial conception.

But are we to believe that your parents had a lifelong marriage during which they never engaged in sex? If so, would this not indicate that each of your siblings was also divine? Should they not each be highly revered, just as you have been? (And should not your father be considered one of our greatest and most disciplined saints?)

More to the point, why would belief in your mother's perpetual chastity be crucial to our faith or salvation? And speaking of human sexuality, why has religion been so long preoccupied with this topic? Is it truly any business of the clergy what men and women do consensually behind closed doors? Why does the church so confidently presume the right to interfere in even the most personal aspects of humanity's daily life? Its bothersome meddling spills over into nearly every facet of society, including seeking *political* influence in an effort to make its arbitrary moral code *legally compulsive*, even upon those who reject its authority outright!

But is the church's *own* house in order? Certainly you are aware of the sordid, and often shockingly perverted, sexual histories of various priests, ministers and other representatives of the faith. The long and sorry record of ecclesiastical hypocrisy is deplorable, and one wonders whether your church, instead of poking its nose into the bedrooms of its parishioners, might be far better served governing the activities within its own rectories, convents, monasteries, vestries and sacristies.

Sexual indiscretions of church officials make headlines with increasing frequency, and it now seems clear that ministerial hanky-panky is merely symptomatic of the same anxiety, confusion, guilt, shame and frustration that organized religion has long engendered amongst the laity. A case in point: the church implies on the one hand that sex is mostly impure and morally diminishing but that, on the other hand, we should save it for someone we love!

Ostensibly, the church views sex as only an animal instinct, included in the divine plan solely to propagate the species. Saint Paul himself portrays sex within marriage merely as a kind of workable compromise with sin. Official pronouncements on the subject are, at best, highly conflicted and bewildering. Is it any wonder, therefore, that so much of our societal dysfunction is centered in the subject of sex?

And what of your own teachings, sir? Unless you meant something far different from what has been recorded, I must take serious issue with some of your instructions to your followers. For example, how is it you found it wise to declare that if someone steals my coat, he is then also entitled to my cloak? Is not this rewarding of criminal behavior quite likely to further encourage it?

As for some of your stricter teachings, do you still think it sensible to instruct us, as you do in Matthew 18, to cut off our hands and pluck out our eyes if they should somehow give us offense? Such draconian measures will no doubt ensure that the left hand will not know what the right hand is doing (indeed, at a given moment it may well be unaware even of its general *location*).

Since many Christians are put off by your numerous austere edicts, few of your followers, if any, fully obey them. Pragmatically, the task appears impossible, and your growing flock must surely disappoint you at every turn.

With so much opportunity for its members to transgress, it is little wonder that the church has placed such high emphasis on confession of sin. In this regard, it would seem that Roman Catholics are especially to be pitied, since they are encouraged to visit their clergy routinely and delineate their moral failings *in person*. As the Church of Rome now boasts well over a billion members, one marvels that a single parish priest is ever able to set foot outside his confessional.

CHAPTER FOUR

J: You know, on second thought, maybe you could save time by just strapping me to a post for a public flogging.

DK: *Heh heh.* I told you this wouldn't be pleasant. You should've dropped in years ago, before I lost *all* sense of reverence.

J: No worries. I love being the target of a one-man roast.

DK: I'll give you one thing: you've got the patience of a bloody saint.

J: Yeah… well, keep goin' there, Shakespeare. You wouldn't wanna lose your momentum.

DK: Alright, then, back to the defamation…

> Here is yet another of your messianic mandates that has long caused me concern. In Luke 14 you insist that your followers must hate their parents, spouses, children and siblings before you will adopt them as disciples. Ignoring that this bizarre declaration comes directly from the alleged Son of God, how would breeding intra-family hatred help further your cause of brotherhood, harmony and peace? Does not this twisted decree conflict with your instruction that we should "love one another"? And does it concur with the Ten Commandments, which clearly state that we are to *honor* our fathers and mothers?
>
> In similar manner, did you not prevent your disciples from honoring their parents when, in the ninth chapter of Luke, you refused to let them return home to bid their families farewell? Surely their request to do so was not unreasonable. Indeed, were they not ready to surrender everything dear to them for your sake?
>
> Also, did you not dishonor *your own* mother when you rebuked her at the marriage party in Cana? And did you not do so again in Matthew 12 when you asked her, "Who is my mother?"

Following is another example of scriptural incoherence: In Mark 9 you tolerantly declare, "He that is not against us is for us." Yet in Matthew 12 you reverse course entirely by adopting a far less lenient stance: "He who is not with me is against me." These two pronouncements clearly contradict, both in spirit and by way of logic. Were you uncertain of your position on this matter—or did you merely change your mind?

Further, did you in fact proclaim, "I come not to bring peace, but a sword"? If you did actually make this ominous pronouncement, then you deviated completely from your assurance to the Apostles James and John, in Luke 9, that you had come not to *destroy* men's lives but to *save* them.

According to Isaiah, you are to be called "Wonderful," "Counselor," and "Prince of Peace." Did the Old Testament prophet have it all wrong, or shall we be on the lookout for a newer, less violent Messiah?

Ironically, world history is awash with the blood and misery of severe Christian intolerance, the chronic carnage of which speaks for itself. Under church supervision, millions of innocents over the ages have, in the name of Christ, been sanctimoniously ostracized, harassed, humiliated, tortured, brutalized and murdered.

It would appear, sir, that your declaration was spoken quite in earnest and that you truly *did not* come to bring peace. And God knows your religion has given full play to the sword! Indeed, your forewarning of Christian violence would seem thus far to be one of the few New Testament prophecies actually to materialize.

[Now I was *really* feeling uncomfortable. I stopped reading and looked up to address Jesus directly.]

Maybe we'd better quit right here. The rest can just wait for another time.

J: No, no—I'm thoroughly enjoying it. Just the right mix of indignant anger, cutting humor and healthy disbelief. Besides, it's nice hearing a little heartfelt candor now and then. You'd be surprised how much brown-nosing and groveling comes my way. You willing to go on?

DK: Are you kidding? I have not yet *begun* to bitch…

Moving along, I feel I would be seriously remiss not to inquire about the great Fall-and-Redemption theme that permeates so much of Christian scripture. It is, after all, the very backbone of the faith.

To begin, it seems patently absurd for God to have created humanity and then complain that it was not up to standard. Clearly if there is anyone with whom God should find fault in this regard, it is yourself and the Holy Spirit. Instead, divine wrath seems to be forever focused upon *mankind*—as if we had begged God for our creation and He then grudgingly complied with the request.

But the entire human fiasco is solely *God's* responsibility, as it is logically apparent that we mortals were created quite without our knowledge or consent. Nevertheless, when bemoaning the sins of the world, you and your heavenly Father seem ever wont to point the accusing finger earthward.

As a result of your displeasure, you continue subjecting countless billions to the potential sufferings of eternal damnation, a practice which seems unjustly over-reactive, to say the least. Surely we cannot all be held liable merely because our Edenian ancestors could not follow simple instructions.

Having now collected twenty centuries of data by which to evaluate the results of your believe-or-be-damned policy, have you and your Father found reason to question whether there is truly any wisdom in it? How are you doing, statistically speaking, in your "salvation" effort? Is your sinner-to-convert ratio satisfactory? Are you happy with the results of this hit-or-miss strategy?

In brief, do you still find it wise to expose your mortal brethren to the possibility of everlasting torture simply because some of them are unable to believe that which they honestly find unbelievable? Is it realistic or fair to require someone to embrace a proposition whether he is sincerely convinced of it or not?

And what of believers from *other* religions? Are you thoroughly insensitive to *their* cherished values and philosophies? Do you expect them to drop years of deeply ingrained learning or centuries of cultural tradition and immediately take up practicing Christianity? Is this even slightly reasonable, coming as it does from the source of all intelligence?

Why, in your omniscience, did you and your Father allow ancient religions to develop at all? Why permit them to blossom without interference if you knew that Christianity was forthcoming and that all non-Christians were to be ultimately condemned? If you earnestly desired all peoples to be Christian, why did you not descend to earth immediately upon learning that Adam and Eve had rebelled? And finally, which God was responsible for inspiring pre-biblical religions in the first place?

Next, are you aware that those most intent on Christian proselytizing are often found by non-believers to be narrow-minded, irrational and disrespectful? Having been once among their ranks, I can attest first-hand that many of these zealots are frequently demanding, inflexible and even openly cruel in their efforts to gain new converts.

Do you find it effective to use such persons to convey your supposed message of non-judgment and unfaltering love? Do you know that many of them are, in your behalf, distributing disgraceful, shallow-minded literature aimed at frightening non-believers into professing you as the Christ? These embarrassing publications contain laughable and inane cartoon scripts depicting, for example, ridiculous end-of-the-world dramas and absurd scenarios of the "Rapture."

Tell me, sir: do you feel your movement is well served by such childish ignorance and outright silliness? Moreover, can a man be considered truly "saved" having been driven into the Christian fold solely by way of stark terror? Are you in fact pleased with the perverse strains of religion dispensed at the hands of such fear mongers?

Might it be better to employ in your expansion efforts those persons who have proven to be examples of light, love, wisdom, gentleness, reason, tolerance and compassion? To be candid, given distressing biblical accounts of your own harsh words and behavior, I now question if it is realistic even to think of you as possessing such noble attributes.

J: *Ouch.*

DK: Oh yeah, brother. And I'm just now finding my rhythm...

Next, are you aware that vast sums of money are generated daily in the name of "Jesus Christ"? Enormous infrastructures and massive organizations have been created to wield power and influence in your name. And I am sorry to report that our radio and television airwaves are now jammed with programming by so-called "Christian" ministries, some of which are hosted by the most pretentious, self-righteous personalities conceivable.

Are you comfortable with these disingenuous men and women systematically bilking millions of credulous believers by promising healing, wealth, good fortune or other special blessings in return for monetary contributions? Some of these swindlers enjoy lives of luxury and even shocking extravagance, while many of their gullible benefactors scrape by on almost nothing.

Is this kind of institutional proliferation and personal profiteering the sort of thing you envisioned when you began your ministry? Does not all this pomp and circumstance oppose your declaration that one cannot serve both God and money? Does it not also ignore your command not to make "a show" of one's religion?

Sadly, Christianity has become a thriving industry and I cannot believe that such was ever your intent. Am I right to suspect that you would consider it all a gross distortion of your original message of simplicity and humble devotion to God? Would not the public displays of piety you found so reprehensible during your lifetime be just as abhorrent to you now?

By and large, it is my view that religion's influence on mankind has been anything but constructive. Admittedly, various faiths occasionally spawn exemplary purveyors of wisdom and beacons of spiritual light. As a rule, however, the limited goodness emanating from religion has rarely compensated for the disastrous and far-reaching effects of its overall dysfunction.

Religion in general, and your church in particular, bears a long and shameful history of arrogance, intolerance, divisiveness, judgment, hypocrisy, persecution and violence. Indeed, one could argue, perhaps, that Christianity has furnished quite compelling evidence for the existence of a wicked devil; but hardly has it provided convincing proof of a loving or compassionate God.

CHAPTER FIVE

J: Feeling any better yet?

DK: Actually, it's kinda fun unloading on you like this. Nothing personal, though, right?

J: Not at all. We messiahs specialize in catering to the ignorant.

DK: Gee, *that's* good to know.

J: Please, go right on dumping.

DK: Alright. But remember, this was *your* idea…

As for your personal character, we are told in the gospels that you once exploded with anger inside the Temple, throwing furniture and assailing the Temple's moneychangers with a whip. Is this account accurate?

If so, does not such an attack directly impugn your decree to your followers that they should be "wise as serpents, and harmless as doves"?

Can your behavior that day justly be reconciled with your admonitions to your disciples that they should "resist not evil" and that, when confronting wickedness, they should promptly "turn the other cheek"? Did you truly consider non-resistance the best policy—or were you merely hoping to boost your odds of winning when starting brawls at church?

Also, did you later consider that your hand had "offended" you during those moments of anger in which you laid a whip to the Temple vendors? Can this outright case of assault and battery be construed as anything less than *sin?* If not, why are we told time and again that you were wholly pure and sinless? And why did you not immediately sever the hand that enabled you to commit this transgression? Perhaps the whipping incident caused you to reevaluate your official policy of limb-lopping. But why, then, were we not informed of this important doctrinal revision?

Pressing ahead, I am impelled to ask about another scriptural austerity that has long had me perplexed. In the fifth chapter of Matthew, you gravely declare that whoever insults a man by calling him a fool shall be liable to the torments of hell. Frankly, I am shocked and distressed that the loving Lord of the Ages appears unable to forgive this relatively trivial offense and apparently stands ready to consign violators to the fires of everlasting vengeance!

Given this unusually severe penalty for a moment's indiscretion, it is clear that God considers such misconduct altogether intolerable. However, if that is truly the case, then how is it that you felt no twinge of hypocrisy, nor apparently any concern for the safety of *your own* eternal soul, in blatantly referring to the Pharisees as fools? You did this not once but twice—first in Matthew 23 and yet again in Luke 11. The latter incident is especially distressing, since one of the Pharisees you were berating had kindly invited you to join him and his friends for dinner. Upon arrival, you began hurling insults and invectives at nearly everyone present.

Poor table manners aside, did you not recall your own uncompromising injunction against calling someone a fool? And did you forget the grave and irreversible consequences of such behavior? Furthermore, should we not find it extremely confusing that in Luke 12 God Himself calls the rich landowner a fool? Are these accounts merely the result of faulty translations, or shall we conclude that you and your Father remain safely exempt from adhering to the rules you so freely impose on others?

Also, what of the report that you once swore at a fig tree solely because it bore no fruit? Is it proper for a spiritual leader to go around scolding perfectly innocent vegetation? The bizarre practice of cursing inanimate objects would appear to set a very poor example of detachment and self-control.

Tell me, hallowed sir: Were there other circumstances in which you felt obliged to denigrate your own creations? Did you ever curse a cow, for instance, simply because it carried no milk? Were you equally disturbed when encountering honeyless beehives or eggless hens?

Next, can you explain your statement to your disciples in Matthew 24 that their generation would not pass away before you returned to earth? How utterly confusing that you would foretell the exact timing of your Second Coming while stating immediately afterward, "Of that day and hour no one knows, not even the angels of heaven, *nor the Son,* but the Father only."

You further predicted that during your disciples' generation the sun would be darkened, the moon would cease giving light (to be expected, of course, given the extinguishing of the sun), the stars would fall from the sky, the powers of the heavens would be shaken, and you would return in clouds of glory.

These declarations were made with quite some degree of authority and resolve, and the objective reader is virtually forced into a single, inescapable conclusion: you believed the end of the world was imminent.

It is curious, therefore, that you next issued The Great Commission, whereby your disciples were to begin traveling the globe and establishing your fledgling church. Yet what was the purpose of this directive? For if a man knows the world is quickly nearing destruction, why would he bother building anything?

As some two thousand years have elapsed since your predictions, modern observers must wonder if perhaps you were mistaken in your prophecies regarding the world's conclusion. Is it possible you grossly miscalculated the timing of this important eschatological event?

On a more somber note, would you mind clarifying the exact nature of your execution? Was it death by crucifixion, as stated in the four New Testament gospels? Or were you hanged in a tree, as claimed in Acts 5 and again in Acts 10? While addressing this point, you might expound as well on the death of your disciple Judas. The book of Matthew says that after he betrayed you, Judas "went and hanged himself." But Acts 1:18 says that Judas died from a serious fall in which his stomach split open and his entrails were spilled.

In a related issue, the land upon which Judas met his infamous demise came to be called 'The Field of Blood.' Merely as an item of interest, who was the rightful owner of this property? Was it Judas himself, as stated in Acts, or was it the chief priests, as declared by the writer of Matthew?

Lastly, the Apostles' Creed states that, when you died, you descended directly to the fiery depths of hell, where you allegedly spent the next two days. Yet you are said to have told one of the criminals with whom you were crucified, "Today you will be with me in paradise." Was your partner in execution not greatly disappointed upon his arrival instead to the sooty, smoking pits of Hades? And was he not profoundly confused at your odd conception of paradise?

> The Christian church staunchly maintains that its scripture is divinely inspired and is therefore inerrant. But as illustrated by these examples, the Bible contains numerous discrepancies and factual misstatements—scores and scores at the very least. That so, what are we to conclude of the idea that God is infallible? And alas, where does this leave the poor Pope!?

[Once again I paused to test the waters.]

DK: How we doin'?

J: I'm not sure whether to keep laughing or call for backup.

DK: We can stop here if you'd like.

J: Are you *nuts*? I haven't had this much fun since Jim and Tammy Faye went national…

CHAPTER SIX

DK: I gotta give you credit: so far you've been a pretty good sport.

J: Don't get too comfortable; I'm just biding my time. Better get your licks in while you can.

DK: Alright, then, on with the drubbing…

> And now, respected sir, I regret that I must become even more irreverent and still harsher in my demands for additional insight regarding the Christian faith. For this next subject is so vastly important, so existentially significant, so crucial to everything for which Christianity stands, that tiptoeing around it would be negligent beyond pardon.
> I warn you now that I will be as fervent in my critique of this subject as your church has been in its

confident proclamations about it. I am referring, of course, to the Christian theology of salvation.

To begin, we are told in the Holy Scriptures that before you commenced your ministry you ventured into the desert, where you then prayed and fasted forty days and forty nights. While this claim would appear most improbable, you certainly deserve the benefit of the doubt. Perhaps, like some modern yogis and other spiritual adepts, you possessed a great deal of esoteric knowledge, providing you nearly superhuman control over your physiology. I can even allow that you may in fact have survived nearly six weeks without food. Beyond that, however, I begin having earnest reservations. Let me explain...

Scripture declares that when your forty-day fast had ended, you were hungry. Now, please be assured that regarding the truth of this *particular* assertion I have no doubt whatsoever. But my suspicion is aroused by what is reported to have happened next: for the gospels tell us that you were then visited by the devil, Satan himself.

Is this a fact? If so, why did your deadliest foe feel so confident and secure in your presence? How could such an encounter so casually unfold? Was this the same kind of light-spirited, God-and-devil interplay that occurred centuries earlier involving the Old Testament character Job? Did you ask Satan, as God did more than once in the Book of Job, where he had just come from and what he had been doing?

Are we to understand that, in a given moment, the God of creation knows neither the devil's whereabouts nor his activities? Can you see how your ignorance in this regard might cause humanity a great deal of concern? For if God Himself is unaware that Satan lurks just around the corner, how may *we* reasonably be expected to know it?

I have often wondered: what did the devil look like when he showed up that day? Was he bearing a tail and horns and carrying a pitchfork, as so often depicted in drawings? Was he wearing clothes? Was he red, as in the pictures—or did he look like any average fellow in the Judean wilderness?

An obvious question arises: why is the devil allowed to roam the earth freely when, as I understand it, all other souls condemned to hell are restricted eternally to the immediate campus?

If I may, allow me to examine in detail that day's reported sequence of events and explain why I believe them to be highly relevant to the Christian notion of redemption…

The first occurrence in this story, according to Matthew's gospel, is that Satan, who evidently knows you have not eaten for several weeks, tries coaxing you into making bread from surrounding stones. What he hoped to gain by prodding you to change rocks into bread is never explained, so let us simply assume that he too was getting a little hungry.

Nevertheless, this is where the story begins to lose my support. Because it is here, scripture maintains, that upon confronting the Great Tempter you immediately begin discussing philosophy.

Unless this drama has been terribly misreported, you who are the Light of the World are given opportunity in that moment to slay the much-loathed Prince of Darkness on the spot. Doing so would have liberated the world at once and forever from the onslaughts of corruption, sin, guilt, suffering and death. Indeed, did not the negation of Satan and his evil influence constitute your entire earthly mission?

Instead of killing him, however, you strangely chose to engage the ancient Lord of Destruction by quoting a scripture. What exactly were you hoping to accomplish?

I cannot sufficiently emphasize my complete bewilderment concerning this allegedly Spirit-inspired accounting of your behavior. In this single, pregnant historical moment, one of incomprehensible theological magnitude, the Great Enemy strolls right into your desert camp, apparently unencumbered, and boldly begins issuing bizarre challenges to the omnipotent Master of Creation!

Now, it is clear from scripture that you knew this obnoxious fellow was Satan. Therefore, as God, you easily could have ended his injurious reign simply by kicking his diabolical derriere. Are we to believe instead that the best plan you could formulate was to commence a verbal wrestling match? What, in the name of sanity, were you thinking!?

If, as the church avows, you are an ever-loving deity, why did you not finish off the heinous celestial maverick then and there? Would not an ever-loving God leap at such an obvious opportunity to "save us all from Satan's power"? Is it possible you are not ever-loving after all? Or were you temporarily out of your ever-loving mind?

We are told that you once proclaimed to your disciples, "All power is given unto me in heaven and in earth." Why, then, did you not choose to *invoke* your unlimited power in that moment? Did you not realize that doing so would have rendered all subsequent suffering—your own, as well as ours—forever unnecessary and moot? Since you did declare that you had come to bring not peace to the earth but a sword, why, in heaven's name, did you not gird up your loins that morning and *use* the damned thing!?

Whatever the reason, your decision not to destroy the universal perpetrator of evil while he was incarnated there before you was nothing short of madness. It remains, in my opinion, the most calamitous show of poor judgment in the history of this miserable, suffering world. For it is beyond mortal comprehension that you allowed the infamous Grand Villain to slip through your fingers when you had the chance to cut him down for good. And your refusal to conclude forever these burdensome heaven-and-hell dramatics remains, in my assessment, eternally unforgivable.

J: At least you're not bitter.

DK: I warned you this would be brutal… but hey, why the big grin?

J: Cynicism is a beautiful thing.

DK: You're not upset?

J: Upset? Not a chance. I love hearing the shallow ramblings of a pseudo-intellectual.

DK: Oh yeah? Well, I'm glad you're enjoying the show, because there's several more acts before the final curtain.

J: Then by all means, please proceed with your little melodrama. Wouldn't have any popcorn, I suppose?

DK: No, but there's plenty of stones around if you care to make the conversion.

J: Only works for bread. Oh well, no matter… back to the frontal assault.

DK: Right… where was I?

J: Zorro of Bethlehem meets Lucifer of Hades.

DK: Ah yes, here we are…

> To be sure, the world has paid a dear price for your staggering failure to eliminate Satan that day in the desert. Certainly you must realize—and please indulge the pun—the grave implications of that fateful decision. Your refusal to slay the feared Wicked Warrior has resulted in countless billions subsequently falling prey to him and his demonic minions. As I shall soon demonstrate, most of humanity will suffer the deathless tribulations of damnation directly because of you and your short-sighted dealings with the devil.
> Make no mistake: your decision to allow Satan to continue his crusade of temptation and terror was a stark and hypocritical repudiation of everything you espoused, defying both your recorded teachings and all precepts of logic, compassion, and common sense.

J: Man, when you start shooting, you really empty the clip.

DK: Oh, you ain't heard *nothin'* yet…

> Moving forward, the writer of Matthew next informs us that after your first recitation of scripture to Satan, he took you to the holy city of Jerusalem. If I may be so bold as to inquire, do you frequently take such excursions with the Archenemy? Did you go willingly that day, or were you coerced? Did you and Lucifer walk

together, and did you swap stories about the good old days in heaven when you and he were still on the same team? Did the two of you ever get anything to eat?

Here again I shall offer the courtesy of erring on the side of leniency. Perhaps, being able to maneuver superhumanly, you and Satan did not journey together but agreed instead to rendezvous at the Temple. Travel arrangements notwithstanding, however, either you meekly complied with the devil's request or you objected. If you did go amiably, would this not constitute yet another serious hypocrisy? Would it not contradict the many New Testament admonitions to avoid temptation? Would it not, in fact, negate the very specific instruction in the Book of James to "Resist the devil and he will flee from you"?

Why, therefore, would you agree to travel anywhere with the great Foe of the Faithful? Is it your habit to comply with Satan's demands in this manner, or were you simply providing the definitive illustration of your directive to "Resist not evil"?

Perhaps now you can understand why your detractors, and even some of your supporters, are so guarded or skeptical regarding the biblical chronicling of your life. Might it not be wise at this point to issue some kind of update or clarification on these narratives?

Straining the limits of scriptural credibility, the gospel writer next avers that, upon arrival in Jerusalem, the devil took you immediately to the pinnacle of the great Temple. But again, does Satan have such control and influence over God that he can whisk Him around in this fashion?

More importantly, did the devil explain to you beforehand why he was cajoling you to the top of the Temple—or did you not think to ask the reason for this strange request? Did anyone try to stop the two of you from hoisting yourselves onto the holy edifice? Were there, in fact, any witnesses to this remarkable event? If so, had they any idea that the two fascinating characters conversing on the revered structure were God and Satan themselves? Or was it perchance nighttime, so that no one could see what was happening?

> Given my present poor cash flow, would you object to my earning a few dollars by commemorating this enthralling episode with a screenplay? Which title do you prefer: *Savior on the Roof,* or *Devil on a Hot Tin Turret?*

CHAPTER SEVEN

J: I see you're not letting decorum stand in the way of pandering to your ego.

DK: Okay, so I took a few cheap shots. Unfortunately, you'll find things getting even cheaper pretty quickly.

J: I'm on the edge of my seat.

DK: Then you want me to continue?

J: Oh, more than life itself.

DK: Well, we've still got a ways to go. But don't worry, you're gonna *love* the ending.

J: You can say *that* again.

DK: Getting a little touchy?

J: Nah, just kidding. Go ahead, proceed with the execution.

DK: Right on….

> Once you and Satan had reached your destination at the Temple's apex, the devil seemingly used your own strategy against you by provoking you with scripture. Then, like a five-year-old badgering a playmate who has just climbed onto a high tree branch, he challenged you to leap off, cynically goading you to trust angelic guardians to break your fall and save you from harm.

Instead of *chiding* the devil for this time-wasting bit of lunacy, you inexplicably decided, yet again, to reel off another scripture. But while you were verbally jousting with the sullied Stealer of Souls, did the larger picture of salvation ever cross your mind? Did it occur to you that you had been given still another opportunity to forever terminate human suffering and condemnation? Think of all you might have accomplished there on the templetop simply by giving the sinister bastard a little shove!

Moving forward in the story, the gospel writer tells us that after your roguery with the devil in Jerusalem, he next took you to "a very high mountain" and there showed you "all the kingdoms of the world." Is this claim *literally* true? Did Satan actually sweep you to the top of a mountain? And could you truly see every city in the world from its summit? Which mountain was it? Did you get a good view of Rhode Island and New Jersey?

J: Skeptic, skeptic, why do you persecute me?

DK: Sorry, I couldn't resist. That last jab was straight from D. M. Bennett. I know a good line when I steal one.

J: Your plagiarisms are forgiven. Please—trample on.

DK: With sacrilegious pleasure…

While I readily admit that I am no expert, I do know that although many have scaled the world's highest mountains over the past decades, not a single climber has ever claimed to see all the world's cities from any summit. Given the simple physics of a round planet, would not such a perspective be impossible? Even from outer space, no such view is feasible.

I realize, of course, that in your homeland it was almost universally believed that the world was flat. When the gospel writer scribed this account of your escapades with Satan, did he realize the true shape of the planet? Or was he, more likely, still laboring under the illusion that the earth was planar?

The next thing we are told about your mountain trip with the devil is that he promised to give you all that you surveyed if you would fall down and worship him.

Now, under normal circumstances this would seem to be a most desirable bargain. A few moments of feigned worship in exchange for complete ownership of all goods and real estate on a planet is generally considered by shrewd negotiators to be the kind of deal worth making. Fortunately, however, you declined the devil's proposition, apparently realizing that, in presenting this wild proposal, Satan was only bluffing. After all, none of the world's kingdoms have ever belonged to him, and not one square foot of property or structure is his rightful possession.

In any event, by this time mere practicality would seem to have established the futility of quoting any further scriptures, especially since Satan was evidently quite familiar with the holy writings himself. Strangely, though, you decided to share with your evil opponent one last sacred verse.

After this concluding citation, you ceased your war of words with the devil and ordered him to depart. Thus did you squander your final—and perhaps easiest—opportunity to take the devil by the horns and slay him. For it was then that you might have spared humanity from Satan's ongoing enticements by merely pushing him off the high mountain ledge and sending him plummeting to his demonic death. Disturbingly, however, you simply told him to get lost.

At this enigmatic turn of events, I am even now both stunned and disheartened. Did you think it preferable that you later die a horrible death by crucifixion than to solve the problem of sin and corruption at its source? Why did you not kill the wicked Ruler of Ruin when you had the chance? Would it not have been the greatest gift you could have bestowed upon humanity—and upon yourself as well?

Candidly, did your own suffering and death pacify your Father's disturbed feelings better than the death of Satan would have? How did your violent demise in any way harm the devil? And why was the architect of our everlasting proscription allowed to go free when you knew full well the eternal ramifications of his iniquitous intent?

Why, in Revelation chapter twenty, is it prophesied that Satan is to be liberated *yet again* after having been caught and bound for a thousand years? Does it reflect even a hint of wisdom to have him under lock and key and then release him for one final round of destruction? When reading such things, do not people everywhere have the right to wonder if you have taken leave of your senses?

If, as you claim, all power in heaven and earth belongs to *you*, why keep lending so much of it to the devil? If you truly have dominion over Satan, why is he allowed to continue unabated in casting his sinister spell? Are you content knowing the devil is garnering billions of souls into his demon-filled dungeon, even as you and your Father sit idly by and allow it? Quite frankly, do you not find all this salvation-damnation business devilishly strange to begin with?

J: Hang on… I'll be right back.

DK: Where you goin'?

J: I'm just gonna grab a mattress.

DK: Hold your camels, we're comin' to the *coup de grâce*…

My dear sir, entire volumes could be written listing the endless questions regarding the gaps, vagaries, contradictions, riddles, uncertainties and logical challenges presented by Christian scripture.

For example, where did you and your Father reside before you created the universe and nothing existed? And how is it that the first three days of creation were comprised of both evenings and mornings, when Genesis clearly states that the sun, moon and stars were not created until day number four?

Also, if there is no predestination, how is the book of Revelation able to assert that a mere 144,000 souls will be with you in heaven at the end of time? Is not the sum of exactly twelve thousand dozens a little too perfectly round to be haphazard or coincidental? And permit me, if you will, to put this relatively microscopic number into perspective…

Since Christianity's advent, many billions have heard the gospel message proclaimed. Barring your quick return, several billions more are likely yet to hear it. Such numbers are staggering. Sadly, however, a total of 144,000 salvaged souls represents but a tiny fraction of all those ever given opportunity to accept you as their Lord and savior.

But let us for the moment ignore non-believers entirely and focus only on your supporters. By your own accounting in the book of Revelation, the number of souls saved by Christianity remains inconsequential even when computed strictly as a percentage of those who have eagerly *embraced* it. Allow me to indulge in a few simple statistics:

Of the countless aspirants claiming to accept the gospel since your death, let us assume that only two billion of them ever committed sincerely to its practice. This number is extremely conservative, I believe, as it amounts to an average of only one million bona fide new converts for each of the 2,000 years since your death. (For means of comparison, the world contains more than two billion Christians at this very moment.)

With only 144,000 of your devotees at last permitted beyond the pearly gates, your "success rate"—even assuming just two billion Christian faithful across the ages—computes to a trifling .0072%. Stated differently, of all those earnestly adopting your message of redemption, the number actually redeemed, according to Revelation, totals just over seven-thousandths of one percent.

As you can plainly see, even among staunch Christian advocates your salvation results are dismal. But accounting for all humans throughout history turns the figures positively grim. It is scientifically estimated that nearly 100 billion humans have walked the earth to date. Dividing this number into Saint John's divinely revealed figure of 144,000 reclaimed souls, your deliverance rate plunges to a meaningless .000144%. Stunningly, this amounts to just one rescued spirit for every 695,000 people who have ever lived.

41

J: I'm surprised a guy this good with numbers could so badly flunk first-year algebra.

DK: Hey, what teenage boy with a pulse could concentrate sitting next to Donna Mackenzie? The girl's entire wardrobe consisted of knee-high skirts and tight sweaters. I got carpal tunnel syndrome that semester and I didn't even own a computer. But don't trip me up, I'm nearly at full boil…

It should be here mentioned that some Christian apologists contend that Saint John's reference to the 144,000 redeemed is merely *symbolic* and does not represent the actual number of those who will be welcomed into heaven. Ignoring the tremendous problems this argument presents for Bible literalists, let us suppose that your inglorious death does ultimately ransom a full 25% of all those who have ever lived. Even using this generous but historically unjustifiable figure, there remain roughly 75 billion—that is, *seventy-five thousand million*—of God's children who will yet suffer inexpressible and everlasting misery amidst the inextinguishable fires of their heavenly Father's hell.

The numerical exercise above is all quite academic, of course, since Saint John makes clear in his writing that the small company of God's redeemed shall include only members of the twelve tribes of Israel. This is all the more confusing when considering the New Testament's many declarations that heaven's final population will consist only of those who confess the name of Jesus—something not a single member of the original twelve tribes could have done.

Adding to the surreal and mystifying nature of this issue is Revelation 14, which states that heaven's elect will consist entirely of truthful male virgins!

But let us leave aside peripheral issues and lay the hammer to the anvil: Has not the devil been far more proficient in his soul-collection campaign than the Holy Trinity could ever hope to be? Are the three of you not gravely embarrassed by this exceedingly poor showing? Indeed, the above figures would seem to indicate of your plan for "salvation" a failure so colossal as to be pathetic.

J: *Wooophh.* Is it time for the seventh-inning stretch?

DK: No need. I'm fixin' to crack it over the fence to seal the game…

Given its contradictions and highly bizarre nature, can we depend on John's revelatory accounting of the Last Judgment? Can the record of his unusual vision be trusted as the literal, inspired word of God? If so, then evidently you have decided to condemn even the great majority of God's own "chosen people." Since its establishment among the ancient tribes, this group alone must now have a running total of tens of millions at the very least. Apart from the lucky handful attaining salvation, most will be left wondering, no doubt, why you chose them in the first place.

I put it to you directly, sir: do you really expect us to worship a God so inflexible, so cruel—so entrepreneurially inept? Does He deserve our adoration or devotion while persisting on a course that has proven so disastrously ineffective? Should He be loved for allowing the senseless murder of his own Son and eternally castigating nearly everyone in history?

To be blunt, dear Jesus, I fear your unhappy journey to our sorry planet was all but futile. Aside from benefiting the fortunate few, it appears the torturing you endured in our wretched behalf was suffered largely in vain. One thing is certain: if the numbers of Revelation hold fast, then mathematically speaking your redemption efforts are wasted.

Merely speculating, perhaps the blame for your gospel's failure to redeem humanity lies chiefly with those you appoint to disseminate it. Judging by the inspired facts of Revelation, your large corps of evangelists through the years has been virtually worthless. With their poor ability to "close the sale," most Christian preachers would apparently be hard-pressed selling ten-dollar paroles to death row felons.

Despite your disappointing salvation debacle, however, there is one interesting facet of The Last Judgment in which you may find solace…

You predicted in Matthew 7 that, come Judgment Day, you personally will lecture the countless doomed *souls standing before the Great Throne (a spectacular multitude which will, by my calculations, consume a space approximately the size of West Virginia). Just prior to casting the pitiable throngs into hell, you reportedly will turn to them and declare mercilessly, "I never knew you." It is little consolation, I suppose, but have you realized that when you do this you will be addressing the largest crowd ever assembled?*

In conclusion, renowned sir, I offer these questions, protestations, and observations hoping that you will find it both prudent and reasonable to respond. Naturally, given my poor historical prayer results, I will not wait by the mailbox for your reply. Please be assured, however, that I will bear no resentment if an answer is not forthcoming. For though I may indeed be disappointed, I shall not *be surprised.*

Yours most sincerely,
D.K. Maylor

J: Wow… quite an effort.

DK: Yeah? So whaddaya think?

J: I think I just became the first guy in history to be crucified *twice*…

CHAPTER EIGHT

DK: Maybe I owe an apology. After hearing myself read that stuff aloud, I guess it *was* a little severe. But then, I never imagined I'd be raking you over in person.

J: Don't sweat it. I actually enjoyed it.

DK: You're kidding.

J: Not at all. It was honest, reflective, intelligent—

DK: Hey, thanks.

J: —but of course delusional and completely misinformed.

DK: *What!?* Listen, I must've suffered through *two thousand hours* of mind-numbing sermons and tedious New Testament study group sessions to accumulate the knowle—

J: *Whoa, whoa, whoa*… calm down there, pilgrim—don't get your hackles in a snarl. There's no reason to take offense. In a way, your letter speaks for millions of skeptics throughout the ages. You're not the first to have serious questions about Christianity, you know. Lots of people have the same kinds of doubts, but most just don't have the guts to admit it. Before we go any further, we'd better spend a minute discussing the concept of scripture. Nearly everything you're throwing at me hangs on ancient, third-party reports.

DK: Well, in *your* case that's about all we have. It's not like you left a signed autobiography.

J: Let's be practical, then, and review the typical scripture evolution process. First, someone writes a personal account of events or opinions he considers spiritually significant. In many cases, his ideas are received second-hand from people who may, or may not, have been actual witnesses. Some of the ideas are embellished, sensationalized, or adapted from earlier mythologies and legends. Years, decades or even centuries later, the guy's letter, like others written in similar fashion, suddenly becomes revered. Folks start treating these works almost like legal documents. They create formal organizations around them, developing strict theological doctrines based upon them. Finally, a select group of men—women, strangely, are nearly always excluded from such proceedings—decides that some of the writings should be canonized and considered "holy."

DK: I guess that's the basic progression.

J: Alright, so stick with me here and try to envision how these things really develop. Initially, when one of these "sacred" works is written, its intended audience doesn't give it much thought. To them it's just another letter, right? I mean it's not like the guy walks downstairs one morning and tells the wife, "Looks like rain comin', hon. Can't be plowin' in weather like this. Think I'll stay in today and knock out a few lines of scripture."

DK: Of course not.

J: In reality, it's more like a friend of yours sitting down and writing out some personal thoughts. He sends you the letter and you read it. That's great. But no matter how inspiring or commanding your friend's words might be, the last thought on your mind is, "You know, I think ol' Barney just issued a transmit from God."

DK: So to the author's peers, a document we now consider sacred was probably just another letter from Barney.

J: Exactly. But then the letter starts circulating, and with time it takes on an entirely different aura—especially if the writer is now a member of the dearly departed.

DK: Interesting how a guy's work gathers so much more weight after he's dead…

J: And once the document has been used as a reference or a guiding light for a number of years, some of the faithful start insisting that the author was divinely inspired.

DK: In a simplified way, I suppose that's pretty much how it happens.

J: So what've we got? With the New Testament, we've got a bunch of letters and narratives written in ancient tongues that are often extremely difficult to interpret and translate and are in fact frequently quite ordinary. We've got John detailing his personal tiff with a guy named Diotrephes; Paul dealing with administrative matters; the writer of the letter to Timothy urging his friend to drink a little wine for stomach ailments. In other words, pretty mundane stuff. Nevertheless, the authors are said to have received a kind of download from heaven, every line of which purportedly carries profound significance. And most believers assume that these writings *must* have been specially inspired or the church wouldn't have included them in the Bible.

DK: I'm not sure many have thought it through to that extent. I'd say a lot of folks believe that God was essentially *in charge* of the process, even if He didn't do the actual writing.

J: By *that* reasoning, though, God has been far less concerned about the sufferings of his children than He has been about the printing business.

DK: Come again?

J: Well, I mean it's a pretty strange God who's willing to bear the horrors of a holocaust, for example, and yet considers the publishing of erroneous scriptures intolerable. "A little genocide is no problem," He says, "but let's make damned sure we issue a quality book product."

DK: Why so facetious?

J: Because I'm shocked that billions throughout history have so blindly accepted religion's proclamation of what constitutes "God's word." You know so little of the writers and their character, so little about their motives, beliefs and superstitions, the validity of their information, the surrounding social and political environment or the long, meandering process of scribing, transcription and alteration. It all took place hundreds or even thousands of years ago, and yet believers soak it up like a dry sponge, never raising a question.

DK: You make it all sound so unintelligent.

J: Intelligence *is* as intelligence *does*.

DK: You're quoting Voltaire?

J: I'm rephrasing Forrest Gump.

DK: Maybe you're not being fair. I know plenty of devout believers who are brilliant thinkers.

J: Brilliance is irrelevant; it's more about *knowledge*. Just because someone quotes the Bible chapter-and-verse doesn't mean he understands how scripture *developed*. Quiz the average Christian about the Bible's evolution and you're likely to get a blank stare. He may know scripture's *content*, but he rarely knows its *history*. And in most cases, he doesn't *want* to. He just drinks it all in and calls it faith. I'm telling you, a fella might be a bloody genius—but raise the topic of religion and suddenly his brain turns to Jell-O.

DK: I guess the proof's in the pudding…

J: It's ironic, but the average person will exhibit the most guarded skepticism in nearly every aspect of his daily life. And yet, suspicious, fantasy-like stories of his spiritual forefathers he'll embrace without a flinch. My raising the dead and walking on water he'll accept without a smidgen of direct proof, despite all experience and evidence to the contrary. But let a neighbor offer him a great deal on a used car, and right away he's phoning his mechanic: he's *sure* there must be a catch.

DK: Pretty cynical coming from the leader of Christianity.

J: I was no Christian! I was a Jew! I never even *heard* of Christianity, and I darned sure never intended to start another religion. I came to lead humanity *beyond* religion—to reestablish your direct connection to God.

DK: Doesn't that require being Christian?

J: Why should it? Cleaving to dogmas and labeling yourself doesn't alter your reality.

DK: The church says that God wants everyone professing the name of Jesus.

J: That's not what I hear from the Hindus, Buddhists, Muslims and Jews. Anyhow, do you realize that all it takes to be a Christian is the simple declaration that you *are* one? I mean who could tell whether you actually qualify? What are the criteria? Who would know whether you're truly dedicated and sincere?

DK: Surely God would know.

J: Are you under the impression that God is a Christian?

DK: Well, if He isn't, you may wanna put out a little press release. The church implies that God's attitude is, "Christianity: My way or the highway—to *hell!*"

J: So the church views Christianity as God's religion of preference.

DK: Of course. Philippians chapter two says that "at the name of Jesus every knee should bow…and every tongue confess that Jesus Christ is Lord." Apparently God wants an all-Christian planet.

J: Most people who call themselves Christian don't even know the *meaning* of the word. To some, it's a label for a person who follows my teachings. To others, it's someone who claims me as their "personal Lord and savior," which implies something different to just about everyone. But the word "Christian" means "Christ-like." And *all* people are Christ-like *in essence*. Most of 'em just don't know it.

DK: Wait a minute. You're saying that by your definition *everyone* is Christian?

J: Not in a religious sense, of course. But the Christ isn't a personality, and it's not religion-specific. The divine spirit is as fully present in the atheist, the agnostic and the "uncivilized" jungle native as it is in the most devout believer. So despite its confident claims, Christianity has never owned a monopoly on the Christ.

DK: Going strictly on the evidence, I don't see how you can reasonably claim that everyone is Christ-like.

J: The parable of the Prodigal Son teaches that even though the son of a wealthy man *believed* himself to be poor and disowned, it wasn't so *in reality*. He simply forgot his true status as the rich man's rightful heir. But the father knew the son was always fully entitled to the entire kingdom. I told that story because I never saw others as anything less than divine. The Christ spirit lives in everyone, and their ignorance doesn't change the facts.

DK: But the Bible also sa—

J: Listen, before we get into bantering with scripture, let's acknowledge the danger of using archaic writings to justify beliefs that are otherwise indefensible. That practice has led to monumental suffering through the centuries—and I should know. I was accused of all kinds of violations of sacred scripture and Jewish law, including working on the Sabbath, claiming oneness with God, and so forth. I threatened the religious doctrines and power structures of my day, and it eventually got me killed. Like you, my peers were giving ancient documents way too much authority.

DK: Are you implying that scripture is useless?

J: I'm just advising you to test its value the same way you'd test anything else. You don't hesitate to employ reason and discretion in *other* aspects of life. Why not use it with your faith? Does it

49

make sense to suspend critical thinking just because someone tells you that a particular writing is "holy" or "inspired"? What if they're wrong?

DK: What if they *aren't*? The afterlife implications could be disastrous.

J: You're living in a theological house of cards there, pilgrim—but we'll discuss that later. The main point is that if God gave you the ability to reason, then He must have expected you to *use* it. Why should God be offended that you'd apply prudence and intelligence to anything connected with *Him*?

DK: Well, obviously I've got plenty of doubts; it's just that I'd rather not roast in hell because of them. But believe me, over the years my faith has crumbled like peanut brittle.

J: Then take heart, O ye of brittle faith. The simple-minded belief that God will punish you for questioning scripture presents an immediate problem.

DK: And that is?

J: Well, if you believe that God created both the Bible *and* your logical, reasoning mind, then whose fault is it if those two things conflict?

DK: On the other hand, you can't always determine what to believe using only reason and logic.

J: Try convincing me of that without using reason or logic.

DK: Okay, you stumped me there. But then, how do we solve the problem? Nearly every religion has sacred texts, and most contain some pretty wild stuff. Are any of them helpful?

J: Sure. Some of the world's scriptures are worthy, love-inspired writings with deep levels of understanding and wisdom. Many of the Psalms, for example, are beautifully uplifting hymns of praise and encouragement. But others are clearly a call for heavenly vengeance. In fact, many of the world's religious writings are really nothing but stories of God's partiality to a particular people—stories of God choosing sides. So a lot of what passes for "God's word" is questionable at best. Some scriptures portray God in a way that makes Him seem more devilish than divine.

DK: Care to back that up?

J: Hmmnn… well, take the famous Passover story from the Book of Exodus. Not a hint of godliness in the entire episode. Scripture says that Yahweh carried out his tenth and final plague on the Pharaoh and his people by instructing the captive Israelites to wipe lamb's blood around their doors. God would then go through Egypt killing the first-born children, and even the first-born *animals*, of those who didn't comply. Exodus claims that not a single household in all of Egypt was spared from this heavenly terror attack.

DK: Pretty spooky.

J: So *you* tell *me*: what is it about this account that folks consider so inspirational or worthy of commemoration? Personally, I never saw the point. In effect, we were celebrating our people's deliverance from God's otherwise murderous rampage through Egypt. If the Passover is a grateful remembrance of Israel's alleged liberation from slavery, then it's also a grim reminder of a homicidal deity at his worst.

DK: Didn't God give Pharaoh several warnings?

J: Sure, but if there's only one God, then He was also the God of the Egyptians. So why is it that the Bible God never claims parenthood over people other than Israelites? Who was responsible for *creating* all the others? According to Genesis, everyone descended from the same two people. Anyhow, couldn't an omnipotent being resolve the Egyptian crisis in a way that was peaceful for all concerned? I mean why impose divine wrath on an entire society? Wouldn't it have made more sense simply to install a more agreeable Pharaoh?

DK: It's a story *I* never understood, either. Killing innocent children and animals doesn't seem like the loving, politically imaginative solution you'd expect from the great creator of the universe. And this was the same God who sternly warned the Israelites, "Thou shalt not kill."

J: He was probably thinking, "That's *my* job."

DK: Could it be that we mortals just don't understand the deeper significance of God's behavior? You gotta think He had a good *reason* for the Passover.

J: Actually, there's no conclusive or convincing evidence that such a thing ever happened. But even if it had, the Passover story is just one among many biblical examples of divine sadism. The Old Testament oozes with bloody accounts of God not just *allowing* but actually *ordering* Israel's leaders to murder their enemies. Hundreds, thousands—even tens of thousands at a stab. Occasionally God virtually leads the charge. And the *New* Testament is no better, as it contains its own gloried claims to heavenly insanity—the most obvious, of course, being the Crucifixion itself.

DK: *Mother of Judas!* I can't believe what I'm hearing! I can already see the headline: "Jesus Returns for Interview, Angers Jews and Christians Alike."

J: If you doubt what I'm saying, just scan the scriptures sometime. If you can stay objective, you'll see that, in many cases, the Bible God is nothing but a deified thug. In the Old Testament, He's chastising, punishing and killing practically everyone in sight—including the Israelites themselves. In the New Testament, He's on the sidelines, watching over the needless murder of his so-called "only son." Who could feel any genuine devotion to this character when He constantly demonstrates such striking hypocrisy?

DK: Personally, I didn't like the guy from the moment He asked Abraham to sacrifice Isaac on the altar. And even though He gave a last-minute reprieve, I found it hard to respect a God who would test a man that way.

J: Perfect example of what I'm talking about. As you say, what kind of God would even *ask* such a thing? Anyhow, it was all a big waste of time. An omniscient being would've known beforehand that Abraham would comply with the deviant demand.

DK: Maybe God isn't the all-knowing deity we've been led to believe He is.

J: Possibly not. In Genesis 22, just before Abe plunges the knife into his son's chest, God's angel intervenes. Speaking for the Lord, as made clear in verse sixteen, the angel says, "Lay not thine hand upon the lad… for now I know thou fearest God…" Now, certainly God wasn't testing Abraham on behalf of an angel. Nor would a mere angel be conducting such an extreme trial without God's knowledge and consent. So it's safe to assume that it was Yahweh Himself who wanted to determine the extent of Abraham's faith.

This implies that God doesn't really know his own creations—which doesn't argue well for his omniscience.

DK: I once heard a preacher say that God did it not for his *own* sake, but for the sake of Abraham. He wanted Abe to know the strength of his own conviction.

J: Then the Bible God is one sick puppy. If a modern-day parent tied his son to an altar in preparation for sacrifice to God, the man would be locked up faster than you can say, "Grab the Thorazine!"

DK: Well, depending on the culture…

J: Frankly, this Bible God isn't someone you want wandering around the compound. He talks a good game about his endless mercy and abiding love—but if He's cranky, they may not last the night! He's clearly a god of death, doom and destruction. He's a brutal, bloodthirsty enforcer; an unscrupulous narcissist; a flamboyant ruffian. He scares the hell out of people.

DK: An elderly fundamentalist friend of mine used to love quoting a line from Exodus. "The Lord is a man of war," he would declare. He said it was part of a victory song of praise to God by the Israelites.

J: Well, they certainly gave Him the right title. I'd imagine Yahweh was a little surprised at the praise, though, considering that the Israelites were constantly rebelling against Him. But then, who *wouldn't*? I mean who could maintain allegiance to a God so whimsical, unfaithful—and dangerous? Heck, the dude would bury large populations at the drop of a pin. You could never love even an *earthly* parent who was so damned mean.

DK: Somebody said that about the only difference he could see between Adolf Hitler and the God of the Old Testament is that Yahweh seemed impressively more proficient at genocide.

J: Well, that's a pretty sad commentary on how people have come to view God. My advice would be to throw this divine bully of yours into the lake of everlasting fire and be done with Him. Catering to his gigantic ego just encourages Him.

DK: That almost sounds blasphemous.

J: The real blasphemy is projecting stupidity, torture and cold-blooded murder onto the all-loving creator. Your fearful image of God is worse than useless: it's downright destructive.

DK: Jackhammering the Bible's foundation won't be very popular with the "God-said-it-I-believe-it" bumper sticker crowd.

J: The truth has *never* been popular. It's like an obnoxious drunk: the minute he pulls up a chair next to somebody, they move to the other end of the bar. Most folks develop ideas about reality early on and then spend the rest of their lives defending their theories. Any evidence to the contrary is ignored or attacked. That's why speaking the truth can be hazardous to your health. My own life proved nothing if not that.

DK: Why do we find truth so threatening?

J: To the ego, illusions are sacred; so truth is held off at all costs. Just look at history. Spiritual visionaries usually aren't around for long. Their esteem fades fast, and they typically get killed or run out of town. Near the end, even my own approval ratings had plummeted. Fortunately, enlightened souls are never concerned with winning popularity contests—least of all among those who advertise their religion on a T-shirt or windshield.

DK: It seems religion can become just another status symbol.

J: Often so. But the point is that God isn't frightening, despite religion's picture of a menacing deity who patrols the neighborhood like a vigilante cop, slapping down the bad guys while ignoring the blatant hypocrisy of his own lawless behavior. A little common sense would tell you that a loving parent doesn't threaten, intimidate or condemn his children. And he sure as hell doesn't torture and kill them.

DK: *Heh heh.* The paradox reminds me of the old TV series "Kung Fu," in which a peace-loving Chinese monk walks around the country kicking everyone's ass. Actually, I think a lot of us view our religion's God as sort of a stern cosmic stepfather. Either that or a kind of universal parole officer who's got us under constant surveillance.

J: Most religious devotees would say they believe that God is omnipresent. And they're right. But they're overlooking the logical conclusion: If God is everywhere, then He can't be *over here* while you're *over there.* So the concept of judgment is based entirely on

54

the belief in separation, and a world of mistaken perception is born of it.

DK: But even if He doesn't judge us, God must occasionally get angry.

J: Angry at *what*? Why would He be angry at his own creation? One of the dumbest and most poorly considered concepts ever advanced about God is that He gets angry. Even modern psychology can tell you that anger, at its core, is always based on fear. *And God does not experience fear.* God is a constantly purring kitten, pilgrim. As pure love—*and nothing else*—God extends only love and creates only lovingly. Reality is only light. The rest is your own delusional nightmare…

CHAPTER NINE

DK: I can see now that I won't be getting any love letters from the Christian right.

J: Don't lose sleep over *that*. Nearly every age has its "moral majority." They're rarely very moral and *never* the majority.

DK: I'm just having a little trouble hearing such blunt talk from a man whose philosophy was based on a platform of non-judgment.

J: What, I'm not allowed to have opinions? You've mistakenly concluded that non-judgment means becoming a deferential, fence-straddling wimp. Don't expect me to sit here all day without taking a stand. I didn't come in to spout a bunch of mamby-pamby aphorisms that don't really help anyone. I'm here to make a *difference*, not to run for president.

DK: So to *your* way of thinking, a person can be devout without becoming a mindless and diffident wuss.

J: I would sure hope so. I mean have a look at *my* life. Even in the highly distorted gospels of the New Testament, I'm certainly not depicted as the sweet, mild-mannered guy that children learn about in Sunday school. Now, I never *condemned* anyone, because I understood the illusory nature of the world. But that didn't stop me from identifying wickedness, hypocrisy or outright stupidity. Sometimes you have to address present circumstance, even while recalling the reality beyond it.

DK: Then what of your admonition not to judge?

J: Non-judgment means refusing to see yourself as separate from or better than anyone else. You look upon everyone as a full child of God and realize that their most fundamental interests are no different from yours. Knowing this, you refrain from forming fixed opinions about inner realities based upon outer conditions. I've always thought that two people oughtta be able to call each other an SOB and still *love* one another. No matter what someone says or does, you should always remember their true, divine nature—because it's also *yours*.

DK: Well, I dunno… some people's hearts seem black as coal.

J: I don't deny it. You may well have to acknowledge the *effects* of darkness. But you learn to respond with nothing but light.

DK: Where does all this theological debunking leave the *historical* Jesus? I mean you're letting all the air out of the scriptural infallibility balloon, so what I wanna know is, were you…uh, that is, *are* you God—or not?

J: Instead of feeding your delusions, I'll make a startling statement that all believers must eventually confront:

Belief in God is a meaningless idea.

DK: Illumination, please.

J: Look at it like this: God, if He exists, is either *known* or He isn't. Beliefs are just barren middle ground; a lazy comfort zone of gray; a shabby substitute for knowledge. Belief, by implication, means *not knowing*. Either you *know* God as your own reality or you don't—simple as that. The rest is empty conjecture. I mean does God want his children merely to believe—or would He, more likely, want them to *know*? Do you think God would create you and then sit around hoping that you'd eventually come to *believe* in Him?

DK: It would seem like a pretty poor game plan. But hey, you're tap dancing around my question. Do you in fact consider yourself divine?

J: The question's irrelevant. If I say, "Yes, I'm God," would you believe me? And even if you did, it would still be only a *belief*. True fulfillment or devotion requires *knowing*, and anyone serious about spirituality would insist on *direct, personal experience*. I never demanded or encouraged blind faith.

DK: That seems to contradict your words to the Apostle Thomas: "Blessed are those who have not seen and yet believe."

J: There's no contradiction if you understand what I meant. You can't know God as your own inner reality until you've stopped relying on external validation. Therefore, blessed are those who don't need signs—because they *know*.

DK: Okay, I can follow that. But still, I'd like to come to grips with who you really are.

J: Instead of asking, "Who is Jesus?," you'd be far wiser to ask yourself, "Who am *I*?" Most people resist that question because it worries 'em to think they may not know the answer. It's a lot easier to assume that I'll do your heavy lifting *for* you. The thinking seems to be, "I'll just stay in tight with good ol' Jesus and I'm good to go."

DK: Is that realistic?

J: Not for a second. I've been referred to as "savior"—but for all the wrong reasons. Despite popular opinion, my mission wasn't to prove how special *I* am and how inferior *you* are. We're *brothers*, not slave and master. You'll have to shovel your way to the wellsprings of knowledge, just as I did. Luckily, I made your task easier by showing you where to dig.

DK: Is it accurate, then, to say that you came to save the world?

J: In a sense, yes. But you're asking a loaded question. We'll get into it later, but for the moment I'll say this: I didn't endure the inconvenience of hanging on a cross in order to install a new set of creeds, start a better religion, or launch some grand behavior modification campaign. And I didn't come to teach that God is sitting self-righteously in his heaven, steaming mad about his children's disobedience.

DK: Then why *did* you show up?

J: Because humanity has a tendency to create hell on earth. You could say I came to help you get the hell out of here.

DK: And how do you do that?

J: Like other enlightened men and women, my purpose was—and still is—to help people reconnect with their godself. I stand beside them, pointing to the only genuine escape from suffering: the inner realization of truth. I called it the "kingdom within." But the choice to seek this inner kingdom is always *personal*—it's yours and yours alone. You're my brother, not my subject, so I can only encourage you to begin the search. I help where I can at other levels, but don't use *me* as an excuse to keep from delving inward. Your first impulse is to look *outside* for salvation. My job is to redirect you continuously back toward the self.

DK: I thought your job is to point us toward *God*.

J: Yes, and I just revealed the only place where He can ever be found.

DK: Within the self.

J: Where else? There's nothing to find *outside* the self, because outside the self is *nothing*.

DK: You talk about our equality and say that we can know God intimately, just as you do. But I can't help feeling that you must have some advantage over us.

J: Only this: I'm in complete realization of my true nature, and you, temporarily, are not. But even this difference can't last, since you and I are one. All your self-perceptions are false, and in the end the false has no chance. Truth *will* manifest, simply because it's true. That's why "the gates of hell shall not prevail against it."

DK: Ah-ha! So you're not above resorting to scripture!

J: Like I said, some can be useful. You'll have to forgive me.

DK: An ironic request if ever there was one… and by the way, exactly what *is* forgiveness? Must we constantly beseech God to change his mind about us? Is He angry one minute and pacified the next, just because we offer up a prayer? How can He react to billions of individuals at every moment? Does God experience an unlimited number of emotions at once? The whole thing seems crazy.

J: Again, it's all based on the notion that you and God are separate—an insane premise that can only lead to preposterous conclusions. Since you perceive God as separate and judgmental, you figure He's got to be worshipped or appeased with sacrifice and prayer before He'll overlook your mistakes or cave in to your requests.

DK: I think a lot of us view God sort of like Santa Claus-turned-KGB. He's seldom very jolly, but He damned sure knows when you've been bad or good, so be good—

J: For goodness' sake, you've gotta be kidding! You've merely projected your egoic, guilt-based thinking onto a deity of your own making. Like most folks, you can barely entertain the notion of a truly magnanimous God—a God who offers nothing but love. You're convinced that love and judgment can peacefully coexist, and you believe there's a price to be paid, or at least some action required, before your "redeemer" will fully accept you.

DK: Well, of course. That's the very message of the Crucifixion.

J: But you can't have it both ways. You can't declare that God created you perfect in unmitigated love and then argue that He expects you to prove yourself *worthy* of it. You wouldn't even succeed in convincing me that He wants you to *appreciate* it. That's senseless and totally at odds with grace.

DK: I was taught that God's grace consisted of offering *you* up for sacrifice. You died willingly, of course—but there *were* a few strings attached. For example, we're required to confess our sins, accept you and you only as our Lord, and profess that your death was God's atoning gift to us.

J: Well, it's a pretty sick and twisted God who gives the "gift" of death. But even if you say you believe it, you never let down your guard—because deep inside you're not so all-fired sure. You gush on about God's wonderful grace, but then spend the rest of your life trying to earn it, deserve it, or keep it. With that kind of pressure, how grateful could you really be?

DK: You're trampling where angels and associate pastors fear to tread.

J: Look, when evaluating any concept of God, you've got to ask if it's *reasonable*. Because if something *seems* absurd, it probably *is*. The Superforce of creation is no idiot.

DK: Heck, with all the conflicting theology we're given, you couldn't blame us for being a little paranoid or confused. First the New Testament says that we're saved by grace alone and that salvation hinges solely on faith. You said so yourself several times in the gospel of John.

J: He who believes in me shall never perish, and all that.

DK: Right. But unfortunately that contradicts your statement in Matthew 19, where you tell a man that all he has to do to secure eternal life is to "keep the commandments." You never even mention the aspect of faith or belief in you as God's savior. Furthermore, in the book of James we're cautioned many times that even if we *do* have faith, it's meaningless if not accompanied by good works.

J: Yeah, that's true. In fact, James' notion of "pure religion" centers not on *faith* but on *behavior*.

DK: But that position thoroughly refutes Paul's stance in Romans 3, where he basically says that works aren't important. However, just one chapter prior, in Romans 2:6, Paul states quite specifically that God will reward us *according to our works*! And if *that* swamp of mucky theology isn't enough to keep our heads spinning, the New Testament throws in the *additional* factors of spiritual rebirth and baptism, which some scriptures say are essential while others ignore them entirely. And just so no one's caught napping, we're also warned that works without faith are completely ineffective. So all your sermons about love and forgiveness are apparently rendered moot if we don't hold the proper *beliefs*. And finally, just to ensure there's not a sane man standing, Paul warns in 1 Corinthians that both faith *and* works, when offered without love, are worthless.

J: An exasperating maze of conceptual goulash.

DK: Well, I mean it's one big, chaotic mess—the kind of stuff that compelled me to write you that letter. Christian salvation is nothing but a smeared picture of blurry grays, with no clear boundaries or requisites. And what about predestination? Revelation 13 says that the names of the saved were written in the Book of Life *before the foundation of the world*. In other words, before anything was created! This would mean that all of God's interaction with humanity has been pointless and that nothing external can save *anyone*—neither faith, love, works, nor good sense of fashion.

J: Good grief. It's no wonder religion drives people batty...

CHAPTER TEN

DK: Maybe now you can see what we're up against. Religion drags us from pillar to post with contradictions, riddles, austerities, mysteries and improbable theories. Where the heck do we turn to find the bloody *truth*?

J: I told my disciples, "The kingdom of God is within you." So why not look there? Begin trusting your heart.

DK: Hold on, now. The Bible says, "The heart is deceitful above all things, and desperately corrupt." That's straight from Jeremiah.

J: The Bible also says, "I will put my law *within* them, and I will write it upon their *hearts*." That, too, is straight from Jeremiah.

DK: Touché.

J: You see, that's the problem with scriptures: they're more common than backstage volunteers at lingerie shows. Let me prove the point. Open your Bible at random and read the first thing you see.

DK: Alright… "There is no fear in love, but perfect love casts out fear. For fear has to do with punishment, and he who fears is not perfected in love." That's 1 John 4:18.

J: So the writer is declaring that anyone living in love should experience no fear, least of all fear of God or his punishment. Are we agreed?

DK: I can't see another way to interpret it.

J: Good. Now read Matthew 10:28.

DK: Lemme see here… okay, these are said to be *your* words: "And do not fear those who kill the body but cannot kill the soul; rather fear him who can destroy both soul and body in hell."

J: A little perplexing, no? The gist of the verse from Matthew is the polar opposite of the line from 1 John. And let's not quibble about the meaning of the original Greek or Aramaic or any of that. The fact is, one passage says that love means having no fear, while the other passage specifically instructs you to be fearful. So you can use the world's religious writings to prove or disprove darn near anything. Many scriptures contradict, like the two we just examined. Others are confusing or indecipherable. Some are just plain ridiculous.

DK: Which ones can we trust?

J: Don't trust *any*. Take everything you read or hear and then weigh it against the truth of your own spirit: trust God by trusting *yourself*. Always examine other people's ideas or opinions—including mine. The sincerest saint may well turn out to be mistaken.

DK: How frustrating. I've studied various philosophies for years, and it seems there's just no end to the proliferation of words.

J: Every seeker should understand from the start that words are just symbols. They represent *ideas*, which again represent something else entirely. So words are several degrees removed from reality. They're signposts. They can lead you *to* the truth, but they're never themselves the truth.

DK: Apparently, people locked onto *your* words and wound up creating a whole new religion.

J: The usual song and dance. Once a group of devotees is convinced they've found "the truth," then instead of using the teachings to guide them beyond the mundane, they carve the words in stone and turn them into dogma. Same thing in my case. To use the old Buddhist analogy, it's like I was pointing to the moon and everyone fixated on my finger.

DK: On the other hand, beliefs do provide some level of comfort.

J: Yes, but that's not *truth*. It's intellectual anesthesia.

DK: Pontius Pilate once asked you, "What *is* truth?" Evidently you never replied.

J: He wouldn't have understood or appreciated the answer. I would've been feeding caviar to the dog. As my mother would say, there's no use peddling Avon at a cockfight.

DK: I'll let that one slide…

J: Truth isn't a concept or a set of beliefs that can be rattled off in a few sound bites. It can't be memorized like an answer to an exam question. Truth is way beyond words, ideas or symbols.

DK: And yet John 8:32 has you declaring, "You shall know the truth and the truth shall set you free." It sounds like something specific.

J: Again there's no contradiction. The truth *does* set you free. And what is truth? The only thing it *could* be: reality. You shall come to know reality, which will show you clearly that you *already are* free. While it's accurate to say that truth is simply what *is*, it's also a fact that you're presently unable to recognize it because your emotional and intellectual filters are skewing everything you perceive. They prevent you from seeing yourself as a perfect creation of God—as a divine extension of the one eternal Truth.

DK: It's tough for me to accept that I'm one with God. Personally, I don't feel all that saintly.

J: Only because you've been raised to believe that you're damaged merchandise. For years you've been fed a steady diet of guilt and sin, along with threats of punishment and condemnation. To correct your thinking, just substitute the recommended daily allowance of awareness, reason and honest self-inquiry.

DK: Don't we all need absolution from the guilt of our sins?

J: There *is* no sin, and no one is guilty of anything but ignorance.

DK: You must not be reading the papers.

J: I'm not denying the apparent evil in the world. I'm only telling you that you don't understand what you see. The world you presently perceive is undeniably tragic. But *God* didn't create it, because He doesn't reside in time and space. God creates only the eternal—only the whole and perfect. The eternal has no end, whereas the world rises and sets with consciousness.

DK: Nice theory, perhaps. But not very biblical.

J: Don't be too sure. Luke 6 states that a good tree does not produce bad fruit. Do you think the writer was talking horticulture? He meant that light gives birth only to light, and never to darkness. He says figs are not gathered from thorns, nor grapes picked from a bramble bush. For that matter, peaches are never taken from pines, nor pomegranates from an antique shop. Adzuki beans are rarely found in delicatessens, and if you want Brussels sprouts, you'll have to go all the way to—

DK: Alright, alright—I *get* it. Look, I'm sorry to keep kicking a dead horse, but you know very well that some will call these ideas blasphemous.

J: George Bernard Shaw famously observed that all great truths start out as blasphemy. It's just a label invoked by religion to defend propositions that can't stand on their own two feet. It's a curse word that fear and superstition heap upon the mind that dares to think for itself. In every age, blasphemy is whatever threatens current beliefs. Only a few hundred years ago, a fellow named Copernicus proposed that planets in your solar system revolve around the sun and not vice versa. His heliocentric theory was considered blasphemous.

DK: Right. Caused quite a stir, I believe.

J: Yeah, but soon afterward a clever guy named Galileo came along and *proved* it. Didn't matter, though. He was quickly labeled a heretic by the church and was imprisoned and tormented for his discovery. He fully believed his findings were accurate but was forced to recant them under threats from the Inquisition. As usual, religion led the revolt against knowledge, and once again dogma triumphed over reason. Boy, does *that* bring back memories.

DK: Still, the fact that something's controversial doesn't always mean it's true.

J: Nor does the fact that it's widely embraced.

DK: Granted. But again, how do we know what's true and what isn't? Maybe that's why we have a Bible. At least it provides guidance.

J: But the Bible's guidance is extremely dubious, brimming as it does with violence, contradictions and far-fetched claims. Besides, in its entirety the Bible is pertinent only for Christians—and no two Christians on earth interpret it the same way. Each person brings years of mental conditioning to every passage, and each sentence passes through mountains of hidden psychological and emotional filters. There's hardly a gram of objectivity involved, and all around the world Christian sects are fighting about what these scriptures mean. In *non*-Christian cultures, the Bible is largely irrelevant. Hinduism has its Bhagavad-Gita, Islam has its Quran, and so forth.

DK: It seems that every holy book claims to possess the truth.

J: The problem is that everyone has a different perception of truth: one man's god is another man's *false* god. To Christians, *I'm* the top honcho. But for Hindus, the main man is Krishna. To a secluded tribe along the Amazon, maybe it's a special sun god or even a particular animal. It's a haphazard system at best. Is this the way God would communicate his truth?

DK: I couldn't say. Growing up in the church, I always felt that God considers Christians to be special, just as He supposedly favored the ancient Israelites. I was raised to believe that Christians are the modern-day "chosen people." The church says we were given the ultimate truth in you and that everyone else should convert to *our* way of thinking and be saved. So we're supposed to spread the good news through our "witnessing."

J: And what exactly is this "good news" the church is so eager to have witnessed?

DK: C'mon, you're setting me up. You already know the Christian spiel.

J: Play along with me here. Sometimes it helps to verbalize this stuff.

DK: Okay. Which Christianity shall we discuss—the literal or the liberal?

J: I don't see that there's really a choice. Where the mainstream church is concerned, a non-literal interpretation of Christianity isn't even an option, because the New Testament is far too specific about my function as propitiator of sin. In the largest sense, scripture writers have carved a very narrow, well-defined path, leading to only one tenable interpretation: "Baby, you're no darned good, and God killed poor Jesus *because* of it."

DK: That may be a bit too restrictive. Some Christian sects don't really stress the aspect of sin. They choose instead to focus on God's love and teach us how to become better people. So while some believers may disregard certain *parts* of the Bible, they still consider themselves Christian.

J: How is that justified? I mean I'm certainly not defending the biblical view. But fundamentally speaking, if you reject certain parts of scripture as invalid, then you also reject the argument that every word is divinely inspired. And if some Bible passages can't be trusted, then on what basis would anyone claim to believe in me as the Christ?

DK: I understand your position, but I just feel you've got to allow for compromise—some kind of *middle* ground.

J: Sorry, but scripture is quite explicit about humanity's serious breach of covenant with a judgmental God who requires compensation—usually in blood. The overriding theme of the Bible, including my own role as savior, is clearly one of guilt and atonement. So any softer interpretation of Christianity is completely arbitrary and biblically indefensible. Using New Testament teachings just to become a "better person" is to ignore its solemn message of soul imperilment. It disregards the gospel's urgent call for repentance and profession of faith, and amounts to inventing a new religion made strictly to one's liking. To examine Christianity properly, we have to discuss the form that scripture actually describes. The *details* may contradict, but the *main premise* is unmistakable. Churches that dodge this primary tenet of the faith are simply being dishonest. There's no biblical justification for a softball Christianity that merely teaches people to play nice.

DK: Well, in that case, the most literal interpretation of the gospel is that we all inherit a sinful nature from the initial transgressions committed in the Garden of Eden. The good news, from the New Testament bearing, is that your sacrificial death exonerates us from sin and saves us from God's judgment. But it's not automatic. We have to accept your lordship over us and believe in you as the one and only Son of God and our solitary means of salvation.

J: Okay, but for some people this wild story about God's self-incarnating suicide mission is a pretty tough sell. What happens when potential converts aren't interested? What if they don't *accept* your good news?

DK: Then we're supposed to move on and shake the dust from our feet, whatever *that* means. Fundamentalists say that those who reject the message will end up burning in hell.

J: Hmmm.... doesn't sound like very good news to *me*.

DK: I'll admit it's a pretty severe non-performance clause.

J: So the first benefit of accepting me as your redeemer, apart from getting to reside in the same upscale neighborhood as this cantankerous deity of yours, is that it saves you from eons of torture in the unquenchable fires of the underworld.

DK: I'm sure there's a prettier way to say it—but yeah, that's the bone and marrow of it.

J: And that's what the church considers *good news*? What's good about a judgmental God who can't forgive his children until an innocent man is murdered? Where's the good in salvation that requires slave-like obedience to a fearful master? And what good comes of learning that no matter how loving or compassionate or forgiving you may be, you're destined for eternal suffering if you don't consent to the twisted creeds at the heart of the church's scary plan of redemption? No, personally I can't find a shred of goodness in Christianity's good news. Now, there may be something to the *news* part of it—because if God planned my crucifixion because others were misbehaving, then it's certainly news to me.

DK: All I know is that the story of your death and its impact on man's destiny is vital to the Christian faith, and rejecting it is not an option. Besides, we're told that we shouldn't *want* to reject it, since God is loving and desires only the best for his children.

J: Really? Shall we assume He felt the same just before He obliterated nearly every life form on the planet, *including* his beloved bipeds, in the Great Flood? Will He still be wanting only the best for his tender brood as He rains down his hell-fury upon them during Revelation's predicted Tribulation?

DK: *Sheesh.* I'm boxing an opponent who isn't wearing gloves!

J: So the core message of Christianity is that, in the beginning, God created all things perfect. But since Adam and Eve fell from grace by eating governmentally banned produce, your own perfection was lost because God considers *you* their partner in crime more than six thousand years later.

DK: Yeah, which I think is really stretching the statute of limitations.

J: And now, apparently, God deems everyone sinful and corrupt the moment He creates them.

DK: I guess so.

J: Then do those who die as infants get thrown into hell along with the unrepentant?

DK: I rather doubt it. After all, we're told that God also has compassion—so I wouldn't think He'd condemn those who never had a chance.

J: Sounds like you'd all be better off stillborn. It's a wonder God hasn't figured this out Himself.

DK: I understand the mockery. But I can only tell you that the church says we're *born* into sin and that we're sorely in need of God's forgiveness.

J: Which He withholds unless you embrace the proper religious doctrine.

DK: According to some of the New Testament writers, yes.

J: And without these corrective measures, billions of God's children are slated to become human glow torches in a distant, ill-defined torture chamber called hell.

DK: That's the story we're given.

J: Going by your own synopsis, then, the Inquisition never really ended. The only difference now is that the torture has merely been *delayed*. Under *this* arrangement, the world is nothing but God's elaborate observation facility, and most people are destined to burn the moment they enter it. Christianity is merely the means whereby God waits to see if they'll be able to change his mind about their fate.

DK: I suppose you could sum it up that way, even if it is a little cold and unpolished.

J: But thankfully, the church declares that you can save yourself from the Great Sinner Weenie Roast.

DK: Right. The path of salvation runs directly through your atoning death on the cross. *I* committed the crime and *you* paid the price.

J: You mean I paid the price and *then* you committed the crime.

DK: Well, technically, yes.

J: So God had *me* crucified because *you're* such a rotten schmuck?

DK: I know, it's a cockamamie scheme by *any* standard. But hey, who could've known God would be so obsessed with an ordinary guy like me?

J: Alright, let's make sure we've got this dogma by the collar. The church insists that humanity's collective soul is automatically inclined to damnation because a couple of kids in antiquity disobeyed meal restrictions. As a result, mankind is entirely dependent upon *my* tender mercies for its ultimate redemption, and anyone who doesn't see it that way is playing with hellfire.

DK: That's our predicament, it seems.

J: And now you're asked to believe that I'll *spare* your miserable soul if you'll invite me to be your "personal Lord and savior."

DK: Yes... but we can't just *say* it, of course. We have to really *mean* it.

J: I see. But if you can't—or won't—embrace this deranged theology, then you're sentenced to slave forever in God's extraterrestrial sweatshop. Is that pretty much how it works?

DK: For the most part. Although none of it actually takes effect until after we're pronounced dead and rigor mortis sets in.

J: Ah. So the Big Judgment is delayed until your body reaches room temperature.

DK: Well, various churches interpret it all very differently. Some say we first go to Purgatory, where we wait until the Final Judgment. The main fireworks don't start until the Rapture, when *you* return to earth and *really* get things moving.

J: In the meantime, though, there's a hundred billion souls stuck in God's heavenly holding tank.

DK: Possibly—although the Bible is extremely vague on the precise mechanics. But in general terms, that's the summarized version of Christianity's Fall-and-Redemption epic.

J: It's a great story: plenty of tension and drama laced with exciting sub-plots. But I'm surprised there's no mention of Bigfoot or Chupacabra.

DK: Hey, it's no laughing matter. The Christian God means business.

J: And you're okay with this demented deity of yours?

DK: What choice do we have? We're told that God is both wise and mysterious. Scripture says that *his* ways are not *our* ways.

J: Oh, I wouldn't go *that* far. In the twentieth century alone, more than a hundred million people were slaughtered at the hands of their fellow human beings. Many were killed in the name of Christianity itself. Going by Old Testament records, it appears that God's ways and yours are actually pretty darned similar. Now, I'll admit I don't see much *wisdom*—but they're sure as hell *mysterious*.

DK: Man, I never figured you for such a smart ass. What happened to "gentle Jesus, meek and mild"?

J: Look where that got me last time.

DK: It's just that people expect a guy of your stature to be somewhat pious and proper.

J: Sorry, I'll try acting a little more messianic. Maybe I could throw in a few "verilys" and "trulys."

DK: Hey, it may all be a joke to *you*—but shooting holes in sacred beliefs can get a guy seriously hurt.

J: You're preachin' to the choir, son.

DK: So how 'bout a little guidance on this scripture thing? A guy's gotta believe in *some*thing.

J: Why do you need to *believe* anything? Couldn't you live just dandy with no beliefs at all? Why not lean strictly on what you know and leave the rest to philosophers?

DK: Wouldn't that lead to chaos and lawlessness?

J: When's the last time you watched the six o'clock news?

DK: Okay, but if every nation embraced Christianity, as the New Testament urges, then maybe we'd all get along.

J: You mean like they did in Northern Ireland or during the American Civil War? Heck, most of the major combatants in the first *world-wide* war were countries that are predominantly Christian.

DK: Hmmnn, I see your point. Even in places where large numbers profess to follow Jesus, the world is *still* a bloody mess.

J: Verily...

CHAPTER ELEVEN

DK: I think one of the main reasons we embrace religion, aside from the obvious desire to continue on after death, is that living in a dangerous world is frightening. Some of us *need* a God who's got things under control.

J: How can you survey the world and believe that God or anyone else has it under control? You perceive the world as frightening because you don't understand *yourself* as the source behind it. Having confused cause and effect, you don't realize that you're the *creator* of the world and not its byproduct.

DK: Other spiritual teachers have taken that same position. But philosophically it's a hard pill to swallow. The church says that we're all just poor, lost souls in need of redemption.

J: Playing small and declaring yourself a "miserable offender" who's sinful to the core is something you were taught by a guilt-oriented religion. You love to prattle on about your inherent worthlessness and then pass it off as humility. But that kind of puny self-image is strictly artificial—the direct result of a witless theology. Imagine a small child growing up alone on a deserted island. The thought of having a flawed soul would never occur to the kid.

DK: But even in a case like that, wouldn't the child be tainted by original sin?

J: That's an old pagan doctrine, later adopted by the Jews. God would laugh at the idea. As your very essence, He knows only of your *original innocence*.

DK: The church would call that heresy. But if that *is* how God sees it, then He might've thought to include a few lines about it when He was throwing his scriptures together. Nearly every book in the Bible centers on humanity's dark side. For Christianity, sin is practically sacred.

J: Sin is just an arbitrary label—a reflection of the mind's tendency to judge. Socially, it's purely subjective. One culture's immorality is another's religious obligation.

DK: Then we're not automatically born into wickedness?

J: How could an infant be wicked? In a dazzling display of theological creativity, someone in history decided that people are inherently evil—crosswise with God from conception. Thus, newborns were considered spiritually defiled before they ever drew their first breath.

DK: Maybe that's why they gave 'em a spankin' right out of the chute...

J: Original sin. Boy, oh boy... what a stroke of genius. The basic idea long predates even Judaism, but the Jews gave it credibility and permanence—it really took hold in the Jewish psyche. Psalm 51 even has King David proclaiming this ridiculous sinful-baby doctrine: "Indeed, I was *born* guilty, a sinner when my mother *conceived* me." Centuries later, Christians took the ball and ran with it. They gave original sin the strength and publicity it needed to become high-profile religious doctrine.

DK: So it was the Garden story in Genesis that led to the concept becoming front-page news.

J: Yes, and if you take the story literally, all mankind is made instantly guilty because Adam and Eve disobey God's instruction not to eat "the fruit of the Tree of the Knowledge of Good and Evil."

DK: I always had trouble with that. We're never told anything *about* the tree—why its presence was even necessary, or why its special fruit was so dangerous.

J: Nor is it explained why God is so paranoid about humans becoming educated. Equally baffling is the sudden appearance of evil. Just a few paragraphs before the forbidden fruit fiasco, Genesis states, "And God saw *everything* that he had made, and behold, it was *very good*."

DK: How could God believe that everything was coming up roses when the possibility of evil hung in the air? Didn't He realize the Tree of Knowledge would cause serious problems?

J: Who knows? As you suggest, it's strange enough that God saw the need to create a forbidden object in the first place. But then He goes and *plants* the damned thing smack in the middle of the garden!

DK: In God's defense, He does warn Adam that the tree's prohibited produce is lethal.

J: Yes, and He leaves him with a stern admonition: "... for in the day that you eat of it you shall die." But as things turned out, God's prophecy never quite came to—*heh heh*—fruition.

DK: You're shameless.

J: And not only did Adam fail to *die* upon eating from the Tree of Knowledge, but he actually went on to live *nine hundred and thirty years*!

DK: Maybe God just meant that if Adam ate the forbidden fruit he would die *eventually*. He was probably warning Adam that he'd lose his immortality.

J: Your basket might hold apples if it weren't for Genesis 3:22. In that passage, the Lord expresses grave concern to *someone*—and God only knows who He was talking to—that Adam and Eve will next try to eat from the Tree of Life, in which case they'll live *forever*. Human immortality was never part of the plan.

DK: Wow, I never caught that before. Evidently God created Adam and Eve as mortals right from the get-go. He *knew* their days were numbered.

J: He certainly did. In fact, the ever-jealous Almighty is so worried about the prospect of humans becoming gods that He takes an extraordinary precaution. He guards the path to the Tree of Life with cherubim and—*get this*—a flaming sword that turns in every direction!

DK: Not your everyday durable goods item. What was He thinking?

J: Perhaps He didn't want competition for the position of Eternal God. Apparently the universe is only big enough for one.

DK: So God installs a magical sword and stations angelic guardians to prevent anyone from approaching the Tree of Life or eating its eternal-life-instilling fruit.

J: Right. Which should generate an immediate question for inquiring minds.

DK: I think I see where you're going. If God didn't want anyone eating from the Tree of Knowledge, then why didn't He protect *that* tree the same way that He later safeguarded the Tree of Life?

J: *Bingo!* I mean He plants the Tree of Knowledge right there in plain sight but then tells the naïve young couple not to go near it. Now, anyone with a trace of parenting skill would know that's a recipe for disaster. It's like a mother putting a box of razor blades in her toddler's playpen and then warning him not to open it. The moment God created temptation, catastrophe was inevitable.

DK: I suppose one could argue that God initially *trusted* his two children. He gave them specific instructions and then expected them to obey. They were, after all, intelligent beings.

J: Yeah, perhaps a lot more intelligent than their creator…

DK: I still can't believe that God would deceive Adam about the consequence of eating the forbidden fruit. If He knew that Adam would die *anyway*, it was dishonest using scare tactics to keep him in line.

J: It was manipulative, to say the least. But then, that's the problem with creators these days: there's no accountability.

DK: You're *killin'* me…

J: So after discussing the forbidden victuals, God puts Adam to sleep, yanks a rib from his chest and fashions it into the first woman. Why God resorted to invasive surgery I'm not quite sure. As I said earlier, all He needed for *Adam's* creation was a fistful of mud. Anyhow, it isn't long after the woman shows up that things *really* turn ugly.

DK: Boy, can I relate to *that*…

J: Shortly after she's created, Eve hooks up with one of Eden's most impressive residents: a talking serpent. The serpent, generally taken to be a snake, employs his reptilian wiles to convince Eve that God was just making an idle threat and that eating the restricted fruit won't really cause instant death. Unable to control her God-given curiosity, Eve gobbles down the juicy jinx and then encourages Adam to take a few bites as well. Surprisingly, neither one drops dead.

DK: Then the serpent was right!

J: Yep. That poor snake has taken a lousy rap in the history books.

DK: Nowadays he'd be suing for millions and a page one retraction.

J: Pay attention now, because here's where the story really gets interesting…

Soon after ingesting their forbidden fruit cocktail, the two lovers realize they're naked and begin using fig leaves to cover themselves. Later, God takes his morning stroll through the Garden and sees that his first two dependents are now wearing clothes. Strikingly devoid of omniscience, God interrogates Adam about the new fashion trend and discovers that he and his mate have snubbed divine orders by eating fruit taken from the Tree of Knowledge. Caught red-handed, Adam quickly blames everything on Eve, while Eve blames it all on the slick-talking serpent. After listening to the couple deny responsibility, God gets pissed off and begi—

DK: Excuse me, one second here. Really sorry for the interruption—but did you just say, "*pissed off*"?

J: Look here, old hoss, you've gotta get past this "gentle Jesus" thing or we'll never get *any*where. You think I grew up in the grit and grime of workaday Jewish culture two thousand years ago and didn't speak in the vernacular? You think I never pulled a prank on a pal or played hooky from school? That I never looked on a beautiful woman with animal desire? That I never drank a little too much at a wedding? Never told a raucous joke or ran a red light?

DK: Uh, ran a red lig—

J: You straitlaced Christianized prudes need to grow up and get a life. You priggish ninnies have turned me into some kind of sissified, hyper-religious hall monitor with a superiority complex. You know, if I ever write a book, I'm gonna call it, *You Don't Know Jack about Jesus*. For the most part, I lived a regular-guy life and did regular-guy things.

DK: I see. Just your average, run-of-the-mill Messiah.

J: Darn right. So you can eighty-six that "meek and mild" bit once and for all. I didn't walk the neighborhood with my hands folded in prayerful supplication while reciting the twenty-third Psalm. My own daily routine wasn't all that different from anyone else's.

DK: Apparently I've seen too many reruns of *Ben-Hur*. My apologies. Please continue...

J: So as I was saying, the two lovers scarf down the apple and God thoroughly unloads on Adam: "You sorry son-of-a-deity! Look what you've done! You've gone and ruined *every*thing! Do you realize I had to sweat like a pig for six full days to put all this together!?"

DK: Must be one of the newer translations…

J: Next, as a result of his children's dietary transgressions, the creator makes one of the meanest, most irrational decisions in the history of religious lore. In an instant of uncontrolled fury, God subjects hundreds of subsequent generations to strife and unhappiness by condemning them to lives of toil, suffering, death and polyester clothing.

DK: He also decides to curse women by causing them pain when giving birth to their children.

J: Oh, sure… as if *raising* them weren't trouble enough already.

DK: You don't hold very high regard for the biblical accounting of The Fall.

J: Well, if you stick to its allegorical value, no prob—it's brilliant. But if you're selling it as historical fact, then truly I say unto thee: it's the *silliest* damned thing I've ever heard. I mean I just don't understand modern religious gullibility. In most other ways, folks are extremely cynical. Some conspiracy groups still believe the original moon landing was a giant government hoax.

DK: Yeah, they claim it was all staged in the desert or in some Hollywood studio.

J: The irony is that some of those fruit loops are Christians who accept without question every fanciful, mind-boggling story in the Bible. I'm telling you, people can be skeptical to the point of paranoia: they'll deny the existence of a sharp stick when it's poking 'em in the eye. But read 'em a story from a "holy" book and suddenly they're pliant as puppies. A limitless universe created in less a week? *Plain as the nose on your face.* A primeval garden with magical trees and talking snakes? *It's right there in the Bible.* A world gone haywire because two kids nosh some illegal fruit? *Thus saith the Lord.*

DK: Okay, but I think you're ducking responsibility. I mean it's not like original sin was the brainchild of some Catholic school dropout. You already admitted it was your own church that *blessed* the concept and made it marketable.

J: Two points… First, I don't have a "church." That's a religious thing, and I'm not about spreading theology. Besides, the number of Christian sects on the planet now exceeds *thirty thousand*, and some have beliefs that are diametrically opposed. I wouldn't know where to *begin* sorting out a mess like that. I use the term "church" only to refer to it in general, as an institution. It's the same way we use the masculine pronoun to refer to God. We could just as easily use "she" or "it," since "God" refers to something so far beyond the grasp of the intellect that, for all practical purposes, the word is meaningless. So my terms are just handy conventions of language that everyone understands.

DK: Got it.

J: Second, if you're trying to establish the soundness of an idea by stating that it was conjured up by the church, you're resorting to an especially poor argument. History is *bursting* with examples of lunkheaded thinking emerging from the sanctums of religion. It's usually the very last establishment to accept new discoveries or encourage real progress. Don't forget your pals Copernicus and Galileo.

DK: I suppose you're right. Historically, the church has conceived and implemented some pretty sick ideas.

J: And some got a lot of people killed, my friend. It's no coincidence that the most evangelical religions are also the most deadly. Take the Crusades and the several phases of Inquisition. All by themselves, these two thunderbolts of church-inspired wisdom inflicted *centuries* of routine persecution, torture and murder onto millions of innocent people. As you said in your letter, Christianity has a long record of unfettered bloodshed.

DK: But of course that's reaching back hundreds of years.

J: True. But the religious thought system that *inspired* those brutal eras is still firmly entrenched; it's hardly changed at all in two millennia. And I could cite plenty of examples of so-called "religious" warfare that've taken place in just the last few years—even Christian against Christian. Heck, we can find reports of ongoing religious conflicts in today's newspaper.

DK: So clarify something. You admit that humanity in general is more twisted than a screwworm. But you also claim that God is focused on our natural innocence and not on our iniquity. How does *that* compute?

J: God doesn't perceive his children the way they perceive themselves. As *extensions of Himself*, they're as pure and holy as they were the moment they were created. Nothing the body perceives is rooted in reality.

DK: If all of God's children are innocent, how do you explain religion's almost universal, laser-like focus on sin?

J: Pure and simple crowd control. Promoting a sense of unworthiness and encouraging fear of divine punishment is religion's favored method of keeping the natives at bay. It's a great way to wield power without using force. After all, a *fearful* parishioner is a *submissive* parishioner.

DK: The First Letter of John states, "If we say we have no sin, we deceive ourselves."

J: The writer of 1 John may have been a little deceived himself. A couple chapters later, he does a complete reversal and declares, "No one born of God commits sin."

DK: I don't follow. Most Christians believe that *you're* the only one who was "born of God."

J: Yes, but the author of 1 John clearly isn't referring only to me. He says unreservedly, *"he who loves* is born of God and knows God." So the New Testament tells you on the one hand that everyone's a sinner and that you're kidding yourself if you deny it. But then it declares that no one born of God commits sin and, further, that everyone who loves *is* born of God. Using New Testament logic, then, anyone who loves is *sinless*.

DK: Very confusing stuff.

J: It's a textbook case of scriptural schizophrenia.

DK: What's the cure?

J: Just keep things simple. The Bible says God is love. If that statement is true—and it is—then love, as God's nature and essence, is pervasive, all-powerful and unchanging. So if God, or love, is changeless, omnipotent and omnipresent, there's no place for evil or sin.

DK: Then the Bible needs serious revision, because it's loaded with stories detailing God's obsession with human transgression.

J: Believe me, *you're* the ones preoccupied with sin—not God. What really needs revising is human consciousness. At its root, literalist Christianity is the result of fearful beliefs about God. So it's not surprising that frightened people would embrace such a scary theology.

DK: Hey, that reminds me… a few months ago I began a gangsta music parody of religion. Here's a few lines…

"The Man Upstairs says He *cares*/He tries to *learn* us but can't *turn* us/It don't *concern* us/So He'll *burn* us in his bad-ass *furnace*!"

J: *Heh heh.* Now, that's what I'd call giving the Good Book a bad rap.

DK: Kidding aside, though, where do you settle out on the Bible?

J: It's a random collection of writings by people pretty much like you. They often held the same misconceptions and superstitions about God that *you've* got. At some point, humanity will have to stop giving its power to a bunch of ancient manuscripts and external authorities. God has nothing to do with doctrine or belief: his truth is *within* you. You could even say that God's truth *is* you.

DK: Hoo-boy. There go the southern Baptists…

CHAPTER TWELVE

J: You're squirming in your chair, pilgrim. Am I upsetting your tea cart?

DK: I guess you've caught me a little off guard. For centuries, the church has been selling divine wrath and impending doom. Of course, it painted lipstick on the skeleton by offering a way out of the fire. But the basic message was always, "You're not good enough." Now you're telling me it was all just a ploy to keep the troops in line.

J: Forget my words a minute and reflect on your own life. Can you prove that God ever punished you for doing something you considered sinful?

DK: Well, there've been times when I've felt *guilty*.

J: Sure, but don't equate guilt with divine judgment. You experience guilt because part of your mind—psychology calls it "ego"—believes that it's separate from everything. Especially from God. This false belief in separation is what prompts you to act destructively in the first place. At its root, guilt is the belief that you've attacked or offended God. To believe you could do either is as arrogant as it is absurd.

DK: Some Christians say that guilt is God's way of "convicting" us of our sin.

J: Only humans convict one another. In God's jurisdiction, accusations against his children are always dispensed with under the pronouncement, "Case dismissed." Punishment has no meaning in the High Court of spirit, and guilt is nothing but circumstantial evidence of your confusion about what you are.

DK: Aren't you forgetting free will? We always have a choice. Surely God has the right to punish us if we disobey.

J: Even if He *has* the right, why would He feel compelled to invoke it? He's *God*, for the love of Mike. Is He incapable of rising above his own feelings of distress or disappointment? Can't He just forgive and forget?

DK: As I understand it, God *does* forgive our offenses—if we *ask* Him to. The only real punishment takes place at the Final Judgment, when those who rejected Him on earth will be sent to their eternal chastisement.

J: Tell me: how would most Christians feel about a mother who couldn't overlook her children's mistakes unless the kids were constantly begging forgiveness? Or what about a father who would torture his children for refusing to glorify him, to embrace his philosophy, or to show enough gratitude?

DK: I believe most would say they were totally unfit for parenthood. But that's completely different.

J: Oh, you're damned right it's different. The gap in wisdom between parents and their children is *minuscule* compared with the gap between God and the average human. Shouldn't the Almighty be held to a slightly higher standard? And yet hundreds of millions of religious devotees still zealously defend the doctrine of eternal soul damnation. They believe their God can't possibly tolerate those who break the rules or disagree with Him. They expect *earthly* parents to be infinitely loving and longsuffering with *their* children but seem perfectly okay with *God's* demonic treatment of *his*.

DK: A valid point, I suppose. We probably should require more insight and maturity from the super-brilliant Mind of the Cosmos.

J: Anyone with a few working brain cells should be offended by religion's loopy representation of God. Even those awash in the disturbing theology of guilt should expect the Lord of love to show a little more compassion. But somehow they've got no beef with a God who takes everything personally and consigns his ignorant, skeptical or rebellious children to infinity in a burning hell.

DK: Check me if I'm wrong here, but your premise seems to be that we're all literally inseparable from God and that, because we're one with Him in spirit, it would make no sense for Him to reject, punish or condemn.

J: Love would never *think* of such things. In a state of unity, who would be the accuser and who the accused?

DK: You're offering a spirituality of unqualified love. Naturally it's far more appealing than a theology of conditional salvation. But my sensibilities tell me there *must* be a price for what religion calls "sin."

J: Sure there's a price. In the realm of duality, actions have consequences. But none of it affects your reality as spirit. Human error is one thing, but "sin" has a spiritual tone. It implies that you and God are separate—that sometimes you're one with Him and sometimes you're not. In such a bewildering universe, God would be constantly joining and then separating from his very own creations. Here one minute, gone the next. This kind of theological paradigm is crazy, and folks need to start asking some tough questions.

DK: Like what?

J: Like, how long can we coddle and tolerate this two-faced, whimsical God being touted by religion? Is it reasonable to call Him loving when He judges and condemns his own children? If He's so darned interested, why doesn't He show up and take charge now and then? He was perfectly willing to micro-manage in the *old* days—so what the hell's kept Him waiting around for two thousand years?

DK: You're right. Tough questions.

J: But religion discourages people from considering this stuff because... well, we wouldn't wanna lose control or impair cash flow, you know.

DK: No wonder the Sanhedrin wanted you out of the neighborhood.

J: Hey, I'm not asking you to go dousing every burning bush or to throw out the baby with the baptismal water. But to grow spiritually, you have to start using your God-given intelligence and begin questioning ideas that seem outlandish. The humanized deity conceived by most people is an egomaniacal idiot at best. At worst, He's a murderous, judgmental tyrant. Do you really believe the force creating the infinite universe is tracking your sin-to-sanctity ratio?

DK: You make the God of religion sound like a celestial buffoon.

J: It's more about your own naïveté. You've spent a lifetime serving a foolishly juvenile and sickly distorted image of God. So who's the *real* buffoon?

DK: Alright... if there is no sin, then how do you explain the problem of evil in the world? Clearly it exists.

J: Which one—evil or the world?

DK: Well, I was referring to evil. The world's existence is obvious.

J: You may wanna reconsider. Logically, before the concept of evil arises, there's got to be a world in which it *can* arise. But the realm of spirit isn't dualistic. The world may *appear* evident—but have you examined it closely?

DK: Why would I bother? Unless we're sitting on a pile of nothing, the world is solid as a brick.

J: Don't put the saddle before the blanket. Some of history's greatest sages have talked about the deceptive nature of the material world. Eastern teachers have long called it "maya," meaning illusion. These people aren't deluded; they're simply tapping into the pre-egoic state of awareness. With that comes the clear understanding that consciousness gives rise to materiality—not vice versa.

DK: And how, may I ask, would the average unemployed writer *attain* this exalted state?

J: By paying close attention and giving it all some thought. You'll come to see that every phenomenon, even your concept of self, is really just a product of the mind.

DK: You're telling me that the world is only a *dream*!?

J: Putting it in modern terms, it's the ultimate virtual reality.

DK: Forgive the impertinence, O Font of Inscrutable Wisdom, but that smells like a stinky load of philosophical fertilizer.

J: Churchill said, "The truth is incontrovertible. Panic may resent it; ignorance may deride it; malice may distort it—but there it is."

DK: But c'mon, now, let's keep our feet on the ground. You can't ask me to believe the world is just a figment of my imagination. I might expect that kind of talk from an Indian swami, maybe. But this whole "dream world" thing just doesn't fit your usual *modus operandi*. Hell, next you'll have me chanting "OM" in the forest!

J: Scoff if you'd like. But I'm telling you, this has been the consistent finding of spiritual masters throughout time. Even I was quoted as saying, "Judge not by appearances." I said that because I knew that all form is illusory. How do you think I was able to cure the sick or heal the lame? That would be impossible if every mind were separate or if materiality was the solid stuff you believe it is. Quantum physics has already proven it isn't.

DK: Okay, then, I'm calling your bluff. If our minds are really united, then your enlightened consciousness should be available to *me* at this very moment. I should be able to experience the same world-negating reality that you do. Shoot, I would think a man of your caliber could lighten my spiritual dark spots and heal my psychological deceptions in a matter of seconds.

J: Your expectations are a little out of whack. I'm just a lowly messiah, not the good witch of the north.

DK: C'mon, you're backpedaling. Either we're connected or we're not.

J: We *are* connected. But you're not ready to see it, because you have conflicting goals: you very much *want* the world of your imagination. The Christ consciousness is always available—but you have to devote yourself to discovering it. You have to want *that and only that*.

DK: Sounds like a lot of work.

J: It's more a matter of focus. It takes clarity, intention, courage, and unwavering earnestness. You have to scrutinize the imagined self and realize its baseless nature. The process can be frightening because it topples all your towers—your presumed knowledge is annihilated. You'll think you've been left adrift on the ocean of consciousness, with no bearings and no destination. In fact, it feels like death… which it *is*: the death of the false self.

DK: If you're trying to sell me on enlightenment, then your sales pitch needs polish. You'd better hone your presentation skills.

J: Sorry to pee on your pajamas, pilgrim, but if you think the spiritual path is always fun or easy, you've been severely deceived. Awakening can be brutal business. As the old joke goes: if you aren't terrified, then you're not paying attention. The universe is loving, yes. But it'll drag you kicking and screaming through the mud if that's what it takes to bring you around. To ego, true love is inimical and ruthless. You'd better make sure everyone understands that.

DK: I've definitely been misled. Some people talk about spiritual growth like it's a metaphysical fun house.

J: Then they aren't doing folks any favors. You can't encourage someone to confront his delusions without explaining the potential trials. It's like inviting a shivering homeless man for a meal on a frigid winter day and then serving up popsicles.

DK: I don't think you ever made that clear.

J: Well, it wasn't for lack of trying. I told my disciples they would have to take up their crosses *daily*. The journey inward can be terribly burdensome—especially in the beginning. Saint John of the Cross referred to this spiritual rite of passage as "the dark night of the soul." You should know about it before you start. You have to remember there's light at the end of the tunnel, or the suffering connected with dissolving the illusory self will be too much to bear.

DK: That all sounds very Buddhist—very Eastern.

J: What the heck are you implying? I *was* Eastern! Listen, using easy labels to invalidate something is just another way to maintain defenses. It keeps belief systems safely intact and unexamined—a great way to stay comfortable but ignorant. If Buddhists have discovered a path to reality, so be it. Plenty of Christians, Hindus, Muslims, Jews, native shamans—even primitive jungle tribes have discovered the same eternal truths I'm sharing with you here.

DK: You're chipping away one sacred concept after another. I'm feeling totally disillusioned.

J: Oh, thank heaven. For a while I was afraid we weren't making any progress.

DK: Whaddaya mean?

J: I mean you can't go forward until you've begun to dispel your illusions. Therefore, you've got to be *dis-illusioned*.

DK: I don't think I'm ready for any self-inflicted wounds.

J: If you knew the bigger picture, pilgrim, you'd realize there's no other kind...

DK: Incidentally, you never answered my question about evil. Is it real, or not?

J: Let's put it this way: there's no such *thing* as evil. How could there be? If God's nature is only light, and if God is omnipresent, then there can *be* no darkness. To believe in the reality of death, suffering or evil is to believe that God's gifts are limited—which is the same as believing that God's *giving* is limited. The notion that

God withholds his full goodness until certain conditions are met is the foundation of most major religions.

DK: But let's be practical a minute and put God aside.

J: I'll ignore the irony…

DK: What I mean is that as far as *I* can tell, God rested on the seventh day and never returned to work. So when I talk about evil, I'm talking about *real life* and *real people*.

J: Action always stems from beliefs: you *behave* according to what you think you *are*. So evil, no matter how grave, is just a behavioral response to a warped view of reality—a frightened reaction to a mistaken self-image and a world misconstrued. You could simply call it unconsciousness or spiritual ignorance. It shows that you've identified with something you aren't.

DK: Then there's no devil dishing out trickery, destruction and death?

J: Good lord, man, who would've *created* this great Emissary of Evil?

DK: According to Revelation, Satan was initially one of God's angels. But then he led an angelic revolt in heaven. After warring against Archangel Michael and his forces, Satan and his angels were defeated and thrown out. *Now*, say the fundamentalists, he goes around creating havoc with *our* lives and tempting us to reject God.

J: So first, war breaks out in heaven.

DK: *I* know, it's a real contradiction. That one I haven't quite reconciled.

J: Next, Satan and his power-hungry band of rebels are defeated. But instead of being thrown into hell, where they belong, they're sent down to earth, seemingly free to sow as much destruction as possible.

DK: Yes, but only until their *ultimate* defeat during your Second Coming, several thousand years later.

J: And all of this while God just sits there like a candy-assed wimp and *allows* it!? Who invented this fairytale theology of yours? Dr. Seuss?

DK: C'mon, ease up with the mordant messiah routine. This account of evil's inception emanates straight from the hallowed halls of Christianity.

J: That doesn't validate it much. But look: darkness is just an absence of light. Bring in the light and the darkness vanishes back into nothingness. Same thing with evil... introduce the light of love and it disappears.

DK: If that's true, then evil is nothing but a concept.

J: That's *exactly* what it is. Evil has no independent reality. It's just a convenient label for unconscious behavior. Ego's tendency is to search for cause and effect. It sees moral mayhem and concludes there must be an unseen force behind it. So it looks at evil and invents a devil, which religion is all too happy to exploit.

DK: Bogus Beelzebub! So Lucifer is just a man-made scapegoat!

J: He's a carefully crafted product of literalism. Needing a cosmic fall guy, Christian fundamentalists took the poor schlep and turned him into the great Archenemy of God. But the Jews had no such character in their cosmology, which is why the term "devil" never appears in the Old Testament. The name "Satan" is used about a dozen times, mostly in the book of Job. But he's basically portrayed as a kind of expedient servant of God. The only time there's any real friction between the two is in Zechariah 3, where God only mildly rebukes him.

DK: Apparently old Lucie has gotten a lot more attention than he deserves.

J: Very few Christians realize that the name "Lucifer" occurs only once in the entire Bible—in the fourteenth chapter of Isaiah. Some versions omit the name completely. Even the tried-and-true Revised Standard Version uses "O Day Star, Son of Dawn!" instead.

DK: That'll never work. Doesn't have the same sinister ring to it...

J: Even though some people use that Isaiah verse as "proof" for the emergence of the devil, it's directed quite specifically to the ruling king of Babylon—and the writer plainly says so in verse four. Five minutes of research would show that "Lucifer" just means "bringer of light" or "light-bearer," which is a pretty strange moniker for a devil in the first place. Sometimes the name is translated "Day Star" or "Morning Star." I'll let you in on a little-known biblical secret: it's just a poetic reference to the planet Venus.

DK: Stars above! Sounds as though Lucifer is lucky to have lasted as long as he has.

J: Yep. I don't know how anyone could read that Isaiah passage and see the introduction of a universal fiend. It's a blatant example of coercing scripture to justify a theology.

DK: Alright, but you're talking Old Testament here. Satan also has plenty of *New* Testament support, some of which is attributed directly to *you*.

J: The devil's in the details, my friend: I didn't write one word of those stories. The fact is there's no Bible account of God creating any cosmic evildoer or even allowing one to materialize. Lots of ancient religions had anti-God characters, however, so it's not surprising that the concept was carried forward by several of the Bible's authors. Unfortunately, some of the literalist factions among the early Christians even had *me* talking about a devil. But then, if a guy's writing about me when I'm not around, he could have me spouting darned near any fool thing he wants.

DK: Now, what kind of unscrupulous bastard would *do* such a thing?

J: *Heh heh.* I wonder…

DK: Say, if there's no devil, then how do you explain the gospel account of that high-stakes spiritual wrestling match between you and Satan in the desert?

J: Ah, yes… the story you wielded like a crowbar to bludgeon me in your opening letter.

DK: *That's* the one.

J: My god, can't you people think *metaphorically*!? Do you read this stuff and just flip your brain switch to the "off" position? That desert narrative is a beautiful allegory about the temptation of the spiritual seeker to abandon his Godward journey for the short-lived treasures and pleasures of the world.

DK: Then there was no physical tempter present?

J: Blimey, pilgrim, when's the last time this devil character showed up at *your* place? No, wait—don't answer. I can just imagine it...

Ding-dong...
"Who's there?"
"It's Lucifer the devil calling."
"What're you selling?"
"Damnation, if you please. I'm here to lure your eternal soul into hell."
"Well, I dunno. What's the latest offer?"
"Just the usual stuff. A few fleeting years of wealth, power and fame. Maybe a little sex with coeds if you're lucky."
"Gee, Luce, old boy, it sure does sound *tempting*. But could you stop by a little later? I'm just hopping into the shower..."

CHAPTER THIRTEEN

DK: Okay, enough with the sit-down comedy shtick. You'd better get serious or this interview will have less credibility than a liberal in a Lamborghini.

J: Oh, but I *am* serious. I'm asking some dead-earnest questions here. You blather on about this Satan chap as if the two of you just spent the day chumming around the park. So I'd like to know: what direct, *personal* interaction have you had with the great Master of Malevolence?

DK: Well... none that I'm aware of.

J: And yet for decades you've carried this childish belief in a cosmic boogeyman who invisibly hovers over the earth, enticing people to sin and renounce God, demanding everything of genuine value while offering nothing of real worth in return.

DK: Well, I haven't really given it much th—

J: Hell's bells, man, how did you ever make it past grade school!? Is your family aware of your condition?

DK: Hey, gimme a break. This God-versus-Lucifer stuff has been shoved down our throats for a long time. Anyhow, the way I see it, the church owes its very *existence* to Satan. Without him and his burning lake, the need for salvation goes up in smoke and Christianity becomes more worthless than a sewing article in *Penthouse*. I'm telling you, the church *needs* the devil. Besides, can two billion Christians be *wrong*?

J: You bet your pitchfork they can. And so can a few billion believers from other religions. Shouldn't you all start showing a little more intellectual discrimination in your theologies?

DK: I'm afraid that revamping our views of God would require gutting most of the world's scriptures. Take the Old Testament, for example. It may not contain any running theme of soul damnation, but we both agree that it renders God as a very hard-nosed kinda guy who's even willing to mow down thousands of his own people when He's got a headache. So it's pretty tough developing a theology of love around *that* stuff. The *New* Testament isn't much better, because God comes across fairly harsh and somber in *those* writings, too. And I think *you* know what I'm talkin' about.

J: Hey, I taught my disciples to *love* one another. In my view, that's pretty straightforward. I told them not to judge and urged them to be kind, merciful and forgiving.

DK: Well, going by their New Testament letters, I'm not sure they got the message. But it's not your disciples I'm worried about. In the four gospels, *you're* the one who appears narrow-minded and disparaging. You weren't consistently *violent* like Yahweh—but judging by all those scrapes with the Scribes and Pharisees, you were almost as stern and unyielding.

J: Making threats of being cast into outer darkness and such.

DK: Yeah, that kinda thing. Now, after hearing your explanations, I can ignore your cryptic references to Satan and an afterworld of punishment where there's "wailing and gnashing of teeth." But *some* of the gospel narratives must be accurate; and if so, I sense that you were something of a moral drill sergeant. And you don't appear to have been all that tolerant, either. Sure, you were great to have around when boating in hurricanes or when supplies ran short in the kitchen. But you don't generally come across as being a helluva lot of fun.

J: A real party pooper, eh?

DK: Well, maybe not completely. I mean in the realm of good drama, you were definitely *da man*. When it came to showy, headline-grabbing photo ops, you were untouchable. And the miracles… my God, what a glorious show! You were a TV executive's dream-come-true. If one of those so-called "Christian" networks had *you* in the lineup, every minute of their phony, corporate-sponsored Hollywood showboat tripe would be airing with late-night infomercials. But after the way you treated the Pharisee who invited you to dinner, I'd be surprised if anyone even had you over to watch football at Thanksgiving.

J: C'mon, you're not being reasonable. You can't expect to know me from a few dozen second-hand gospel stories and a thimbleful of highly questionable "history." Using that kind of limited information, could anyone get a realistic reading of *your* life?

DK: But why all the finger-pointing, tongue-lashing and name-calling?

J: Again, I didn't write a *word* of that stuff. But it's not hard to see how it happened. Humans have a longstanding preoccupation with guilt. My ancestors merely made it an art form.

DK: They sure did. It shows up in the very first pages of their scriptures with God's punishment of Adam and Eve. From there, it runs like a thematic thread throughout the Bible, right down to the final book of Revelation. And nearly every step of the way, God is demanding blood, sacrifice and atonement. At first He's content to settle for butchered and burnt animals. In the end, however, He requires you—the human version of the sacrificial lamb—to be nailed in agony to a cross.

J: But look… even if you buy into the laughable idea that simple mortals can offend God, why would He lay their guilt onto *me*? Sacrificing an innocent man for others' wrongdoing doesn't do squat to change anyone's consciousness. It only creates further injustice. God could never *imagine* such madness.

DK: Actually, the whole atonement scenario is confusing. And I never understood how the Jews could allow the killing of their long-sought Messiah—especially when he was innocent.

J: You're overlooking an important fact: by *their* standards I *wasn't* innocent. I was constantly breaching their well-entrenched code of ethics, barbaric though it could be. Near the end, the Jews completely lost faith in me as the great deliverer. Their expected Messiah would've been rankling the *Romans*, not highlighting hypocrisy within *their own* circles. Once they sensed that I wouldn't save them from their worldly lot, even most of my supporters turned on me like a rabid dog. So the Jews hardly considered me the vanquishing liberator they were hoping for, and many felt I deserved what I got. They were the ones screaming for my execution, remember?

DK: Well, I still feel that, as "king of the Jews," you really got the royal shaft. From what I can tell, death by crucifixion was an absurdly severe penalty for your relatively harmless behavior.

J: In nearly every culture, infringement of sacred codes is serious business. By the time *my* generation rolled around, Judaism had done a thorough job of establishing its God as a deity of vengeance. Mosaic law made it perfectly clear that moral offenses *had* to be compensated—oftentimes with blood. Jewish leaders considered me a threat because I stepped over the line too many times, especially by claiming oneness with God and undermining conventional religious structures. They needed a solution that would send a powerful message to other potential troublemakers. And they got it.

DK: So to a people already comfortable with guilt and retribution, your violation of the law, coupled with your perceived arrogance, was apparently plenty of justification for putting you to death.

J: Absolutely. That mindset also explains why the breakaway factions that established literalist Christianity had no qualms historicizing the old story of an innocent savior who dies to atone for a guilty humanity. And even though they felt that their new religion supplanted the harsh rules of Judaism, in a more subtle way it was still a theology that demanded "an eye for an eye."

DK: It seems that's the only justice the world understands.

J: Spiritually, though, vengeance has no relevance. I reminded people that their "sins" were forgiven, because I knew that what God created perfect *remains* perfect. Guilt isn't real, because God's children are all part of Him, and guilt can never spring from innocence. So it's an ipso facto, Jacko, that the children of God can't possibly be guilty. I assume you're familiar with the gospel account of the woman caught in adultery?

DK: Of course.

J: In that little adventure, the Pharisees, who were sort of that period's equivalent of modern-day literalists, bring an adulterous woman to me, hoping to pin me down by reminding me that Jewish law requires adulterers to be stoned. Now, we both know that if folks began stoning everyone caught in adultery, the world would pretty quickly run out of rocks. But the Pharisee is a tough customer—a hypocrite of the highest order. He's a Ph.D. in the *letter* of the law but a flunkout in perceiving the spirit *behind* it. He's an academic bully with the tender-heartedness of a junkyard dog and the sensibility of a drunken teenager in a new Corvette. And despite the fact that he lives in a glass house, the Pharisee is always ready to start throwing rocks.

DK: It's pretty clear that the Pharisees weren't nearly as interested in punishing the woman's infidelity as they were in eliminating *you*.

J: They were a hungry pack of wolves, sensing blood and preparing for the kill. It was a perfect example of literalists using the "authority" of ancient writings—in this case the savage, uncompromising laws of Moses—to overrule the higher authorities of love, compassion and plain old common sense. The Pharisees knew that if I openly contradicted scripture, I would be subjecting myself to serious punishment. They also realized that if I allowed the woman to be stoned, my consent would discredit the message of love, forgiveness and non-judgment I was teaching and, in effect, would've made *me* responsible for her death. I would've appeared both weak *and* hypocritical. It was a classic no-win situation, and everyone knew it.

DK: So like a smug chess master closing in on checkmate, the Pharisees set the trap.

J: Yeah, they baited me: "So what is *your* opinion on the matter?"

DK: Scripture says that you then bent down and started drawing on the ground. What the heck were you doing?

J: I was just stalling. I thought I might buy a little time by doodling in the dirt. The woman's situation was bleak, and I had to figure a way to resolve it without getting either of us killed. So I doodled awhile.

DK: What was running through your head?

J: I knew that each of the Pharisees was too cowardly to act alone. Their pathetic show of force stemmed only from mob strength and herd psychology. I also knew that if I denounced their sacred scripture advocating murder, they'd have an open-and-shut case against *me*. So I knelt there thinking a minute, and finally the answer came: I'd use their own cowardice and perverted sense of justice *against* 'em. Instead of denigrating the moral code, which they desperately wanted me to do, I took a chance. I stood up and proposed that whoever was without fault should throw the first stone.

DK: Pretty darned clever.

J: After that, I bent down and quietly started doodling again. I was careful not to look at anyone directly—but I kept close watch through the corner of my eye. As the harsh implications of my words went crashing through their consciousness and reverberated in the tense silence, one by one the bloodthirsty cowards began to leave. It would seem that "secret guilt by silence is betrayed." Know who said that?

DK: I'm guessing it wasn't Nixon.

J: The English playwright Dryden.

DK: I should've bought a vowel...

J: The moral of the story, of course, is that everyone makes mistakes. The Pharisees, if only grudgingly, were forced to acknowledge they were no different from the woman they were about to kill. Their own misdeeds took different *forms*, perhaps—but they shared the same human imperfection.

DK: Powerful. You made Solomon's stuff look like penny ante poker.

J: I only mention it to address the belief that I was judgmental. The story should demonstrate that I neither judge nor condemn; I just highlight self-destructive thinking. This helps correct the basic error, which is always some form of the mistaken belief that everyone has separate interests. Non-judgment is a sure sign of higher consciousness and one of the big keys to inner peace. But for those focused on guilt, judgment is never more than a stone's throw away.

DK: Scripture says that after the mob dispersed, you told the woman that you didn't condemn her. But you also told her, "Go and do not sin again."

J: Yes, but not because I would've *judged* her the next time. I just knew she wasn't likely to be that *lucky* again. And here's something else that's been misunderstood: although I didn't judge the adulterous woman, *neither did I judge the Pharisees.* I may have caused waves by revealing hypocrisy now and then, but I was usually just articulating the obvious. I always looked upon the face of my brothers and sisters and remembered God. As expressions of Christ, every person on earth should strive to do the same. Your own mission is not much different from mine.

DK: Well, in our case I hope we can rework the ending a bit.

J: Don't worry—no crucifixion required. You're only being asked to remember the truth of your brother's divinity *for* him until he remembers it for himself. Look past his illusions and see the goodness and grandeur that so often lie hidden. Being united in spirit, doing this will increase the light for you both. And don't bother preaching. Just practice awareness, compassion and forgiveness, and let spirit take it from there.

DK: You know, for the last few years I was beginning to wonder if you were just another iron-fisted religious extremist. But by God, you're beginning to sound almost human.

J: I can see that I've definitely been getting some bad press.

DK: Let's just say that your biographers didn't do you any favors. They gave us a savior who healed the blind, alright. But when it came to anticipating the problems he would create for later generations, he himself couldn't see past tomorrow. He walked on water but couldn't save *anyone else* from drowning. He resurrected the dead but left a theology that wound up condemning most of the living. He promised the kingdom of heaven, but what actually arose was a hypocritical, sanctimonious, money-grubbing, religious bureaucracy from hell. I hate to break it to ya, chief, but after hearing some of the stuff you've said today, I can assure you that your factory's no longer shipping the original product.

J: Well, that's what usually happens when the inventor dies: management starts focusing on the bottom line. Then they go and change the formula…

CHAPTER FOURTEEN

DK: I have to admit that this new perspective is shifting my views. But it definitely won't play well in Peoria—not to those who still see you as a prophet of ruin. Most people have fixed ideas about your life and what it meant, and I doubt there's much hope of winning them over.

J: Just tell 'em you had a little chat with Jesus down by the river.

DK: Yeah, right. I'd have better luck claiming I had lunch with Elvis.

J: Oh well, forget proselytizing—it's not your job to change anyone. That's religion's whole problem: it has believers everywhere focusing on *others*. *Your* responsibility is to seek the truth for *yourself* and to accept your brother as he is. *A Course in Miracles* says, "The Holy Spirit speaks to *you*. He does not speak to someone else." If you were capable of leading others to truth, you would've already found it yourself and wouldn't need a savior in the first place. Correcting errors and revealing truth is *spirit's* function, not yours.

DK: You talk about human error like it's nothing but a bad calculation on a math quiz. But a lot of man's "errors" have had some pretty dreadful results. Personally, I'm sick to death of living in a world of cluster bombs, nerve gas, landmines and depleted uranium. So I say to *hell* with their inventors, manufacturers and those who order their use as if they were perfectly acceptable options. From what I've observed, most wars are really just state- and corporate-sponsored land grabs, aimed at putting obscene profits into the pockets of the world's banksters and the fear-mongering death-squads of the military-industrial complex. Like almost everyone, I'm *dog tired* of paying the high price of their so-called "protection."

J: I see. And how did *that* make you feel?

DK: Very funny, Freud. And by the way… this may not sit too well with *you*, but most of us have had it up to *here* with granting religious tolerance to every fruitcake devotee with a holy book in one hand and an automatic rifle or suitcase bomb in the other.

J: Yes, wonderful. You seem to be getting in touch with your inner child…

DK: Joke all you want, but most of us are majorly OD'd on a world run by hypocritical, elitist, sound-bite-spewing career politicians out to control the world. These professional leeches gorge themselves at the public trough, unimaginatively preserving the status quo and living like bloody *royalty* on sweaty tax dollars while urging everyone else to tighten their belts. I'm telling you, we're fed up with their testosterone-jacked, war-first, schoolyard bully mentality. We're burnt out on all their secret agenda, secret alliances, secret policies, secret surveillance—and secret damned *everything*.

J: Perhaps you'd like to discuss your relationship with your mother…

DK: And as if all *that* weren't enough, those of us who still find the will to bother caring are stressed to the max on ocean dumping, trade wars, myopic foreign policy, slash-and-burn deforestation, political propagandizing, population explosion… and telephone customer service reps who don't speak the friggin' *language*!

So listen, savior boy—you wanna do some *real* good in the world? You wanna make a *difference*? Then set us all free, O heavenly confessor. Liberate us, each and every one, from the shackles of big-brother government, welfare-state entitlement spending, and the sinister, wealth-sapping ensnarement of the arrogant, God-forsaken Federal Reserve!!

J: Anything else?

DK: Yeah… give us this day our daily bread—but without forcing us to relinquish half the loaves into the outstretched palms of useless bureaucratic parasites. Deliver us from evil at the hands of all the devious, self-serving special-interest groups and their sickening nonstop gush of slippery, disingenuous spin. Lead us beside the still, non-municipally-fluoridated waters and make us to lie down in green pastures where we're free from the controlling grip of morally vacant Wall Street gangsters; a politically perverted legal system; an ominous New World Order; robotic God-and-country patriots—and twenty freakin' *thousand* pages of *tax code*!!!

J: I'm sorry, Mr. Maylor, but it appears our session time is up. That'll be three hundred dollars, which you can pay conveniently by credit card to the secretary on the way out. Please remember to take your medication, and I'll see you at our usual time on Thursday…

DK: Okay, okay—so I got a little carried away. But I just can't get past this life-is-beautiful, see-no-evil philosophy of yours. The mushroom clouds are looming, and you see nothing but clear skies ahead!

J: Hey, the world as it stands is a veritable loony bin—and nearly always has been. All I've said is that, regardless of severity, evil is merely the result of mistaken self-perception. And *nothing in the world* can shift your perception. Only *you* can do that.

DK: So in *your* mind, the world is a hopeless cause.

J: The world is in *your* mind, pilgrim, not in mine. And it isn't a cause but an *effect*. Therefore, it's neither hopeless nor promising.

DK: To hear *you* describe it, evil is simply a product of spiritual ignorance.

J: Well, isn't it obvious? Who would choose to exploit, neglect, abuse or attack if he knew everything to be one with his very *self*?

DK: I'm not sure I understand this "oneness" thing. Here I am, and there you are sitting across from me. Clearly we're separate.

J: You're referring to our bodies, which are indeed separate. But surely you've realized by now that *you* are not your *body*.

DK: Say *what*?

J: Oh, c'mon, sonny. Don't tell me you grew up in the arms of the Christian church and failed to grasp the whole point of the Resurrection.

DK: Not sure I'm following.

J: Look, if the Resurrection proved anything, it proved that life is not the body. No matter what else you believe about the event, you have to ask yourself one thing: What was it that was resurrected?

DK: The answer seems evident: your body.

J: That's the common view, yes. If you accept the biblical accounts of the Passion, then you'd have to conclude that the Jewish and Roman authorities believed they were snuffing out my life because they were killing my *body*. What they didn't understand—and what the vast majority of human beings *still* don't understand— is that *we are not our bodies*. Bodies are just skin and bones... a temporary accumulation of food and water.

DK: Maybe so, but there's a cute little blonde at the dry cleaners whose accumulation is pretty damned impr—

J: What I'm saying is that your body is not the same thing as *you*. Bodies have no volition of their own. They don't reason, feel, or think, and they don't have the power to make you do *any*thing.

DK: You haven't seen the chick at the cleaners.

J: Hey, I can appreciate a tight-jeaned babe as well as the next guy. But I'm telling you, bodies are just interesting piles of stardust—and extremely transient. Now, form can be *fascinating*, I'll give you that. But the important thing is the life behind it. You have to realize that you aren't the structure that's being energized and animated: you're the energizing, animating force itself.

DK: If the body is basically inconsequential, then why the big Christian focus on the Resurrection?

J: Because ego can't imagine existence without form. And since ego thoroughly identifies with the body, it makes sense that an ego-based theology would center on physical reality and require a bodily resurrection to counteract the seeming finality of death. When someone speaks of immortal life, what they're usually envisioning is an eternity in some non-destructible *form*.

DK: In other words, a body.

J: Exactly. People may talk convincingly about the importance of the spirit, but what really keeps 'em up at night is their ongoing concern for the body. I mean the way some folks talk about their religion's heaven, you'd think they'd be scrambling to line up for the poisoned Kool-Aid. But no, most of 'em cling to the body for as long as they can—and at damned near any cost. Even when their bodies are used up and their quality of life is near zero, they'll drive their families into poverty just to lay in bed a few more years and drool on themselves. They consider the body essential for existence and the key to their happiness and survival.

DK: But somehow you didn't see it that way.

J: Not at all. I came to understand that spirit doesn't have the slightest need for the world of form. So the authorities could destroy my *body*, but I knew beyond doubt that they could never touch *me*. They misunderstood reality the same way you do: they identified with their bodies. It's the fundamental mistake of the world and the very basis of the separation idea. Understanding all this, I knew that death of the body is ultimately meaningless.

DK: Yet you're reported to have said from the cross, "Father forgive them, for they know not what they do." It sounds like you believed a serious offense had occurred.

J: Just for the sake of debate, I'll take the *other* side: Why would my executioners need God's forgiveness?

DK: Because they knowingly murdered an innocent man!

J: But if having me crucified was God's grand plan all along, as most Christians believe, then it seems to me that all those involved in my arrest, sentencing and execution were essentially

assumed yourself to be. Your entire personality is a gigantic delusion based on memories, ideas and habitual thinking. The self-realized understand that they aren't their bodies or their minds— or *anything* they could describe or point a finger at.

DK: A little too esoteric for *my* taste.

J: There's really nothing weird or mystical about it. Enlightenment is just the sudden recognition of your natural state, which is completely beyond definition or description.

DK: But the notion that I'm some sort of body-mind combination seems indisputable.

J: Again, the idea that the sun revolved around the earth once seemed equally apparent. Upon examination, however, the geocentric model of the universe was eventually proven false. In the same way, your egocentric idea that you're a body-mind will disintegrate once you seriously question it.

DK: Since you had this "I am not a body" understanding, did you remain unafraid when you realized you were actually going to die?

J: I didn't fear death *in itself,* because spirit can't be killed. But I was sure as hell *focused.* Believe me, nothing puts enlightenment to the test like the threat of a few well-placed crucifixion spikes. I knew beyond doubt, however, that the body wasn't critical to my existence.

DK: Still, it was a noble sacrifice.

J: Those who insist that I was sacrificed at Calvary don't have a clue. Who would've *required* this gallant deed?

DK: God, of course.

J: God never requires sacrifice, because God only *gives;* He doesn't *take.* If God is everything and if everything is one, then who is sacrificing to whom—and for what? There's nothing about love that needs appeasing. And what would you or I possess that God could possibly want? Would a loving God offer life and then put us through hell by cruelly demanding it back by way of death? How would He justify such foolishness? By offering hope that He might bestow life again at some point in a nebulous future?

DK: I can't speak to the wisdom of it. But still, no one held a gun to your head. We're told that you freely *offered* yourself in sacrifice—to atone for our sins.

J: We've already agreed that it isn't reasonable for God to require the shedding of *my blood* to make amends for *someone else's behavior*. I can assure you that God, in his vast intelligence, wouldn't deem such stupidity of value to *anyone*—least of all to Himself.

DK: Well, *something* must have been lost at Golgotha.

J: That's the great irony. The critical point of the Crucifixion is the one that most Christians never seem to grasp: *nothing was lost*. The only thing you could remotely consider sacrificed in that episode would be my body. But why would I offer up my body, knowing its inherent worthlessness? Besides, scripture asserts that I knew I would be resurrected very quickly. So what kind of sacrifice is it to go without a body for a couple of days? Someday soon, you'll be without one yourself—and for a helluva lot longer than a weekend.

DK: True, but I won't be shedding my lifeblood for a sinful humanity.

J: And neither did I. In that regard, the Crucifixion has been horribly misconstrued. According to the church, I volunteered to descend to earth and submit to slaughter so that God could forgive his children. Can you think of anything more insane? It's like a son telling his father, "Listen, dad, I heard that my brothers and sisters have been acting very badly and that they've really got you upset. Now, I know that you love them dearly—so if it'll help you forgive them, you can go ahead and have me killed."

DK: I think you're loading the dice. I mean *of course* it'll sound nuts when you present it like *that*.

J: But that's exactly how the church *does* present it! They just don't spell it out quite so bluntly. Besides, what kind of whacko father would actually *agree* to this psychotic plan? And anyone who'd go along with it would be just as crazy as the one who conceived it.

DK: Then I'm forced to wonder what was really accomplished by your death on the cross.

J: Nothing whatsoever. As we've already established, the body has no value in itself. It's just a neutral thing, neither good nor bad. It can be helpful and enjoyable if used properly, and potentially disastrous when it isn't. You could view it as a kind of learning aid—a temporarily useful means of experience and communication. When its function is finished, you gently lay it aside, like a worn-out garment. *My* body had no more cosmic significance than yours.

DK: Possibly not. But you still chose to participate in the Crucifixion when you easily could've opted out. That's pretty sacrificial in my book.

J: Millions throughout history have sacrificed their bodies for others. In that sense, my death was hardly unique. Now, I'll be the first to admit that I certainly didn't *deserve* to be killed, since I hadn't harmed anyone and had in fact helped and healed many. But no one can die for anyone else because, first, there *is* no death; and second, if there *were*, it quite obviously couldn't be transferred like some industrial carbon credit. In fact, the Bible states very specifically in 2 Kings, and again in 2 Chronicles, that "every man shall die for his own sin." Another thing to realize about the Crucifixion is that God wasn't punishing *me* because *everyone else* was *evil*. That's lunacy. Love doesn't murder to save.

DK: But God must expect *some*thing for his trouble.

J: C'mon, Sparky, try not to reason like a cheerleader. What the hell kind of trouble has anyone ever caused *God!!??* I mean if God's mood can be soured by a wretched little speck of life on an insignificant dot floating through a nondescript galaxy in a darkened corner of an unlimited universe… well, I can only say that if you've got that kind of power over the Almighty, then the real God would essentially be *you*.

DK: It's probably residue from my upbringing, but I just can't believe that God could be so magnanimous as to accept us no matter what.

J: And that's your biggest problem: you can't even *imagine* infinite love. As long as people believe that God requires sacrifice, my life and message will appear threatening and fearful. They'll perceive God as a tyrant. And they'll continue feeling justified butchering one another in his name.

DK: You're contradicting just about everything we're told about you in the New Testament. The scriptures make clear that you came to prevent God from sending us all to hell.

J: Another good candidate for the litmus test I suggested earlier: "Is it *reasonable?*" Honestly, does the Christian story of God's redemption really make sense? It's no more rational than much of the behavior attributed to Him in the Old Testament. How coincidental—and how convenient for those who use scripture to justify violence—that the Lord of Love would consistently work his will and effect his agenda by the very same method so long utilized by mankind: through the killing of the innocent.

DK: Alright, but your death wasn't only about atonement. It was also said to be proof of God's immeasurable love.

J: Well, if the God of the Bible really loves his children, He's got a damned strange way of showing it.

DK: So in the eyes of heaven, *your* life was no more important than *ours*.

J: My life had more of an *impact* than most, because so few have attained that level of spiritual insight. But contrary to church teaching, there was nothing unique about my basic *nature*. Whatever I accomplished, so too could others—and I plainly said that. My life was no more blessed than yours, nor was there anything special about my death.

DK: The New Testament says that your death *was* unique because you were the "only begotten Son of the Father."

J: Which would make *you* a kind of bastard child, would it not? The phrase you're quoting is much more sensible as, "the begotten Son of the *only Father.*"

DK: But that description could apply to anyone.

J: *Exactly...*

CHAPTER FIFTEEN

DK: Well, I have to say it again: proclaiming everyone divine is fairly revolutionary.

J: It was equally revolutionary when Semmelweis and Pasteur told their colleagues to wash their hands.

DK: The thing is, you claim that all of God's children are innocent. Yet the Bible says the problem of sin was so acute that it required God sending you as his divine emissary to resolve it. Wasn't negation of sin the main reason for your worldly appearance?

J: Depends on what you mean. By stabilizing my awareness in reality, I cleared a trail for others to do the same. As a universal way-shower, I help people awaken to their own Christ potential. Once they do, they realize there can *be* no sin because there's no such thing as defiled spirit. In that respect, I take away the sins of the world by demonstrating that the world itself is ultimately without substance.

DK: I still say that sounds like some kind of New Age pseudo-theology.

J: Maybe I'm not making myself clear: I'm not here pushing *philosophy*. I'm not touting some theory you should strive to believe or accept on faith. You can fully verify what I'm saying by moving steadfastly inward. I can't do your spiritual work *for* you, of course. But my awakening, like anyone else's, also contributes to yours. Discovering your inner light is contagious, which is why I said, "Let your light shine." Although it generally goes unnoticed, the Christ presence resides in everyone. And when the flame of truth begins burning brightly in one, it also ignites the fires of awareness in others. A single spark can set the entire forest ablaze.

DK: Not to be pessimistic, but I wouldn't expect that forest fire of new consciousness anytime soon. Not in *this* crazy world.

J: Temporally, the process *can* take a very long time. But from the standpoint of the Absolute, it's already accomplished. That which was, still is… and ever shall be. "I AM" is the Alpha *and* the Omega—not separately, but all at once. You've got to discover this for yourself, though, because there's no progress in leaning on the belief that I was a special case.

DK: John's gospel has you claiming, "I am the way, the truth and the life." It sounds like you believed you *were* special.

J: What I said and what got passed along in the gospels decades later were often two different things. State it this way: I AM is the way, the truth and the life. The Old Testament line, "Be still and know that I am God," requires the same kind of correction: Be still and know the I AM is God. Once you realize what these cryptic scriptures are describing, they take on new meaning—they start to make sense.

DK: What is this "I AM"?

J: It can't be defined—but it can easily be sensed and experienced. Using words only as pointers, you could describe the I AM as the silent stillness within. The conscious, life-filled, energetic presence at the root of you. It's your immediate, unchanging connection with the divine, and to know it intimately is your "salvation."

DK: The church says that salvation lies only in "professing Jesus."

J: There's no salvation in a name.

DK: Then what of that "turn or burn" stuff? I mean how does all this Bible reinterpretation affect the "Jesus Saves" movement?

J: In the way that salvation is typically preached, it nullifies it completely. Once more, let's apply a little reason. If we accept the literalist view, God creates man as perfect and then throws him into the Garden with his infamous free will. This "free" will turns out to be pretty damned expensive, though, because it essentially allows man to destroy himself.

DK: But if God is omniscient, then He should've seen the trouble coming.

J: You'd think so. But for some reason He creates man anyway and then has the audacity to act surprised and wounded when man actually *succumbs* to temptation and eats the forbidden fruit. Now,

I ask you: what kind of God *behaves* like this!? I mean we're talking about the all-powerful creator of the universe. We're told that He reigns supreme and that his will can never be thwarted. Suddenly, though, his divine plan is shattered and his infinite power usurped by a couple of scrawny test creatures with boundary issues!

DK: Check my thinking here… but if God's intent was to have a perfect creation, and yet feeble little Adam and Eve were able to keep Him from having it, then not only is the Bible God not omniscient, but He's also not omnipotent.

J: The logic is sound. And God's two young rebels voided his supremacy not just once but *several* times. As you said, they denied God his desire for a flawless creation; but they also forced Him to do things He clearly didn't want to do. So in their influence on the world's destiny, Adam and Eve were at least as powerful as God. Almost as soon as they're breathing, the pitiful savages make chaos of the Almighty's erstwhile problem-free paradise—which of course took nearly a full week of demanding shift work to produce.

DK: It seems humanity made Frankenstein's monster look like a sixth-grade science project.

J: Yep. Very soon on, God's creation of intelligent life spins wildly out of control. In fact, by only the sixth chapter of Genesis He's already fed up with the whole irritating arrangement and decides to drown every man, woman, child and beast on the planet—that is, with the obvious exception of Noah's family and their floating zoo.

DK: But even that apparently didn't solve the problem.

J: Unfortunately not. Like most of the Bible God's crackpot schemes, drowning all humanity in the Great Flood was a total waste of time. Noah's offspring were just as prone to violence, idiocy and fleshly indulgence as their antediluvian ancestors.

DK: So the fly's in the ointment once again as mankind spoils God's earthly nirvana for the second time.

J: Correct. He obviously needs a more effective plan to set things right. After giving it some thought for, oh, a couple thousand years, God finally hits on a remedy that He figures just can't miss. He brings in a divine superhonky—that's *me*—who's totally incapable of sinning and enviably perfect in every way. Now, why

He didn't create *everyone* in this manner has yet to be explained. But I digress… So for several centuries God ponders the problem of sin, and suddenly it hits Him: "I've got it!" He exclaims. "Jumpin' Jehoshaphat, what a stroke of brilliance! Why didn't I think of this before!? I'll let them murder my son!!"

DK: And then, by way of some trumped-up charges in a Roman kangaroo court, God allows you to be brutally rubbed out.

J: Actually, if you believe that God and I are one and the same, then you'd have to say that *God killed Himself.* No getting around *that* conclusion, right?

DK: I'll have to think this one through…

J: Well, anyhow… as the church tells it, God in his bottomless wisdom decides that I should die a horrible, sacrificial death to atone for evil in the sullied soul of humanity. Therefore I, in my heavenly innocence, choose to incarnate and suffer for *your* sorry butts. Otherwise you lesser life forms could never make it into heaven because… well, because you're just too darned vile.

DK: Despite the derisive tone, maybe God perceived a real *need* for symbolic absolution.

J: But let's be honest: it's not a very big God who goes around nursing grudges and keeping tabs on his children's mistakes. I mean salvation wouldn't be needed in the first place if not for the dull-minded deity who came up with the silly idea. Any eighth-grade "B" student could see that the plan would never work. The craziest part is that, in its essence, Christian "salvation" is really just a divinely provided loophole to escape its Designer's own wickedly sadistic nature.

DK: Definitely a creative new slant.

J: But it's true: the need for absolution is questionable from the start. And even if God *did* want an officially sanctioned act of forgiveness, He just as easily could've descended in a whirlwind of glory and declared the job finished: "No problem, folks, you're all forgiven! Let's eat!"

DK: Although that wouldn't have required any sacrifice or effort on *our* part.

J: Neither did my crucifixion.

DK: Hmmm. So you're proposing that God might just as well have worked out a *non-violent* solution. A kind of one-time, no-exclusions, non-expiring absolution of sin.

J: Well, why not? After all, He's *God*. He can do as He pleases, right? Who's gonna stop Him? But no, the God of literalist Christianity can't bring Himself to simply forgive and move on with his life. Instead, He's sorely offended by his naughty urchins and constantly makes a dramatic production of it.

DK: At least He got everyone's attention.

J: But why does He *internalize* everything? Why is the Bible God so egocentric about his children's rambunctious behavior? It's not like the little miscreants have any mindfulness of *Him* while they're busy transgressing.

DK: It appears the Big Guy just can't tolerate being challenged or ignored.

J: No, and He doesn't handle offenders with a mere slap on the wrist, either. He's out for blood and wants to make damned sure his children *know* how wretched they are. He wants *them* to feel the pain of his *personal* burden. So He plans the Crucifixion—centuries in advance, according to the church—to make sure his unruly subjects will fully appreciate the ominous implications of their iniquity. If they want salvation, they'll have to pay the price in *guilt*.

DK: Once again I can't explain the *thinking* behind it. But surely God realizes that some people are too young or innocent even to understand the basic *concept* of sin. Others are raised in situations that would never realistically allow them to *accept* the Christian message.

J: Doesn't matter, say the literalists. God is a God of *justice*, they'll tell you—as if eternity in hell for holding a dissenting view could possibly be construed as just.

DK: Okay, but even the God of fundamentalism purportedly has a tender side. Some literalists maintain that even if a person wasn't a Christian at death, a few special, cooperative cases might still qualify for salvation. They say that God judges the *heart*.

J: If God were the judge you believe He is, then evaluating people's *hearts* might at least show some sensibility. But in a scheme like *that*, good works and professions of faith could well be worthless.

DK: According to one fundamentalist camp, even if a life-long killer repents on his deathbed and accepts you as his savior, God will forgive him and take him into the kingdom.

J: Here again you're describing a God who's several bricks short of a load. First, He painstakingly commands his children to follow strict ethical standards based on fairness, respect and high moral order. Those who disobey face the gravest of consequences. But then He allows the entire system, no matter how grievously abused, to be instantly circumvented by a simple escape clause of his own invention. So if New Testament theology can be trusted, salvation is a mere technicality.

DK: Growing up in the church, I was so thoroughly programmed by the teachings that I didn't even consider the *possibility* that God might've pardoned us without having you killed. I mean the thought never crossed my mind. I was raised under the specter of Hebrews 9:22: "…without the shedding of blood there *is* no forgiveness of sins."

J: It just shows how naïve and unquestioning you've been. Somebody spoon-feeds you this biodegradable waste, and you swallow it like a baby slurping down strained carrots. *The entire philosophy is nuts!* Not only that, but it reeks with the stench of hypocrisy. The Bible declares that God wants his children to practice love and forgiveness—but no one is disturbed by the fact that He Himself can hardly ever "turn the other cheek" when *his own* feelings are injured. I mean when the God of heaven is disappointed, all hell breaks loose!

DK: It does seem that He usually isn't happy until He's administered some meaningful violence. You'd think He'd find a *quiet* solution now and then.

J: No, sir—not Yahweh. He's strictly a God of retribution: someone's gotta *pay*. All through the Old Testament, He's constantly beating his chest and responding to human shortcomings with intimidation, nasty threats and the use of lethal force. "I'll send down *plagues*," He thunders, "and strike you *dead* if I have to! You disobedient bunch of free-willed reprobates! Don't you know who I *am*!!?"

DK: But by the time *you* showed up, centuries later, God had mellowed a bit.

J: That's true. His redemptive "justice" still centers on guilt and vengeance, but generally He begins taking a more manipulative, self-righteous approach: "*Now* look what you've made me do," He tells humanity scoldingly. I mean He acts as though He had no *choice* but to have me killed—as if there was no alternative. So he puts *me* through hell so that *you* can get to heaven. Makes perfect sense, don't you think?

DK: You know, I felt a little guilty when I was railing about this stuff in my letter. But after talking it out, I think I actually may have been too kind. The entire salvation arrangement is completely cranked! The God of literalism has the temperament of a pit bull, the patience of a hound-cornered fox, an ego the size of Dallas, and the brain of a small rodent.

J: Yeah, sort of an oversized public official.

DK: I'm beginning to like your previous suggestion that God could've bypassed earthly theatrics altogether simply by making *everyone* perfect—like you. That would've eliminated the very *need* for salvation.

J: "No, no, no—that'll *never* do," says God. "What we need here is some serious *drama*. Before they gain entrance to my eternal day spa, the pitiful little hellions will have to *earn* it!" "Besides," He reasons, "if I don't give my children the ability to *refuse* my kindly grace, how will I know if they really *love* me?" So here's the omnipotent king of creation exhibiting a neurotic insecurity that makes Woody Allen look like John Wayne.

DK: Well, I'm sure He didn't want a race of mindless androids walking the planet—but God really dropped a fork in the blender by giving humanity free will.

J: And that, according to the Christian scenario, is where *I* come in. By the strictest interpretation, those who believe in me are saved, and those who don't will be forever toasted to a golden crisp. For a large percentage of his children, God's glorious plan of "salvation" leads directly to their eternal affliction. Thus has God's wisdom grown so damned mysterious that it now shows genuine signs of psychopathology.

DK: It's pretty obvious why Christianity has flourished: the fear factor is powerful. And it certainly worked in *my* case. For years, the main reason I embraced religion was to escape the sufferings of Hades. Although I must say that with all the craziness I witnessed within the church, there were times I didn't see much difference.

J: *Heh heh.* There's a fine line between heaven and hell. In fact, according to the gospel story of Lazarus and the rich man, the two locales are within shouting distance.

DK: Now, *there's* a picture: eternal bliss on one side, with wailing and gnashing of teeth on the other.

J: Yes, and that presents *another* vexing theological puzzle.

DK: Which is what?

J: How will anyone in heaven manage to sleep with all that noise next door?

CHAPTER SIXTEEN

DK: Well, okay… so you've made a pretty good case for re-thinking the Christian message, especially the Crucifixion and the meaning of salvation. But I still have a problem with the Resurrection. I mean rising from the dead isn't your everyday parlor trick. It's an exceptional claim, to say the least.

J: Not necessarily. Other traditions have stories of saints resurrecting. And medical annals are full of cases involving someone clinically dead returning to life.

DK: Not after three days.

J: No, but going by gospel standards for "Most Days Dead Before Resurrecting," I don't even hold the record.

DK: Huh?

J: What about my friend Lazarus? Scripture claims that *he* was dead *four* days before *his* comeback.

DK: You're right, I forgot about him. He outlasted you by a day or more. What happened? Things get a little boring on your weekend excursion to hell?

J: I got tired of all that wailing and gnashing of teeth.

DK: *Heh heh.* I swear, in the history of outlandish messiahs, you get the first place trophy.

J: Really? Who takes second?

DK: Jesse Jackson.

J: Uh huh… You know, you seem a little surprised that I can laugh and have fun.

DK: Well, the gospels depict you as a real sourpuss.

J: I guess that's only natural. After all, salvation's not exactly a topic for late-night talk show gags. You can't really expect folks to bust into giggles when my name is mentioned.

DK: No, but offhand I can't think of a single church teaching that even *suggests* you had a sense of humor. To my knowledge, there's no biblical reference to you ever having a good chuckle or even cracking a smile. I mean it's not like the gospels are chock-full of you telling your favorite rabbi jokes.

J: It's true. Not once am I presented as a light-hearted personality relishing the moment. In fact, nowhere in the New Testament is there any real emphasis on appreciation of the present or on the simple, immediate savoring of the gift of existence. The spotlight is usually on some *future* life in which the fortunate redeemed will somehow derive unending pleasure by giving glory to God. With this kind of brainwashing, you can see why so many Christians experience a deep sense of unworthiness: the church has managed to make them feel guilty for even *being* here! But the truth is, I enjoyed life and had plenty of good times. Some folks were downright irritated by it. They considered me almost a hedonist and resented that I hung out with drunks, prostitutes and other shady types.

DK: But even though you make the occasional sardonic statement, we're never given any details of you really cutting loose. The four gospels have you sounding more like a chastening parent than a compassionate teacher—they barely give you a *whisper* of mundane humanity. When you aren't caught up in some big drama, you're busy moralizing on mountains or lambasting local religious groups.

J: Remember, the gospels are extremely condensed accounts of my life *as passed along by others*. Entirely second-hand stuff. And naturally the writers focused on what they considered the most important points. Which is only sensible, I suppose. I mean nobody wants to hear about Jesus mowing the backyard or making off-color wisecracks about Romans. So you'll never understand me by way of the scriptures. Reading the New Testament, a fella gets the impression that every time this Jesus character shows up, a sermon breaks out.

DK: What bothers me is that the impression was unanimous. The gospel writers all paint the same picture of a sober and surly savior in desperate need of an oil massage and a few puffs of the sacred weed.

J: Believe me, that was no accident. The solemn nature of the New Testament was part of church strategy to expand the flock. Scripture had to motivate folks to sign on, and a jovial, laid-back messiah would never cut the mustard.

DK: Well, it's like I said before: if we wanna know anything about you, the Bible's all we've got.

J: But try to be practical. I walked the earth for more than *thirty years*, for gosh sakes. Yet if you took each quote ascribed to me in the New Testament, you could read the whole collection in about two hours. Add the fact that much of it is fabricated and you discover that you've got very little turkey and way too much stuffing. So how much could you really learn?

DK: I do know the four gospels weren't written until long after you died—which is cause for suspicion right from the opening bell. And interestingly, *not one* is written in the first person. Apart from a couple of vague lines from John, the gospel writers never really talk about you in a *personal* way. Even in the introduction to the book of Luke, the writer *implies* that some of his material was obtained from people who knew you; but strangely he doesn't *say* that. Instead he says that he got it from "eyewitnesses and ministers of the word," which could mean something altogether different. Just once I'd like to read a first-hand account of *A Day in the Life of Jesus*. Maybe something like…

"And then Jesus and I went to Capernaum, where we delivered an entire third-grade class from Attention Deficit Disorder. Next, we knocked back a couple of stiff ones with a few off-the-wagon Zealots at a local watering hole. That's where the J-man told us about the time he was thirteen and played a practical joke on his father by turning his prized bottle of 20-years-old fig wine back into water."

J: Well, my disciples could've told a few stories, alright. But as you said, the New Testament authors penned their writings a long time after I was gone. And not a single original document remains.

DK: Nevertheless, the Apostles seemed ready to meet their maker on your account. They must've been confident their message was true.

J: That argument is based almost entirely on other New Testament information, so it's classic circular reasoning. Besides, fanatical behavior tends to reflect a position's weakness, not its strength. Only the *theoretical* needs *promoting*. I mean how many fanatics have tried convincing the world that the sky is blue? For thousands of years, millions of misguided souls—acting on their *beliefs*, mind you—have laid waste entire cultures and murdered untold numbers of people who, they believed, were so flawed in their thinking that they deserved death. Most of these "defenders of the faith" were deeply "religious" and highly dedicated to their cause. But were their beliefs proven or validated by their willingness to kill or be killed?

DK: I get your point, of course. But with the possible exception of Paul's persecution of Christians before his conversion, the Apostles weren't killing anyone. They were just preaching what they believed to be the message of God's salvation. No harm there, right? I mean it was all done in good conscience.

J: Virtue can rarely be determined by one's conscience, which is usually no better than the environmental programming that produced it. True virtue requires honest self-evaluation, hard-won wisdom and some applied intelligence. Nearly every act of political, social or military aggression is performed perfectly within the bounds of the perpetrators' "good conscience." So you can't assume, just because someone is acting in the name of country or religion, that his behavior is therefore noble or exempt from scrutiny.

DK: Then you disapprove of the message your followers were spreading?

J: Depends on which message—and which followers. You'll recall that I warned my disciples before my arrest that they would misunderstand my teachings. Sure enough, they completely distorted my words because of their own fears, hopes and predilections. A few centuries later, my simple ideas about life had morphed into full-scale religion. Christianity had become just another mainstream institution, garnering political muscle and spawning clout-seekers by the boatload. As usual, power and ignorance were a deadly combination.

DK: It does seem that wherever religion is introduced, it leaves a mountain of corpses behind. Within a century of the Europeans arriving in the Americas, tens of millions of indigenous peoples had become what is now euphemistically referred to as "collateral damage." They were slaughtered indiscriminately at the hands of soldiers, missionaries, settlers and explorers, many of whom considered themselves faithful Christians. The battle cry, apparently, was "Kill a heathen for Christ!"

J: But again, in this respect we can't single out Christianity, because it certainly isn't the only religion with a record of violence. Other traditions have also left trails of blood in their paths. And talking about it as *history* tends to make it all sound merely academic. What should worry you is that the same insanity is still happening *today*. By their very nature, ideologies breed separation and discord. They lead directly to belief in specialness and feelings of superiority. That's hardly what I had in mind.

DK: Well, as I mentioned in my opening letter, you *are* quoted declaring, "I come not to bring peace, but a sword." That's

Matthew 10:34. You also reportedly told your disciples, "Let him who has no sword sell his mantle and buy one." Luke 22:36.

J: Are we having a scripturefest? Oh boy, this'll be *fun!* "Be at peace with one another." Mark chapter nine. "Would that even today you knew the things that make for peace." Luke 19. "Peace I leave with you; my peace I give unto you..." John 14.

DK: *Hmmph.* The Bible says "God is not mocked," but it seems He's not above doing a little of it Himself.

J: Just keepin' the dialogue perky, pilgrim... But listen, you folks brandish those obscure sword-related verses as if they were blatant proof that I condoned violence and would approve of conflicts and wars you consider justified or even "righteous." The minute some perceived enemy steps out of line, you're no longer asking, "What would Jesus do?" To the sword-verse-quoting, right-wing contingent, the answer's obvious: "Why, he'd fire up the bombers and break out the nukes!"

DK: Okay, but when a bunch of thugs wallop you upside the head, don't you have to wallop 'em right back?

J: *I* didn't.

DK: Well, I'm not sure we can really compare your situ—

J: Listen, my friend, you may as well face the facts: the ethics of the average Christian have shamefully little connection to the so-called "teachings of Christ." Almost from the start, Christendom has conveniently overlooked the clear, unambiguous instructions in Luke 6: "But I say to you... *love* your enemies, *do good* to those who hate you, *bless* those who curse you, *pray* for those who abuse you... And as you wish that people would do unto you, do so also unto them."

DK: Morally challenging stuff.

J: Yeah, try floating *that* in the next State of the Union address.

DK: I'll pass it along to the appropriate party...

J: Also, the verse you cited from Luke 22 reminds me of something else I'd like to clear up. In verse 37, the gospel writer has me slightly misquoting a line from Isaiah 53, an Old Testament chapter frequently said by the church to contain prophecies of *my*

119

life and mission. But the passages have absolutely nothing to do with me, and no Hebrew scholar worth his weight in matzo would argue otherwise.

DK: Hang on, let me read it through... Hmmnn... The chapter is definitely confusing and vague. For the most part, the prophet is referring to things that had already happened. A few verses seem to match certain *aspects* of your life—but others aren't relevant at all. So I get your point: it's hard to see how the words had any connection to you.

J: As I've said, with so many scriptures flying around, you can support nearly any crazy argument you want. The "God-said-it-I-believe-it" crowd is simply on intellectual cruise control. They take an easy path by avoiding the foremost requirement of those who seek the truth: *thinking for yourself.* So don't trust everything you hear from the experts, cuz. Always challenge concepts that require you to check your intelligence at the door. God is neither cruel nor stupid—but to accommodate the average belief system, He'd have to be both.

DK: I *will* say that I always resented that God would command *me* to be infinitely loving and forgiving while *He* condemns *billions* to eternal agony. God's hell isn't just insanely vicious—it's also horribly hypocritical.

J: Believe me, after what humans have made of *this* world, hell would be overkill.

DK: Actually, I think some people feel sort of gratified believing in hell. They kinda *like* the idea that someone they aren't fond of might eventually get shafted with a red-hot poker. Others may not fully *embrace* the notion of hell—but it *is* a biblical concept. So they seem to think that, by *accepting* the teaching, they're just being humble.

J: Well, be it ever so humble, there's no place like hell. Nor is there a heaven. These things aren't *locations*—they're *states of mind.* Hell is the absence of the awareness of love's presence, while heaven is the re-emergence of that awareness, which is your natural reality and has never changed. The paradise dangled before you by religion is not a *place*; it's the remembrance of your eternal connection with God. And it isn't waiting for you somewhere in the future. Heaven is always *here* and *now*, because there *is* no other place or time.

DK: You know, it's strange that the Bible has so little to say about hell. If the soul's eternal security hangs in the balance and hell really does exist, then you'd think God would spend a little more time explaining it.

J: You aren't giving God enough credit. You're projecting your perverted sense of human "justice" onto *Him* by assuming He operates within your personal value system of cost-versus-reward. But sacrifice is a very materialist view of the relationship between God and man. It's "the art of the deal" taken to the extreme. The root thought is that, to receive something from God, you've got to *give* something first—even if it's only faith or obeisance. Most Christians would ridicule the ancient ritual of human sacrifice, which was practiced to appease or curry favor of the gods, but they don't seem to realize that Christianity was founded on this very concept. They never stop to ask why the God of creation needs to be placated by the shedding of innocent blood.

DK: Literalists would argue that a gift like salvation bears a cost. It seems unrealistic that God would give something for nothing.

J: Their God is like a schoolyard drug dealer. He may dole out a sample or two—but he definitely expects a return on his investment. Try to understand that God has no ego, no emotional requirements, and no need for anyone to suck up or tell Him how terrific He is. Besides, wouldn't it contradict the very *definition* of grace if you have to earn your way into it?

DK: Well, it's not exactly like we have to *earn* it. To my understanding, all that God's really asking, basically, is for each of us to accept your sovereignty and give you honor. So it's only *that* which makes his grace conditional.

J: However you slice it, there's something hugely inconsistent about conditional grace. And anyway, how gracious could He really be if you've got to secure his approval through subservience, acquiescence or barter? Do you really *like* this bigheaded, wheeler-dealer God you've inherited?

DK: Until a few years ago, I never gave it much thought. I repressed my doubt because I was afraid God would punish or condemn me for losing faith. I dunno, maybe I've been brainwashed. But it's hard to believe we can just stop worrying about this heaven and hell thing. It seems too good to be true.

J: For someone whose God is supposed to be loving, a place like hell should seem *too horrible* to be true. An eternity of searing torment as payment for a few short years of ignorance? How much devotion or respect can you really muster for a deity who would instigate something so insanely cruel and unfair? And even if your juvenile fundamentalist notion of salvation were true, do you honestly believe you could walk the golden streets of heaven in peace? Could you really sit quietly by the River of Life, joyfully strumming your harp while your friends and loved ones are screaming in agony amidst the fires of hell across the tracks?

DK: Of course not.

J: Then how in heaven's name could such madness be tolerated by a God of love?

DK: The literalists say that God doesn't *like* condemning anyone but that He's a God of justice—so He *has* to.

J: Oh, I get it. He's *morally obligated* to torture his rebel children. He's *compelled* to behave like a lunatic.

DK: Like I said before, I was taught that God offers everyone the opportunity to accept Him. But with free will, we're also at liberty to reject Him.

J: In which case He ushers you straight off to hell, eh? He doesn't *want* to sentence you to everlasting anguish—but He feels He *owes* it to you, is that it?

DK: Apparently it's the Christian thing to do.

J: Explain something: If God is so worried about his children's salvation, then why doesn't He personally intervene?

DK: But we're told that's exactly what He did when He sent you!

J: Even if you're right, that was two thousand years ago. In the meantime, God's children are dropping like flies. As you've said, *billions* are incurring damnation because of his ongoing negligence!

DK: Well, I guess He just figures that your appearance in Palestine should've been sufficient. *Now* all He can do is spread the word and trust that we'll make the right decision.

J: Really? You mean hoping for the best is God's only remaining option? If so, then Christianity's fundamental theology is this: First, God creates mankind frail and ignorant. After the great Fall in the Garden, He then predestines each person for hell. Many centuries later, He offers a plan of remediation which—and let's be honest about this—large numbers of his children are predisposed to reject. Meantime, He allows Satan the freedom to harvest as many souls as possible while *He* sits back watching the show, waiting to see which of his "precious" creations will manage to avoid self-destructing.

DK: Actually, I doubt that *God* would take that particular view. As I say, He *did* provide an avenue of escape.

J: So God, in his deeply mysterious way, gives humans free will either to accept Him or reject Him, which, technically, means accepting or rejecting the church's *doctrinal theology*. Those who *do* "accept" Him are issued white robes and wings, while those who don't are consigned to spend eternity longing for cold beer and a cool breeze.

DK: A bit waggish—but yes, I'd say that's about how most hardline Christians see it.

J: Therefore, under threat of eternal torture, God's teensy-weensy prison cell of "free will" gives you the option to form just *one opinion*, to take only *one perspective*—to make *one choice and one choice only*. In effect, God's message to mankind is this: "You can take me or leave me, your pick. But don't forget those blazing pits of fire!"

DK: That's how it looks from here.

J: Well, what the hell kind of free will is *that*? Sounds more like *spiritual extortion* if you ask *me*. It's no different from an earthly parent telling his children, "You're each free to live as you please. But if you don't do as I ask, I'll disown you. Then I'll hunt you down, lock you away, and torture you for the rest of your life." Now, honestly: would you excuse this father's deranged behavior toward his children by telling yourself that he's only doing it because he *loves* them?

DK: Obviously not.

J: Then why go so easy on God? You see, this is the literalist's unavoidable dilemma. He can't grasp that a loving God and a hell of eternal torment are complete contradictions. If one exists, then the other, by definition, cannot.

DK: So if God is loving, He couldn't have created hell. And if He *did* create hell, then He isn't loving.

J: No two ways about it. A God of goodness couldn't also be the author of the definitive evil and the ultimate child abuse.

DK: Perhaps God isn't "good" in the way we normally use that word. His particular brand of goodness may transcend our usual interpretation.

J: Well, maybe you've got a point. Let's have a look at scripture and find out. Psalm 145 says, "The Lord is gracious and merciful, slow to anger and abounding in *steadfast love*."

DK: Steadfast meaning firmly fixed and unwavering.

J: Right. And who is the beneficiary of this everlasting goodness? The Psalmist answers in no uncertain terms: "The Lord is good to *all*," he declares, "and his compassion is over *all* that he has made." He further states, "The Lord is… gracious in *all* his deeds… just in *all* his ways… kind in *all* his doings."

DK: Not much wiggle room for interpretation, I wouldn't think.

J: No equivocation whatsoever. So the Bible clearly claims that God is "good" in the way folks typically mean when speaking of goodness. Furthermore, it says specifically that God is good "to *all*." But wait—what's *this*!? Just before he closes shop, the Psalmist slips in a single but critical caveat to keep everyone on edge: "The Lord preserves all who *love* him; but all the *wicked* he will *destroy*."

DK: Now, *that's* a little worrisome—especially if you're not sure what God considers "wicked." It also implies that anyone who doesn't love God *is* wicked.

J: A similar irregularity occurs in Exodus 34, when the Lord claims for Himself the same qualities ascribed to Him by the Psalmist: merciful, gracious, fully in touch with his feminine side, and so on. But lest anyone breathe a sigh of relief, the Lord also says that *He'll by no means clear the guilty* and, moreover, that he'll punish the sins of the parents *by way of their children*—and not just for awhile but for several generations thereafter!

DK: So going by the Bible, God is loving but hateful, forgiving but vengeful, and slow to anger but quick to destroy.

J: Or so says the "internally consistent and inspired Word of God." But hey, never mind all the scriptural double-talk. If the Bible God is so doggone lovable and his personality so irresistible and compelling, then why must He threaten his children with everlasting torture to get 'em home for the holidays? Why, in his desire to make them attentive, rueful and contrite, does He feel duty-bound to dispatch all the radicals to the choking-hot, lung-searing, sulfuric combustions of hell? I mean why always *drama*? Couldn't He accomplish the same thing by simply relegating them all to a summer in Houston?

CHAPTER SEVENTEEN

DK: Well, now you've got me really thinking about the Christian afterlife. I'm probably the only guy who'll ever ask you this, but how's about taking me just a little deeper into hell?

J: Haven't had enough heat yet, eh?

DK: To me, hell is critically important because it sits at the very center of Christian literalism. I mean the church can talk all day long about God's *love*, but that doesn't mean diddly if salvation is basically just an escape from punishment. So I feel the topic deserves a bit more scrutiny.

J: Alright, let's put on our fire suits and jump back into the flames. By the way, I've been meaning to ask: where in the Bible do we find a record of hell's creation?

DK: You're baiting me. I don't think scripture ever describes it.

J: Clever lad! And why do you suppose that is?

DK: Haven't a clue. I've never really considered it.

J: It's because the Israelites saw themselves as God's elect. They would never have dreamed that God might forever condemn his own people. So the Christian vision of hell would've been unthinkable. Divine punishment was primarily associated with the *immediate* world.

DK: But doesn't the Old Testament make mention of hell?

J: Sure, many times—although later Bible versions changed most of the original King James "hell" references to more closely reflect original Hebrew concepts such as "Sheol," the earliest reference to an afterlife in the Hebrew scriptures. It can be translated as "the pit," "the grave," or "the abyss." Old Testament verses that *do* contain the word "hell" are relatively few and vague, and it's quite obvious that the writers who used these terms weren't familiar with the fiery, devil-run establishment invented by Christian literalists.

DK: What about the *New* Testament? In addition to the word "hell," you've also got terms like "Hades" and "Gehenna." Most Christians just assume they all refer to the same thing: God's place of eternal punishment.

J: Garden variety ignorance, pilgrim. Like the Old Testament terms, each of those words has its own subtle and varied meaning. So biblically, hell is a mixed bag—a real mystery. A few passages undoubtedly imply a place of punishment; but others suggest only a kind of purgatory where souls are cleansed and purified, as gold might be refined by fire. Some verses insinuate a simple resting place of inactivity. So you'll need to request clarification the next time someone tells you to go to hell.

DK: I have the feeling it won't be long…

J: Historically, Judaism didn't have any fixed dogma regarding the concept of hell. Many Jews certainly did *believe* in an afterlife, but the laws of Moses don't threaten moral offenders with unending next-world punishment. Instead, they promise *earthly* misery— both for the perpetrators and for their descendants.

DK: Then the Israelites had no clear and unequivocal post-mortem theology.

J: No, and *I* certainly didn't go around preaching one. I knew that no religion or belief system has any influence on the condition or destiny of man's spirit. You might say that I was an early supporter of separation of church and fate. My family and I grew up following the precepts of the Torah, and it's a simple fact that it never reports the creation of any eternal hell. Now, if you're a biblical literalist, that should really worry you. Because if God created a place of everlasting torment for his rebellious children, don't they deserve to know a little more about it? Okay, so there's a lake of fire—which makes for some tricky yachting. But shouldn't God provide a few more details on the sufferings in store for those who don't make the Judgment Day cut? Shouldn't He have clarified why He was bent on punishing non-believers *forever* and why He would use such cruel and sadistic means to do so?

DK: Possibly. But as you've established, you wouldn't expect this Bible God to go explaining Himself or asking anyone's permission. His decisions are pretty much unilateral.

J: But c'mon... a place like hell you don't just spring on someone at the last second like a pop quiz. To milk hell for its true prevention value, it has to be *publicized*: you've gotta get the word out—scare up a little obedience. Circulating a few vague and conflicting scriptures isn't nearly good enough. To really keep folks in line, a concept like hell needs widespread pre-release marketing.

DK: I never thought of it like that.

J: I wonder about you, pilgrim. Were you an ostrich in a previous life, or do you just have a knack for overlooking the obvious? I suggest you launch that high-powered mental speedboat of yours before it splinters from dry rot.

DK: Hey, don't forget that I grew up here in the deep south. In these parts, calling someone a Jesus freak is considered a compliment. These people are so fanatically religious, they make Quakers look like street thugs. So take it easy. I've had this fundamentalist stuff blasted at me since I was a kid. Although now that you've brought it up, I do find it a little surprising that the Bible doesn't provide more details about hell. As you say, God should've at least given us some initial background info and explained his reasoning for torturing his own children.

J: But the issue of hell burns far deeper than its mere dearth of scriptural particulars—because *someone* had to *build* it. I mean the place didn't just appear from nowhere, right? And we all know there's only *one* creator.

DK: Well, if we ignore that Trinity thing…

J: So now we've got another disturbing problem. If God did indeed create hell, then *when,* exactly, did He *do* it? If He constructed it right away, during Creation Week, then you'd have to wonder, "Hey, why the hell is He creating hell!?" Know what I mean?

DK: Not exactly.

J: C'mon, Maylor, don't embarrass your publisher. If God created hell at the very outset, then He had to *know* there would be a *need* for it. See where I'm going?

DK: Ah, now I get it! If God knew up front that hell would be required later on, then He must've known that his forbidden fruit arrangement would ultimately trigger man's downfall.

J: Hallelujah, *now* the drug's wearing off! You see, if the Almighty didn't want his naturally curious children exercising their so-called "free" will, then why give it to 'em in the first place?

DK: On the other hand, it's not like God issued Adam and Eve a two-inch-thick Garden Conduct Manual. I mean even the lewdest public displays of affection were apparently no problem. There was *one lousy rule*—and they *broke* it.

J: Okay, but let's assume for the moment that God is omniscient, as many people believe, and that He can in fact see into the future. If so, then He had to foresee The Great Fruit Disaster before it ever unfolded. And if He *knew* that Adam and Eve were going to stumble, then why didn't He draft up a different freakin' *plan?* Why not leave the stinkin' tree out of the Garden altogether? So right from the start, his scheme was crazier than a corgi on crack.

DK: The story does seem preposterous.

J: Like hell it is!

DK: Oooh, nice pun...

J: Forbidden fruit, my butt. And they say that God never *tempts* anyone. Geez! Only a ditzball deity would conceive a plan that would lead to his own children's destruction. On earth, a parent like that would be locked up without a moment's pause. But a *God* who does such things is considered a creative genius—fit for *worship*, no less!

DK: Maybe God didn't create hell right away. He might've constructed it later on, after He saw the pattern of rebellion developing.

J: C'mon, we're talking about *God*, not the Governmental Department for Eternal Correction of Disbelieving Heathens. God is supposedly all-knowing, remember? He *knew* his children would rebel and misbehave. He *knew* his salvation plan would cause major casualties. But He followed through *anyway*.

DK: Divine privilege, I suppose. Not everyone can be among the chosen.

J: Oh yeah? Why not? Where's it mandated that God must send his defiant children to hell? That's not the only option, you know. If He truly finds 'em so terribly annoying, He could merely zap 'em out of existence and put 'em forever out of their intellectually honest and open-minded misery.

DK: I guess that makes sense. What God created, He could just as quickly terminate.

J: And don't forget your previous observation: The New Testament says that *your* forgiveness should be *without limit*. So it's pretty baffling that God would set such a low threshold on *his*.

DK: Yeah, now *that* part really rattles my cage. We mortals should have at least as much right to hypocrisy as God has.

J: But there's more. If God created hell, then you'd have to wonder *how* He did it.

DK: You're losin' me again.

J: Okay... according to scripture, hell is a place of unrelenting misery, right? So you gotta figure it's a pretty grim arrangement—dark and sweltering, gloomy and depressing, non-stop stream of complaints to management. Probably no tablecloths, either. But how, exactly, did God design the place? Did He give it a lot of thought? Are there quartering racks? Is the place fully equipped with fiery beds of coal and dungeons of pain? Or does He just pipe in rap music all day?

DK: I see the problem, alright. Doesn't give me a very good feeling to think He actually *conceived* the idea.

J: That's my point. I mean can you envision God *pondering* this challenge? Here He is, like the wicked witch hovering over a crystal ball, plotting and scheming against his earthly enemies, rubbing his hands together with evil cackles of laughter in delightful anticipation of the terrible sufferings to come. "*Heh heh, heh!* Now, how best to bring misery and affliction to my little mutineers?"

DK: Maybe we're going too hard on the guy. Because I can't imagine that God would've thoughtfully *designed* his hell. I'm told that He condemns people to hell reluctantly and with great sorrow.

J: Sorry, buster, but that dog won't hunt. Doesn't God have any free will of his own? It makes no sense to say that sending folks to hell really bums Him out. That suggests He doesn't *want* to do it but that He has no choice. But again, He's *God*. He's not union, so no one's *forcing* Him, right? Why not, as the old song says, just call the whole thing off? So here again we've got a *slew* of ponderous theological dilemmas. First, either God *knew* that people would sin but created them anyway, knowing they would suffer forever if they didn't repent. *Or*, He suspected they *might* sin but, again, elected to gamble with their eternal souls. *Or*, He believed they *wouldn't* sin, in which case He was completely mistaken and therefore *isn't* omniscient and in fact doesn't know his children at all. Take your pick.

DK: Not a pretty set of choices.

J: And there's an even more pressing problem. If God sees the future, then He already knows the Judgment Day results and who's gonna draw the short straws. The moment someone is born, He *knows* if they're destined for hell. So he could spare the poor blokes an eternity of horror just by skipping their creation altogether!

DK: Now, *there's* a creative solution: the preemptive non-existence option.

J: Here's more complexity: The church teaches that God feels the pain and suffering of his children. But does He continue to feel the pain and suffering of those He hurls into hell? If so, then God has actually *condemned Himself* to an infinity of anguish! On the other hand, if at some point God begins *ignoring* the horrendous cries of his children burning in the fires of the abyss, then how is He any different from a despotic dictator who sleeps perfectly well at night knowing that his death camps are *stuffed* with people wailing in tortuous misery? Your alleged "God of love" actually appears rather hateful.

DK: I've always heard that God *hates the sin* but *loves the sinner*.

J: Well, whether God truly *loves* his sinners is a wide-open question. But here again is an enormous double standard, because when dealing with God and his flaming hell, *you're* commanded to *hate the torture* but *love the torturer*!

DK: Alright, then, maybe God *isn't* omniscient. It's possible He didn't know mankind would be such a problem. He may have genuinely thought his little human experiment would turn out just peachy.

J: Then why did He create hell? In case things got a little too rowdy at the fair?

DK: Perhaps He wasn't sure how life on earth would develop. Maybe God sees only certain *fragments* of the future.

J: Pretty tough to make that argument if you believe, as most Christians do, that God's prophets predicted *my* life—and even the course it would take—hundreds of years beforehand. To foresee *that* kind of stuff would require knowing almost every step anyone could ever make.

DK: You're right, I'm probably really pushing the envelope. After all, we're talking about *God* and not a traveling carnival gypsy. But still…

J: Actually, it's quite within the bounds of scripture that the Bible God *isn't* all-knowing. You mentioned the book of Job in your opening letter and had some fun with the fact that God asks Satan more than once where he's been and what he's been doing.

DK: Another allegory, perhaps?

J: Not if we're talking about the "literal word of God." No symbolism allowed, remember? That would really blur the line between fact and fiction. I mean you can't argue that the Job story is mere fable but then turn around and claim the Resurrection is a concrete fact. Although I must say that *both* require a pretty massive suspension of disbelief.

DK: So if the Job account is actual *history*, then the Bible God's knowledge would appear to be somewhat imperfect.

J: And don't forget our previous discussion about God's uncertainty regarding the faithfulness of Abraham. In fact, limitations on divine awareness appear time and again throughout the Old Testament. In Genesis 18, for example, God openly admits to Abraham that He's clueless about the situation in Sodom and Gomorrah. Start reciting at verse twenty…

DK: Un momento there, padre. Some of us are forced to resort to the text… "Then the Lord said, 'Because the outcry against Sodom and Gomorrah is great and their sin is very grave, I will go down to see whether they have done altogether according to the outcry which has come to me; and if not, I will know.'"

J: So in the Bible's very first book, God freely admits that He's not omniscient. It's a critical point, because it carries important implications about every other action or statement attributed to Him in the scriptures. It's especially relevant if He's pontificating about the future of the planet or knowing people's "hearts." I mean He confesses ignorance about what's happening *right now,* and yet throughout the Old Testament He lays down oodles of blow-by-blow predictions set to unfold years or even centuries later.

DK: I suppose it doesn't really matter whether God is all-knowing or not. Either way, I have a hard time finding affection for a deity who isn't gratified until his enemies are suffering. I may grudgingly *respect* Him, but I sure as hell don't *like* Him.

J: You respect Him the way a whipped animal respects an abusive owner. Deep inside, you resent Him; and worse still, you *fear* Him. At its core, religious fundamentalism is built upon a terrible, ungodly fear of a terribly fearful God. And let's be frank: you can't truly love something you fear. You may *resign* yourself to this tyrant—but you'll never really *trust* Him. You'll always wonder if, someday, like a disloyal Doberman, He'll turn and rip you to shreds.

DK: I think I always had big problems with God condemning his children. But for years I couldn't bring myself to admit it.

J: So you held God at bay by offering contrived affection and fearful obedience. You bucked up your feeble beliefs by proselytizing and gathering with those who, like you, had decided to hedge their theological bets. Frightened and unsure, you scared up as many reinforcements as you could find and called it evangelism.

DK: I was only doing what I felt was right.

J: "Nothing in the world is more dangerous than sincere ignorance and conscientious stupidity." That's Martin Luther King, Jr.

DK: Still, as irritating as I might've been with my witnessing, I always believed I was serving God.

J: Pascal said that men never do evil so completely and cheerfully as when they do it from religious conviction.

DK: You're a living quotation book! But listen, you're grinding a lot of sacred cows into hamburger. This interview won't be very popular with the "born-again" crowd.

J: Being born again is fine, but you've gotta make sure the second birth doesn't squeeze all the oxygen from your brain...

CHAPTER EIGHTEEN

DK: Okay, so you've extinguished the fires of hell and we can all breathe easy. Terrific. But your attitude on the "born again" thing is a little puzzling. In John's gospel you reportedly told Nicodemus, "except a man be born again he cannot see the kingdom of God."

J: Yes, but I never said he couldn't *enter* the kingdom, which is how most Christians interpret it. This only reinforces the mistaken notion of the kingdom as an other-worldly location in a distant corner of the universe—a place where right of entry is determined by God after the body's demise. You're always "in" the kingdom, but you don't "see" it without inner purification. That part's not optional.

DK: Then *your* version of salvation is *also* conditional.

J: It's conditional in the same way that a man wearing blinders must remove them before he can see again. But that's not like saying that *God's love* is conditional, which it most surely is within literalist Christianity. My view of redemption was that salvation is *of the mind* and always available to anyone with a pure heart and a peaceful spirit. These are the only "conditions." When they're met, the student will understand that his reality as a creation of perfection has never changed. The only obstacle, really, is the student's own unwillingness to see.

DK: *Religion's* salvation, on the other hand, is all about safety of the soul.

J: Yes, and it usually centers on the acceptance of certain creeds or beliefs. Also, it doesn't take full effect until sometime after death, making the devotee completely dependent on future-based assurances that can never be verified. This "pay-now, collect-later" proposal is the sheep-herding tactic underpinning nearly all religion. The message is, "Do as you're told while you're alive and you'll inherit an everlasting paradise when you're dead."

DK: And you see it as a sham.

J: It's a fool's game. There are no hidden altars in God's temple. He doesn't withhold joy from his children in the present to determine if they deserve it in the future.

DK: Then what was your point to Nicodemus?

J: That beliefs are not the same as liberation. I told him that unless he was born again—or "born *anew*," as the later translations put it—he would remain blinded by his intellect. I wanted Nick to know that reality was nipping him on the heel every second, but that transformation was required before he could perceive it. The essence of my ministry was always, "Behold, the kingdom of God is *at hand*."

DK: So what becomes of religion's heaven?

J: It fades into irrelevance where it belongs. Religion's notion of heaven entails a glaring and fatal flaw: it presupposes that timeless reality will somehow be more beneficent to the future than it has been to the past. But why would anyone find comfort in this idea? Religion's God has apparently been sitting unconcerned in his heaven for several millennia while his children endure the most horrific kinds of earthly hell. What makes you believe He'll be more helpful or attentive anytime soon?

DK: Some Christians claim that God was waiting for Israel to officially become a nation again. Of course, it's been more than fifty years since that took place, and nothing has really changed.

J: You mean this Bible God allowed billions of his children to suffer thousands of years of dreadful misery while waiting for a relatively tiny population of special people to establish themselves on a few acres in the Middle East?

DK: Well, I think it's all a matter of one's theological perspec—

J: You'd better adjust your thinking, old chap. God's "timeline" is only *now*. His reality is always in full bloom, and it isn't unfolding according to some grand cosmic plan. It isn't going to get "better." Now, the *world* may shift and swing for better and for worse, but reality is always perfect—*right here, right now*. You won't see it, though, until your perception shifts.

DK: Then correcting *perception* is the key.

J: It's the open secret to a new life. I taught that reality is always tapping you on the shoulder, reaching out to you constantly from the unknown. I told Nicodemus, "that which is born of the flesh *is* flesh; and that which is born of the Spirit *is* spirit." I meant that when you focus on things of the flesh—that is, the material world and its endless distractions—you fail to perceive the far more important *invisible* reality underneath. Therefore, you have to be "born anew." It's clearly a metaphor, so obviously you have to uncover its deeper meaning.

DK: Well?

J: It means dying to everything you think you know—releasing your stranglehold on all that you believe the past has taught you about reality. You have to crucify your interpretations about what things mean, how life works, who you are, what God is, and so forth. Let go of every concept you ever held about *anything*—good or bad, true or false, worthy or ignoble.

DK: Are we that misguided?

J: You have no idea how far you've wandered from home—not actually, of course, but in your *mind*. So when it comes to demolishing old ideas, there can't be too much destruction. You have to leave everything behind.

DK: I doubt you'll find many customers for *that* philosophy.

J: I certainly haven't yet. As I've said: to ego, transformation appears fatal. But really it's a metamorphosis. Just as the caterpillar's passing leads to the birth of a butterfly, what emerges during the course of surrendering is a new creation entirely. You'll see nothing as you saw it before. To borrow a phrase from Revelation, you'll wake to "a new heaven and a new earth"—that is, a new consciousness and a new perception of the universe. In a sense, you will indeed be "born anew." Ironically, you'll experience this new reality as spontaneously natural, as if it were your true state all along—which it was.

DK: I'm still not locking on. What exactly is this rebirth?

J: The term "born anew" implies that something existed *before*. So what was it? Simply your natural state of pure awareness.

DK: Awareness of what?

J: Of "the kingdom"—a divine sense of cosmic perfection and completeness that's been with you from the beginning. God placed it there Himself, and He placed it there *forever*. Now, the kingdom can't be *lost*, but it *can* temporarily be lost *from sight*. This is the basis of religion's long-ballyhooed "Fall."

DK: How will I know when I've arrived back at this "kingdom" of yours?

J: You'll have absolutely no fear, a clear sense of immortality, and no further perception of evil or sin. You'll find yourself falling hopelessly in love with every moment—with all creation. And even when things go awry, nothing will appear as a "problem." No longer slave to your desires, you'll feel unity with all things, and you'll perceive no separation, not even between you and what you presently think of as God.

DK: Then being born again isn't just taking on a new belief system.

J: You're still missin' the boat, sailor. Rebirth is about *relinquishing* every belief you ever held. You become "empty," as the Buddhist would say. Once your mind grows quiet and free of all the usual noise, reality will come rushing in like a tidal wave to fill the void.

DK: It sounds a little scary.

J: It *can* be, because the old ego-self is fearing for its very life. It thinks it's going to die—and it *is*! In awakening, every concept you've taken for granted is destroyed. This is why religion is so popular. It keeps you safe within your philosophical cocoon. You don't have to think, because your belief system does it for you. But what would you lose by surrendering your present beliefs? What have they provided that's so highly appealing? Can you honestly say that you're peaceful, loving, and free of all conflict and fear?

DK: Not even close. Sometimes I feel I'm stuck in ignorance forever.

J: Well, at least you *know* that you don't know. The critical first step toward enlightenment is realizing your ignorance. Once you've seen the *need* for understanding, the rest is guaranteed.

DK: This enlightenment thing is a real mystery. I have no idea what it means.

J: It's not something the intellect can grasp, and any description has no relevance to the experience. But don't worry. Enlightenment is just another concept, and even those familiar with the idea typically see it as reserved for yogis, avatars or gurus. For most Christians, enlightenment isn't even part of their vocabulary.

They read about it in biographies of dead saints, perhaps, but they certainly don't connect it with their own salvation. In the long run it doesn't matter much, because awakening is inevitable. I'm just helping to shorten the pain of delay.

DK: I know that Buddha, Krishna and other spiritual standouts have emphasized enlightenment. But *you* never even *mentioned* it.

J: What *those* guys called enlightenment, *I* referred to as "salvation" or "the kingdom of God." Traditional Jews of the period wouldn't have understood the concept of self-liberation: they weren't geared for it. They were still dealing with an ill-tempered, anthropomorphic God who measured out material reward and punishment according to one's obedience to the law. Apart from a few sages and some esoteric groups in the region, my contemporaries didn't think in terms of enlightenment. It would've been as foreign to them as it is right now to most Westerners.

DK: So you met your people on their own intellectual and cultural terms.

J: Yeah, but there's not much correlation between my original teachings and their hacked-up New Testament rendition. The gospel writers have me droning on about a sinister devil and his blistering hell. But pushing a theology like that would've gotten me laughed out of the temple. All that soul condemnation bunk was added well after I was gone. And it's not like I didn't give clues about my version of salvation. I hinted at enlightenment by way of parables and analogies, comparing it to a lost gem, for example, or a hidden treasure—things that were out of sight and had to be sought. If I had believed that salvation rested solely upon "professing Christ," then what would there be to *seek*?

DK: In the fifteenth chapter of Matthew, you do seemingly allude to enlightenment when you tell your disciples that *worldly* affairs are not the true source of humanity's ills.

J: Right. Man's *real* troubles arise from his dismal *state of mind* and his addiction to thought. I warned about "the leaven of the Pharisees"—a reference to their dulled consciousness and their destructive, judgmental *thinking*. I also spoke about the five wise maidens who carried oil for their lamps, another simple analogy for heightened awareness.

DK: So you concealed the notion of enlightenment by decorating it with parables and other disguised teachings.

J: There was no other practical way to do it. Attaining this mystical understanding would take one completely beyond the "law," and that was a very dangerous proposition. So the message had to be encrypted. It was always there for those with "ears to hear"—but most folks didn't have the ears. They didn't realize they were rejecting their own freedom.

DK: It's just my opinion but, with or without enlightenment, most people seem fairly well adjusted.

J: I'd have to disagree. Nearly everyone you know is living in a state of fear, either subtle or overt. Some are more *aware* of it than others; but they've all reconciled themselves to a chronic, low-grade "infection" of anxiety, which they assume is normal. Most folks are just a little restive or unsettled, but many are actually neurotic and some are downright psychotic. The anguish alone should motivate people to question their outdated modes of operating.

DK: Assuming we can release old thought patterns, what remains?

J: Let it all go and find out. One thing's for sure: what's real can never be threatened or lost, and what *can* be lost was never real. Anything eternal, anything truly *worthy*, will still be there, waiting, on the other side of surrender. What *does* remain could be defined loosely as the Mind of God. Some call it "the Absolute."

DK: Can you describe it?

J: Only by negation: I can tell you what it *isn't*. It isn't anything you can conceive, identify or define.

DK: But c'mon, I've gotta have more than *that*.

J: I'm telling you, words just don't apply. Reality can't be captured in the net of your intellect. It's timeless, spaceless—without structure, dimension or attributes. Completely empty yet full to the brim. Perfectly still yet teeming with power. All-encompassing. Bigger than the biggest yet smaller than the smallest. Unassailable peace. Pure bliss. Real in a way you can't imagine. Compared to it, all else is worthless.

DK: *Ay, Chihuahua.* That still doesn't tell me a thing.

J: Nothing I say will help. It's like describing the flavor of strawberries to a guy who's never had one. You could talk about strawberries for hours, but in the end he'd be no closer to knowing the taste. He'd simply have to experience it for himself.

DK: Perfect. I'll just think of enlightenment as spiritual fruit salad.

J: I *can* tell you this: once you know your reality, you'll never again resort to weak-kneed beliefs. You'll know the truth—and you'll *know* that you know. And once you do, everything previously considered obvious or indisputable will be consumed like kindling in the fire. Even Saint Thomas Aquinas, one of Christendom's finest thinkers, found that his most brilliant thoughts were ultimately empty. After his transforming mystical experience, he said, "All that I have written seems to me like so much straw compared to what I have seen and what has been revealed to me."

DK: So the dawning of this power-filled stillness is something that has to be *experienced.*

J: Yes, and when it happens, you'll no longer need to pacify the mind with belief, supposition or theory. Enlightenment renders all your concepts obsolete, and when you awaken into it you won't give it up for love, power, fame or insider stock tips.

DK: Sounds better than sex.

J: Not nearly as messy, anyway…

DK: Couldn't a guy just be content with finding happiness in *earthly* gratification and forget all this kingdom-seeking baloney?

J: I don't know—*can* you? Worldly pleasure is extremely transient. Using your sex example, one minute you're ecstatic, and then you're off to scavenge the fridge, craving root beer and pizza.

DK: But why seek knowledge if ignorance is bliss?

J: First of all, very few people are actually blissful in their ignorance. And secondly, ignorance always leads eventually to *pain.* Deep within, *everyone* longs to know the truth of who they are. And unlike the gratifications of the world, the bliss that comes from *knowing* is a treasure that can't be lost with time or circumstance. It frees you from fear, manipulation, exploitation and disillusionment. It's the pearl of great value referred to in Matthew 13. As soon as he finds it, the merchant sells everything he owns to secure it.

DK: You paint a compelling picture.

J: That's how it is with reality. Once you rediscover your inner wealth, you grab hold of it and release all other attachments. Not because you're being coerced, but because you suddenly understand that everything else is relatively unfulfilling. You're then free to enjoy the wonder of life in a way that those who fearfully clutch things are never able to do. It's the passing from bondage to freedom.

DK: And this is what's called "enlightenment"?

J: Oh, people have used lots of different terms: awakening, enlightenment, realization, liberation. "Awakening" because you understand, upon reflection, that you've been dreaming. "Enlightenment" because you find that your inner darkness was only the prolonged denial of the ever-present light. "Realization" because you suddenly grasp what was true all along. "Liberation" because it frees you from your self-created prison. But whatever label you give it, turning within is the only road to real happiness. Introspection is the first sign of wisdom.

DK: The Bible says that *"fear of the Lord* is the beginning of wisdom."

J: Fear is the beginning of *neurosis*. Humans need a fearful religion like a monkey needs an encyclopedia. Somebody once said that a society without religion is like a crazed psychopath without a loaded forty-five.

DK: You talk about spiritual awakening as opposed to religion. But doesn't religion have the same goal?

J: Maybe, maybe not. But don't confuse spirituality with religion: they're not at all the same thing. Religious spirituality is generally a contradiction in terms. I frequently chided the religionists of my day because I saw that religion often leads to sanctimonious arrogance and feelings of superiority. It tends to patronize your false sense of self. When it's misused, religion leads to judgment and promotes belief in separation which, in turn, leads to further judgment.

DK: A vicious circle.

J: Yes, and once you build a wall between yourself and something else, you're guaranteed not to find God—because then you're dealing with *fragments*, when God's very nature is *all-ness*. So whatever fosters judgment is inherently blinding and self-defeating.

DK: What's the need of religion in the first place?

J: Religion at least recognizes that there's something beyond the limited self comprised of the body-mind complex. True religion brings you back to the One Self. There's really no other goal.

DK: Then religion *can* be a viable tool for returning us to the real.

J: It can certainly point the way. But all too often it loses *the point*. Institutionally, religion can be used to wield political power, to control the hordes… or even to generate revenue. For the individual, it can become a mere social event. Some use religion to relieve their guilt, manipulate others, or strike bargains with God in hope of securing his support.

DK: On the other hand, I've known lots of religious people who were solemnly sincere.

J: Sure, but sincerity alone isn't necessarily constructive; your good intentions aren't enough. You've gotta have the proper *goal*, which is self-liberation. You also need to know how to recognize progress, which is ever-increasing peace. Here's a good test: Would you practice your religion if no one else were doing it? Would you practice it if no one else could see *you* doing it?

DK: So religion should be a private, personal matter.

J: Well, it's not that group support is worthless. But fellowship is one thing; participating in mass delusion is quite another.

DK: That begs the issue of religion in the media. To me, a lot of religious programs these days are a crime against the intellect.

J: District attorneys sometimes see 'em as crimes of a very *different* kind.

DK: Yeah, we've certainly had some shocking cases of religious hypocrisy over the years. Jim and Tammy Faye Bakker's "ministry" had its own 2,000-acre theme park. Turns out the two flashy evangelists were living sordid lives of wild excess on donated funds. Even the family hound had its own air-conditioned, high-dollar doghouse. The whole venture was exposed as a giant fraud, and almost overnight the couple went from grandstanding to grand larceny. I believe ol' Jimbo did about five years of state-enforced penance on that account. I guess you could call it "doing time for Jesus."

J: *Heh heh.* It's a short trip from the penthouse to the pen.

DK: I also remember—it was back in '87, I think—when Oral Roberts threatened his followers by claiming that he had to raise eight million bucks or the Almighty was gonna call him "home." I assume that meant heaven, but maybe God had somewhere else in mind. Anyhow, the guy eventually scared up about nine mil—but not before missing his divinely imposed deadline. Somehow, though, he avoided being taken.

J: If only his contributors had been so lucky…

CHAPTER NINETEEN

DK: You seem quite insistent that we don't need religion to find God.

J: Does a dolphin need a compass to find the ocean? You're immersed in God at every moment. "In Him I live and move and have my being," says scripture.

DK: You're citing the book of Acts, I believe. I thought you were an anti-Biblicist.

J: The only thing I'm "anti" to is ignorance. The Bible contains some beautiful nuggets of wisdom and inspiration. Metaphysically and esoterically it's *full* of buried treasure. But much of the Bible is not only unhelpful, it's actually counterproductive. So you've gotta distinguish between the sublime and the ridiculous.

DK: But with the Bible, don't you have to take the bad with the good?

J: I don't have to do anything of the sort—and neither do you. Those who insist on the all-or-nothing approach to the Bible couldn't know the first thing about its checkered history. Even a *trace* of academic understanding of its evolution would prove the literalist position embarrassing, and anyone espousing that view is merely exposing his brazen ignorance. It's foolish treating the Bible as though every word is sacred.

DK: That's not what church experts say.

J: An expert is just a fella from out of town. Be wary of anyone who insists that every line of scripture was written by God. Blind faith may be faith—but it's still *blind*. When the unquestioning explain the unknown by way of the unverifiable, it can only result in the unbelievable.

DK: You're challenging nearly all religious authority.

J: Religious authority? An oxymoron if ever I heard one! Anyone grabbing at power by way of religion has really sailed past the port. True religion comes from *within* and always results in gentleness and humility; it seeks authority over no one. It radiates only peace and asks for nothing, because it already encompasses *everything*. The Christ spirit is compassionate, loving, humble—and usually very quiet.

DK: Wait a second. I asked you in my letter about a story in the gospel of John describing the time you went berserk in the great Temple. You reportedly threw furniture, knocked over cash registers, and then ousted retailers by assault with a deadly weapon!

J: C'mon, now. Scripture says I used a *whip*, not an AK-47.

DK: Well, either way, it doesn't sound too gentle and loving to *me*. And I doubt very much that it happened *quietly*. If the Christ spirit is so bloody humble, then how do you explain your little temple-tantrum with the money-changers?

J: Listen, I can't be defending myself against every story written about me. As I've said, I had nothing to do with the documenting.

Anyway, what of it? You can't determine another man's consciousness from within the state of ignorance.

DK: A man's actions speak volumes.

J: Usually—but not always. What does a toad in the canyon understand about the behavior of a soaring hawk? Likewise, no one living in spiritual darkness can possibly know the mind and motivations of the enlightened. In the same way you could meet a serial killer in a bar and think he's a terrific guy, you could also meet a self-realized master and think he's flipped his lid. In fact, Easterners have a tradition known as "crazy wisdom" in which the master will do things that seem completely nuts. He knows that shocking his students with unusual words or behavior can help free them from the strait-jackets of their "civilized" programming.

DK: C'mon, you're evading the issue. Did you really go Indiana Jones on the vendors in the temple of doom?

J: Why would I resort to the self-defeating violence of attack when I had spent my entire ministry trying to prove its futility? My one function on earth was to serve as the way-shower for my brothers and sisters. Anger and retaliation wouldn't have shown a way that was any different from the one they already knew. I said before that I AM is the way, the truth and the life. But don't make it all about *me*: because it's *your* way, *your* truth and *your* life.

DK: I only press the matter because the church says that we should imitate Christ. Do you agree? Does it make sense for us to pattern our lives after yours?

J: Given the contradictions in the New Testament, that could be a pretty confusing task. I mean which Christ does the church advise imitating? The one who nobly *forgives* the sins of others or the one who takes their sins personally, threatens their souls with hellfire, and whacks 'em with a whip? The main thing is *intention*. If you're sincere, all effort devoted to knowing your true nature is fruitful. But you can't fake enlightenment, so trying to copy others is mostly futile. Either you know reality or you don't.

DK: Then having a role model is worthless.

J: Not at all. It's true that simply emulating someone's behavior doesn't trigger illumination. But internalizing a master's *wisdom* can pay big dividends. The key is developing new levels of understanding, and the timely words or actions of a saint are powerful and may be just what's needed to spring you free of your conceptual prison. Generally, though, focusing on events, people or circumstances outside of you will only cause needless delay.

DK: From where I'm sitting, liberation seems a long way off.

J: How far could you be from your own reality? Trust me, it's closer than your next breath, and nothing can keep you from it— not even the finest religion.

DK: You continue distinguishing between spirituality and religion. But isn't there some correlation?

J: About the same as between a Broadway play and a soda machine in the lobby. The mind may associate religion with spirituality, but there's no direct relationship. In fact, each tends to make the other seem irrelevant. Religion is what happens when self-knowledge disappears.

DK: But you admit that religion *can* lead to greater spiritual awareness.

J: Sure, but so can a heart attack. And given a choice between the two, I'd really have to think awhile...

CHAPTER TWENTY

DK: You don't show much regard for the sanctity of religion.

J: That's because religion has never shown much regard for the sanctity of *people*.

DK: Once again your view doesn't jibe with scripture. You're quoted as telling Peter, "On this rock I will build my church." It sounds like you were planning something big.

J: Well, you'd almost need a theologian's help to miss the statement's obvious metaphoric nature. And only one gospel even quotes it. You'd think something considered so important would've gotten a little more press. Using one cryptic sentence to create a mammoth institution seems a little over-zealous, wouldn't you say?

DK: But did you, in fact, install Peter as the first pope?

J: I never saw Peter as more important than anyone else. If I had, why would the disciples have argued later about who was "greatest" among them, as they do in the ninth chapter of Mark? Clearly *they* didn't believe any formal hierarchy had been established.

DK: Still, the Roman church points mostly to that story of Peter's promotion to justify itself and its papacy.

J: Maybe so, but that was never my intention. *My* goal was to re-establish a "higher law" that would gently supersede the strict and unforgiving laws of form. I definitely sought change—but within the *individual*. I wasn't organizing a movement.

DK: Then how do you regard the pope now that his position is firmly entrenched? Is he truly infallible?

J: Does a bear genuflect in the woods?

DK: Well, is the pope at least acting as your temporary envoy until your return? And doesn't his selection involve the will of God?

J: We'll talk about my "return" a little later. And let's avoid any *personal* judgments and focus generically on the office of the papacy itself. Let's see if we can determine how much of it involves "God's will"…

First, the papacy has hardly been a "temporary" arrangement. Over the centuries, more than two hundred sixty men have headed up the Holy See.

DK: Are you serious!? Two hundred and sixt— Hey, wait a minute. Headed up the holy *what*?

J: The Holy See.

DK: Look, I know I'm a real pope dope. But what exactly is the Holy See?

J: It's the formal term for the principal episcopal jurisdiction of the Roman Catholic Church—what you might call, "Popeville." The Holy See is presided over by the Bishop of Rome, also known as the Pope. It's the central body governing the Vatican and representing the Catholic Church in its worldly affairs. So whether it's to be or not to be, if over land or over sea, the Holy See will oversee nearly all things Catholic, from A to Z. From sea to shining sea, *ami*, the Holy See is sovereign. *Oui?*

DK: I think I've got it now. *Merci.*

J: So more than two hundred sixty men have occupied the papal throne, also called the Chair of Saint Peter, and their collective histories contain all the bloodiness and dark intrigue of a drugstore mystery novel. The church was so embarrassed by some of these papal putzes that it actually began referring to them as "antipopes." A number of them purchased or even murdered their way into the job. Some lasted only a few months—or, in one instance, less than two weeks—before being ousted, killed or mysteriously perishing. With some of these guys it was *up* one day and *down* the next.

DK: Holy See-saw!

J: The first half of the tenth century was an especially fascinating phase for the papacy—and probably its darkest hour. Referred to even by Catholic historians as the "Pornocracy" or "Rule of the Harlots," it was a period dominated especially by two Roman noblewomen: Theodora, wife of powerful Count Theophylact, and her daughter Marozia. They weren't actually prostitutes, but in some ways they came pretty close. You don't need *me* for this information, though. You can read all about it in the writings of former priest and Catholic scholar Malachi Martin.

DK: Ah, c'mon! You can't tease me with that tantalizing lead-in and then leave me hanging! Let's hear what the good Reverend Martin has to say.

J: Well, Marozia's story holds particular allure. She gave birth to a son who was fathered illegitimately by Pope Sergius III, and later, with her son barely out of boyhood, Marozia had *him* installed as

Pope John XI. But Marozia's saga doesn't stop there. She was also aunt to a third pope and grandmother to a fourth.

DK: Wow. I can maybe understand obsession with rock stars or athletes. But *popes*?

J: Oh, you wouldn't believe the fiendish excitement surrounding the papacy during the days of these two schemers and their various hand-picked pontiffs. It was one long succession of papal thrills and spills—a regular pope opera. Between Marozia and her mother, this powerful faction held sway over the Church of Rome for more than fifty years. These two nettlesome but influential women designated and helped install nine popes in a short eight-year span. They also had a hand in *removing* some of these revolving-door papal puppets. Two of the nine wound up strangled to death; four were deposed and died under mysterious or unexplained circumstances; and one was suffocated—the same horrible fate that awaited one of the two shrews herself many years later.

DK: Vixens of Vatican! A pontifical Peyton Place!

J: Actually, Vatican City—which, incidentally, is the world's smallest independent state—wasn't officially established until 1929.

DK: Well, *whatever* they called it, the place apparently had better drama than most syndicated TV series.

J: And there's lots more. For example, Pope Stephen VII— nowadays referred to as Stephen VI—was installed on the throne by another formidable noblewoman, named Ageltrude. At the time, she was Queen of Italy but had earlier been Holy Roman Empress. Soon after Pope Stephen's consecration, Ageltrude and her son Lambert II—who was variously King of Italy, Holy Roman Emperor, and Duke of Spoleto—urged the pontiff to exhume the body of their bitter former enemy and one of Stephen's predecessors, Pope Formosus, who by then had been peacefully in his grave nearly a full year.

DK: They dug the guy from his grave!? What was *that* all about?

J: It seems that Lambert and Ageltrude, in a belated effort to exact revenge on Formosus, wanted his corpse brought to the Basilica of Saint John Lateran and placed on trial—*posthumously*—for alleged crimes during his tenure as pope. As Ageltrude's pawn, Pope Stephen, who was diseased and mentally unstable, dutifully responded. Along with several of his cardinals and bishops, Stephen had the unearthed Formosus fetched to the Basilica, where they dressed the old boy in full pontifical garb and then sat him down on a papal throne in preparation for his "trial."

DK: I've heard of re-activating dead cases, but this is ridiculous.

J: Famously known as The Cadaver Synod, this bizarre episode entailed Pope Stephen and a papal accuser actually shouting allegations at Formosus' corpse—even cross-examining it—while a group of cardinals looked on and a terrified teen-aged deacon stood next to the dead pope and responded in his stead with a pre-written script.

DK: Unbelievable… a ventriloquist and a dozen dummies. Sounds like a macabre skit from Monty Python.

J: Once they were satisfied with the proceedings and the official pronouncements of guilt, several of Pope Stephen's cardinals charged at Formosus, tore the papal vestments from his decaying body, and savagely ripped off the first three fingers of his right hand—the ones generally used for official papal blessings.

DK: *Ouch*. Gives a whole new meaning to the "non-digital" age.

J: By at least one account, they next dressed Formosus in layman's clothes and then hauled him outside, where he was discourteously dragged along the road whilst a Roman crowd pummeled him with stones and mud. Finally, Formosus—or what remained of his remains—was ingloriously dumped into the River Tiber.

DK: At least his career ended with a splash…

J: By the way, the aforementioned Marozia was also in attendance that day. A mere child at the time, she'd been brought there to witness the strange event by Ageltrude, who evidently wanted to give Marozia some early training on the ways of life amongst Roman nobility. No one recorded if the young girl was nearby when Cardinal Sergius presented Ageltrude with the gruesome "gift" she had requested of Pope Stephen: the violently severed fingers of her former rival.

DK: Good gosh, I never realized the papacy could be so colorful. Or so *dangerous*.

J: It was a pretty rough period, for sure. In fact, one papal candidate decided he just couldn't stomach all the brutality and bloodshed that might ensue should he ever become pope. So he quit the priesthood and joined the mafia.

DK: Jiminy Christmas, I'm interviewing the reincarnation of Henny Youngman! Alright, so has Father Martin got any other lurid pope tales? This stuff brings out my shadow side.

J: Well, there's some interesting history concerning three other popes of the era, two of whom were hand-picked by Marozia's mother, Theodora. First was Leo V, who lasted all of one month in July 903 before he was thrown into prison by Cardinal Christopher, who presumably had Leo strangled in the slammer and then replaced him as pope. Unfortunately, Christopher was himself imprisoned by Cardinal Sergius, who subsequently gave Christopher a taste of his own medicine by having *him* strangled in prison.

DK: You're pullin' my leg here, right? You're makin' this up as you go along.

J: Perhaps you'll be more inclined to believe the historian Vulgarius: that's *his* account.

DK: Truly amazing… So Leo V gets strangled by Cardinal Chris, who naturally succeeds him as pope. But then *he's* overthrown by Cardinal Sergius, who quickly has Christopher strangled, too.

J: *Now* you've got it. As the last man standing, Sergius then murders all the cardinals who opposed him and has his enemies on the papal court strangled as well.

DK: Damn! Sounds like the local rope maker stayed pretty busy. A wild stab in the dark says Sergius wound up in the chair of Saint Pete.

J: And took the name Pope Sergius III. He also took the nubile Marozia, still a mere teenager, for his mistress. She eventually bore him a child who, as I mentioned earlier, would one day become pope himself. Theodora, no doubt, was proud as a peacock.

DK: So according to Malachi Martin, whatever became of this mother-daughter team of papal powerbrokers? You said one of 'em didn't fare too well.

J: Theodora went on to a relatively quiet death. But Marozia's pathetic fate was far more dramatic. After years of harsh imprisonment by her own son, Marozia, now withered and barely alive in her prison cell, was finally suffocated "for the well-being of Holy Mother Church."

DK: Clearly an act of Christian charity. Who sealed her fate?

J: The sentence had been decided by top ecclesiastical authorities several days prior at a special synod. It was allowed to stand, if somewhat reluctantly, by a couple of very powerful kids who had presided over the gathering: the brand new, fifteen-year-old Holy Roman Emperor Otto III—a spoiled-rotten kid who became King of Germany at age three—and his twenty-three-year-old cousin Bruno, better known by Catholics as Pope Gregory V. But events precipitating Marozia's "holy" execution were set in motion many years earlier, with some fascinating circumstances leading up to her unsavory demise.

DK: Five-to-one the story involves a few popes.

J: Yessir, it does. Pope John X became concerned about the growing power of Alberic, Duke of Spoleto, so the pope and Marozia's mother arranged for Marozia to marry the threatening nobleman. I guess they figured that if you can't *strangle* your enemy, you might as well *sleep* with him. Ironically, though, the move would ultimately trigger Marozia's downfall years later at the hands of her own son by Alberic, a lad named Alberic II.

DK: You mean Marozia's husband, Al the Elder, actually *allowed* this?

J: Unfortunately the old man wasn't around to prevent it. After foolishly attempting to take Rome by force, he failed and was killed. Not long afterward, Theodora died, too. But the indefatigable Marozia went on to marry yet another commanding nobleman: Guy of Tuscany. The two then joined forces with the enemies of Pope John, overthrowing him and of course tossing him into prison.

DK: I don't suppose it's reaching too far to assume they also had him killed.

J: I see you've caught on to the pattern.

DK: I imagine strangulation would be too obvious. Let me guess: poisoned linguini?

J: Nothing so Machiavellian. They simply had the man suffocated.

DK: Geez, didn't anyone have a butcher knife or a bottle of hemlock? What's with all these strangulations and suffocations? It's enough to take your breath away.

J: At least John X had a good run. He lasted about fourteen years—a virtual eternity for a pontiff in those days.

DK: So, was this when Marozia's son became pope?

J: Not quite. She and some other enemies of John X first installed Pope Leo VI. He stayed on the throne about seven months, was eliminated and then replaced by Pope Stephen VIII, or Stephen VII as he's called in some records. About eighteen months later, Stephen mysteriously vanished—and not because he got lost in the woods, if you get my meaning. Anyhow, that's when all of Theodora's and Marozia's murderous meddling finally paid off. Marozia's son, fathered some twenty years earlier by Pope Sergius III, was at last eligible to assume the papal throne, taking the name Pope John XI in March 931.

DK: I suppose the family that preys together stays together...

J: From this point, it appeared that Marozia, with her young son now pope, could at last attempt to conquer the world. Her dream grew closer when her second husband, Guy, died, because it was then that she married Guy's half-brother, Hugh of Provence, the longstanding King of Italy. Marozia figured that if Hugh could become emperor, then ultimately Marozia's son Alberic II would inherit the throne. This would give Marozia complete imperial sovereignty by controlling both the political *and* "spiritual" realms of the empire.

DK: But apparently her storybook ending never came to pass.

J: Well, you know what they say about the best-laid plans of mice and megalomaniacs. Sadly for Marozia, her son Alberic II pulled off a coup d'état against his new stepfather during the royal wedding festivities, thereby overthrowing his mother and the king and becoming ruler of Rome. The deposed King Hugh somehow escaped and fled the city, reportedly hidden away in a basket and dressed only in a nightshirt. That's when Al Junior had his own mother, only forty at the time, thrown into prison. And there she would stay, without reprieve, for many years until her death.

DK: They say parents shouldn't smother their children—but Marozia probably wished that she *had*. I guess in a family like *that*, there was nothing quite so rewarding as sending dear old mom up the river.

J: Marozia's final insult came on the dramatic night of her church-approved murder. Nothing but a pile of skin and bones lying on her prison cell floor, the poor, wasted woman was forced to listen to a scathing list of her heinous offenses along with those of her grandson Octavian, son of Alberic II, who was later consecrated as Pope John XII. Now, I should stress that neither Octavian *nor* Marozia would ever win the Good Samaritan award; but compared with the crimes of her grandson, Marozia's misdeeds were mere breeches of etiquette. With his evil, lascivious lifestyle, this Octavian kid probably set the low mark for the entire history of the papacy.

DK: I want every mucky detail.

J: Well, after being deposed by a Holy Synod and replaced by Pope Leo VIII, Octavian was forced to flee Rome. However, he later returned to evict Leo from the papal throne and then set out on a terroristic mission of revenge. Going by Malachi Martin's account, the alleged offenses of Octavian, operating as Pope John XII, might have impressed even some modern-day crime families. His sins against the emperor and "Holy Mother Church" were legion: treason; perjury; looting the papal treasury; cutting off the nose, tongue and two fingers of a Cardinal-Deacon; skinning a bishop; severing the hands of a notary; and beheading no less than *sixty-three* Roman clergy and noblemen.

DK: Wow. Pope Terminator the First.

J: But as the good bishop in the prison cell had painfully reminded Marozia, her grandson's negative karma finally came calling one night when His Holiness was caught giving his fully unclothed papal "blessing" to a married woman whose husband appeared unexpectedly. Dispensing with the usual pontifical protocol, the irate fellow promptly proceeded to shatter the promiscuous pope's skull with a hammer.

DK: *Heh heh.* So the pope came and went, all in one night. Funny how betrayed husbands always go after the *man.*

J: Meanwhile—back in the dungeon—the young twenty-something bishop concludes reading through his official list of accusations against Marozia and her odious offspring. After performing the rite of exorcism to drive out any lingering demons, the bishop then accepts Marozia's penitent confession, rescinds her longtime excommunication and, lastly, grants her full absolution. Thus did he prepare her for the two mysterious visitors who would make their way into the prison later that night, bringing with them the notorious red cushion that would be used to snuff out what little life remained in Marozia's pitifully withered *corpus miserabilis.*

DK: Incredible! What an eye-opener this little discourse on the popes has been. Apparently there was lots of high drama surrounding some of these old-time pontiffs.

J: Oh, *that's* for sure. Some of these guys were virtual *models* of moral depravity, bent on swelling their power base and overtly expanding their personal fortunes. Exactly the kind of stuff you might expect from a highly influential position that was—during certain periods, at least—almost entirely political.

DK: Well, thankfully those days are history.

J: Hopefully so. And it's certainly not true that every pope has been up to his halo in graft and corruption. Some have been brilliant thinkers who've done great things and inspired worthy actions. But papal influence still packs just as much punch in the world of politics as it does in the realm of religion. It's an office of nearly unlimited power: a pope can issue edicts almost at will. He lives like a king in a palace that most kings would envy, he's waited on hand and foot from dawn 'til dusk, he's rarely questioned by those around him, and even dominant world leaders will often defer to him.

DK: There've only been a few popes during *my* lifetime. Seems like most of 'em are fairly old by the time they're selected. Why is it they never install these guys until they're too pooped to pope? Anyhow, I never much cared for their strange, almost misogynistic banning of women from the priesthood or their arbitrary morality—for example, prohibiting birth control in a world already suffocating from overpopulation. I mean you'd think they'd put a little less emphasis on *growing* the flock and a bit more on nurturing the one they've already got. But I'll admit, the most recent popes have generally seemed like pretty *decent* fellas. Although I doubt they're much fun at luaus.

J: I'd imagine they must get tired of wearing the same clothes every day.

DK: *Heh heh.* 'Course, being a bachelor myself, I can definitely relate. But you're right: just once I'd like to see the pope show up at Saint Peter's square wearing a T-shirt and faded jeans. Maybe a backwards ball cap and a small tattoo. It might make him a little more accessible, you know? There's just something ironic about a powerful spiritual leader wearing flashy, ornate threads and living a life of luxury while preaching to the world about simplicity, humility and equality.

J: In some ways, it's the ultimate satire. The pope is zipped around in private jets and expensive limos and has his own bullet-proof Popemobile. He's even protected by a special battalion of Swiss Guards. I mean where's the *faith*? As head of the Vatican, the pope presides over a multi-billion dollar empire of high-rent real estate, exquisite artwork, priceless jewelry, and hoards of other immensely valuable collectibles and artifacts. He and his advisors control huge wads of cash and even impressive business and investment portfolios.

DK: They've got their own bank, too. I read recently that the Vatican Bank has been involved in money-laundering scandals for decades, engaging in suspicious and secretive transactions totaling hundreds of millions of dollars. Amidst law enforcement allegations of major connections to organized crime, the bank frequently refuses to disclose the sources and destinations of huge chunks of money, playing continuous cat-and-mouse games with government authorities to escape the prying eyes of regulators.

J: And all this while much of the pope's faithful third-world constituency struggles for survival in poverty and squalor.

DK: Then you disapprove?

J: C'mon. Even with the highly slanted picture of my life handed down in the scriptures, does this sound like the kind of thing I envisioned? Nowhere in the New Testament is the pope or the papacy ever mentioned. So that nebulous, lone gospel passage regarding Peter's supposed career advancement is one of the most over-leveraged scriptures in history, and any objective reader could only come away with more questions. Building a global religious superpower upon it is nothing short of remarkable.

DK: But in that respect, Catholicism certainly isn't unique. A large part of Christendom is run basically like a multi-national conglomerate. In some ways, that's essentially what it is.

J: Then it's a real surprise to *me*. Where did folks get the idea that I wanted to establish a retail religion? I simply urged my followers to go out and share the good news of personal transformation. Somehow I got incorporated.

DK: What got the institutional ball rolling?

J: The starting point was Christianity being made the official religion of Rome and its far-reaching empire. Next, of course, came the money: bishops were placed in charge of the cash box. After that, the new religion *really* gathered steam. I'm not sure how it all got justified, though, because I always emphasized a strictly *personal* spirituality to be pursued quietly, out of public view. I told my students that whenever they prayed they should do so *in private*, and I frequently rebuked the religious establishment of my day. This should've made it quite apparent that I wasn't advocating formal organization.

DK: I suppose we really have made "a show" of our religion.

J: And not just a show, but a full-scale *production*. I mean some of that TV stuff—criminy, what a circus! Complete with props, sponsors, costumes, scripts... heck, they've even got budget quotas. But the real prize-winners are the Bible-thumping, crowd-pumping televangelists. The high priests of hokum.

DK: That bad?

J: Most unhelpful, to put it mildly. I mean how many people ever became enlightened listening to *that* stuff? You're familiar with the movie "Oh God!"?

DK: Sure. God was played by the lovable George Burns.

J: Right. At one point, he sends his earthly messenger to visit a pompous, money-grubbing TV evangelist.

DK: I remember that scene. The messenger informs the duplicitous preacher that God wants him to shut up.

J: Well, the way I see it, in a lot of cases that wouldn't be a bad idea.

DK: Some are probably adding a little Hollywood just to spice things up. After all, they've gotta compete for a limited audience.

J: The problem is that all that screaming, finger-pointing and fist-pounding feeds the ancient image of God as an angry, judgmental tyrant. It mires people in their fears and encourages a sense of personal unworthiness. Folks tend to assume that the smug preacher is connected with God in a way that makes him special. And let's not forget the big shakedown: selling salvation can be a pretty efficient way to turn a buck. Your own countryman Ambrose Bierce once said that a clergyman is someone who undertakes to manage *your spiritual affairs* while bettering *his own earthly ones.*

DK: Always loved that guy. The man was a cynical genius.

J: Well… I suppose there's *one* good thing about a guy flailing his arms from the pulpit.

DK: Yeah? What's that?

J: At least you know where his hands are…

CHAPTER TWENTY ONE

DK: Discussing evangelism reminds me of the great Joseph Campbell. He said that, when listening to someone, we should focus as much attention on *what* is speaking as we do on *who* is speaking. He said we should ask ourselves if what we're hearing is the voice of love—or is it something else? When I watch these slick-haired, silk-suited TV shills jawboning for Jesus, I don't hear much love or humility. They sound more like monstrous egos screaming for attention. What's amazing is that a lot of these glib evangelist types are *loaded*. They're amassing fortunes in the name of a man who apparently shunned materialism and owned almost nothing. They're raking in millions and soaking up celebrity while preaching about *your* humble life of simplicity.

J: Well, whenever you find a herd of sheep, you're bound to find a few wolves.

DK: To be fair, though, I've met plenty of people who claim they were "saved" by one evangelist or another.

J: There's no doubt that religious messages can change lives— but judgmental theology never saved *anyone*. Preachers can hold powerful sway over others, and it makes sense that folks desperately wanting answers would be attracted to someone offering an easy fix. But any choice made from fear, guilt or loneliness doesn't hold much hope of success.

DK: Is it all a waste of time?

J: I wouldn't say that. God can use *anything* for the ultimate good—even religion. At some level, everyone is seeking the truth, and it's fine when religion helps someone take the first step towards real understanding. But too often the convert's *first* step is also his *last*. He shuts himself into the box of faith and never peeks out again.

DK: I think a lot of religious figures are willfully exploiting the seeker's trust—especially some of these jokers in the media. They seem to believe they're mankind's direct link to heaven.

J: It should be the goal of every worthy teacher to make himself obsolete—to bring his students to the point where the teacher himself is no longer needed. Even the Holy Spirit's task is to nurture you back to communion with God, at which time learning will again be unnecessary. The Holy Spirit is your divine intercessor and the only one you'll ever need. Anyone posing as an intermediary between you and God is either malevolent or deluded.

DK: No offense intended… but don't many people see *you* as their intermediary?

J: They do. But I'm really just a facilitator. You can't lift yourself by your bootstraps, so I serve as a temporary support line in your journey back to Christ consciousness. But I always work from a standpoint of equality and service, never superiority.

DK: Still washing our feet for us, eh?

J: You could say that. I performed that ritual to show my disciples, in a way they couldn't possibly misinterpret or forget, that the Christ spirit *serves* rather than seeking to *be* served. By washing their feet, I emphasized my friends' holiness to them, hoping they would be inspired to do the same for one another. I continue bestowing honor onto all my brothers and sisters, because I know that each has the same Christ potential that I had.

DK: That's a tough sell this day and age.

J: Then let's see if we can give the idea some footing. Let's back off from religion for a bit while we cover some essential metaphysics.

DK: Quite honestly, I'd prefer to avoid so many abstractions.

J: You worry me, son. Can't you see that religion is comprised almost entirely of the abstract? In that regard, Christianity is especially vulnerable. It's so far-removed culturally and temporally from the modern world that there's barely a splash of tangibility involved. Christians who badmouth the metaphysical movement have completely missed the fact that *their own religion is one hundred percent metaphysical*. They have an invisible God sitting in an unseen heaven populated by angels and just down the street from a nebulous place of misery called hell. This imperceptible deity communicates solely through a mysterious spirit-being who, again, no one has ever laid eyes on. His most famous worldly appearance is said to have occurred in ancient Palestine by way of yours truly, a man who, even today, is still without firm historical foundation.

DK: So Christians denigrating metaphysics is like an airline president maligning the Wright brothers.

J: Absolutely. I mean they haven't even got a cross to bang a nail on!

DK: Alright, point taken. Go ahead and open the metaphysical floodgates and I'll try to stay afloat. But don't expect miracles...

J: Well, I've already explained that everyone is fully divine in essence but that very few realize it. Now, this information is certainly not hot off the press. Two thousand years ago I said, "Many are called but few are chosen." Since God doesn't play favorites, the statement can mean only one thing: *everyone* is called, but very few *respond*.

DK: And the needed response is what?

J: Simply the recognition that truth has never changed. You're merely being asked to acknowledge your own reality as a perfect creation of God. And though it may appear unlikely, eventually *everyone* must respond. As one who did, I serve as an interim guide to show you the way back home. But like I've said, I can't force you to make the trip. That would be a serious violation of the precious "free will" you keep trumpeting.

DK: Then you don't actually require us to *do* anything.

J: I never coerce; I just wait until someone's ready to see the obvious. That's the meaning of, "Behold, I stand at the door and knock." Once you awaken from your dream state, you'll understand that your will and God's are the same. To believe otherwise is to believe that *you* could change God's will that they *be* the same. And you *do* believe you've altered God's will whenever you think of yourself as sinful. That's not humility—it's the ultimate arrogance.

DK: If we're all one with God, as you say, then I suppose our divinity would be undeniable.

J: Let me simplify something. Despite the fact that you believe you have *many* problems, you really have only one: your belief in separation. From that single mistake, an entire problematic world appears. My role is to help you wake up and realize you've been dreaming. I help bridge the gap you've interposed in your mind between yourself and God. The gap is only imaginary, of course—but you've fallen so far into fear that you've cut yourself off from your natural state of divine communion. In reality, nothing has happened.

DK: I'm still not sure I can tag along on this dream thing.

J: The second chapter of Genesis says that a "deep sleep" fell upon Adam. Re-read that account and you'll find there's never any reference to him waking up. As the symbolical first man, Adam in his deep sleep represents a spiritually slumbering humanity, which has yet to experience any large-scale awakening. Most people are still fast asleep in their dream of separation.

DK: But the "dream," as you call it, seems convincingly *real*.

J: So did the ones you had last night while you were sleeping. Is it possible that upon awakening this morning you simply passed from one dream-state to another? *A Course in Miracles* refers to this very idea: "All your time is spent in dreaming. Your sleeping and your waking dreams have different forms, and that is all."

DK: Somehow, though, my sleeping dreams seem far less valid.

J: Not while you're having them they don't. Only upon awakening do you look back and realize you were dreaming. While you're sleeping, your dreams appear unquestionably real. An especially scary dream can wake you up in a sweat and can even have you panicked and gasping for air. So when you're sleeping, the mind fully believes your dream is reality. I'm merely explaining that a similar process continues when you get out of bed.

DK: But let's not get ridiculous. Obviously I know I'm not dreaming whenever I'm fully awake.

J: My whole point is that you're *not* fully awake. I assure you that, once you awaken spiritually, you'll look back on your "old" life with the same sense of misty reverie that you now have about your experiences during sleep. Your entire past will seem as wispy and surreal as any nighttime dream you ever had.

DK: Wow. This notion of waking dreams has my head spinning.

J: Maybe you'd better sleep on it…

CHAPTER
TWENTY TWO

DK: Frankly, I'm still skittish about talk of "oneness." It sounds like just another round of syrupy crap from the New Age movement.

J: You find unity confusing because you still think of yourself as a body-bound personality. But I'm telling you with certainty that leaves no room for doubt: *there is no such thing as a "person."*

DK: Jesus, you must be joking!

J: Say, are you taking my name in vain?

DK: Uh, no, not at all. I was onl—

[I looked up from my furious shorthand scribbling and caught Jesus quietly snickering in delight.]

DK: Okay, you got me on that one.

J: Listen, I know abstractions are frustrating, so here's the meat and potatoes: You believe that you're so-and-so, born in a particular place to certain parents, and so on. I'm urging you to question all that. Did the *world* create *you*—or have *you* somehow created the *world*? Think it over. It's a critical piece of the puzzle.

DK: Yeah, the piece that passeth understanding.

J: Don't be so quick to write it off. The reason for your arrival in this world was not necessarily—excuse the pun—apparent. God's creations are not born to die, and your story of having emerged helplessly from a womb is literally inconceivable. I'll say it again: *You are not your body.*

DK: I'll defer on this one to your inside information.

J: No, no—you can't just take my word for it. You have to prove it to yourself. But do take my word for one thing: you *can* know the truth. But instead of searching within, you turn… uh, shall we say *elsewhere.*

163

DK: I get the insinuation. We give our lives meaning by inventing philosophies and religions. Then we comfort ourselves with their dogmas and their hand-me-down stories of spiritual superstars.

J: Yes, and they're the wildest stories ever. Myths of gods and goddesses descending and ascending. Last-days battles between deities and devils. Dramatic heavenly judgments and next-world locales of ecstatic pleasure and unspeakable pain. It's the kind of stuff you'd normally read in children's storybooks. But comfortable in your ignorance, you spend the years sleepwalking through life, striving to gratify endless desires while fighting imaginary dragons of your own making. Eventually you tire and wither, and finally the body succumbs to the pitiless hand of Fate. As consciousness fades, you look back on the spectacle you called "life" and frequently find yourselves wondering, "What was all the fuss about?"

DK: And then we die.

J: Yes. And your belief is that upon this mysterious moment called death, God will magically zip you off to heaven—or hell, depending on whether He's had his morning coffee—where the meaning of your confusing earthly stopover will finally be revealed.

DK: I sense an air of disparagement.

J: Are you kidding? This heaven and hell piffle has about as much credibility as government inflation data…

CHAPTER TWENTY THREE

DK: Maybe you've gone a little overboard with your cynical view of life.

J: I'm not cynical about *life*. I'm just cynical about the way most people *live* it.

DK: Some seem fairly happy.

J: But the happiness is mostly superficial. And strictly relative. If folks are on top of their game, they may well consider themselves happy. They've got the right job, the right partner, enough money, good health and so on. But what if hardship or tragedy strikes? What happens when the job dissolves, the partner walks out, the money disappears, or health gives way to illness? Suddenly they discover that happiness was just a fortunate but temporary confluence of circumstance—a brief fulfillment of their ever-changing desires.

DK: Is that so bad?

J: Neither bad nor good—there's no judgment involved. The problem is, nothing lasts. It's obvious that all beginnings will lead to an end. Anything acquired is lost; whatever is built will crumble; that which is born must die. When the fabric of your life starts unraveling at the seams—and it will—the tenuous nature of your happiness becomes painfully clear. Even if you're able to hold things together well into old age, you know for certain that death, the Great Equalizer, will surely come calling.

DK: Then what's the downside to ignorance? As far as I'm concerned, we might as well eat, drink and be horny. I mean if we're doomed anyway, why not live to the fullest and forget the weighty, philosophical matters?

J: Your question implies that everything will sort out at the moment of death. But don't assume that death brings instant peace. Death happens only to the *body*. It doesn't eliminate desire, which is what got you into this mess. Desire resides in the *mind*, so it isn't automatically purged at the body's passing.

DK: You're telling me that my desires have landed me in a world of my own making? Surely I'm not that powerful!

J: How would you know? Not understanding what you are, you can't possibly realize your potential. Even on earth, the combination of desire and imagination are nearly unlimited in their ability to create. At the cosmic level, they can literally produce a universe. Desire's not bad in itself, but until you understand that a world of separation doesn't give you what you really want, you'll continue recreating it. So don't count on death to bail you out of your body-centered delusion. If you can fool yourself once, you can do it a thousand times. And most people have.

DK: Why would we choose a bodily experience in the first place?

J: Because you find it interesting.

DK: What's wrong with that?

J: *Nothing* is wrong. No one is judging you, and everything is in divine order. You don't know this because you've forgotten who you are. And believe me, forgetting your real nature is a calamity of cosmic proportion. You can't imagine what your little dream world is costing you.

DK: Still, most of us make a life of it. We *adjust*.

J: Krishnamurti said that it's no measure of health to be well adjusted to a profoundly sick world. And even if you're one of the relative few for whom life proceeds swimmingly, time generally takes its toll. As the years pass, folks grow increasingly anxious about their approaching departure. When the moment comes to exit stage left, they're often filled with a terrible fear of annihilation—regardless of their religious creeds. Believe me, I get just as many last-minute prayers of desperation from the sanguine halls of faith as I do from the trembling pits of fear.

DK: Not many atheists on deathbeds, eh?

J: No... but not many real believers, either. Death's imminence exposes beliefs for the comfortless charlatans they are. No thought system is reassuring if you secretly fear you're being destroyed. But dying needn't be traumatic. You can choose to wake up *now* and avoid a death involving panic or fear. You were born crying— but it's quite possible to die laughing.

DK: Is life so meaningless and absurd? And doesn't *God* bear some responsibility? You claim that at some level I *chose* this world—but I sure don't *remember* it. *I* say my arrival wasn't nearly so mysterious and was simply Nature taking its course. I mean it all seems pretty obvious. My father had an itch that needed scratching—and *wham!* "Congratulations, Mr. Maylor, it's an eight-pound-four-ounce, sacrilegious little heretic."

J: You defend your opinions with great authority. But you can't know the truth until you've thoroughly investigated.

DK: Okay, then, let's say you're right. Let's agree that I've somehow invented my little world and that earthly life is just a bizarre parody of reality as God created it. But right or wrong, we still have to make the best of things. So it seems reasonable to want a comfortable existence with good health, a nice home, a loving companion and such. I mean as long as we've hopped aboard the Dreamtime Express, we may as well relish the ride.

J: Yes, but it's all worthless if you've lost sight of who you are.

DK: You mean, "What doth it profit a man?" and all that jazz.

J: Exactly. The greatest part is that once you free yourself from the tyranny of thought, you'll no longer care what you have or don't have. Either way, there won't be any sense of privation. Living from a bottomless well of strength, love and goodness, for the first time in your life you'll possess true wealth. Instead of continuous wanting, seeking, and taking, you'll at last have something valuable to *give*.

DK: You say the physical stuff isn't all that important. But even if I were enlightened, how's a guy supposed to *give* if he's wandering the streets with a begging bowl?

J: Your material state isn't the point: we're talking about *consciousness*. Just as a flower's perfume blesses the air around it and the candle's flame brings light to everyone in the room, your enlightenment will help bring salvation to a world starving for it merely by your very *presence*.

DK: Don't we have the obligation to provide for ourselves?

J: You have the *right* to do so; there's no obligation involved. But the issue isn't survival. It's *focus*. I once warned against investing your life's energy—that is, your *attention*—in things that fade. I compared it to building a house upon the sand. Like casino gambling, it's a loser's game in the end. The body and the world are quite divine when seen in their true light, but to believe that your salvation lies in either is to place your treasure where "moth and rust consume and where thieves break in and steal." Those words press you to look beyond the physical to the source from which it all arises.

DK: It sounds like you're asking us to forego the enjoyment of life.

J: On the contrary. I'm trying to remove the suffering from it, thereby making it *possible* to truly enjoy it. That's the meaning of the words, "I came that they may have life and have it abundantly." The statement clearly implies that before the Christ consciousness emerges, there's no real life at all.

DK: How did you come to your understanding of these truths? What was your secret?

J: Nothing mysterious, really. I just recognized early on that in this world there's nothing to cling to. I questioned *everything*. I spent time with the sages and learned from their wisdom. They taught me to withdraw my attention from outer things and to meditate and take my focus inward. Finally it dawned on me that I was the subtle cause behind the entire universe. I realized that, whatever appeared, *I* first had to be there to witness it. Before a single question could be asked, even about God Himself, *I* had to be there to ask it.

DK: Is that what you meant when you said, "Before Abraham was, I am"?

J: That's not exactly what I said. A simple correction is needed: "Before Abraham was the I AM."

DK: And his disciple was greatly confused, saying, "What the hell is he *talking* about!??"

J: *Heh heh.* Abraham symbolizes the material world. Therefore, long before the world, which is just a manifestation of consciousness, was the one, changeless, primordial self, of which you are an intimate part. That self is of course the same self that first *imagined* the world and is in fact the only one who could have done so.

DK: Still a bit convoluted, I'd say.

J: Only because we're using words, which are symbols, to describe reality, which is straightforward, unified and beyond representation. But God isn't the least bit complicated: He's simplicity itself.

DK: So where can I find Him?

J: How can you find something you wouldn't recognize? God is all around you—and in fact *is* you—but your distorted perceptions and concepts are preventing you from seeing it. Anyhow, forget finding God, because He isn't lost. *He'll find you* if you'll stop insisting on how He should do it and what form it should take. Just keep your attention on the self. You don't yet know *what* you are, but the fact that you *are* is obvious, and the one wholly true statement you can make is also the shortest sentence in the English language: I am. Everything else is mere theory and fluff.

DK: The question's a little cheeky, but why should I trust all this advice you're dispensing?

J: An excellent question, Grasshopper. I'll share a little story…

There once was a man drowning in the middle of a large river. Gasping and grunting, he was slapping at the water in a frantic effort to save himself. Hearing the commotion, a woman appeared from the nearby forest and saw the man struggling to stay afloat. As she watched him thrashing in the water, the woman shouted, "Say there, you in the river! Are you drowning!?"

"No," the fellow shot back sarcastically, "I'm performing a one-man, synchronized swimming exhibition. *Of course* I'm drowning, you nitwit! Don't just stand there like an incumbent politician. *Do* something!"

So she weighs up the dire situation and concludes the same as any mature woman would: "Isn't it *just like a man* to be so *cocky* when asking *favors!*"

DK: I just love these inspirational religious parables.

J: *Heh heh*. Didn't they include this one in the gospels?

DK: I'm afraid not.

J: Ah, too bad—it's one of my favorites… Well anyhow, seeing the drowning man's despair, the woman takes pity on him and explains, "By a strange coincidence, many years ago I too was drowning in this very river. Unable to swim, I was utterly without hope. Oddly enough, at that precise moment a stranger emerged from these same woods and came to my rescue by tossing me one of the large fruits from that huge tikiberry vine over yonder. Would you like me to throw one out to you?"

"Hmmm... how do I know it'll do the trick?" the man complained.

"Awfully *cynical* for a *drowning* chap," the woman muttered to herself. Being the merciful type, however, she patiently clarified: "You see, the fruit of the tikiberry vine is large, like a gourd, but being mostly hollow, it's also very lightweight—so it floats and makes for a natural life preserver. As you can plainly see, I'm still very much alive, and the tikiberry fruit is the sole reason I'm standing here today."

"Okay, lady," the man said with resignation, "I suppose I'll have to trust you on this one—but only because I'm without options and I'm desperate!"

"Ah, the proverbial mustard-seed faith in action!" the woman declared. And with that, she tossed a tikiberry fruit to the drowning man and saved his life...

DK: A very touching story, I'm sure. But how does it relate to my concerns about the soundness of your advice?

J: O faithless interrogator, how long am I to bear with you!?

DK: At least a few more hours, I would hope.

J: The gist of my little parable, you see, is that it doesn't matter whether you *believe* a life preserver will float: floating is its very *nature*. When you're drowning, all you've gotta do is grab on. If you stop sinking, then you'll know it worked. In the same way, when the enlightened offer a bit of guidance, you'd be wise to try it out and test its merit. When I tell you that your identification with the mind-body complex is the crux of your trouble, maybe you should do a little exploring.

DK: Apparently our fall into physicality has been a disaster. Is the body that problematic?

J: The body itself is not the problem. It's your belief that the body is *you* that creates all your fears and desires and causes you to suffer. Your suffering will cease once you stop identifying with the body and the mind. But don't let this become another philosophy, because that won't help you at all. Like the drowning man in the parable, you've gotta give it a fair crack and judge the outcome for yourself.

DK: How long before I see results?

J: Hard to say. Your entire world revolves around the body and your thoughts about its circumstances. You're hugely invested in the notion that happiness is dependent on the increasingly favorable progression of your physical life story. Humans have developed so many attachments to the realm of form that the stripping-away process can be lengthy—and painful.

DK: Then why would we do it?

J: The time will come when you won't have a choice. Eventually the pain of ignorance becomes too much to bear, and the diminishing returns of the material world begin causing you to question its ultimate value. It's the Prodigal Son syndrome. Sooner or later you have to admit your discomfort and be willing to leap over the chasm of your fears.

DK: I'm having trouble getting motivated for the jump.

J: You've spent a lifetime doing things *your* way, with no lasting results. Why not try *my* approach? You've assumed from childhood that your identity lies in the body, and you've never even questioned it. But here's a good way to prove that you and the body-mind are not the same thing. Ask yourself, "*Who* is experiencing this body? *Who* is having these thoughts?"

DK: The answer's obvious: *I'm* the one in this body. *I'm* the one with these thoughts.

J: Yes, but who is speaking?

DK: What the heck do you mean? *I* am speaking!

J: But again, who is this mysterious "I"?

DK: It's *me*, you messianic mule! The one sitting right here in front of you!

J: You're pointing your finger at your chest and referring me to your body. My question is, who is the one doing the pointing and referring?

DK: Cripes, man, you shoulda been a lawyer.

J: Look, I'm not here to play philosophical mind games. Addressing the question "Who am I?" is paramount. It's the secret to undoing all your misperceptions.

DK: Your theories and an hour of digging trenches might buy me a coffee at Starbucks.

J: Still skeptical, eh? Tell ya what... try a little experiment. Tonight when you're lying in bed preparing to sleep, close your eyes and quietly contemplate the question, "*Who* or *what* is lying here?" You'll find there's no answer, because what you are isn't something that can be located or defined: you can't identify yourself as any particular *thing*. Nothing will change, of course, but you may finally realize that you aren't what you thought you were. You'll see that you just *are*... and that it's perfectly okay.

DK: The thought of being nothing in particular is strange—perhaps even a little threatening. I'm not sure I can embrace the unknown like that.

J: But you do it quite happily every time you doze off! In the state of dreamless sleep, your entire universe disappears, and every one of your sacred self-concepts goes with it. All the circumstances, people, and things with which you so closely identify are rolled up like a strip of carpet, and you lose all attachment to what you presently conceive to be your "world" and your "self." And yet there's absolutely no sense of fear, loss or annihilation. Your whole world is gone, your ego is dead—and you're perfectly content!

DK: Say, what the heck have you got against ego? *Mine* has served pretty well. That is, at least I'm surviving.

J: There's far more to life than survival, my friend. And until you're free of ego, you're just a slave to your programming. The truth is, maintaining the false self is burdensome and draining. In fact, it's the great sense of relief from having to do it that gives sleep so much of its appeal. It's why you gladly welcome the prospect every night of diving headfirst into the unknown. And you do this with absolutely no assurance that you'll ever again emerge from your state of no-*thing*-ness.

DK: Still, I have my history to rely upon. I mean I've always awakened from the "nothing state" when morning arrived.

J: Sure, but the point is that when you hit the sack each night, you're perfectly willing to fall helpless into the Great Mystery, with no guarantee it won't swallow you up forever. You *assume* you'll awaken with the sunrise—but you're only betting with the odds. And surely you can see that the day will come when you *won't* wake up.

DK: You're referring to death?

J: Of course. What happens to "you" *then*?

DK: Well, I've always just figured that *God* will handle things.

J: O ye of groundless faith! Your thinking entails a long string of disquieting, unproven—and *unprovable*—assumptions.

DK: Like what?

J: First, it assumes a God who's *outside* of you and separate—a kind of cosmic Wizard of Oz hiding behind the scene, throwing the switches and running the show. It also assumes that God created you *as a body*, with careful planning and design. But if God *did* create you as a body, then He brought you onto the planet solely at his discretion. As you said in your letter, He couldn't possibly have asked your permission if you hadn't yet been created.

DK: Obviously not.

J: So going by your present beliefs, God has, in effect, made you a victim of his own agenda. If you believe that God created you as a body, at his whim, then He allowed you no part whatsoever in choosing your birthplace, your parents, your home or your childhood living environment. Unfortunately, by forcing your participation in his little earth-drama, God also subjected you to the possibility of eternal damnation. It's evident, of course, that if God created *you* in this fashion, then He created everyone else the same way.

DK: I suppose I'm forced to agree.

J: Which means that God, even as we speak, is still creating all those suffering babies. What on earth could He be *thinking*? And how lucky for *you* that God brought you into one of the wealthiest nations on the planet—and a largely *Christian* one at that! This was truly a stroke of great fortune, especially considering that, theologically speaking, God gives you only one shot on the earth-plane to get things right. I can only assume that you must be very special.

DK: *Sheesh.* When you're dripping sarcasm, there's no closing the valve.

J: Sarcasm? *Me!??* Heck, I'm *thrilled* that God sent you to the Big Show with a coveted front-row seat. But gosh—why is He so mean to those millions of innocent, starving children? What about all the infants born with crippling disease or other terrible afflictions? And what of those born into squalor, oppression, neglect or abuse? Cursed from the outset by your all-wise, all-loving deity. "But that's life," says God. "*My* ways are not *your* ways, you know."

DK: You must've been a real joy at the dinner table.

J: I only call 'em like I see 'em…

DK: Well, now you've got me in a dither. If I truly had some degree of personal volition regarding my appearance in this world, then everyone else must've had the same freedom of choice. But if they did, why would anyone choose to incarnate into a life of intense suffering? Wouldn't everyone choose to be rich and famous? Or at least *comfortable*, for gosh sakes.

J: If I tell you the world is ultimately just a dream, does it really make sense analyzing the motivations of the shadow figures *within* the dream? Would they even exist if *you* weren't around to conjure them? Do they exist when you're not *aware* of them? Where do they go when you drop off to sleep? Where do they go when they die? Where do they go when *you* die? Can *anything* exist outside your own consciousness? If you say yes, how would you set about proving this gargantuan paradox?

DK: Score one for the man in the nomad threads.

J: For the moment, then, let's stick to addressing reality as you've come to *perceive* it. Your present belief system holds that a separate God created the universe, piece by piece—you and everyone else included. Some get the gold mine, some get the shaft.

DK: Yes, and it's totally unfair that some are given lives of luxury and ease while others are born into abject misery. Or that God would allow some folks eighty or ninety years to become "saved," while others get maybe ten or fifteen, or even less—sometimes *none at all*. It would seem that God's soul redemption strategy is subject to the same time and space constraints as any other aspect of existence.

J: If that's true, then salvation's just a matter of luck.

DK: So if God operates the way most of us have assumed He does, I'd have to wonder why He doesn't realize that some situations simply aren't conducive to the Christian message. For example, how could a child of the ghetto understand the idea that you died for his sins? I mean it's not realistic. The poor kid's probably just trying to scrape together his next meal.

J: I'm afraid the Bible God is pretty much oblivious to all that. He doesn't appear all that worried about whether people have enough food, a decent home or a safe place to raise their kids. Unlike his Old Testament days, He's no longer preoccupied with major events like wars, famines and plagues. He's got no time to fret about volcanic eruptions, killer tsunamis or the latest deadly virus. Nowadays He's mostly concerned with preserving his good name, basking in his own glory, and building loyalty among the troops. In fact, that's the one area where He's always been consistent: He's ever focused on how much attention everyone's giving *Him*.

DK: Okay, so the *problem* seems pretty clear: our understanding of God is a mile off the mark. But what's the *solution*?

J: Well, as I see it, you have two choices. Either you resign yourself to worshipping this self-absorbed, learning-disabled God of literalism, or you throw Him out on his deafened, insensitive ear. If I were the average human, I'd fire Him on grounds of incompetence alone—make Him go back for some remedial logic courses or something.

DK: I trust I'll have your protection when the lynch mob arrives…

CHAPTER
TWENTY FOUR

J: I can practically hear those brain sprockets grindin'. Say what's on your mind.

DK: Well, I'm thinking what if they're right? The literalists, I mean. What if they're right about God? Don't we have to give some weight to *their* view? My aunt used to say that even the *thinnest* pancake has two sides. So, what if God *really is* the quick-tempered cuss of the Old Testament? Shouldn't we mortals tread lightly? Because He's pretty ruthless when He gets his nose out of joint.

J: C'mon, man, we're talking about *God* here. According to believers, this is the same force that creates quasars, black holes and supernovas, whirling galaxies, and star systems light-years across. Even the body—overemphasized though it may be—is utterly imbued with intelligence. It flawlessly processes millions of functions per second without your slightest effort or awareness.

DK: No argument on this end: the universe is truly a living miracle. And the whole extravaganza seems perfectly coordinated—from the macro level of a solar system, right down to the mysterious, subatomic world of the quark.

J: Then we agree that a vast and brilliant hyper-intelligence is pulsing through all existence.

DK: All but Capitol Hill, I'd say.

J: Okay, so are you gonna sit there and contend that the Cosmic Magnificence behind infinite creation is a character who actually takes personal interest in your sex life?

DK: Hell, I wish *somebody* would.

J: But level with me now. Is it reasonable to believe that this universal Super-Mind wants you to bemoan your sins, cling to the ol' rugged cross, and send off large chunks of cash to some podium-pounding preacher at your favorite television megachurch?

DK: You're probably right. Apart from the things of man, when I look at the natural world, I don't see a trace of judgment or religion in the whole ball of wax.

J: By golly, I think your sail's finally catchin' a breeze. Hear, O Interviewer, thus saith the Interview*ee*: Unless your intelligence exceedeth that of the Scribes, the Pharisees, and the average teenage celebrity idol, ye shall never enter the kingdom of heaven!

DK: Man, if you were this flippant twenty centuries back, I can see how your style might've teed off some folks.

J: It ain't Aunt Thelma's bridge club…

DK: But perhaps you contradict yourself. You talk about the miracle of creation—and yet you insist that none of it is real.

J: We should distinguish between the real and the eternal. The universe certainly appears real enough *in the moment*. The universe is *un*-real, however, insofar as it exists only as an idea in the mind; there's nothing eternal about it. How lasting or substantial could it be, when it vanishes every time you drift off to sleep?

DK: I'm beginning to glimpse some truth in what you're saying. I can see how materiality might be just a passing play of consciousness.

J: Yes, but the beauty, intelligence and love that infuse it are deathless aspects of the eternal realm that gives it life. In that sense, the universe could well be called divine. Seen from a wider view, there's nothing evil, clumsy or accidental about it.

DK: How do you expect these ideas will be received? I mean even most *liberal* Christians will find them fairly radical. As for the conservatives—well, let's just say I won't be invited to any parties over at Christian Coalition.

J: How people respond to new ideas is *their* problem—don't make it yours. If a guy wants to attend The Church of the Open Bible and the Closed Mind, that's his prerogative. But when a man's unwilling to *question* his thoughts, then he's condemned to continue *thinking* them. Let me give an illustration of how the mind tends to resist certain types of new information…

Suppose I tell you that an obscure and distant planet—we'll call it Zeta Globulus—is two hundred light years from earth, four times larger than Jupiter and comprised mostly of quartz. Would you be upset?

DK: Of course not.

J: But you don't know if my statement is true.

DK: No, but neither do I know that it's false.

J: Good enough. In other words, even though you're uncertain about the validity of my claim, you remain open-minded.

DK: Sure.

J: Great. Next, let's say I tell you that the moon orbiting Zeta Globulus is made of green cheese. Are you going to get angry about *that*?

DK: Well, I wouldn't be angry, but I'd probably think you're a few kosher pickles short of a barrel.

J: Why? You've already admitted that you know nothing about Zeta Globulus. How can you be sure that my cheesy claim isn't true?

DK: Because we've got lots of scientific data regarding planets and moons and such—and not one bit of evidence suggests that any are made of cheese. On top of that, the idea's clearly ridiculous.

J: Alright… so let's summarize what we've got. You're convinced, through means you believe are reasonable and reliable, that the moon orbiting Zeta Globulus *isn't* made of green cheese. And while you may think I'm a real crank for suggesting that it *is*, you won't be *personally offended* by my crazy assertion, even though my statement, if it *were* true, might threaten your entire understanding of reality. Right?

DK: Right.

J: So we've established that you feel no need to defend or attack when presented with information that *sounds* reasonable but that you aren't sure about.

DK: Correct.

J: You're also willing to consider information that *contradicts* what you believe, as long as you're not *emotionally attached* to the subject. In other words, you may not agree with me, and you might even think I'm crazy, but you aren't getting all hot and bothered about it. Are you with me so far?

DK: I think so.

J: Okay. But now, suppose I tell you that your grandmother— sweet as she might have been, making homemade preserves or serving up chicken soup when you were running a fever—was secretly responsible over the last twenty years for robbing seven small-town banks. *Now* will you be upset?

DK: I don't know. I might.

J: Why is that?

DK: Because I know it's not true.

J: No, you don't! You merely want to *believe* it's not true. Maybe I'm a G-man who's been pursuing the case for years. Maybe I've got information on ol' Grams that would drop your jaw. Or maybe I was the driver of her getaway car. Who knows? My story may well turn out to be true. You're simply not in a position to judge, because you may not have all the facts. Follow me?

DK: I guess so. But I still don't see where you're headed.

J: Well, a minute ago I made a claim about the dairy content of the moon orbiting Zeta Globulus. By referring to widely accepted scientific knowledge and using a little common sense, you quickly concluded that my statement was very likely false. And you weren't even slightly inclined to be angry, even though you considered my assertion outrageous. But the moment I provide a little rundown on the history of creative bank withdrawals by dear old Granny, you're puffing your chest and strapping on the gloves. You're offended, even though you can't be sure whether she robbed those banks or not.

DK: So most of us are pretty objective about topics we regard as psychologically neutral. But once we have a vested interest, or the element of emotion is introduced, everything changes.

J: Yeah, you become far less willing to consider information that threatens your established position: you lose your sense of detachment. For example, if you're a biblical literalist and I tell you my lunar green cheese story, you'll probably figure I've lost my marbles—but you aren't likely to become hostile. However, if I tell you there's not a smattering of convincing proof that Moses ever parted the Red Sea, then suddenly, as one who considers the Bible infallible, you're insulted and upset. At this point, you might offer what you consider to be supportive "evidence" of the Red Sea account. But if I still reject your argument, you abandon rational discussion altogether and begin demanding unquestioning acceptance. If I continue resisting, you're soon accusing me of doubting "God's word" and giving me climate reports on the underworld.

DK: What you're saying is that we're perfectly happy using reason—but only while it works to our advantage.

J: Right. After all, most people like to think of themselves as reasonable. But when it comes to religion, the moment reason fails them, they resort to their trusty fallback position, the one that can never be questioned or assailed: *"This* requires *faith!"*

DK: So you're saying that if I knew—not just believed, but somehow really *knew*—that the Red Sea story was true, then why should I become angry with *you* for doubting it... is that it?

J: Exactly. I mean if you're thoroughly convinced that the parting of the waters took place, then fine. Just walk away calm and unconcerned, and leave me to wallow in my ignorance. But don't start steaming under the collar and shoving the Bible in my face as if you've just provided some sort of incontrovertible proof. The

Bible is *full* of stories about "moons of green cheese." It doesn't prove anything about the stories, but it *does* provide good reason to question the Bible.

DK: A scary thing to do if you were raised to believe that it all came straight from heaven's High Command.

J: Yep. It's just human nature to protect deeply ingrained ideas. This is especially true of *spiritual* ideas, whose precepts people often feel *obliged* to uphold and protect. In fact, Bertrand Russell said that one of the main stumbling blocks to intellectual progress is the religion-inspired notion that there are some things that it's one's "duty" to believe.

DK: I can certainly see how that attitude could stifle authentic investigation.

J: Yes, and it's not a matter of sincerity, because people desperately *want* to believe—and many convince themselves that they *do* believe. But deep within, they aren't so sure that what they're proclaiming is true. That's why religious or political fanatics and militants expend lots of energy cultivating converts. They buttress their own fragile beliefs by gathering kindred souls who, like themselves, don't ask questions and won't take "no" for an answer.

DK: I suppose we all need moral support.

J: Only ego needs reinforcements; spirit simply knows its own invulnerable oneness. When a position is unreasonable or can't be proven, its defenders are all the more zealous promoting it. Sometimes the side with the weakest position is the one that makes the most noise.

DK: That reminds me of the old story about the preacher's wife. One Saturday evening, she's reviewing her husband's planned Sunday morning sermon. She circles one of the paragraphs in heavy red ink and writes in the margin, "Weak point. Yell louder."

J: Once you become entrenched in your ideological foxholes, you fight like the devil to hold your ground. But one of the marks of true intelligence is *open-mindedness*—the ability to consider opposing arguments without getting angry or feeling threatened.

181

It's a sure sign of a problem if you never find yourself asking, "Is it possible I'm *mistaken*?" Wisdom teaches that people's emotional response to philosophical disagreement is sometimes directly opposed to their true conviction. So be cautious with folks who have all the answers. Those who know rarely tell, and those who tell rarely know.

DK: I guess we're back to the old analogy of the blind leading the blind.

J: I'm afraid so. Until you're firmly grounded in real knowledge, your good intentions are just mucking things up by adding more half-truths and confusion to the mix. It's like the Bible says: focus on removing the refrigerator from your own eye before worrying about the toaster oven in someone else's.

DK: I'll assume you're paraphrasing.

J: It's a rough translation. My Greek's a little rusty…

CHAPTER TWENTY FIVE

DK: It seems we all believe we've got a lock on truth and that *our* view of God is the *right* one.

J: And that's why religious extremists are so driven: they're *certain* they understand what God is all about. Feeling like divinely appointed messengers, they're so blinded by their dogmas that they'll happily bulldoze entire cultures in the name of their faith. They actually believe they're doing heaven a *favor*: "We'll make these poor bastards see the light of our God's mercy if we have to bloody well *kill* 'em!"

DK: Pretty bizarre, alright. In our reckless efforts to populate the cities of heaven, we're serving up hell here on earth.

J: You like Bible quotes? Here's a good one: "He who says he is in the light and hates his brother is in the darkness still."

DK: Then I can't reasonably claim to love God if I mistreat my neighbor.

J: No, and it's safe to assume that would include killing him in the name of your religion.

DK: You just quoted from the First Letter of John. That same book also proclaims, "If any one says, 'I love God,' and hates his brother, he is a liar…"

J: Well, he may not be lying but he's certainly confused.

DK: You mean because we can't possibly love an unseen heavenly God if we don't even love our brethren on earth.

J: No, no, no—it's far more *radical* than that. You love God *by* loving your brother. To say "I love God" is like declaring that you're all for peace, brotherhood and cheap access to the web. It's mom-'n-apple-pie kinda stuff. Besides, what the heck do you know of God that makes you speak of Him so confidently? Talking about God as if He's separate only proves that you know nothing about Him. God *is* your brother, your sister—your *self*. The universe is holographic, and the whole is contained in every part.

DK: Well, naturally I like to think that I love *God*. But in my humble opinion, certain aspects of his creation are just plain repugnant.

J: But the notion of loving God apart from something else is a negation of all that God is. *God is unity itself.* Your distorted perception shows you a world of unrelated parts, so you've confused diversity with fragmentation. The paradox is summed up in the word "individuality." Most people think it implies separateness; but its root means "indivisible." Identifying with the body, you perceive yourself to be an isolated individual— an obvious etymological contradiction—and you therefore assume that you're separate from all you survey. But one of your favorite spiritual works declares, "Now are we *one* with Him Who is our Source."

DK: Once again you're quoting from *A Course in Miracles*. I find that ironic. Because even though *Course* is Christian in tone, it was recorded by a Jewish atheist. She said that *you* gave it to her through a process of "inner dictation."

J: Maybe I did.

DK: Fundamentalist Christians claim that it's Satanic and that it was inspired by a demon who was impersonating you.

J: What a clever little devil!

DK: It's no laughing matter to the fundies. They say that Satan is extremely powerful and that he's able to deceive by shrewdly mimicking God, thereby leading people astray. They say you've got to be terribly careful and discriminating to discern the spirit of God from the *false* spirit of evil.

J: You mean it's possible to mistake their devil for their God? How interesting that the two should be so similar as to be nearly indistinguishable. It's no mystery if people are confused. They've got a devil with godlike powers, and a God who frequently acts demonic! Kinda makes you wonder who they're really worshipping on Sunday morning.

DK: Be careful with the mockery. Literalists comprise a fairly sizable percentage of the American populace.

J: Are these the same folks who claim the earth is only several thousand years old? That corpses will rise from their graves during the last days and be airlifted into the clouds? That hell is a burning lake and that heaven is paved with streets of gold?

DK: Well, I don't know about the streets...

J: So according to Christian right-wingers, it's possible that a book about peace, love and spiritual enlightenment was actually written by *demons*?

DK: That's how *they* see it.

J: Just to keep the balance, let's view things from across the fence. If these seemingly ubiquitous demons are so cagey and cunning, then who's to say they didn't write the Bible? After all, here's a book that depicts God as angry, sadistic, murderous, irrational and horribly unjust—none of which creates a very magnetic persona for the guy. So you'll have to admit it's a pretty demonic vision of the divine. I mean if I were in the business of steering folks away from God, that's certainly the sort of picture *I'd* paint.

DK: You once advised to judge the value of something by its results: "Ye shall know them by their *fruits*."

J: Given Christianity's grim history, I'm not sure the church is too anxious for anyone to go judging its fruit: too much of it winds up rotting on the ground. In the last two thousand years, Bible-based arrogance has resulted in the deaths of *millions*. I've yet to hear of *A Course in Miracles* causing widespread slaughter.

DK: It's just that, for some people, it all sounds a little suspicious. A lot of us are skeptical when someone claims to have "channeled" something—to have had "conversations with God."

J: *Heh heh.* Someday you'll look back and see the irony… But hey, isn't "direct inspiration" essentially the claim behind most of the world's holy books? Take Paul's statement in the first chapter of Galatians. He says the gospel he preached wasn't one he received from man, but rather that it came to him—and I quote—"through a revelation of Jesus Christ." And many Christians claim that every line of the Bible is similarly inspired. Believers seem comfortable enough accepting that explanation for *those* writings.

DK: Yeah, but that's different. I mean after all, the scriptures are… uh…

J: Yes?

DK: Well, you know…. *ancient.*

J: Sounds kinda stupid when you say it out loud, eh?

DK: What I mean is, a lot of people just can't relate to that New Age stuff.

J: Man, you slap labels on things faster than a drugstore clerk. You're pigeonholing, pilgrim. "Liberal," "conservative," "radical," "agnostic," "atheist"—they're just intellectual cop-outs. Not exactly the hallmark of an open mind.

DK: But I'm sure you understand why folks would be skeptical about your involvement in modern-day media. We don't usually think of you contributing in such concrete ways.

J: You know, that mystifies me every time I think about it. I mean I was committed enough to your freedom two thousand years ago to endure the pain of a needless crucifixion. Would I undergo that kind of dramatic nonsense and then call it quits? Isn't it more likely that I'd continue helping in every way possible?

DK: I dunno. I always figured that, after Calvary, your job was pretty much finished and the rest was up to us.

J: What am I, some kind of cosmic Fred Flintstone? You think I punch the clock, put in my hard eight, and hit the door at five? "Crucifixion's over! Yabba-dabba-doooo!" Is that how you see it?

DK: Not necessarily. I've always had a vague conviction that you're still interacting with us—but on a *spiritual* level, not writing books and such.

J: Well, obviously I'm not really interacting with a world that doesn't exist. But I do provide help at the *source*: in the mind. The level of perception that shows you the material world also appears to contain evidence of God involving Himself *with* that world. It's all arising in consciousness, though, and one form is ultimately no more real than the next.

DK: *Oooph.* Now I know why Judas hanged himself.

J: It's impossible to explain in a way you'd understand. Let's just say that nothing is beyond the purview of spirit because nothing is beyond God. He engages his creations in ways they can recognize and use.

DK: So God knows our unity but still relates to us individually.

J: God doesn't share in your delusions, of course. But his spirit does mediate with each mind that believes itself separate from the source. This is necessary because most people's consciousness functions within a pretty small domain, and each mind has very different perceptions of reality. That's why you don't typically have Muslims dreaming of Lord Krishna, Jews having visions of Mother Mary, or fundamentalist Christians encountering White Buffalo Calf Woman. God communicates with each of his children on their own terms.

DK: Reminds me of Paul's statement in 1 Corinthians: "I have become all things to all men, that I might by all means save some."

J: Except that Paul's view of salvation was far too narrow and his ambition far too weak. God becomes all things to all people that He might by all means save *everyone*. With God, the goal and its accomplishment are always united, and the only goal is this: to restore communion with the one, divine spirit.

DK: You keep mentioning spirit. And you're quoted as saying before the Ascension that you would send us the *Holy* Spirit.

J: But I wasn't promising delivery of a spiritual caretaker from heaven. I was only telling my disciples that spirit would soon be emerging in their own consciousness. In other words, they would become *aware* of it. And let's clarify something else: the term "Holy Spirit" is actually redundant. Spirit by its very nature is pure and whole, or "holy." So referring to spirit as holy is like describing water as wet. I wouldn't even mention it except that, by using the term "Holy Spirit," a lot of folks have concluded that there's *another* spirit that *isn't* holy. But God's spirit is *one* and therefore all-encompassing.

DK: So this "Holy Spirit" you promised is within us at every moment.

J: More intimate than your wildest fantasy and closer than two cab bumpers at a Park Avenue stoplight. God's spirit is *your* spirit. It's not something beyond you.

DK: You sure about this?

J: Let's just say I have it on good authority. God ain't "out there." Get over it…

CHAPTER TWENTY SIX

DK: Say, I don't mean to be quarrelsome, but there's something I'd like to nail you down on.

J: Not a wooden beam, I hope.

DK: Sorry, poor choice of words.

J: No problem, hammer away.

DK: Well, you've essentially said that there's no actual devil. And yet several gospel passages have you referring to "Satan" or "the evil one." In fact, you allegedly told Peter, "Get behind me, Satan!" What was going on?

J: I was just using a metaphor to describe ego. Do you recall the circumstances surrounding my confrontation with Peter?

DK: Sure. He was hoping to dissuade you from going forward with your arrest.

J: Right. I was just scolding him for undermining my mission, because at that moment he was speaking entirely from ego— which is, figuratively, the "devil" of all mankind. I was telling Peter emphatically that I couldn't go around preaching liberation and then give in to fear. If I hoped to be taken seriously, I had to follow through with my message of infinite trust in the power of love. So my references to Satan were strictly symbolic, since no one operating from cosmic consciousness would reinforce illusions of fear and separation.

DK: You seemed pretty keen on metaphors and parables.

J: Only because they were less threatening—both for Roman authorities and for the Jews. Some things had to be said in ways that only those properly instructed could understand. You see, most folks use religion as an easy way to have their questions answered. But *my* teachings involved a much more *uncomfortable* process: having your answers questioned. People aren't ready for that. It frightens them. And as the Crucifixion demonstrated, frightened people can be ruthless. When you boil it down, I was killed because I threatened revered concepts and traditional power structures.

DK: Won't this interview do the same thing?

J: Probably. You might consider a gated community.

DK: You know, I'm beginning to realize that nearly every conflict on earth is based on disagreements over concepts. I mean we're butchering one another over mere *interpretations*, for gosh sakes. Do mind and spirit always conflict?

J: Spirit and *egoic thinking* conflict. But spirit isn't fighting anything, because reality doesn't fight with illusions. In your natural state, the body, mind and spirit are seen as different aspects of the whole. They easily fulfill their various functions in perfect harmonious balance.

DK: Life's just a bed of roses, eh?

J: Look, I understand that, from your present worldview, problems appear all too real. But there are no problems in reality, and reality is never a problem.

DK: So where ego sees separation, spirit sees only oneness.

J: That's right. The egoic mind is constantly "dissecting" reality, attempting to understand totality by breaking it into pieces. The contradiction should be obvious. Viewing yourself as separate and unrelated inevitably causes you to see everything else that way, too. But reality is whole, and you lose sight of it the moment you divide it; you unleash a chain reaction of attack and defense. For ego, those are the only viable options—the two sides of its double-edged sword.

DK: You mean that God's paradise has gone to hell in a hand basket for a simple mistake in *perception*?

J: In a word, yes. The "Fall" referred to in various religions is the origin of the belief in a personal "I" and the beginning of guilt, fear, and the subtle, insane belief that you've attacked or offended God, marred his handiwork and usurped his authority. You then perceive Him as angry and needing appeasement. But it's all in the mind.

DK: Then our problems are mostly mental.

J: Absolutely. What problems do you have that don't originate in the mind?

DK: I could list a dozen.

J: Yes, but when you speak of a problem, you're actually describing a *condition*. Conditions simply are what they are, and one man's trouble is another man's bliss. So it's the *mind* that looks upon a situation and defines it as "a problem." The mind says, "This is unacceptable. I need the present moment to be different before I can feel okay."

189

DK: So it's our *interpretation* that makes something problematic.

J: Generally, yes. The mind's tendency is to judge reality according to its own ideal. Since that ideal is rarely met, the mind is constantly resisting what *is*, leading to unhappiness and frustration. The mind keeps anticipating salvation or happiness in the *future*, which of course never arrives. So unhappiness is a mental thing. A circumstance may well be difficult or unpleasant, but that's only an external *condition*. It's *the mind* that turns it into a problem.

DK: One teacher I respect says that we're each responsible for our own misery—but only *all* of it.

J: She knows that in the fully awakened state there's no such thing as a problem.

DK: Yeah, but I dunno. I mean I can go along up to a point—but once again the philosophy appears impractical. Take a starving child, for instance. The kid is dying because he has no food. That's a real and immediate *problem*.

J: For whom?

DK: Well, at the very least, it's a problem for the kid himself. And I, too, have a problem with someone starving to death.

J: Every moment, millions of people are hungry or even starving. I doubt it prevented you from enjoying last night's supper.

DK: Maybe not. But I do have trouble with a world where some have plenty and others have nothing.

J: A guy can have everything he wants and still be miserable, while someone enlightened could be living on the streets and be perfectly peaceful. It makes all the difference when you realize that the relative world is simply a product of imagination, projected outward.

DK: Ah, the recurrent theory of The Dream. I still say it sounds like a bunch of metaphysical mumbo-jumbo.

J: Poets have been expressing this idea for centuries. Edgar Allan Poe wrote, "All that we see or seem is but a dream within a dream."

DK: Exactly the sort of fried-brain rambling you'd *expect* from a boozer on opium!

J: C'mon, you aren't giving it a chance. Some of history's greatest spiritual seers have made the same assertions I'm making today. Aren't you curious why so many enlightened ones would proclaim that the world is a projection of consciousness? They have no reason to deceive you; there's nothing in it for *them*. Maybe you should heed their words and investigate.

DK: Listen, you might sell that "projection" stuff to the guru contingent, but to most of us working stiffs the world is plenty real.

J: To which world do you refer?

DK: To *this* world, of course. The same one you're experiencing right now.

J: Hey, don't project your fantasy onto *me*. The world *you* perceive is your own *private* world, closed and inaccessible to anyone else. It can't be shared, and so it isn't real. God is an "equal opportunity" creator. Anything personal or exclusive is strictly part of your ongoing illusion.

DK: But there must be *some* link between dreams and reality.

J: Of course, and it's the only link there *could* be: You.

DK: This dream world bit sounds totally nuts.

J: But physicists have already proven that anything solid viewed from the microscopic level is about 99.999% *space*—there's practically nothing there! Sub-atomic particles are flying around at warp speed and flashing on and off millions of times per second with no stability whatsoever. Researchers have noted that even the very *observation* of these things seems to alter their behavior. And yet it's within this weird and paradoxical world of mere energy patterns that you're placing all your hopes and aspirations. It's a poor strategy, because at the quantum level your identity essentially vaporizes. It's built on a "reality" that's both short-lived and razor-thin.

DK: If the world is really an illusion, why didn't you just *say* that two thousand years ago?

J: Wait 'til this interview hits the street and find out for yourself…

CHAPTER
TWENTY SEVEN

DK: I think I see now why people turn to religion: it's a whole lot easier than *thinking*. This dream thesis could give a guy nightmares.

J: You should've listened to your mother. She always said you were living in a dream world.

DK: Yeah, but *she* was only *kidding*.

J: Still don't believe me, eh?

DK: It just sounds preposterous, that's all. It's a ridiculous notion.

J: How can you be so sure?

DK: Well, because the world is... I mean everything is so solid and... hell, *I* don't know!

J: At least there's no attempt to conceal the ignorance.

DK: Okay, I give up. Tell me again why you say the world is nothing but trickery of the mind.

J: It's not only me. Thousands across history have discovered the same thing. Even Einstein said, "Reality is merely an illusion." But there's no taking this on faith. You have to see it for yourself when the timing's right.

DK: And what determines that?

J: Well, there aren't any rules... but generally it takes an unmitigated desire to see things as they are. To arrive there requires extreme humility and the admission that your intellect won't save you. You come to the same realization as Socrates: "All I know is that I know nothing." Then spirit can begin undoing the misperceptions you hold about yourself and the world.

DK: So which world do *you* live in?

J: The only one there *is*: the world of reality. It's open, free, and accessible to all.

DK: Did you have to die to attain it?

J: The real world is beyond life and death. Those are just deceptive ideas based on your identification with the body and your belief in duality. They don't apply to spirit. To experience reality, you don't have to *do* anything. Just know yourself as you really are.

DK: This "real world" you speak of sounds a little boring.

J: How would you know until you've experienced it? In my world you could never feel unfulfilled, deprived or deficient. Someday you'll marvel that you ever thought reality was disagreeable or threatening. It's truly a state of perfection.

DK: Then you have no desires?

J: It sounds uninteresting to ego, but the sheer joy of knowing your own completeness is fulfilling beyond description. It's a state without equal and makes desire meaningless. Nothing you've experienced even comes close.

DK: What abou—

J: Nope, not even sex.

DK: What prevents me from *entering* your world?

J: Your desire for a *different* one. You want to be special and separate.

DK: Is that a bad thing?

J: Only in the sense that it creates suffering and causes you to forget what you are.

DK: If your world is so glorious, why don't you just let me in?

J: But I'm not keeping you out! Take it, take every last inch!

DK: Enlighten me so that I can!

J: What an odd demand. It's like saying, "I want *you* to show me my *self!*" Could someone else possibly reveal who you are?

DK: Well, if anyone *can*, surely it's a guy like you.

J: You don't understand: reality isn't being *withheld* from you. You don't see it because you've chosen *not* to. It's useless to complain about suffering brought on by conditions of your own making. If you truly wanted freedom, you would never have chosen bondage.

DK: Impossible. I don't recollect doing any such thing.

J: I always smile inside when I hear someone deny responsibility for their appearance in the world of form by declaring that they don't remember making the choice. The mind's nature is to remove the past from consciousness and store it in the subconscious where it doesn't clutter the floor, so to speak. Even the most important times in your life—your wedding night, for example—can usually be remembered *at best* only in blurry snippets. So don't bother defending yourself by telling me that you can't remember what happened in antiquity, when you can barely recall what you had for breakfast.

DK: But I think we'd agree that choosing to incarnate is a far more significant event. And yet I have absolutely no memory of it.

J: You also don't remember the social firestorm you created by stealing your best friend's pocketknife when you were seven. But that doesn't mean you didn't do it.

DK: Wow, I hadn't thought about that in... heck, practically forever. Man, you don't miss a *thing*.

J: The universe is not deaf and blind, my friend. The gospel of Luke says that even the hairs on your head are numbered. Of course, in *your* case it's getting a lot easier to keep track.

DK: Easy to make balding jokes with a fully loaded mop!

J: *Heh heh.* Maybe you've just gotten too tall for your hair...

DK: Okay... so why in God's name would I create such a mess? I mean let's agree that I did indeed, sometime in a distant past, make a soul-level decision to experience the world of form. Why would I choose something so potentially painful?

J: For the same reason you might go mountain climbing or diving off a cliff. You know the activity is dangerous, but you're willing to chance it because you want the *experience*. It offers the possibility of pleasure, joy and exhilaration. Think how many times you've considered a course of action that you knew full well could bring you pain—but you did it anyhow. With one motive or another, you wanted to do things *your* way. Your decision to experience the realm of materiality is basically no different.

DK: Well, whether I *chose* this world or I didn't is merely academic. If my dream is causing me the problems you claim, then just wake me up.

J: But how can *I* change your desires? Whatever choice you made in the past is largely irrelevant if you're still making the same one today. Have an honest look inside and see how many attachments you have to the world—to a lasting and meaningful "reality" of the body.

DK: So I experience a world of individual isolation because I'm *choosing* it?

J: Most definitely. And you can't be *forced* to relinquish your fantasy or you'd accuse God of undermining your cherished "free will." The *bad* news is that your egoic dream of material world glory has you in a temporary headlock. The *good* news is that delusion is never ultimately victorious. Once you snap out of your dream state, you'll know that your will and God's have always been one. And *knowing* this unity within the material universe can make for a glorious adventure.

DK: I'm still having trouble with "oneness." I don't recall you teaching this concept to your disciples.

J: You have a short memory. You asked me at the start of the interview about my statement, "I and my Father are one."

DK: But you were talking about you and *God*, not about you and everyone else.

J: I'll swear, son… the juice is *flowin'* but the bulb ain't *glowin'*. God *is* everyone else! We're all *connected*, don't you see? Perhaps a quote from John 17 will help make the point: "The glory which thou hast given to me I have given to them, that they may be *one* even as *we are one*, I in them and thou in me, that they may become *perfectly one*."

DK: Hmmmn. Guess I never paid much attention to that passage.

J: Most people don't. They'd rather drone on about their sinfulness and how they gotta be "washed in the blood o' the Lamb" and all that trash. But the unity argument is both simple and compelling. If the Father and I are one, and if you and I are one, then it's logically apparent that you and the Father are one. If A equals B, and B equals C, then A *must* equal C.

DK: Divinity by rational deduction, huh?

J: It's elementary, pilgrim. But you have to verify it by going within. Consistent self-observation and awareness will bring the desired results.

DK: What compels anyone to move beyond his own status quo?

J: Regrettably, in most cases it takes a genuine, unexpected crisis. You have to be driven to complete surrender, to a place in life where the old paradigms no longer work. You come to see that you're not in control and that you never really were. It takes penetrating self-honesty and a willingness to acknowledge that fear and pain are present—however subtle, dull or repressed they may be.

DK: Surely pain doesn't cultivate joy.

J: No, but unfortunately very few will begin self-examination without it. Before anything can change, you've got to see the obvious *need* for change. It's like a junkie who denies his addiction while projecting the blame for his unhappiness onto those around him. Until his pain becomes unbearable and he admits that he's the cause of his own misery, not much can be done. Strange as it may seem, life's most enlightening experiences are often preceded by intense suffering, which is generally induced by some kind of pain, either physical or mental. Sometimes both.

DK: What about those who are successful and content? Why should *they* bother?

J: Because until they know who they are, they're just spinning their wheels. Don't equate material achievement with genuine joy. Only rarely are they found under the same roof.

DK: At last a trait I recognize! Even in the gospels, you didn't think much of worldly triumph.

J: Let me resolve this in a way that can't be misconstrued: The universe is pure abundance. It's not lacking anything, because it's a reflection of the all-sufficient *Source* of abundance. So deprivation isn't part of the plan, and there's nothing inherently holy or virtuous about poverty or struggle.

DK: Amen to *that*.

J: But "success"—and I use the word loosely—can be extremely bewitching. It lulls you to sleep. When things are humming along smoothly, no one's much interested in looking within. It's only after crisis or calamity arises that most folks start questioning. Until then, they'll tolerate surprisingly high levels of anxiety, spiritual emptiness and personal dysfunction. But tolerance isn't without limit. Eventually, though not necessarily within what you perceive as a lifetime, everyone senses that there *must* be a better way. They realize they can't be "saved" by anything they do or acquire. When that happens, their route is altered and their sails are set for new horizons.

DK: *A Course in Miracles* says, "Discomfort is aroused only to bring the need for correction into awareness."

J: Yes, but don't take that to mean that *God* is doing something to you—there's no punishment involved. The discomfort was there all along, but over time you become less willing to deny its presence. As pain surfaces, you realize the emptiness within and begin acknowledging the call of spirit. It's like a hatching chick pecking away at its shell: given enough time, it finally breaks out. In the same way, spirit eventually dissolves all your carefully constructed defenses. Reality, to your benefit, won't be ignored forever.

DK: So until we're psychologically ready, you just "stand at the door and knock."

J: True—but judging by the usual response, you'd think I was selling funeral plots. When *I* come knocking, most folks pretend they're not home and refuse to answer the door. I'm offering "Get out of Jail Free" cards, and the prisoners aren't interested.

DK: Brings to mind the dying words of H.G. Wells. "Go away," he said, "I'm alright."

J: A fitting analogy…

DK: I still think the average person is fairly content with life and doesn't feel any real *need* to question.

J: You'll need more than bailing wire and duct tape to keep *that* argument intact. Nearly every culture on the globe contributes to the world's illegal drug trade; it's a multi-billion dollar business. In your supposed world of contentment, artificial liberation maintains one helluva market share.

DK: Perhaps I spoke too soon.

J: And don't overlook the *legalized* drug cartels: the pharmaceutical firms. They're selling anti-depressants, sedatives, "mood enhancers" and anti-psychotics by the truckload.

DK: No doubt about it: misery loves a drug company.

J: The booze business is pretty brisk, too. The world has about *two hundred million* alcoholics. Unless folks are feeding a steady diet of liquor and joy pills to their pets, it sure sounds to me like *someone's* unhappy.

DK: Alright, you've got me pinned to the mat: we're obviously trying to escape *some*thing. But life can be difficult. Who could blame us for wanting a little help to cope?

J: No one's assigning guilt. In your present state of mind, the world *is* stressful. I'm just telling you that it isn't ultimately *real*. The only lasting solution to the world's insanity is to go beyond it. You can verify the truth of what I'm telling you by contacting reality directly.

DK: But again, how do we *find* it?

J: Reality is coursing through you at every moment. Just get out of your own way and stop living by the compulsive dictates of the monkey mind. Give at least as much awareness to the *self* as you do to the world around you. And don't be one who runs from silence. Make time each day to get quiet and to settle into the I AM presence. The Christ in you is very still and can't be heard above the noisy clamor of the world.

DK: In the old days, I would constantly have a TV or radio going, even if I wasn't paying attention to it. I've noticed that *lots* of people do that.

J: It's been said that a man's problems arise mostly from the fact that he can't sit comfortably alone with himself in a quiet room. There's a lot of truth in that.

DK: Why do we so resolutely avoid silence?

J: Subconsciously, you're afraid of yourself. You've concluded that reality is fearful, so you distract yourself to avoid looking within. Keeping busy ensures that little or no time is freed up for peaceful contemplation.

DK: Well, we do have responsibilities.

J: Of course. But that excuse can also become a convenient crutch for avoiding introspection. Hiding behind responsibilities can be an egoic diversion to keep you off-track. You've got to make time for silence and reflection the same way you'd make time for anything else. Life is, after all, a matter of priorities.

DK: I do pray a bit.

J: Yes, but even prayer is an outward-directed activity.

DK: Maybe it's a cultural thing. The frenetic Western lifestyle doesn't leave much room for peace and quiet. In the course of a given day, the average Westerner probably doesn't spend even one minute focusing calm attention on the self. In the East, though, it's pretty common to spend time daily in meditation, contemplation or devotion. A lot of Easterners even have masters to function as their spiritual mentors. Is it necessary to find a guru or other special instructor?

J: The student needn't seek out a teacher. The teacher will find the student if the time is right. Hence the old saying, "When the student is ready, the teacher appears." In any event, the student is never without the ultimate spiritual guide: his own *internal* teacher. Christians call it "the Holy Spirit." But whatever you name it, the full intelligence of creation is at your beck and call.

DK: Before I became so cynical, whenever I needed help I just prayed directly to you. Is that practical?

J: I'm never absent to anyone for any reason. I'm quoted saying, "Behold, I am with you always." Obviously I wasn't talking about myself as the man you call Jesus, but was instead referring to the *inner* counselor: Behold, I AM is with you always.

DK: But you do consider yourself a direct expression of God, true?

J: An *expression*, yes—along with you and everyone else. It's a big mistake to limit the concept of divinity to a single personality. God permeates you and everything you see.

DK: This notion of a divine, universally common spirit would give entirely new meaning to the word "Christ."

J: I would hope so. Because the historically isolated Christ of religion is meaningless…

CHAPTER TWENTY EIGHT

DK: I can tell you right off the bat that you're swimming against the tide with this unity theme. The proposition that everyone's inseparably connected with God will have plenty of folks offended.

J: That's mainly a Western thing. Some cultures wouldn't find the concept the least bit novel or threatening. In India, people commonly use the word *Namasté* when greeting or parting. It's a deep and complex term denoting humility and equality, but over the centuries it came to mean something like, "The divine in me acknowledges the divine in you." So some people see man's godly nature as a given.

DK: Well, in *this* culture we're not so benevolent. There's an awful lot of believers with spiritual chips on their shoulders.

J: Just write the interview and let the chips fall where they may.

DK: Then you don't want me traveling around and spreading the new message?

J: God help you if you try. Your one responsibility is to accept the Atonement for *yourself*. Atonement—or "at-one-ment"—is simply the process of restoring unity awareness. This is something you can learn only by *living as if it's true*. Realize that teaching and learning are two sides of the same coin. So *living* the Atonement is the best way to *teach* it, and *teaching* it is the only way to *learn* it.

DK: And how do we accept the Atonement for ourselves?

J: There's only one way: through forgiveness. But not through forgiveness as it's typically understood. To most people, forgiveness means first viewing someone as blameworthy and then magnanimously absolving them. It says in essence, "You're *guilty*, but because of my spiritual superiority, I'll forgive you." That kind of forgiveness is worthless and is clearly just another form of judgment. True forgiveness is based on the understanding that nothing in reality has changed and that, in spirit, no one is guilty.

DK: Then the axe-murdering rapist gets off scot free?

J: Of course not. The ancient karmic law requires that you reap what you sow—that is, you experience what you believe you *are*. But that applies strictly to the world of bodies and form. None of it affects your reality as spirit.

DK: Is that *fair*?

J: Fairness is relevant only in the realm of polarity. God created you perfect, as spirit. He would never allow you to destroy yourself, because that *would* be unfair. Think of it like this: you can jump up and down all you want, and you may well end up with sore feet. But it won't even slightly affect the laws of gravity.

DK: If form is ultimately unreal, then how does forgiveness fit in?

J: True forgiveness acknowledges that you and your brothers are one. It allows you the freedom to think and act as though you're intimately and inextricably joined—with each other, with me, and with God. Real forgiveness is the overlooking of what, *in reality*, has never occurred. And the one who benefits most by your forgiveness… is *you*.

DK: So how does God interpret destructive behavior?

J: The question is irrelevant, because God isn't experiencing your mind-body dream. But in terms you can understand, it's as though God merely observes your temporary delusional state and thinks to Himself, "My children are having a nightmare. I must awaken them." He knows that your greatest need—your *only* need, really—is to wake up from your dream of separation.

DK: In that case, how would forgiveness help?

J: It redirects the mind from the false perspective of separation back to the truth of oneness. Beyond the mind, ideas like sin and forgiveness are meaningless. But at the level of thought, forgiveness is the best tool at your disposal for speeding your awakening. It reminds you and your brother of your spiritual unity.

DK: What makes forgiveness so powerful?

J: When you truly forgive—when you look beyond your brother's mistakes—it liberates you both. It opens possibilities, both mental *and* physical, that previously didn't exist. There's a famous story in the gospels about me healing a paralytic on a stretcher. The first thing I'm quoted telling him is, "Your sins are forgiven." But no one seems to notice that the man never *asked* forgiveness and in fact showed no penitence of any kind. You might reflect on why I would pronounce someone forgiven without requiring confession or remorse.

DK: Apparently you consider the notion of man's sinful nature to be mistaken. But if sin is unreal, then what of guilt?

J: Guilt is hell itself. Locking someone in the handcuffs of guilt imprisons *everyone*. It reinforces the idea that you and your brother are separate or different and that one is superior. By holding on to guilt, you become like a jailer who's forced to remain in prison to watch over his prisoner. Both men lose their freedom.

DK: I can see how overlooking offenses might apply to the little stuff. But what about *extreme* situations?

J: Some of history's most impressive stories of enlightenment have come from those under terrible duress. Even tortured POWs and death camp survivors have told amazing stories of forgiveness and personal transformation in the midst of hell. But don't get sidetracked. By pointing to circumstances that don't involve you, ego keeps you mired in fear and dysfunction. It diverts your attention from the real issue—your own awakening. Remember the verse I quoted earlier from *A Course in Miracles*: "The Holy Spirit speaks to *you*. He does not speak to someone else."

DK: I still say the unity view is unrealistic. Considering the sad state of the world nowadays, it's just not a viable philosophy.

J: Even in severity, the Atonement is always relevant because it's always *true*. And it's the only reality that *is* true. *Your* temptation is the same one *I* faced on the cross: to believe that reality is only true *sometimes*. This basic error is reflected in the idea that love and forgiveness are appropriate only under "normal" conditions. I learned the hard way that intense suffering can easily cause doubt as to whether truth holds in every circumstance. But I never lost sight of my spiritual connection with those who persecuted me. And I never condemned them, even when confronting the greatest of all temptations to question the eternal nature of love: the seeming finality of death.

DK: So not even tragedy or annihilation can change our reality.

J: Who you are is untouchable. The *real* you can't be harmed or assaulted, so it never needs defending. By worldly standards, I had as much right as anyone to feel indignant and betrayed. But I chose forgiveness. Not because I was *holier* than anyone else—but precisely because I *wasn't*. My only accomplishment on the cross was this: I never forgot that my accusers were no different from me and that their short-term ignorance could never alter their reality in God. Therefore, "Father forgive them." Because the crazy buggers don't know what the hell they're *doing*.

DK: I doubt that *I* would've been so gracious. What gave you the strength?

J: It's the nature of love to disregard everything unlike itself and look past it to the reality of Atonement. In my case, you should move past the killing of a body, which accomplished nothing, and focus directly on the resurrection of the spirit, which accomplishes everything.

DK: You continue referring to the Crucifixion as senseless. If that's how you saw it, then why would a powerful guy like you participate in such madness?

J: The church's answer, of course, is that I was punished for your sins. But that would've been both cruel and pointless. I endured the Crucifixion to prove that love is our eternal nature and that fear and death are meaningless.

DK: But even if you weren't *punished* for our sins, you still wound up *dying* for them.

J: Not exactly. "Sin," which is derived from an old archery term meaning "to miss the mark," is a thought or action based on ignorance. By that definition, I didn't die *for* your sins; I died *because* of them. You have to stop viewing my death as a lesson in guilt and punishment. That kind of thinking breeds fear and creates images of an angry God who requires pacification through violence and brutality. Instead, see the Crucifixion as an extreme lesson in the strength of Atonement—a powerful teaching example that *love is the only reality* and, therefore, that nothing real can be threatened. Again, your own mission is really no different from mine. You're simply being asked to demonstrate Atonement under far less trying circumstances.

DK: Not to be callous, but it was easy for *you* to be optimistic and forgiving. You had the luxury of knowing beforehand about the Resurrection. Most of us don't have that kind of spiritual advantage.

J: Hold on there, pilgrim. I had no special access to knowledge. Reality is fully available to everyone at any moment, and your own resurrection is as inevitable as mine was. God creates *equally*, remember?

DK: C'mon, you and I both know that I won't be walking out of my grave.

J: Resurrection isn't about bodies rising from the dead. It's about your inviolable nature as spirit and the miraculous ability of love to transcend the perceived limitations of time and space.

DK: I'm confused. What exactly is the connection between the Crucifixion and the Atonement?

J: There *is* no connection. Even in Christian theology, the Crucifixion didn't establish the Atonement: the *Resurrection* did. As it's typically perceived, the Crucifixion is a meaningless solution to a non-existent problem.

DK: But we're told that your death brought us life.

J: How could death, which doesn't exist, possibly establish life, which exists eternally?

DK: I've heard it put this way: As the symbolic equivalent of an ancient animal sacrifice ritual for absolution of sins, *your death* opened the door for *our redemption.*

J: That idea sprang from my ancestors killing oxen, lambs and other animals to recompense for their own transgressions. They sometimes burned the animals on altars and presented them as "offerings to the Lord." Ancient peoples long believed that whenever God was angry, they could soothe his indignant feelings by spilling innocent blood. Unfortunately it led to some pretty cruel religions.

DK: I think we're at a major sticking point. Not only does the church *endorse* the concept of sacrifice, but it actually *insists* upon it. It claims that you were the human "lamb without blemish," crucified for the sins of the world.

J: Well, it's an awfully convenient theology that has someone else paying the price for *your* wrongdoing. Do you honestly find it reasonable that God's best plan of action in dealing with human imperfection was to have me murdered?

DK: I can't defend the *intelligence* of it. But like you said, those were the rules. Sacrifice was an important tenet in early Jewish culture.

J: But why should God require *my* suffering to forgive *your* mistakes? It's bush league theology for dimwits.

DK: Call me flip, but I'd say you're drastically reducing the wages of sin.

J: Well, Flip, I can tell you that God is no cosmic accountant: He's not keeping a logbook of your behavior. God knows you only as the perfect child He created. Would a loving mother focus on her child's mistakes and continually threaten the kid with punishment or condemnation because of them? It makes no sense that a loving God would hold your wrong-minded deeds against you, and it makes even less sense that he would have held them against *me*. Again, death can never establish life, and love doesn't kill to save.

DK: Too bad this blood sacrifice thing ever got started. It seems that nearly every culture soothes its guilty conscience by killing—humanity *loves* a good scapegoat. Totally sucks if you're a blameless bystander, though. In a system like that, young virgins and spotless lambs had better keep a very low profile.

J: It's a sure bet that when sinners start bargaining with heaven, the innocent will pay like hell. And if you think mobs are dangerous when they're feeling guilty, try showing up when they're expecting a savior…

CHAPTER TWENTY NINE

DK: So once the public fettered you with that "Messiah" label, it became a serious liability.

J: It usually does.

DK: Well, I suppose every generation looks to heaven for deliverance. Even now, a lot of Christians are talking about "the last days," the period just before your alleged Second Coming. With all the high-intensity events unfolding, some people claim we're actually witnessing the "end times." Are you in fact preparing for a big earthly return?

J: A literal interpretation of the Second Coming is pretty lame right out of the gate. Is it the least bit rational that I would show up on earth to get myself killed so that I could return in glory a couple thousand years later?

DK: A bit overly dramatic, perhaps.

J: Read the New Testament carefully and you'll find plenty of passages referring to my impending reappearance. Just about everyone was expecting my return to occur *quickly*. Matthew's gospel even has me telling a group of my followers, "There are some standing here who will not taste death before they see the Son of man coming in his kingdom." I believe you badgered me about it in your letter.

DK: Gosh, my memory is so fuzzy…

J: Even the Apostle Paul makes several exhortations to his church family to stay alert and live soberly because of my fast-approaching arrival. His first letter to the Thessalonians even gives details. Open to chapter four and start reading at verse sixteen.

DK: "For the Lord himself will descend from heaven with a cry of command, with the archangel's call, and with the sound of the trumpet of God. And the dead in Christ will rise first; then we who are alive, who are left, shall be caught up together with them in the clouds to meet the Lord in the air…"

J: So here's the Almighty blowing the horn upon my arrival, and Christians, in full defiance of gravity, floating off to heaven on a wing and a prayer. Now, where Paul obtained this privileged information is never revealed. But it's clear that he and the other Apostles were fully expecting my immediate, glorious and triumphant return, complete with rapturous ascensions and a heavenly brass band.

DK: It seems that Christians have been proclaiming your imminent homecoming for nearly two thousand years.

J: Yes, and you'd think sheer honesty would cause folks to wonder if they've seriously misinterpreted the whole affair. Instead, they're distributing simple-minded literature depicting absurd judgment scenarios of my great Second Coming. Their purpose, evidently, is to scare the hell out of earth's poor "unsaved" wretches by showing them what a loving God they've been depriving themselves of. Never mind that He's planning to boil their butts in a burning lake if they don't come around to admitting what a terrific fellow He is. It might be amusing if it weren't so pathetic.

DK: Crazy stuff alright.

J: At its core, this kind of thinking reflects the belief that the material universe is ultimate reality. It assumes that God created you as a body and that He'll revive and redeem you *as a body*.

DK: That's how your disciples seemed to see it. They must've gotten the idea *somewhere*.

J: Well, they didn't get it from me. I never denigrated the body, but neither did I glorify it, as made clear in the compiled sayings of the Sermon on the Mount. I taught that life is much more than the body and that the kingdom can't be found in the physical world.

DK: You once said that your kingdom is not *of* this world.

J: No, but neither is yours. I told my disciples the same thing. But like most people, they just couldn't envision a reality in which they weren't in some *form* they'd recognize. In contrast, *A Course in Miracles* says that a child of God "is not a traveler through outer worlds" and that "no world outside himself holds his inheritance."

DK: Are you saying that our world holds no hope of redemption?

J: I'm saying it's a worthless salvation that depends on the future. God isn't mysteriously delaying your happiness for delivery at some distant time and place. Liberation is available only in the eternal *now*. The *Course* puts it this way: "Atonement might be equated with total escape from the past and total lack of interest in the future. Heaven is *here*. There *is* nowhere else. Heaven is *now*. There *is* no other time." It further explains, "God has no secrets. He does not lead you through a world of misery, waiting to tell you, at the journey's end, why He did this to you."

DK: The implication is that we're already saved.

J: You were never endangered. You were created eternally *in* Love, *by* Love, *as* Love. Reality has never changed. You're purely divine—and you're as divine *right now* as you ever will be.

DK: But there must be *some* compensation for our worldly sufferings. When do we get the big payoff?

J: Your thinking is severely flawed. You assume that God threw you into a world of suffering and that He *owes* you something because of it. But the world is a choice that *you* made, and most of your suffering is just mental anguish born of ignorance and resistance. It's ego rebelling against what *is* by comparing it to what it believes *should* be. In truth, you're perfectly okay at every moment. There's nothing to fear, and you remain exactly as God created you. The payoff you're expecting is based on the mistaken premise that your identity lies in the body. It doesn't.

DK: So there's no real need for you to return in the flesh.

J: None whatsoever.

DK: Then why the big hullabaloo by the church about your predicted earthly dominion?

J: As you observed earlier, people want security in a world they find threatening. They long for a savior to descend from the stars and set things right.

DK: What's wrong with *that*? I think we'd *all* like to believe there's an omnipotent force maintaining order in the universe and keeping things tidy.

J: Perhaps you're confusing God with Martha Stewart.

DK: *Heh heh.* Well, you'll have to forgive me. If her unauthorized biographers can be trusted, she occasionally made the same mistake herself…

CHAPTER THIRTY

J: You look bewildered. What's up?

DK: I was just wondering: If our spiritual awakening is inevitable, then why do so few of us attain it?

J: Because that's not what you're *seeking*. As unlikely as it sounds, you have a subtle fear of reality. You don't really *want* heaven's answer to your problems; you just want your dreams altered and your toys fixed. Secretly, you doubt whether truth offers any more than illusions do. It's difficult surrendering to the unknown, so you hold on to the familiar—fearful because of it, but fearful too of letting it go. I know it sounds crazy, but most people are deathly afraid of real healing.

DK: How do you mean?

J: Well, let's agree that awareness of unity with God is ultimately the only true healing. If someone prays for that but inwardly fears what he's asking, then the prayer isn't really for healing. It's simply a request, usually born of suffering or a sense of incompletion, that his illusions be made more to his liking. Spirit can never honor such a prayer, because the petitioner is actually requesting something hurtful. That is, he's asking for the *same problem* in a *different form*. His fundamental thinking assumes the reality of the dream, thereby keeping the dream firmly in place. Spirit, ever gentle and unwilling to coerce, merely smiles… and waits.

DK: So even though we give lip service to our desire for truth, at some level we're afraid of it.

J: Believe it or not, that's your biggest dilemma. Throughout time, the only choice you're asked to make is the choice between reality and illusions. Only one is true, of course, and it's true now and forever. But the mind is powerful beyond your present ability to grasp, and any thought you hold, even if based on illusion, will be reflected at some level in what appears to be your "outer" world. There *is* no outer world, though, because there's nothing outside *you*, even if your perception says otherwise. Ultimately, you *will* choose to release your illusions—not because anyone is forcing you, but because illusions eventually result in grief. At some point you'll figure this out, and you'll no longer choose pain and suffering. Enlightenment is unavoidable because nothing can prevent you from being "in heaven," where God would have you be.

DK: Doesn't that contradict free will?

J: Where truth and illusions conflict, how can illusions prevail? Can that which has no existence possibly stem the tide of reality? Your state of perfection is God's will *and* yours, because his will and yours are *one*.

DK: Still, it seems like some people are hopeless.

J: It may appear that way for awhile—but the outcome is as certain as God. Although lots of believers seem to think it's possible, ask yourself if it's likely that God would have a salvation plan that could fail.

DK: I could make the argument that God merely leaves it up to us.

J: You think He'd do that, knowing how many people have brains of Spam?

DK: Well, if we aren't bodies, as you insist, and if our spirit is forever one with God, then why do we need salvation at all? What exactly needs saving?

J: The same thing that believes it was *condemned*: the mind. The problem of separation is only in your mind, so God placed the solution there as well. That's only logical, since God would never put the answer where you couldn't find it. But like I've said, you've got to sincerely *want* the answer. Otherwise, you'll believe it's being forced upon you against your will and you'll refuse to see it.

DK: Alright, so we're stuck in Plato's Cave. How do we get out?

J: There's only one escape from darkness: moving toward the light. You have to abandon your treasured convictions about reality and walk in faith toward the call of the unknown, erring on the side of love, forgiveness and compassion.

DK: Once again you're advising to leap trustingly into the Void. I think that's asking too much.

J: Realize that the power and brilliance that give rise to the universe are also operating through *you*. Knowing the universe is trustworthy makes it easier to trust *yourself*, and faith swells like a flooding river as you learn that you and this Universal Power are intimately connected. So stop defending against the dangers you perceive, and throw yourself onto the mercy of the court. Just surrender, vulnerable and trusting, to the Nameless Mystery that keeps the stars and planets in their paths.

DK: One writer said we've got to be willing to jump naked into eternity.

J: That's it exactly. But don't make your awakening another problem. Just relax into it. Grow quiet. Become aware of the I AM presence as often as you can think to do it. And remember to breathe slowly and deeply and take lots of big sighs. Ask calmly and earnestly to be shown, knowing beyond doubt that answers will come in meaningful ways you can understand. No two trails are the same, but each leads to the same destination: the joy of the eternally inviolable *self*. Again, you'll know you've arrived when you've become fearless. This is what the author of 1 John meant when he said that perfect love *casts out* fear. He knew that anyone in Christ consciousness would realize that God, as love, is all-encompassing and is therefore without opposites, which is obvious.

DK: So where does this new understanding of salvation leave us? Millions still believe we need *you* to save us from hell.

J: Well, in a sense they're right. Hell, after all, is what ego has made of your present reality. Whenever you aren't wholly peaceful and joyous, then you are indeed living in hell—and from that you *do* need deliverance. The indwelling Christ is still "the way, the truth and the life." Now, if some choose to focus on a personality, whether it's me or someone else, then it may take a little longer to bring about the required healing. But either way, enlightenment is guaranteed. Reality can't be restrained.

DK: Are there barriers that even God can't overcome?

J: *A Course in Miracles* states in its very first lines, "There is no order of difficulty in miracles. One is not 'harder' or 'bigger' than another. They are all the same." So the specifics of your illusions are of no concern to spirit. It overcomes each of them with equal ease.

DK: I still contend that a lot of Christians won't take kindly to the ideas that they aren't being judged, that they're one with God, that you weren't killed because they were bad, and so forth.

J: It's the height of irony that people turn angry upon learning they're free. And yet this freedom is precisely the "good news" referred to in my teachings. Regardless how it's been recorded or interpreted, my basic message was about spiritual liberation—about your unbroken connection with your all-loving Source. It's surprising enough that you *resist* the idea. But the really startling part is *why* you resist, and it's quite astonishing when you think about it: You believe a God of unconditional love is *too good to be true*.

DK: It's a point I can't deny. People seem quite comfortable with a God who's willing to torture a soul forever. They say that if God deems it necessary, then it must be justified. In many circles, damnation is very respected theology.

J: *Theology? Bah!!* There's the logical and the *theo*logical—the two are barely acquainted. Theology is the attempt to ascertain the nature of the sun through the assiduous study of shadows.

DK: But surely in order to know a thing, we have to direct our intelligence there.

J: That's true for things on the *material* plane. But God will never be known through the intellect. In that regard, spiritual intuition is worth far more than mental gymnastics. One version of the *Tao Te Ching* proclaims, "The tao that can be told is not the eternal Tao. The name that can be named is not the eternal Name… The more you talk of it, the less you understand… It is hidden but always present… Look, and it can't be seen; listen, and it can't be heard; reach, and it can't be grasped… You cannot *know* it, but you can *be* it."

DK: A fancy collection of contradictions!

J: Yes, like many of my own sayings. Wise words are often paradoxical.

DK: Evidently you don't support the Christian view that God's plan for salvation is a kind of celestial "tough love."

J: It's a strange proposition from the start. Sadly, most folks just can't embrace a reality of infinite goodness. Speak of their oneness with a God who's nothing but love and they'll yank you from your bed at midnight and string you up in the nearest serviceable tree. But give 'em a religion crammed with guilt, judgment and fear, and they flock to it like geese to a country pond.

DK: I'm definitely in no position to point fingers. At one church I attended, we'd sit glued to our seats, never raising a question while the preacher rattled off thirty minutes of hellfire and dread. Looking back, I feel pretty foolish. We lapped up the abuse like a bunch of hot, thirsty dogs at a cool-running stream. And to think I was giving the place a tenth of my monthly wage!

J: So you actually *paid* for the privilege of suffering the assault.

DK: I'm afraid so. A fool and my money are soon partners. Pretty crazy, no?

J: An extraordinary occurrence, to say the least. And again, it all starts with the separated mind—the part of the mind we call "ego." It harbors feelings of deep-seated guilt because it honestly believes that it somehow betrayed and angered God. And since ego believes that God has an ego of his own, it concludes that God must think exactly the same way that *it* thinks. Therefore God is perceived as defensive, easily threatened, and vindictive. This phenomenon of projection is symbolized in the story of the prodigal son. The son feels he betrayed the father and assumes that the father is angry and probably vengeful. But the father himself never held the slightest grudge about the son's mistakes.

DK: So ego is all about separation and guilt.

J: Yeah, they're ego's lifeblood. Stories of God's rejection of an angelic rebel, such as Satan, reflect the same theme. Ditto with ancient accounts of God ousting mankind from paradise. They're all based on an angry God who's separate from his guilty creation—in other words, separate from *Himself*.

DK: It appears that ego sees itself in direct competition with God.

J: Absolutely. It views God as the ultimate Enemy and believes that He wants retribution, just as an offended earthly parent might. Ego believes the guiltless are guilty and that the very suggestion of human innocence is actually blasphemous to God. In fact, much of ego's unwarranted predominance is based on the concept of guilt made real. But this persistent feeling of guilt is intolerable—so ego projects the guilt *outward*. Its fundamental premise is this: guilt is real, and *somebody somewhere* has damned well got to *pay*.

DK: And here, according to the church, is where you stepped in.

J: Yes—but not right away, of course. Somewhere in early human history, someone hit on the concept of atonement. They figured that God's anger might be appeased if a little blood were spilled. First to be offered up were animals. Next it was people. Eventually, tribal priests settled on the ultimate "sacrificial lamb": God Himself.

DK: You should've included a few paragraphs on this in one of your sermons.

J: Oh, I talked about it plenty—but not much found its way into the New Testament. Most people aren't interested in hearing about their natural goodness or their divine innocence. They shun a God who doesn't judge them or keep records on their behavior—they just can't sign on. And if you *really* wanna boil their blood, try telling 'em they're actually *one* with God. Unity schmunity. With a message like *that*, you're lucky to live past lunch.

DK: So we reject a God of love for one whose love is largely provisional.

J: Well, most folks figure that any God worth fearing is probably as unyielding and judgmental as *they* are. Now you understand why so much religious writing is filled with stories of a petty, hypocritical God of anger, punishment and revenge. It just mirrors the character of the people who wrote it.

DK: I know one thing: if the Bible God were human, we'd lock Him up and throw away the key. He'd be considered a threat to society.

J: That or a promising candidate for high political office…

Chapter Thirty One

DK: Ever do any rock climbing?

J: Rock cli— Wait a minute, did I miss something?

DK: Sorry, just a little joke. The mood was getting kinda somber.

J: Hmmm, maybe I'd better lighten things up. Here's a quick one…

Jewish woman and her young son are walking along the shore, enjoying the sunshine and happy as clams. Suddenly and without warning, a strong wave crashes the beach and sweeps the kid out to sea. Instantly the poor woman's frantic, of course, so she turns toward heaven and wails: "Oh God, how could you take my only child, my precious baby boy, the light of my life!?? Please, God… bring him back and I'll do anything you want. I'll visit the temple three times a week. I'll give twel—no, make that *fifteen percent*. I'll even stop nagging my husband!" You know, the whole nine yards of desperate contrition.

DK: Uh-huh…

J: Few seconds later, another huge wave washes in and dumps the boy right back at her feet. He's rattled and coughing up water but completely unharmed. *Now* the mother's crazy with ecstasy, right? She's hugging and kissing her shivering son and crying tears of joy. Suddenly she sees the kid's wrist and turns dead serious. She looks back to heaven and shouts, "He had a watch!"

DK: You really should consider a run at the comedy circuit. You'd be the biggest return engagement in history.

J: Can't do it. Got an exclusive wretch-saving gig on the astral plane.

DK: By the way: we haven't discussed it yet, but today is Easter.

J: A big deal for some. For the awakened, a total non-event. *Now is now*, you know?

DK: But all around the world, Christians are celebrating your Resurrection.

J: Yep, and most of 'em probably aren't giving even a passing thought to their own. If I were preaching a worldwide sermon by satellite right now, I'd probably start off by saying that focusing on *me* has really thrown things off-kilter. I'd say that I'm here to shake people up, to wake them from their egoic sleepwalk—to *resurrect them* from their deadness of spirit. I'd ask everyone to step back from the deception of their mental hypnosis and question their sacred ideas about reality. I'd mention that if you're practicing religion just to save your butt from burning or to chalk up points with God, then you're wasting your time and you might as well take up yodeling. I'd point out that religion should be a bridge and not a wedge. It should inspire peace and harmony, not judgment and discord.

DK: What, no "love thy neighbor" speech?

J: The world's had enough of that milk-and-cookies stuff. My new message would be that if you're gonna love your neighbor, then stop blabbering, theorizing or pontificating about it and just *do* it. I'd also note that loving your neighbor *doesn't* include incinerating him with nukes and napalm, gassing him in death camps, or blasting him to bloody shreds with cruise missiles, grenade launchers and backpack bombs. I'd remind everyone that rejecting or attacking others is the spiritual equivalent of suicide. Doing it in the name of religion is the *ultimate* insanity and shows a level of stupidity usually reserved for certified morons and bureaucrats. I'd mention that fanaticism of *any* kind is repulsive, and that it leaves God— whatever name you give Him—entirely unimpressed.

DK: Keep going. You'll find that releasing can do wonders for the soul…

J: Well, I'd tell believers everywhere that if they're gonna continue claiming the name of God, then they oughta quit all their sniping and bickering and start acting a little more *God*-like. I'd warn all religious devotees that forsaking brotherly accord for the divisive principles of ancient writings will continue to bring disaster upon *everyone*. I'd sledge-hammer their perverted beliefs and ask 'em to reflect on how they expect any peace in their imagined heaven when so much of what they created on earth was hell. And finally, I'd challenge nearly all religions to clean up their act. If they can't do a better job of leading people to peace and enlightenment, then they should blow out the candles, board up the stained-glass windows and go home. Forever and ever, Amen.

DK: Wow. Don't expect a diatribe like that to get any play during family hour. You just took religion by the horns and gutted it.

J: Several times today, you've jabbed me about the words, "I come not to bring peace, but a sword." What I meant was that I'm not here to *confirm* your illusions; I'm here to *obliterate* them. You either side with the Christ spirit, or you side with fear. And in that sense, you are indeed either with me or against me. That's not a threat, just a statement of fact. Some of my students didn't wanna hear that, and most folks nowadays will be no different.

DK: Your message of man's inviolable union with God is certainly reasonable enough.

J: Well, you'd be surprised how much hostility it breeds. For some reason, people sharply resist a gospel that proclaims their divinity—they don't see it as "good news" at all. They'll fight to the death defending their story that everyone is a deplorable sinner, fully deserving of God's condemnation. And apparently He's just salivating at the chance to *give* it to 'em, good and hard, on his dreaded day of doom.

DK: Let's pursue this Last Judgment thing. It sounds like scary stuff.

J: And it *would* be—if it were true. For thousands of years, religion has cynically used this sleazy fear stratagem as a tool to keep the sheep moving quietly through the shearing yard. But the Last Judgment will be made not by God, but by *you*. It'll happen when your consciousness expands beyond all your time-bound, fear-based interpretations of reality. Then you'll no longer have need to judge, because you'll fully *know*. So God isn't waiting around for the opportunity to make his long-predicted "Last Judgment," because He never even made the *first* one. Why would He judge his own creation?

DK: Well, we're told that—for the righteous, at least—judgment leads eventually to heaven.

J: Judgment leads directly to *hell*, and *releasing* it is the only way to any "heaven." When you finally understand that only the truth is true, and that nothing else ever *was* true, then you'll have made your "last judgment." Judgment has created the hellish world you see, because it's a world *of* judgment, based mostly on guilt and its logical implication: punishment. You can escape the whole nasty mess by relying solely on the judgment of the Holy Spirit, whose one unwavering judgment is this: All of God's creations are forever holy and innocent, just as they were created.

DK: Is there no such thing as right and wrong?

J: You could say that whatever creates suffering is wrong, and whatever alleviates it is right. But mitigating suffering for one at the expense of another accomplishes nothing. The relief must be universal.

DK: A lot of Christians associate the Last Judgment with the ultimate fate of the soul. The grand finale, of course, occurs at the end of time, when you and your Father open the Book of Life and root out the faithless from the true. Scripture says that authentic believers will then receive everlasting life, while everyone else is condemned to eternal hell.

J: The Bible's Last Judgment scenario is the ultimate example of ego's need to be right by making others wrong. Ego *delights* in the idea that its enemies will be eternally tormented. As you detailed in your letter, the Book of Revelation specifies that only 144,000 souls will be saved. So the odds of strolling the golden streets don't appear too encouraging. In fact, the church should probably change the words to that famous old hymn: "When the roll is called up yonder, I'll be damned."

DK: Hey, accountability is what Christianity is all about.

J: The basic idea is that God must be appeased before He can forgive. It originated with fearful people whose deity was somewhere outside them, judging them from afar. It's a picture of God sitting on a throne, separating his children into groups of bluebirds and crows. It's mind-numbing, eye-gouging literalism, and it practically requires a shoe-size I.Q. to overlook the absurd theology it begets.

DK: But an afterlife of reward and punishment is a concept that's been around an awfully long time—and well before Christianity.

J: The perception of God as a separate being with egoic attributes is the starting point of nearly *all* religions. In fact, even *using* the word "God" creates the instantly misleading idea that the cosmic Superforce is a discreet entity. But a simple whiff of logic could dispel the entire notion of God as a localized personality: a limitless universe cannot have been created by a limited and definable point *within* it.

DK: So claiming that God is omnipresent but also locatable in time and space—

J: —would be like saying that a single drop of water is simultaneously the entire ocean and, in addition, that the droplet was responsible for *creating* the ocean. How reasonable is *that*?

DK: Alright, but if God isn't a separate personality and there's no day of judgment penciled on his cosmic calendar, then what's all that end-of-time stuff referred to in the scriptures?

J: The end of time is the end of the illusion of past and future—or rather, the end of your *belief* in them. Time is a dualistic concept that exists strictly from a *relative* perspective: it applies only to the world of *things*. The mind, through memory or anticipation, mistakenly imposes an illusory linearity onto eternity. But anything that ever happened, or that ever *will* happen, always happens in the continuous *now*. Every moment stands clear, bright, and free of all conceptual constraints and artificial attachments to past or future.

DK: Now that you bring it up, it's pretty obvious that *this instant* is all there is—or ever could be.

J: Of course. What you think of as "time" is really just a never-ending flow of *is-ness*. So learn to make is-ness your business. Your point of power is always in the present, and all power in heaven and earth *is* given you. But only in the *now*.

DK: Then it makes no sense to say that God will save us in the future, since past and future don't even exist.

J: Past and future mean nothing to reality, which exists only in the present. When *you* finally learn to do the same, then you *really will* have reached "the end of time." So release the past, disregard the future, and enter into the one thing you know is real: the present moment.

DK: I can see how it makes sense to ignore an unknown future. But if we abandon our history, how would we define ourselves?

J: You mistakenly believe that the mind determines your identity. It doesn't. You are what you are, and the mind is uninvolved. Since you don't really understand anything you perceive, using past learning to define yourself and your world prevents you from recognizing what's really there.

DK: A little too academic. You got an exercise or something?

J: Observe your surroundings, from the most familiar to the least, and try to see them with "new eyes"—free of judgment, preconceived opinions and past associations. Look upon even people you know well as if you're meeting them for the first time. Ask yourself, "Who *is* this? Who are they *really*?" Your discoveries may surprise you. Learn anew what things are and what they mean. Whenever distress or upset arises, ask to see the situation differently. And keep one thought in mind: "Whatever crosses the screen of consciousness, *I am only the witness.*" Sooner or later, a new sense of reality will begin to emerge.

DK: Are you claiming that the universe will change just because I shift my thinking?

J: I'm claiming a lot more than that. I'm saying that your thought is powerfully creative and that the world you look upon is its *direct result*. All is transformed when consciousness becomes unified.

DK: I hear the words, but I've got my doubts.

J: That's good. Questioning what you're told is the beginning of freedom. Make it your habit to doubt *everything* until you know the truth of it for yourself. The beauty of reality is that you don't have to take anyone's word for it. I assured my disciples that they would *know* the truth and that it would set them free. So you don't *do* anything with truth. Liberation comes merely from *knowing* it.

DK: Sorry, but I remain a certified skeptic.

J: Great. Put every philosophical assertion to the test. Hang on to your disbelief and place your attention on the essential questions: "Who am I?" "Where did I come from?" "Who was I before I was born?" "Who will I be after I die?" "How did I come to be a frail little body in a chaotic world of woe?" "Did the *world* create *me*—or did *I* somehow create an *illusory world*?" Ponder these things. You've spent years focusing on externals; now spend some time turning inward. You may be shocked to find that your most treasured assumptions are without substance. Go back and start with the basics. Put some "fun" into fundamentalism.

DK: Let me verify that I'm not going crazy. You're sitting there telling me with a straight face that the world I'm experiencing is just a passing figment of my imagination?

J: Basically, yes.

DK: Okay. So *when*, exactly, did I first imagine it?

J: Now, of course.

DK: No, no—what I meant was, when did I first make the projection of a world outside my mind?

J: I'm telling you: *right now.*

DK: *Now?*

J: Of course. What other moment exists?

DK: But I remember experiencing the same thing yesterday.

J: You're remembering it *now.*

DK: Alright, never mind semantics. When will it all end?

J: Obviously it could only end *right now.* But of course, that's a *personal* choice.

DK: Let's take a different tack. Maybe a better question would be, why did I invent a world outside myself in the first place?

J: Actually, the better question would be, why do you continue doing so *now*?

DK: This is crazy! How do I know you aren't leading me on a wild goose chase?

J: Are you serious? You've spent so much time chasing wild geese, you're practically covered in bird poop. Trust me: this teaching is the only goose worth chasing—so you'd better give it a gander. Besides, what've you got to lose?

DK: I could waste a lot of precious time.

J: Believe me, sport, when you reach middle age and still have no idea what you are, you've wasted a helluva lot of time already.

DK: But self-examination is painful.

J: And living in ignorance *isn't*?

DK: At least I'm comfortable.

J: So is a pig being fattened for slaughter.

DK: Man, I just can't *win* with you!

J: On the contrary, my friend. With me, you can't possibly *lose...*

CHAPTER
THIRTY TWO

DK: It's good to hear that your loyalty is unconditional. For most of my life, I was taught that your patience runs out with the Rapture.

J: Most people figure they couldn't possibly deserve my consistent effort and tireless resolve, so they project onto me their own low estimation of themselves. But I'm not limited by your opinions of what's possible or deceived by your false perceptions of what's happened.

DK: But you have to admit that, in most people, the Christ spirit is pretty faint.

J: The Nativity symbolizes that the Christ usually emerges in relative obscurity and where it's least expected—amongst doubt, confusion and feelings of unworthiness. So it doesn't require perfection before manifesting. It just needs a little "virgin" territory: a sincere heart and an open mind. The world seldom recognizes the holy "child" when it first appears, and it typically spends its early days in a pretty modest vessel. This concept is represented in the Nativity story as a manger, commonly thought to be another word for stable. But mangers were just animal feeding boxes, which were frequently used back then as makeshift cradles. I wasn't born in a barn or a cave, though, and the word "stable" never appears in the gospel accounts of my birth. In fact, Matthew 2:11 says, "...and going into the house they saw the child with Mary his mother..." Did you get that? I was born in a *house*.

DK: I should've known you'd go and de-stable-ize the Nativity.

J: But the symbolism of the stable is a good one all the same. In most cases, before the Christ is "born" into someone's life, they've got to be overwhelmed by the smell of manure. For most folks, Christ enters the world surrounded by metaphorical piles of dung.

DK: So much for the beauty of the lilies and your birth across the sea.

J: It's true that the Christ's beginnings are frequently quite humble. But the young "child" receives the nurturing it needs at just the right moments and, as the years pass, it grows "in wisdom and stature." Eventually it becomes "savior" to the world by showing that real meaning lies *beyond* the world.

DK: You reportedly told your disciples, "Fear not, for I have overcome the world."

J: Another botched rendering of my teachings. What I originally said was, "Fear not, for I AM overcomes the world." *Present* tense. The I AM overcomes the world, because the I AM *created* it. So don't worry if your inner spark seems dim. Even the smallest ray of sunshine is backed by the full power of the sun. The light is always fully present. Helping you *see* it is what *I* get paid for.

DK: Then what's *our* job?

J: Just make the choice for peaceful awareness. Free yourself from ego and see if there's anything left to save.

DK: That's it?

J: Don't kid yourself—it's no easy task. I told my disciples, "If any man would come after me, let him deny himself...For whoever would save his life will lose it, and whoever loses his life for my sake will find it." That means detaching emotionally from almost everything you hold dear.

DK: You're right, it's no idle request. Our cultural programming is powerful.

J: Releasing the false self requires every ounce of will and commitment you've got. Quite frankly, not many are up to it. If you manage it, though, you'll find that the rewards far exceed your grandest expectations. And the star that leads you there is I AM.

DK: Seeking enlightenment is all well and good. But aren't we supposed to help alleviate suffering? What about the story of the Good Samaritan?

J: By all means, eliminate suffering where you can. But don't forget that your first goal is to put *yourself* beyond the need for help. When a student tells the master that he wants to help the world, the master will often respond, "First come to know yourself. Then return and tell me what problems you see." The master knows that the student is dreaming—that he's seriously misperceiving reality. He understands that the student will provide infinitely more assistance from the enlightened state than he ever could from the dream state, where he's usually part of the problem.

DK: Then the Good Samaritan was just wasting his time.

J: Not at all. But you're missing a vital aspect of the story. The Samaritan didn't go *looking* for someone to help. He simply rendered service to a brother in need when he happened across his path. It was purely a matter of fate. And here's something else: the Samaritan's help consisted entirely of addressing his brother's *worldly* needs. There's no mention of any attempt to save his soul, instill new beliefs, or change his mind about *any*thing.

DK: Evangelicals won't like hearing *that*.

J: No, probably not. The evangelist is usually focused on the presumed insufficiencies of *others*. Instead of addressing *his own* ignorance, he goes slashing through some remote jungle to bring "salvation" to an isolated tribe that's done just fine without him for the last seven hundred years, thank you very much. The missionary appears from the forest and tells the tribal leader, "I'm here to share my religion." But the poor chief doesn't know the facts and can't possibly realize the enormous calamity that lies ahead. If he did, he would quickly respond, "Why would we want your religion? Look what it's done to *your* world."

DK: But as the title implies, a missionary *is* on a mission.

J: Yes, but in so many cases it's not enough for him to simply feed the hungry, care for the helpless or shelter the poor. Not when there are souls to be saved and cultures to trash. The religious world-saver is fully convinced that he's armed with the truth—that he's seen the light. Now he's hell-bent on *spreading* his epiphany with anyone he can corner. Not content with attending strictly to people's *mundane* needs, the world-saver wants to play *God*. He's utterly confident that he's well-qualified to shape a man's spirit, to mold his character—to command his *destiny*.

DK: Well, I suppose evangelizing is a lot more fulfilling than handing out sacks of grain or pulling rotten teeth. The belief that we may be influencing people's eternal fate is a much bigger boost to the ego. Still, it's hard to be too upset with someone who's just trying to help.

J: But when religion offers "help," it's often accompanied by forceful threats of judgment, punishment or damnation. Is that really helpful? In their present state of consciousness, most people don't know what real help is. They're far more likely to cause *injury*. Heck, every tyrant in history believed he was helping. For the unenlightened, progress consists not so much in doing what you believe is good, but rather in refraining from doing harm.

DK: Then what's to be learned from the Good Samaritan?

J: That you merely walk your path and deal with what arises. If someone needs help and it's within your power to assist, then trust your inner guidance to reveal what's appropriate. But don't delude yourself into thinking that you have the wisdom or power to go fashioning a man's soul. That's the one part of him that needs absolutely no adjustment.

DK: So there's no reason to go *searching* for problems.

J: I'm sure you'd agree that plenty show up on their own. Quoting the book of Matthew, "Therefore do not be anxious about tomorrow, for tomorrow will be anxious for itself. Let the day's own trouble be sufficient for the day."

DK: It's just that humanity is hurting and so much needs doing.

J: Okay, but there's a big difference between treating a kid for parasites and trying to salvage his soul. I mean if you're driven to open an orphanage in Haiti or a soup line in Los Angeles, then go for it. But quit trying to *rescue the world*, for God's sake.

DK: I'm sorry to keep pressing the point, but with a single swipe of the sword you're demolishing two thousand years of church tradition. The New Testament is quite clear about urging Christians to spread their doctrine.

J: But isn't that what you'd expect? After all, the New Testament was written by *evangelical Christians* looking to grow their flock. But converting people to a new belief system was never my plan. Let's examine my gospel parable in which the king tells his faithful stewards, "For I was hungry and you gave me food; I was thirsty and you gave me drink; I was a stranger and you welcomed me; I was naked and you clothed me; I was sick and you visited me; I was in prison and you came to me."

DK: Yeah, that's from Matthew.

J: Right, but do you notice anything unusual?

DK: Not really.

J: Well, you should—especially if you're the evangelical type. All the actions praised by the king, who in this story is metaphorically God, were directly related to his subjects' *physical* needs. Just like the parable of the Good Samaritan, not a word is said about beliefs, or even about spirituality in general. From the Christian perspective, the king is conspicuous in his omission of any reference to the preaching of doctrine. He doesn't say, "I was agnostic and you made me a believer." Or, "I was worried sick about making the rent and you told me about Jesus." Or, "I was grieving my husband's death and you gave me a pamphlet on the Rapture."

DK: So the king gave no credit for creeds, professions or converts.

J: None of that was the least bit relevant. The essential consideration was, "How well did you *love*?" The faithful stewards' salvation came solely from understanding their connection with others. They realized that their own interests were never separate or different from those of their brothers and sisters. And the help was rendered without a single mention of God or religion.

DK: Then the key was showing compassion by relieving suffering.

J: Yes, and no one *suffers* for want of beliefs. They suffer *because* of them.

DK: Ah, truly a tender message… But perhaps you've forgotten something: the passage concludes with the king condemning all the deadbeats to everlasting damnation!

J: A poor choice of endings, to say the least. Another latter-day "edit," it has the king showing the same calloused lack of compassion for which he harangues his subjects. Castigating them to eternal agony is an incomprehensibly harsh penalty for nothing but simple ignorance. The careless ones never understood what *real* spirituality was all about. They ask the king, "When did we see you hungry, naked, or lonely?" They honestly didn't know. Their blindness was unfortunate, perhaps, but it makes no sense that the king would *condemn* them for it.

DK: The punishment certainly doesn't fit the crime, there's no doubt about that. But scripture is unyielding. Come judgment day, you're slated to be God's main cowboy, feverishly separating the men from the sheep. Or *something* like that.

J: Gosh, all we need now is a campfire and a good pack of smokes.

DK: What, you don't relish being a wrangler of souls?

J: I'd sooner cover celebrity love spats for the gossip rags.

DK: Then you won't be ramrodding the Big Roundup, steering all the religious mavericks into the Condemnation Corral?

J: I'm no judge and jury, hoss. I'm just a heavenly hand, riding herd over the Great Awakening. I come not to *brand* humanity, but to set it free on the open plains of truth…

CHAPTER THIRTY THREE

DK: You'd better be careful with this non-judgment theme. You're liable to ruin your reputation by appearing rational and forbearing.

J: *Oy vey.* I can tell I've got lots of work to do…

DK: It's just that unconditional forgiveness, even coming from you, seems pretty radical to our normal thinking.

J: Why is the notion of grace so hard to accept? I mean I forgave those who *killed* me. Would it be consistent to condemn far lesser acts of ignorance later on? Am I not quoted in Matthew 12 declaring that *all* of man's sins will be forgiven?

DK: Well, it totally muddies the issue of salvation... but yeah, that's what the passage says.

J: And mind you, scripture doesn't limit the promise only to followers of *my* teachings.

DK: That's true, but you did make one notable exception. Three of the four gospel writers have you warning that blasphemy against the Holy Spirit will *never* be forgiven—either in this world or in the world to come. You didn't specify the penalty, but the implication is a non-negotiable, one-way trip to the underworld.

J: Prick up your ears, pilgrim, and try to lock on: all of God's creations are joined with Him. *Forever*. It's ridiculous to think that anyone's short-term ignorance could lead to his eternal damnation. God doesn't punish or condemn his constituent parts.

DK: Another patent repudiation of scripture.

J: We've already discussed the problems of taking the Bible as the representative authority for God on earth. It isn't. You've got gems of beauty, ancient wisdom, and metaphysical riches juxtaposed with passages that no reasonable person should tolerate.
Even my own gospel personality is a confusing mix of bizarre contradictions. On the one side, I'm depicted as a loving and compassionate friend and redeemer. On the other, I'm more akin to the Old Testament war god Yahweh: a judgmental, obsessive moralizer. In some passages, I show about as much compassion as a hungry lion for a newborn calf.

DK: So to a degree, the gospel writers merely created a more humanized version of the ancient Hebrew deity.

J: Yeah, they just toned it down a bit. Instead of having me dish out warnings of *earthly* punishment, as was Yahweh's habit, the writers have me using the subtle but far more intimidating threat of soul conviction.

DK: Well, I guess if you wanna keep folks on a really short leash, then threatening interminable punishment is a pretty effective ploy.

J: However warped it became at the hands of others, the whole gist of my original teaching was finding the light within.

DK: Yeah… makes sense, I suppose…

J: You have a faraway look in your eye, pilgrim. What gives?

DK: Oh, it's just that I've got a million thoughts bouncing around in my head—like a bunch of screaming children on a trampoline.

J: So, *vent*. Suffer the children to come unto *me*.

DK: Well, I was just thinking that nearly everything you taught was presented by other great teachers many centuries before you were born. I mean telling us that love is the answer was hardly a lightning bolt of new wisdom. And preaching virtues like charity, tolerance, and forgiveness was certainly nothing new. So if you didn't come to save us from a burning hell, then what did you offer the world that was so revolutionary or novel?

J: Nothing. I came and left empty-handed.

DK: I have to admit, you'll never be accused of padding your stats.

J: It's not that my life made no difference. Clearly it did. But in the very strictest sense, my birth didn't change a thing. Whatever could be said of reality after I arrived was true long before I showed up. And you're right: who didn't already know that you should treat others as *you* would be treated? Confucius had a version of the Golden Rule *five hundred years* before I did. A few decades before me, the great Jewish religious leader Hillel declared, "Whatever is hateful to you, do not do to others. That is the whole Torah. The rest is merely explanation." As for the dangers of focusing on materiality, nearly every great spiritual tradition has taught that investing your life's energy in the temporal world is a losing bet. So yes, it's all pretty intuitive stuff.

DK: But you must've had *some* claim to fame—*something* in your message that caused such widespread appeal. I mean the annual expenditure on Christmas gifts alone dwarfs the budgets of most small countries.

J: Well, now you can see why the church clings so righteously to its proclamation that I was "God's only Son." It has nothing else to offer. Ironically, the success of the Christian religion has practically nothing to do with the main focus of my life: urging people to wake up. My *real* life story was just an unusually dramatic demonstration of the eternal nature of Being. I simply revealed the illusion of the false self and the unreality of separation, fear and death. Other inspired messengers have taught exactly the same thing.

DK: Then there've been *other* Christs?

J: Everyone on the planet is the Christ.

DK: C'mon, you know what I mean.

J: Well, each era has its spiritual pioneers. But no one is more *divine* than another.

DK: What sets these "pioneers" apart?

J: Most people live in their own narcissistic worlds of self-consciousness. They don't have the will or desire to expand beyond these imaginary worlds and leave them behind. For the most part, they live only for the earthly gratifications of themselves and the people they hold dear. They're mostly engrossed in activities directed toward the satisfaction and glorification of their deluded egos. Becoming transfixed by the material and discounting the invisible, they unwittingly erect barriers to their own freedom.

DK: But occasionally someone sees through the veil.

J: Yeah, once in a while, by effort or by fate, that which is human peers into the realm of infinite knowledge and perceives the unbroken splendor of reality. Outwardly, these fortunate few appear to function pretty much like everyone else. But whereas, in the ordinary state, the unreal is afforded all attention while the real is largely dismissed, these enlightened ones have exactly the *opposite* experience. The greater part of them resides in the immovable inner realm of divine unity—the state you call "heaven." Once they've awakened, they cease trying to establish themselves in any worldly sense, because they realize that the world is just a flittering spark of consciousness. They know themselves to be established in God, and even eternal life is nothing to seek. For them, it's already here.

DK: Do they still experience pleasure?

J: Of course, and they also experience pain. But they're no longer seeking the one or avoiding the other. So the key difference is that they no longer *suffer*; they thoroughly enjoy creation's totality. Generally, their main inclination is to show the way "home" to those who *are* suffering and are temporarily lost. They serve as "the way," "the truth" and "the light."

DK: Most of us are a long voyage from *that* zip code.

J: Any perceived difference is just a lack of understanding.

DK: So if we're all essentially like you, then what was your chief accomplishment?

J: Realizing one's true nature—one's true unity with the Source—is the only meaningful accomplishment. After that, there's nothing left but to help others do the same. So I did what I could to point the way for those who would listen. But understand this: spiritual liberation isn't reserved for special people. It's freely available to everyone, simply for the taking.

DK: But of course *you* had a little extra help.

J: Not true! I was no more connected to the Source than you are, and my self-realization was no different from anyone else's. I articulated the same knowledge that illumined souls had conveyed for thousands of years before me. I was slightly ahead of my time, perhaps, but in most ways I was just an average Joe.

DK: Well, Joe, that's a major downgrade from your Christian designation as "God Junior."

J: Ah well, the church has *its* agenda and I have mine. As I've said, I'm no different from you except that I'm in full awareness of reality, and you, temporarily, are not.

DK: But I'm not worshipped as God.

J: Worshipping *me* as God isn't appropriate either. As your elder brother, I'm entitled to your respect and loyalty because of my deep loyalty to *you*. But I don't reside *above* you in some grand cosmic pecking order. If I have your affection, it should flow from a feeling of gratitude and brotherhood, not from a sense of compulsion, subservience or inferiority.

DK: Let's follow this path awhile... Evidently you never required your disciples to render you any special treatment or esteem. And even though lots of Christians glorify you, as far as I can tell you never openly sought it.

J: One could point to certain gospel passages that might indicate otherwise. But if scripture has me directing anyone to pay me homage, you can be sure that *I* had nothing to do with it. Worship means reverence, honor and devotion—a spontaneous expression of gratitude and love. Only a true sense of oneness could inspire such behavior. No legitimate spiritual teacher would ever think of seeking or demanding it.

DK: All the same, lots of people do worship you. How do you respond?

J: I receive it in the same spirit of love in which it's offered. But the honor given me is always returned in full. You may not believe you deserve it, but *I* worship *you*, too.

DK: Once again you're bordering on sacrilege. In the first of the Ten Commandments, God instructs the Israelites to worship Him and *Him only*.

J: But why? Is Yahweh so paranoid of rebellion that He has to threaten his children to secure their fidelity?

DK: I can't really say. He calls Himself a *jealous* God.

J: What the hell is He jealous of? And why is He constantly warning people not to follow other gods if there *are* no others? Besides, if Yahweh's so easy to love, why the need for a commandment *requiring* it?

DK: Given his poor disposition, maybe He's not so naturally endearing. Maybe the chosen weren't all that *inclined* to love Him.

J: In which case a commandment would do no good.

DK: That's true. I suppose coerced worship is effectively hollow.

J: My point exactly. Millions of Christians seem to believe that God desires their constant flattery and attention and that He wants them continuously talking about Him and telling everyone how magnificent He is. But what if you had a friend who demanded that kind of extreme consideration and concern? How long would you want that person around? I mean genuine, spontaneous reverence is a beautiful thing—but compulsive glorification is worthless. God neither needs nor desires to be told that He's wonderful, and He has no ego with which to accept contrived or empty praise.

DK: Yet you're reported to have said, "Those who worship Him must worship Him in Spirit and in Truth."

J: Sure, because there *is* no other way. Either you're *aware* of your reality as spirit, or you aren't. Either you *know* the truth, or you don't. Once you understand yourself, you *are* worshipping God.

DK: You must be aware that these ideas will be attacked. I can think of half a dozen big-name preachers who'll rant with fury denouncing the notion that we're all divine and that our souls are eternally secure.

J: Let 'em rant. You aren't responsible for other people's ignorance.

DK: But these people appear to be highly devoted Christians.

J: Occasionally so did Hitler. Even Stalin spent several years in seminary.

DK: Surely you're not comparing hard-core evangelists to a couple of history's greatest madmen.

J: Well, their methods of presentation are certainly similar. I mean when a guy's thrashing his arms and foaming at the mouth while preaching his message, you'd better cover your wallet, grab your family and run for cover. That kind of delivery only plays on emotions and discourages critical thinking, leaving no room for reason or objective inquiry. It's pure manipulation.

DK: They say that zeal in pursuit of truth is no vice.

J: And citing fancy quotes in defense of ignorance is no virtue! Listen, when a fellow's so sure of his "truth" that he's compelled to start gathering converts, there's big trouble brewing. Contrary to gospel accounts, I never did that. I simply offered myself to those who would listen. If they chose to hang around… well, that was *their* decision.

DK: Then is fervor never justified?

J: Even if it is, there's a giant gap between fervor and fanaticism. Fanatical *thinking* breeds fanatical *behavior*—and that's not good for *anyone*. Church history is soaked with the blood of innocents killed at the hands of pious faithful who thought of themselves as God's personal messengers. Pope Innocent III once commanded his subordinates, "Use against heretics the spiritual sword of ex-communication; and if this does not prove effective, use the *material* sword."

DK: *Heh heh.* Christendom's version of gunboat diplomacy.

J: Believe me, spiritual arrogance knows no bounds. History is replete with episodes of religious terror.

DK: I think some Christians feel *obligated* to proselytize—just as *I* did many years ago. Evangelicals point to the Great Commission, where you order your followers to travel the globe and preach.

J: Like a lot of scriptural quotes assigned to me, those words never crossed my lips. The so-called Great Commission occurs in only two gospels—first in Matthew and then again as an add-on section at the end of Mark, where it's nearly always listed as a footnote. This is where I allegedly tell my disciples, "Go into all the world and preach the gospel…" Scholars *know* it's not a legitimate part of the original text and should never have been included. A lot of Christians haven't thought it through, but any instruction I might have given my followers to "preach the gospel" was obviously not referring to anything in the New Testament. At that point, none of it had even been *written*.

DK: What about the last part of Luke's gospel? You're quoted saying, "Thus it is written, that the Christ should suffer and on the third day rise from the dead, and that repentance and forgiveness should be preached to all nations…"

J: That one's dead in the water, too. But it carries even larger implications of biblical disharmony, so we'll discuss it later. This leaves Matthew 28:19 as the only gospel verse containing the not-so-Great Commission. Given the supposed importance of this glorious mission mandate, it's mighty strange that three of the four gospel writers neglect to mention it.

DK: Well, *someone* sure took it to heart. Over the centuries, the church wound up with *several billion* "defenders of the faith."

J: Whatever needs defending will weaken you. I never wasted time persuading people to label themselves. Proclaiming yourself Christian doesn't make you Christ-like any more than calling yourself a doctor makes you fit to perform surgery.

DK: I'm not sure anymore about religion, but I would think we've got to stand for *something*, if only because it helps us know who we are.

J: Clutching beliefs doesn't *aid* self-discovery—it *retards* it. The only statement you can make with certainty is "I am." The rest is grievous self-deception.

DK: We've agreed that these ideas weren't entirely radical when you taught them, since others had introduced them long before you did. But you *were* ultimately *killed* because of them. So *someone* must have found them threatening.

J: Well, I'll admit that's how it appeared to those caught up in the strict observance of doctrine and rules. But here again is the focus on form over content and the manifestation of ego's belief that God's love is connected with judgment.

DK: Isn't it possible to judge someone and still love him?

J: Can you butcher a cow and still milk it? Love and judgment are mutually exclusive—like I.R.S. agents and compassion.

DK: *Sufferin' Saint Andy,* I'll be audited for sure...

CHAPTER THIRTY FOUR

J: Speaking of judgment, you'll recall that I created quite a ruckus one Sabbath afternoon by allowing my disciples to pick grain from a field, and again for healing a disabled man in the temple. In the gospel accounts of these events, the authorities are extremely upset and won't be thrown off the trail by—excuse the pun—common sense.

DK: Still, you were violating the sacred laws.

J: Right, but where was the *crime*? I was merely showing compassion and relieving suffering. Nevertheless, the Pharisees— basically sectarian literalists—aren't worried in the least about my hungry disciples or the poor guy with the bum hand. They don't give a whit about the *spirit* of the law, which is love. Instead, they're hysterical about my violating the *letter* of the law, which deals only with form.

DK: In other words, a complete failure of human intelligence.

J: Well, decide for yourself: there I was, simply enabling my hungry friends to feed themselves and healing a man of a lifelong affliction. But the silly dogmatists are going *bananas*. And *why*? Because someone's breaking the bloody *rules*!

DK: It's hard to believe that people are capable of such lunacy.

J: *Capable*? Are you kidding? Some folks practice stupidity like it's an Olympic event and they're going for the gold. I mean here we've got this guy whose hand is deformed, something that's caused him years of anguish. Suddenly he walks out of the temple, crying with joy because his hand has been made functional in an instant by a man who demanded nothing. Now, anyone with more empathy than a pit viper is gonna be crazy with happiness for this dude, right? But no, not *those* guys—not the nutty Pharisees. They're beside themselves with anger because… well, because it's freakin' *Saturday*.

DK: You know, when you put a story like that into context, it really drives home the lesson—gives it a whole new meaning. But I can see why you caused so much concern among the ruling elite: you threatened the conceptual foundations of nearly every group in the area. Messing with social mores is downright dangerous.

J: But *someone* had to start the wall crumbling. Because you can't take every rule or scripture at face value, or a lot of 'em lose credibility. The literalist is forced to defend things that are entirely unreasonable without heavy sedation. He can't allow for symbolism—or even the use of a little horse sense. Literalists see a picture of a dove and swear it'll fly.

DK: Well, literal interpretation of scripture does tend to keep things simple. Looking back on my own fundamentalist days, I think a lot of us were just avoiding taking responsibility for our fears and honestly addressing them. We were too busy appeasing God by being good little boys and girls. I see now that it's easier adhering to doctrines and codes than to do the inner work needed to go beyond them.

J: The ironic part is that I essentially *told* everyone as much in the episode we just discussed. I'm quoted saying, "I tell you, something greater than the temple is here." In other words, there's something far more important than *concepts*, which in this case were the rigid confines of ancient regulations. The "something" to which I referred was the light of man's awakened consciousness. The crowd was focused on *form*, while I emphasized *content*.

DK: How 'bout an everyday example of this form/content thing?

J: An angry child screams to his mother, "I hate you!" Now, only a thickheaded parent could fail to understand that the child's fearful behavior, which is the *form*, is just a reflection of the deeper *content*—the child's need for reassurance that he's loved. In the human condition, you're capable of only two basic emotions: fear and love. Knowing this will help you better understand what's going on inside and around you. A situation that seems to reflect a lack of love is, at its base, some form of fear and a concealed cry for help. But that reality is rarely understood in the heat of the moment.

DK: So how should we react when threatened?

J: Ego's first instinct, of course, is to attack or defend. But these two responses have exactly the same root: fear. The miracle occurs when you overlook the error entirely and respond only with love. Naturally the ego will tell you that you're crazy for doing so and that you, too, should be attacking or defending. Someday you'll see that your only real safety lies in your complete defenselessness. Only innocence is strong, and nothing else has any strength at all.

DK: Sounds like a policy of resignation.

J: Not resignation—just *non-resistance*. You're merely accepting what *is* and refusing to energize it through mental opposition. When you know what you really are, there's never any need to defend. It's an iron law that you manifest the very thing you defend against.

DK: Even so, it's not a very appealing strategy. Surrender implies weakness.

J: And yet, complete surrender is the deepest meaning of the Crucifixion and the very core of the Christian message. The image of the open-armed savior on the cross is the ultimate symbol of non-resistance—yielding to what *is*. It proclaims the final undoing of ego, with all its fears and carefully planned defenses. By giving in to my captors and allowing the Crucifixion to proceed, I demonstrated unqualified relinquishment of personal will and total surrender to the present moment. In the face of the most devastating limitation, I threw myself fully into the arms of eternal love.

DK: Pretty radical.

J: Love *is* radical. It appears where no one expects it, behaves like no one anticipated, and accomplishes what no one thought possible…

CHAPTER THIRTY FIVE

DK: I still don't see how love is always justified. What about callous, unprovoked murder? Who could simply look past a thing like that? I mean even the gentlest, most loving saint must have a breaking point.

J: The Apostle Peter wondered essentially the same thing when he queried me on the theoretical boundaries of love. "How many times should I forgive someone?" he asked. He proposed the number seven—as if that were really pressing the limit. It's another illustration of people's need for an easy, unequivocal set of rules. Peter wanted an exact figure: "Seven's okay if you *have* to, Pete. But personally, I never go much beyond three."

DK: But instead, you're reported to have told him, "I do not say to you *seven* times, but seventy *times* seven."

J: But no need for the math. The point is that love has no perimeter and that you should refuse to make error real by judging it. Judgment creates the illusion of separation where none exists, and you can't join with something you judge.

DK: Again your words directly oppose orthodox Christian teaching. The Bible says that God is love, true. But it also declares that He's the ultimate *judge*.

J: More biblical ambiguity. A loving God doesn't judge, and a judgmental God is not loving. Try as you might to reconcile them, love and judgment cannot coexist: where one emerges, the other disappears. When you understand the grace of God, you'll know that love has no borders. That "seventy times seven" bit was just hyperbole to drive home the point—for *Pete's* sake, you might say.

DK: I suppose I'm okay with the supernal *sentiment* of unlimited forgiveness. But it's the everyday *application* that brings me crashing back to earth.

J: C.S. Lewis said that everyone thinks forgiveness is a lovely idea—until there's something to forgive.

DK: But wouldn't you agree that some people's behavior is so offensive to human dignity that they *deserve* our condemnation?

J: Your question ignores everything we've discussed about unity. It's no different from asking, "Are there times I should condemn *myself?*"

DK: So whatever we give out is what we can expect back.

J: Sure, and that should be obvious to anyone over the age of six. In truth, though, you can't give something that doesn't exist. Believing that you *can* judge is just another delusion, and that belief creates a temporary veil between you and your reality. Holding the concept of guilt with the intention of punishing someone only defiles *your own* altar. It's like guzzling a poisoned cocktail and proclaiming, "*This* one's for bin Laden!"

DK: Therefore you taught us to *love* our enemies.

J: Actually, if you and your brother really are united at the level of spirit, then "Love your enemies" could mean only one thing: Realize that you *have* no enemies.

DK: But I can't control whether someone considers me his enemy.

J: No, but you can choose not to return the favor. Remember, the Holy Spirit always speaks to *you*—and only in *this moment*.

DK: You continue emphasizing the importance of the present moment. The question's a little brash, but how does all this talk of enlightenment help me *now*? Will it make me healthy, wealthy and wise?

J: Ah, the central concern of humanity and the motto of devoted capitalists everywhere: "What's in it for *me*?"

DK: I had a feeling this might turn ugly…

J: Oh well, you can't help yourself—you're *American*. The need for instant gratification is in your blood.

DK: But the question is valid. I mean if the story we're given is accurate, you receive angelic assistance to roll away your tombstone while you walk out of your grave free as a bird, without a care in the world. Spitting in the eye of death, you make a pit stop in Hades and then reappear on earth awhile to hang out with some old buddies. Finally, you go flying off to heaven with nary a doubt in your mind. But let's be candid: the rest of us don't have that luxury. All *we* can see is the here-and-now.

J: So you're wondering if spiritual investing pays any secular dividends.

DK: I guess that's cutting to the chase.

J: It's a great question. If you examine the logic beneath it, the question could be re-stated like this: "I understand that discovering the truth will show me that I'm one with God and with all things, that I'm eternally whole and perfect, forever loved and loving, completely safe and blissfully without need of any kind throughout eternity. But what *else* does it offer?"

DK: Hey, I told you the question was a bit cheeky.

J: But it's the thinking *behind* it that's so wonderfully revealing. It goes to the very core of human suffering.

DK: How do you figure?

J: Well, it's the belief in lack and limitation that creates most of the world's misery. The seed thought is, "I'm not complete." This leads to the next obvious thought: "There must be something *external* that will bring me the completion I desire." With that first impulse to seek for wholeness outside the self, the entire human circus begins. Convinced that your happiness lies someplace down the road and somewhere in the future, you set out to find it. But what a useless journey it is! You spend most of your time acquiring, building, striving, accumulating, negotiating, compromising, arranging and contriving—only to have the whole tower come crashing down at the end.

DK: Heck, that's just *life*.

J: It's more a *living death*. Each new "success" brings only temporary gratification at best. Then you're off again, ever anxious of an uncertain future, or fretting over a long-expired past. "Surely my happiness is getting close!" you tell yourself reassuringly. And back onto the treadmill you hop, anticipating a fulfillment that forever lies just around the corner. It's a fool's game, of course, since everything you worked so hard to attain is quickly wrenched from your hands and hurled into the dust. There's only *one way* to roll that giant stone from the entrance of your self-made tomb, my friend—by entering the present moment and liberating yourself from the constant oppression of thought.

DK: I'm sure that little speech would earn big points at Toastmasters. But I don't believe it answers my question about finding more satisfaction in the world.

J: You still don't get it, pilgrim. In the way that most people perceive and interact with the world, you *can't get* no satisfaction.

DK: Well, whaddaya know, folks! We've gone from rolling out stones from the tombs to doling out tunes from the Stones! Step right up, friends, and meet Jesus—the rock-rolling, rock-'n-roll prophet of doom!

J: Look, I hate to break it to ya, Hefner, but focusing all your energy on the world of form, with its fool's pleasures and passing fancies, diverts your attention from your deepest, abiding desire: remembering your connection with God. I told my friend Martha that only *one thing* is needful… and it isn't a Tuscan villa.

DK: You also reportedly said, "No one can serve two masters; for either he will be devoted to the one and love the other, or he will be devoted to the one and despise the other."

J: Well, it's pretty difficult to seek the truth while devoting your life to worldly riches. In any case, no one spiritually liberated could be fooled into believing that anything material can add substance to the self.

DK: Maybe you could lend me those rose-colored glasses you're wearing. Because from where I'm sitting, your priorities are way off plumb. I mean how can a fella concentrate on "care of the soul" when he's constantly beset by burdens of the body? I'll admit I don't know much about the serving of God—but I can damned sure appreciate a generous serving of mammon…

CHAPTER THIRTY SIX

J: Perhaps you're misinterpreting my words on the pitfalls of worldly striving.

DK: No, no—I'm straight: you want us all to live under bridges and sing "Amazing Grace" until we starve to death.

J: Listen, I'm nothing if not pragmatic. But what's more practical than discovering who you are?

DK: Alright, sure. But what's the *motivating* factor?

J: How about freedom from the tyranny of fear and from the continual fight against reality. Motivation enough?

DK: All of it easily attained with just one tab of Ecstasy.

J: Yes, but enlightenment's more lasting—and *legal*. It's also a lot easier on your liver.

DK: If only we could buy it on the street for thirty bucks a pop…

J: Let's keep things simple: has your pursuit of worldly pleasure made you happy?

DK: Well… like most people, I've had *periods* of happiness. The problem, of course, is that they never last. Something always screws up the works, with circumstances constantly changing from pleasant to unpleasant. And back and forth it goes.

J: How could it be otherwise? The entire universe is subject to the Law of Impermanence. Can we agree, then, that in spite of all your efforts to achieve and acquire, the happiness you experience is really nothing but a gap between two periods of *un*-happiness? In duality everything is polar—and all poles have opposites. So any seeking after pleasure must eventually result in the pain of disappointment. Here's how it works…

In pain or discontent, desire is born. Once conceived, desire seeks fulfillment. If fulfillment is thwarted, you're thrown back into pain. If the desire *is* fulfilled, the fulfillment invariably fades, leaving you once again yearning or unsatisfied—both subtle forms of emotional pain.

DK: Say, what are you, one of those glass-half-empty messiahs? Ever hear about the power of positive thinking?

J: Deny it if you'd like, but pleasure and pain are inextricably linked. They go together like politics and grand jury indictments. Like TV preachers and lousy haircuts. Like boxing and paroled felons.

DK: Every party needs a pooper…

J: I'm telling you, pinning your happiness on the fulfillment of desires is dangerously hypnotic. You become like the skydiver who's so entranced by the fall that he doesn't realize his chute failed to open. The experience may be ecstatic and the scenery terrific—but not for long.

DK: Don't we *deserve* happiness?

J: You deserve *joy*, which is inherent in your nature. Happiness is just a passing state of mind that's totally contingent on circumstance. But you can't count on things always going your way. Besides, it all goes Humpty-Dumpty pretty fast. One second you're a handsome prince, and in less than a blink you're napping forever in a wooden box.

DK: You're a real barrel of monkeys, you know that? Excuse me while I find my Prozac.

J: Hey, cheer up. Life may not be *long*, but it sure is *short*.

DK: Oh, that's hilarious.

J: C'mon, why so glum? This stuff's depressing only from the standpoint of ego. The frail, egoic mind wants to extend itself into infinity. But you know that's impossible: the Law of Impermanence has no exceptions. Heck, even if you could live a thousand years—a mere flash in the timeless span of perpetuity— you'd still be no closer to the immortality you seek. The good news is, there's a very simple solution. By now it should be obvious.

DK: I'll venture it isn't sex, drugs and chocolate bars.

J: You have to find the part of you that's *changeless*. Discover the inner being that's calmly and dispassionately watching your life story unfold. Once you contact it, you'll know with rock-like certainty that you need nothing. But I'll warn you again: intellectualizing won't help. Ultimately you've got to see the truth for yourself. You want my advice?

DK: I'm not entirely sure…

J: Quit deceiving yourself with the belief that happiness depends on circumstance. In fact, surrender the very *concept* of happiness. You've merely turned it into another "thing" to be acquired— another potential problem and source of frustration. Remember that salvation, if it's meaningful at all, can only be here and now.

DK: What about the rewards of achievement? In America we say that if you work hard enough you'll eventually find your place in the sun.

J: That's like the guy who lost his gold ring on Elm Street one evening but goes looking for it eight blocks away on Main

Avenue because the light is better. I tried to convey this to my disciples when I told them, "The kingdom of God is not coming with signs to be observed..." In other words, cosmic consciousness is not available in the future and can't be found in anything external.

DK: So what is this "cosmic consciousness"?

J: The sudden realization that you're one with the cosmos—with the whole of reality. Eventually, the fullness and vitality of the present moment will compel your attention like nothing in a non-existent future ever could. Your cup will overflow with appreciation, wonder and gratitude.

DK: Your sales skills are improving. Keep talking...

J: Although most people don't know it, what they're really wanting in life is peace—a deep sense of safety and fulfillment. The usual approach is to go chasing after *things*. But *things* don't ultimately satisfy. Once you see that, then you can begin solving the problem at its source. By accepting what *is* and bringing greater levels of awareness to the *self*, you won't need the sense stimulation or ego gratification that you've required in the past. You'll no longer desire the energizing dramatics you've been creating to give yourself that artificial feeling of aliveness and self-worth, because each moment will be brimming with beauty and delight.

DK: Okay, so enlightenment brings peace. No one can dispute the benefits of *that*. But again, what is spirituality's *practical* advantage?

J: You consider joy and peace impractical?

DK: I'm just looking for something a bit more mundane. What will my spiritual quest gain me in a *physical* sense?

J: The short answer is, nothing... and everything.

DK: Well, *that* clears it up.

J: Enlightenment adds nothing—it merely strips away your sense of lack and imperfection. Consequently, it gives you everything because it reveals your oneness with all things. You come to realize that to *have* is the same as to *be*: everything is yours because everything is *you*. In a sense, the universe itself becomes your "body." Suddenly you're intimately connected with God and his full creation, and a dripping rainspout becomes no less dazzling than a waterfall.

DK: You're painting a nice picture, I suppose. But it sounds like a helluva lot of work to get there. Why would I struggle through this spiritual labyrinth of yours?

J: As it stands, you're nothing but a slave to your shifting fears and desires. Driven almost entirely by the fickle egoic mind, you spend nearly every waking moment pursuing pleasure and avoiding pain. You do this because you believe what your mind is telling you about reality. But I can say categorically that all of its suppositions are wrong. So start questioning what the mind is concluding. Observe how it makes you feel to *believe* those thoughts, and then consider what life might be like without them.

DK: *That* approach seems simple enough. But I'll still have desires, no?

J: Some may stay and some will go. Desires and the yearning to satisfy them are part of your nature. All desire, including the pursuit of knowledge, is rooted in the buried urge to know the self. Even fear is just an expression of the natural tendency for self-protection. But the *real* self needn't be sought, acquired, enhanced, defined, nor defended.

DK: If I really want the truth, then what's keeping me stuck?

J: You've just been searching in the wrong place. Instead of seeking *outside* yourself, begin turning inward. Understand that happiness in the future is a terrible deception and that any religion or philosophy promising salvation down the line is thoroughly bogus. They're serving you a thick, steaming portion of *tomorrow*. Real salvation is available only in the present moment.

DK: So the secret is to find the happiness within.

J: The secret is to *stop looking* for happiness and bring your attention continuously back to the present moment. This pays immediate dividends by keeping your focus on the one "place" where real joy abides. By simply observing the workings of the mind, you'll begin to see all the barriers you've erected against your own peace: anger, resentment, culturally programmed cravings, frivolous ego demands—the whole boiling stew of fragmentation and discontent. But it's possible to be transformed all in a moment.

DK: And that's what's known as enlightenment?

J: Yes, but again: don't let the mind turn it into another prize to be attained. Enlightenment isn't something to be "had." In fact, it isn't really a change at all. It's just the recognition of the perfection that *already is*. I said before that truth is reality itself. But technically there's no such thing as truth, because that would imply a *second* reality of *non*-truth. Seek not so much for truth as for *what's true*. Whatever you perceive truth to be, however, keep it strictly private. Once you begin imposing your "truth" onto others, you've lost your way completely. You've created a monster.

DK: And what about you? Did *you* ever have desires?

J: Sure, it's part of being human. But I finally reached the point where I felt no compulsion to *act* on my desires; I was no longer controlled by the whimsical mind. The self-realized person quietly watches desires arise but doesn't feel the least need to *do* anything about them. He simply observes them drifting across the screen of the mind and allows them to dissolve back into the field of pure potential from which they emerged. You, on the other hand, spend most of your life chasing after one thing or another and you rarely, if ever, appreciate the fullness of the *now*. It's the old story of failing to stop and smell the roses. Or even the onions.

DK: Western culture isn't really big on that stuff.

J: No, but neither is it big on creating inner peace. Running after idols—that is, external symbols of power and happiness—will eventually dissipate your energy. In the end, it leaves you spiritually and physically bankrupt.

DK: But that's the whole Western shtick: make a splash, get rich—*become* somebody. That's how we're supposed to find fulfillment.

J: Be honest and admit that nothing you've ever accomplished or acquired has really given you the lasting happiness you sought.

It's time you came to the obvious conclusion: the world can never substitute for the fulfillment that lies at the heart of your nature.

DK: Then what of "the American Dream"?

J: It's just what the name says: a *dream*. See it for what it is and be done with it. As they say, even if you manage to *win* the rat race, you're still just a rat. Stop chasing your dreams into the world and learn to direct your attention inward. Let the simple statement "I am" be your new Declaration of Independence.

DK: You make it sound easy. But the reality is that most of us have to earn a living—feed, clothe, shelter ourselves and so forth. I mean it's hard to see beyond your nose when it's up against the grindstone. Maybe sweat and spirituality just don't mix.

J: You do have to function in the world, there's no getting around that. But don't allow your "responsibilities" to keep you from fulfilling your *real* responsibility: discovering your true nature. Don't fall into the trap of believing that happiness lies waiting somewhere outside the self or in some forthcoming circumstance.

 DK: But again I resort to logic: if I'm not happy *now*, then happiness *must* lie somewhere in the *future*.

J: I'm telling you, the notion of *contentment tomorrow* has no meaning. Would God place your joy on the horizon, like a mirage in the desert? Heaven is *here and now*, remember? That's the foundational flaw behind "the American Dream." It essentially says that if you *become* this or that, or *acquire* one thing or another, *then* you'll be happy. But all that stuff implies an imaginary *future*. So when you believe it, you've placed your happiness somewhere down the yellow brick road. And even if you do manage to arrive in the Land of Oz, you quickly discover that it was never more than a dream and that happiness was always back home in Kansas.

DK: And the moral of the story is?

 J: Save yourself the trip. You don't have to be a wizard to know that reality is yours every moment. Dorothy's big lesson can be summed up in one sentence: *"Everything worth having is yours from the start."*

DK: Then we shouldn't strive for success?

J: There's no judgment involved. In lower states of consciousness, striving is normal: the mind presents a desire and you struggle to make it real. But the true self knows nothing of success or failure. Spiritually, many worldly "successes" have been abject failures. Should someone be considered successful just because they manage to hit it big? What if they neglect their family, ignore their spirit, destroy their health or sell their integrity? Is that really success?

DK: I imagine that, from a higher orientation, our brief little lives seem fairly meaningless. Dust in the wind, as they say.

J: Your *life* certainly isn't meaningless; but you've given way too much significance to your *life situations*. The point is, whatever you do, find the means to do it *peacefully*—with integrity, awareness and compassion, both for yourself and for all living things. If something can't be done peacefully, then you might reconsider what you're doing. If you gain by forcing someone else's loss, then your own loss becomes greater than you can imagine. Remember, too, that you've instantly made your happiness conditional when you become emotionally attached to the outcome.

DK: Well, that leaves *me* in the clear. I'm not nearly as concerned about *out*come as I am about *in*come.

J: The problem with focusing on results is that you can't go about your work in peace. Insisting how each moment should look, you create stress for yourself and for those around you. By fighting for control and resisting the present, you're essentially saying to life, "Whatever it is, I'm *against* it." So learn to let the universe flow. With gentleness and the strength that comes from *knowing*, let come what comes and let go what goes.

DK: Then you're not suggesting that we just sit around doing nothing.

J: Well, for lots of people, even *that* would be preferable to the insane things they end up *doing*. But as I said, do what you feel you must—but with minimal attachment. In any case, let your attention settle continuously in the moment. It's a simple thing, but with unwavering earnestness, turning your attention to awareness of the self and the present moment will transform you in the most unexpected and miraculous fashion. You'll find life taking new form and new direction. Much of your old world will gently fall away, and you won't give it a second thought.

DK: Is it naïve to simply trust God to take care of us?

J: From the standpoint of the Absolute, the question is moot. In your natural state, you already *are* taken care of: you don't *have* any needs. God isn't aware of you as a separate entity, and He isn't deceived by your delusions of lack, fear, vulnerability and impermanence. God assigns no reality to the idea that you were born into a world apart from Him, struggling from cradle to grave and ultimately doomed to die. If He *were* convinced of your illusions, then they would effectively be real—and you'd be doomed indeed.

DK: Are you saying that God doesn't even know we're here?

J: I'm saying that God knows only the *real*—and only the eternal is real. God knows *you*, alright. But He doesn't know you as a body-mind personality. Your whole line of reasoning assumes that God shares your sense of separation. He doesn't. Whatever you've imagined that seems to have altered your perfection is unreal and doesn't exist. God knows nothing about it.

DK: Well, I should've known we'd come back to this. Again you claim that I've fallen into an ethereal world of dreams.

J: That's putting it too passively; you should take more responsibility. The world didn't just appear by accident, you know. I mean someone had to dream it up, right? So who was it?

DK: Well... *God*, of course!

J: You're still assuming that a separate God threw you into a pre-existing world of madness, suffering and death. But what about *you*? Are you saying that you were completely removed from this momentous decision?

DK: I'm saying that if birth was my beginning, then it goes without saying that I had no say.

J: And what makes you so confident that your birth and your creation were the same thing? On what evidence do you base this cocksure proposal? And don't tell me again that you don't remember anything prior to your birth, because you don't remember too much prior to *last Thursday*. The no-memory argument is a truly weak defense—especially coming from a guy who, for the last three years of his marriage, couldn't seem to remember his own anniversary.

DK: *Sheesh!* You and your total recall! Okay, so maybe I'm *not* taking enough responsibility. But I just can't wrap my head around this idea that the world is of my own making. Surely only *God* would have such power!

J: Does this discrete deity of yours get the blame for your twisted night dreams as well?

DK: C'mon, what is it with you and this dream thing? You honestly maintain that physicality is just something I've *imagined*?

J: To be blunt, yes. For anything to be created, the mind must first *imagine* it. But there's only one mind, so for the universe to come into being, *your mind* must've had something to do with it.

DK: Then my experience of the world is something like my experience in a dream.

J: It's the same phenomenon, taken to a level you can only imagine. *Literally.* But a dream, by definition, *is imaginary*, and God isn't interested in improving your hallucination. God knows that his children are sleeping, and He uses their illusions of time and space to gently waken them from their mind-invented state of fear and separation. With their transformed perception, they'll experience "a new heaven and a new earth."

DK: And then?

J: Eventually the world will vanish back into the Source from which it arose. The universe is "breathed in and out" in great cycles of eons. *You*, on the other hand, will continue on, as ever, safe in the heart of God.

DK: I can't believe you waited two thousand years to show up and tell us that we're dreaming. It sounds completely *nuts*.

J: Your resistance to the idea makes perfect sense. Because even though a dreamer is not awake, *neither does he realize that he sleeps.*

DK: It's all pretty fascinating, I guess—if not a bit mind-boggling. But let's agree that your story is sound. Even so, what *preceded* this hilarious little adventure? I mean before I wound up bloody and crying in the hands of some overpaid obstetrician, who the hell *was* I!!??

J: A terrific question. Answer it to your own satisfaction and I can take a long vacation…

CHAPTER THIRTY SEVEN

DK: So the crux of your teaching is that life is but a dream, and if we find our inner reality, the rest takes care of itself.

J: Yes, and that was *always* the intended lesson. These days, though, you've got scoundrels getting rich on my teachings by remolding them into something my first disciples wouldn't even recognize. Certain factions of the Western church have turned my message of enlightenment into a kind of giant Christian success seminar. I never understood how someone could read the Old Testament—or even the gospel story of *my* life—and conclude that God rewards his children by making their lives *comfortable.*

DK: God doesn't want us comfortable?

J: Not if it means being comfortable in your ignorance. In that sense, comfort was never part of the deal. The road to joy is often paved with sorrow.

DK: That sure isn't the *popular* view—at least not according to the wealth-oriented megachurches.

J: Most of that stuff's nothing but private enterprise spirituality. "Ask anything in the name of Jesus," they shout, "and he'll deliver as requested!" So in *this* little scheme, a Mercedes beats a meditation, and a parcel's as good as a prayer.

DK: But you did make that affirmation, did you not? I mean it's right here in John 14, in black and white. Or—*heh heh*—in red, as the case may be.

J: Yeah, I'm said to have declared, "And whatsoever ye shall ask in my name, that will I do… If ye shall ask anything in my name, I will do it."

DK: Right. Sounds pretty much like a blank check.

J: New Testament scholars can affirm that I never said about three quarters of the stuff attributed to me in the four gospels. Try to remember that when you're hitting me with these Bible quotes.

DK: Okay, but what about that carte blanche guarantee? It's one of Christianity's juiciest selling points.

J: It's not exactly what I said. I never made it a personal statement, because no one fully awakened would still believe in an individual self. But here's the key: in biblical times, a thing's name typically reflected something of its character or its nature. Therefore, "in my name" meant "according to my nature." God's nature is loving perfection, and anything envisioned by someone at *that* level of consciousness does indeed tend to find expression in form.

DK: I have to admit that, in my most authentic moments, I often don't know what I really want. I mean I know I want *happiness*. But I'm not sure what I should be asking God to *do* about it.

J: At the level of spirit, everything you *really* want is already done: you just have to *tune in*. The ever-shifting world of phenomena fools the mind into believing that reality is always changing and therefore always generating new conditions of need. But you, as spirit, are a direct reflection of the Supreme, and the Supreme isn't *evolving*. Now, the *universe* may continue to unfold—but *reality* is forever complete.

DK: You talk about the nature of reality like it's simpler than a button. But I had trouble with basic high school geometry, for gosh sakes.

J: We're discussing things that have to be *experienced*. For now, it's enough to say that, in truth, nothing needs "doing." While you're always free to create and alter your *situation*, reality itself doesn't need revising.

DK: Believe me, there's a hundred things in *my* reality that need serious revision.

J: Even from the deceptive dualistic viewpoint, in which you and everything in the universe are separate, what could need doing that a loving, all-knowing and all-powerful creator wouldn't already be addressing? What requirements would He need *you* to bring to his attention?

DK: Well, nothing, I guess. But then what's the point of asking for something in your name? In fact, why ask for anything at all?

J: There *is* no point, really. You wouldn't believe the millions of flakey, destructive and even sinister prayers that constantly bombard the heavens. Some are asked in *my* name and some in the names of other revered gods, saints or prophets. Most of the prayers are just faithless appeals by folks wanting their dream worlds altered. Luckily for you, God doesn't deal in dreams. He abides only in unchanging reality. Right here, right now.

DK: If that's true, then most prayers are just silly requests asking God to be something He isn't.

J: That was my original point: most prayers are contrary to God's *nature*. You're essentially asking Him to participate in a world that doesn't exist. Far better to question your *beliefs* about reality than to continue begging God to change it.

DK: Apparently God can't be wheedled or cajoled by our pious-sounding pleas.

J: I'm certainly not saying that God doesn't interact with his creations. He does. But He isn't taken in by your delusions, nor is He contractually obligated just because you spout a prayer for a million bucks and then conclude it "in the name of Jesus." Don't project your lifeless material values onto God.

DK: Maybe you're riding us too hard. After all, life can be a real bitch—especially when you're broke. I believe it was the great philosopher Marx who said, "I've been poor and I've been rich. Rich is better."

J: You sure that was Karl Marx?

DK: I was referring to Groucho.

J: Oh, I see. Actually, I think the quote belongs to George S. Kaufman's wife, Beatrice.

DK: Well, either way, it sums up our situation perfectly. I mean if we have to *live* in the world, we may as well be *comfy*, right?

J: Like I said, there's no inherent advantage to poverty. But you run into trouble when you start believing that money will *save* you—because it *won't*. After two thousand years, I'm afraid it's still God or mammon, my friend.

DK: Listen, I know people who would sell their mothers into slavery to be rich. But don't lump *me* into that group. After decades of walking the spiritual path, I'm just barely solvent.

J: You may think of yourself as spiritual—but nearly every aspect of your life revolves around material gain and comfort. Even your *language* is stained with corruptions of capitalism.

DK: I'll buy that.

J: Here's *my* counsel: do what's required to make your way in the world, but at least develop some awareness of what's *driving* you. Take a hard look at your obsession with money and the Western definition of success. Determine how much faith you've placed in your savings account. Will you do that?

DK: You can bank on it...

CHAPTER
THIRTY EIGHT

J: Speaking of faith misplaced, I'm sure you're familiar with my caution not to build your proverbial house upon the proverbial sand.

DK: Of course. You said it always leads to the proverbial *crash*.

J: Well, I'm sorry to say that brings us back to a topic sure to make you the hit of the party on New Year's Eve.

DK: Oh, great… we're back to *death* again. You know, a lot of people are really turned off by your preoccupation with that subject. They say your focus on the afterworld takes all the fun out of *this* one.

J: Despite what you've been told, I never talked about an *after*world. I talked about the *only* world—the world where you and God have always been one.

DK: But the four gospel writers have you selling a futuristic Nirvana to the faithful while threatening fires of retribution for the damned.

J: I would never have tolerated that kind of two-bit theology. I say, post-mortem schmortem. Reality is always *now*, and betting on some rapturous tomorrow is a real sucker's play.

DK: But you did spend considerable energy warning folks not to get too comfortable here. It seems to be one of the central messages of the Sermon on the Mount. Or did we get a bum steer on that too?

J: Most of it is pretty accurate—even if it's not well understood. I wasn't pointing to any heaven in the sky. I was reminding folks that putting faith in the body as a refuge is an endeavor that's bound for failure. The body, no matter how lovely or magnificent, is pretty quickly food for worms.

DK: Then I'd have to agree with the critics: you do come across a bit morbid. Why all that emphasis on the big chill?

J: It's a fair question… but it would take some explaining.

DK: I've got more time than mammon.

J: Alright, but don't blame *me* when you're blackballed on the lecture circuit.

DK: Geez, will it be that harsh?

J: Well, I'll only be verbalizing things that people already know. But it really aggravates 'em when their taboo subjects are openly discussed—especially the topic of death. Like a cockroach on the wall at dinnertime, nobody wants to deal with it. I mean everyone knows they'll check out of the Life Hotel *eventually*. But they'd prefer not to have the manager coming around to remind 'em.

DK: So we hang "Do Not Disturb" signs on the doorknobs of our minds, is that it?

J: You got it. People tend to focus only on certain *parts* of their illusions. It's like a woman buying sirloin: she's perfectly fine with the packaged product—but she's definitely not interested in a tour of the slaughterhouse. You sure you wanna get into this?

DK: As sure as death and taxes.

J: Alright, pilgrim… but good luck on a second printing.

DK: Wow, this sounds serious.

J: Well, yes and no. To the imaginary self—the person you *believe* you are—it'll be like opening the morning paper and finding your own obituary. To the eternal self that's *really* you, it's pure entertainment… some light reading for a good cosmic chuckle.

DK: Okay, I'm braced. Fire away…

J: I'll start with something that may seem unnecessary because it appears to be self-evident. But I assure you that, despite your *intellectual* understanding of it, you have yet to grasp the full significance of the following statement:

You… will… die.

DK: You're right, it's an obvious fact. I don't see where you're going.

J: Well, for decades you've witnessed the "obvious fact" that all living things eventually die. Some live longer than others, of course—but they all die in the end. No exceptions, right?

DK: Not as far as I know. Although, one of the few Old Testament oddities that sticks with me is the statement that Enoch was "taken" by God. It's strange because everyone else mentioned in that part of the scriptures is clearly said to have died. Also, the book of Hebrews claims the high priest Melchizedek was "without father or mother or genealogy, and has neither beginning of days nor end of life…"

J: Okay, but let's agree that you have no idea what the biblical writers were actually describing. I mean the words are fairly cryptic, no? The scripture says, "Enoch walked with God; and he was not, for God took him." Now, let's be honest: that's about as clear as the fine print on aluminum siding contracts. And the writer of Hebrews is equally vague. He doesn't elaborate on why Melchizedek alone should be immortal or why he had no mother and father.

DK: It's an extraordinary claim, to say the least—right up there with being born to a virgin. It appears you may have been trumped in your ability to dispense with parentage.

J: Well, my people *are famous* for eliminating the middleman…

DK: I'm not sure what's behind the story of Melchizedek, but the New Testament attributes Enoch's special circumstances to the fact that he had faith.

J: All I can say is that *lots* of people have faith. But the faithful suffer the same inevitable destiny as everyone else. Even I was no exception.

DK: Sorry, I didn't mean to split hairs. I get your point: I'm not likely to be the next Enoch or Melchizedek.

J: So you know with certainty that your body-mind personality—the thing you call "I"—is going to die.

DK: Of course. But again, why state the obvious?

J: Because you don't really *believe* it.

DK: What do you mean?

J: Well, everyone knows that all living things must die. I mean—
heh heh—that's *life*, right?

DK: I regret I must agree.

J: So, consciously, the fact of death is irrefutable. *Sub*consciously,
though, it's a different story. You know beyond doubt that
everything you *imagine* to be "you" will come to a screeching halt
in a moment's burst. But ego simply can't bear the notion of non-
existence; it reels at the idea that it won't last forever. Although
it doesn't articulate it, in a roundabout way the egoic mind
concludes, "Death is something that happens to *others*, not to *me*.
Or at least not for a very, *very* long time."

DK: I've never fully thought it out, I guess… but I can see that we
certainly shove the file to the back of the closet.

J: And how do you *evade* this tyrannous thought of death? You
stay *busy*. You distract yourself by pursuing ambitious goals,
seeking thrills or pleasure, and formulating intricate plans. You
live as if you'll be here forever. But at some level just beneath
awareness, you're quite conscious that all these things will quickly
disappear. Nevertheless, you expend most of your energy building
your little empire and shoring up your fragile self-image.

DK: Personally, I feel as though my efforts are somehow adding
permanence to my existence. It's like I'm reinforcing who I am.

J: Exactly. You believe you're establishing real security for yourself.
Yet somewhere in the hidden corners of the mind, lost among its
compulsive ruminations and incessant reverie, a subtle but persistent
thought calls ceaselessly for your attention: *You… will… die.*

DK: There's no arguing the point, of course. I mean how can
anyone ignore it? As we get older, the damned voice grows louder
with each passing year.

J: Yet you suppress it. You stay occupied trying to escape it. But
the voice follows you relentlessly, like a shadow. And you know
that what it's telling you is true. Deep inside, you *know* that
someday your world will come crashing down around you—and

not one of your idols can save you. You realize that everything you've identified with is just a momentary picture on the movie screen of life. In the end, it's more worthless than a campaign promise on election day.

DK: Jeepers, is our situation as bad as all that?

J: Let me lay it out for you in terms that only a trial lawyer could distort: *You are going to die.* You're going to die, and you're going to die *soon.* It may be tonight, it may be next month or it could be another forty or fifty years. But you *are* going to *die.* So you may as well envision your cold, pale corpse stretched out in a decorated, overpriced crate and wearing some cheesy-looking suit with a smudge of cheap mortuary makeup on the collar. *Because it's going to happen.* And whether it's sooner or later doesn't much matter, because when the final moment arrives, it'll seem as if you've lived no time at all.

DK: Yeah, I've read that the dying often feel as though their lives, in retrospect, were nothing more than a surreal dream.

J: It's true. One of the most common deathbed perceptions is that life lasted only a moment. As the end approaches and the realization of finality sets in, the dying take one long look back. Suddenly they realize that life was a mere flash of consciousness— no more enduring than a disappearing wisp of breath on a cold winter's night.

DK: Damn, that's pretty depressing.

J: That was the *cheery* part.

DK: You mean it gets worse?

J: *Oh* yeah. It's like the guy who gets a call from his doctor. "I've got some bad news and some worse news," says the sawbones. "The bad news is that we received your test results, and they indicate the condition of a man who's only got about twenty-four hours to live." Naturally the guy is stunned. "My God, doc, what could possibly be worse than *that*!?" The doctor hesitates a moment and then responds: "I forgot to call you yesterday."

DK: Ha! Thanks a hundred for the comic relief.

J: Who wants a savior that can't get a laugh?

DK: Alright, so give it to me straight: how does the story get worse?

J: It gets worse because not only will *you* die, but *everyone you know* will die, too. Your *children* will die. Your *children's* children will die. Your parents, your spouse or lover, your friends, your heroes and your enemies, those you admire and those you despise—all of them will die. The supermodel, the big-name ball player, the wealthy business magnate. The most lovable saint and the most despicable sinner will each die the same eternal death. No exemptions. All of them will fade faster than a crippled nag at Belmont.

DK: It is strange to think that everyone I know and love, and everyone I've ever seen or met, is going to disappear forever.

J: And very few will die quietly in their sleep at the ripe old age of ninety-five. Many will die young. Some will contract debilitating disease, while others will be killed in accidents, wars, murders, and bizarre mishaps or disasters. Some will take their own lives. Before they die, some will suffer immensely, either physically or psychologically. Perhaps both. You could even be one of them.

DK: Maybe I'll be lucky and croak in a whorehouse.

J: But whether it happens peacefully after a long and productive life, or in the midst of painful suffering and hopeless despair, one thing remains certain: you *will* die. And when you go, you'll leave everything—and I do mean *everything*—behind. Nothing in which you now take pride or pleasure will remain with you. Think of that. *Absolutely nothing.*

DK: Well, you were right—that's pretty dismal stuff. Up against you, the average mortician comes off like a nightclub comic. Better stick with that savior bit. You'll never make it on the motivational speaking circuit.

J: Just to drive home the point… think of your favorite sports hero, entertainment star, business wiz, spiritual role model, or *anyone* you idolize, envy or admire. In fifty, sixty, maybe seventy years—not even a *blip* on the radar screen of eternity—that person will either be well on the way to dying or already stiffer than a Presbyterian's martini.

DK: By then, I'd imagine that few people will even think of him.

J: Yes, and fifty years after that, he'll be long dead for sure, and even his descendants won't have known him. If he was famous, they'll speak of him only rarely—at familial gatherings, perhaps—and mostly just from an artificial sense of pride at having him as an item of interest hanging from an upper branch of the family tree. A hundred years after that, if he was *truly* exceptional, maybe a small percentage of the world's population will know his name. But it won't do *him* any good, of course, because he'll be dead and merely of *historical* interest. Most people will have never heard of him—and never will. A thousand years later, he'll be less relevant than a nondescript herdsman in the Arabian Desert. It'll be as if he, along with you and your entire civilization, had never even *existed*.

DK: Wow. I should've just stayed home and watched *Grapes of Wrath* or a documentary on smallpox. After *that* little speech, I'm gonna need a good fire-and-brimstone sermon just to perk me up. I'll bet you were loads of fun at parties.

J: Only because of my skills behind the bar…

CHAPTER THIRTY NINE

DK: Let's make sure I've got this straight. Just reading between the lines, it sounds like you're implying, in your ever-so-subtle way, that we're all gonna die. Have I missed anything so far?

J: Nope, to this point your comprehension is brilliant.

DK: Frankly, I'm a little distressed. Why beat us over the head with something so evident?

J: Because you don't really believe this stuff applies to *you*. Engrossed in your desire for worldly immortality, you don't like hearing that your physical "reality" won't last. Now, I've said that God's creations don't die, so maybe you should do some reflecting. What is it that *does* die?

DK: Don't tell me, let me guess. What dies is our *illusion* of who we are.

J: Give the kid a cigar...

DK: Is our existence just a puff of steam? Are we nothing but a false impression?

J: Of course not. I've never said that *you* are an illusion. It's just that you aren't anything *in particular*. I know there's lots of resistance to this idea, but you can easily verify it by the simple process of self-inquiry. Maybe this'll help: Imagine developing a sudden case of amnesia and not remembering a single detail up to that moment. Who would you be *then*?

DK: Bill Clinton under oath.

J: And to think they chose Leno to replace Carson...

DK: Alright, alright. I suppose if I developed amnesia, I'm not sure who I would *think* I am. But obviously I'd still be *me*.

J: Yes, but can we agree that you'd no longer be the "person" you presently assume?

DK: Well, I guess if I lost all memory, then I'd have no frame of reference for determining who I am. But surely *others* would still know me as me.

J: Would they? You're assuming that they know you *now*. But they're misunderstanding *you* the same way that you're misunderstanding *them*. Suppose everyone you know developed amnesia right along with you. *Then* who would you be? And who would *they* be? At that point, there would be no memory-based references, either from yourself *or* from others, to define who "you" are. But as you say, you would still be *you*, since nothing of your essence would be affected. Your personality and your life-situation might change dramatically, but your spirit would continue undisturbed. In such a case, you'd no longer be able to derive your sense of self from your history. What I'm suggesting is that you stop doing that *right now*. Not that you have to forget your past. Just quit *defining* yourself by your "I-am-this-body" idea. Consider that when you say "I," you aren't *really* sure what you're referring to.

DK: You're right. I actually have no idea who or what "I" am.

J: So think of the irony: all your life, you've referred to yourself as "I." And yet you confess that, once you reason it through, you haven't a clue who this "I" really is. It's ludicrous, no?

DK: It's downright freaky.

J: And if *you* aren't sure of your identity, think how misguided *others* must be in *their* assessment of you. Even now, there aren't two people in the world who would agree completely on who you are. Let's say you ask twenty of your closest friends and family to describe you by writing a couple of pages each. You can be dead sure that you'd receive twenty drastically different responses— and all of them based on the past. Some would contain common elements, no doubt; but overall, each report would be strikingly different. They might even conflict.

DK: Sure, I can see that.

J: Let's go a step further. Suppose *you* were to write two pages describing yourself and then do the same thing again in five years. How similar do you think the two accounts of "you" would be? And suppose you had written a self-description ten or twenty years ago. How close would it be to the one you write today? What if you had written one when you were only five? Can you reasonably argue that you're still the same "person" you were then?

DK: I suspect all those descriptions would differ immensely. But would that mean I'm not the person I've always been?

J: It means, as I've tried to make clear, that *there's no such thing as a person*.

DK: It sounds crazy when you say it. But I'm beginning to see the truth of it.

J: You're starting to understand that you aren't comprised of interpretations, experiences, memories or beliefs. And we've already established that you can't be your mind or your body, because *you're* the one who's *using* them. So there must be something more primal in back of it all, something witnessing the whole thing—something from which it all arose. Find out what that *something* is, and all your questions will fall away.

DK: *Allllll-righty, then.* What say we go bowling?

J: *Heh heh.* I know this stuff is mind-bending, and it sounds outlandish at first. But it's nothing new. Lots of spiritual luminaries over the centuries have tried to help their students see these same truths. Imagining yourself to be a person is just the result of your identification with the body-mind idea. And because you see *yourself* this way, you see everyone else from the same perspective.

DK: Apparently we "know" others only through various conditions and events surrounding their lives.

J: Yes, and you see them through the same distorted filters through which you see yourself. But all those factors are *body-*related. They're just *concepts*, based on a past that doesn't even exist! So you may know someone's *history*, but you know nothing of his *fundamental nature*. You may know a thousand facts about him, but none of them will bring you to an understanding of his reality—or your own. Nothing you presently believe about yourself or others will survive the ravages of time, and you deceive yourself by focusing so heavily on the temporal. You're literally placing your faith in *nothingness*.

DK: So you emphasized death to get us to focus on its opposite.

J: I never emphasized death. Death is only the opposite of birth. I emphasized *life*, which is eternal and *has* no opposite. Who you are *in reality* has nothing to do with the coming and going of the body. You need to accept that everything with which you presently identify will suddenly... and everlastingly... vanish.

DK: Then we can't really enjoy life until we correct our self-image.

J: One self-image is as delusional as another, and every one of them is rice-paper fragile. A perceived slight, a judgmental comment, the loss of a job, a debilitating injury—even just a menacing glance from a stranger, and instantly your frail self-image can shatter. So you can't fully enjoy life as long as you *have* a self-image. While you do, you'll feel driven to develop, maintain, defend and protect it. Feeding this imaginary self prevents you from experiencing life in its fullness and glory.

DK: I think you're overstating the case. Erratic self-image or not, I've had times when I was genuinely happy. I imagine that's true for almost everyone.

J: I'm not claiming you won't have periods of *relative* happiness. But I *can* tell you they won't last. Operating from ego creates an endless cycle of pain and pleasure, and eventually your fictitious identity leaves you destitute. It's the primary cause of your suffering.

DK: The Buddha said that life *is* suffering.

J: Yes, but only from the standpoint of the limited, mind-made self. Pay attention and you'll find that you're most prone to suffering when you're viewing things as a "person"—that is, when you're anxious, upset, afraid or attached to specific outcomes. You begin defending your self-image, worrying about what's going to happen, what people will think, and so forth. Conversely, everything shifts when your attention is in the *now*.

DK: How is that different from our usual mode?

J: When you're fully absorbed in the moment—in a crisis, for example, or perhaps just doing something you really love—you're simply *being* and aren't thinking of yourself as a time-bound personality. Past and future lose their energy-sapping power, and your self-image almost melts away. In such moments of true presence, even the notion of death begins loosening its terrible grip on the mind. Death, a future-oriented concept that's meaningless to spirit but causes great consternation to ego, has no meaning in the aliveness of the *now*.

DK: Then you're not advocating that we go through life keeping *death* in the back of our minds.

J: Death is already *in* the back of your minds: you're constantly trying to suppress or escape it. I'm urging you to seek your real nature. Then you can discover, as I did, the liberating truth that who you are in reality is *beyond* the ideas of life and death. It's true that the real "you" cannot die. But it's obvious that you can identify yourself with things that do. As long as you believe that you're the body-mind, you live with the subtle but ever-present anxiety that you're going to die. The anxiety may be absent or imperceptible when you're young, beautiful, healthy and feeling invincible. But it tends to increase with age. As death's inevitability draws near, most people's anxiety turns to despair, depression or even outright panic. They think they're being annihilated. They often become angry and begin injecting the event with all kinds of high-energy dramatics.

DK: You're right. And I've noticed that those around them sometimes do the same thing.

J: Sure. They're watching a painful reminder of their own mortality. They feel defeated and frustrated as they stand by helplessly and watch. The process frequently becomes an ordeal of stark terror for the one who's dying, and a source of great upset and conflict for those who witness it. But death is only rarely the unpleasant experience it's perceived to be, and thousands of near-death accounts have proven it.

DK: So what exactly happens at the moment of death?

J: *Nothing* happens.

DK: C'mon, stop yankin' my chain. *Something* must damned well happen—because the party invitations sure as hell taper off.

J: If you haven't awoken from your dream at the point of death, then the dream continues in some other fashion. Only the content changes.

DK: Horse manure!

J: I take it you're skeptical?

DK: Well, *get real*, for cryin' out loud. You're telling me that one day I'll be pronounced brain-dead and that nothing will change!!?? And please, resist the obvious snide reply.

J: Listen up, laddie: Cessation of bodily functions doesn't necessarily change the fact that you're misperceiving who you are. After all, you're *dreaming*. And it can't be your *body* that's dreaming, because dreams reside only in the *mind*. One day you'll wake up to discover that your former "reality" was just the devil with a blue dress on.

DK: Not to skirt the issue, but you say that bodies can't think or dream and that only the mind can do these things. But isn't the mind located in the body?

J: Bodies don't have minds. They only have brains—and brains don't think or dream or create.

DK: I don't believe many scientists would agree.

J: Most of science's foundational conclusions are built upon a bad premise: the presumed "reality" of the material world. Science assumes that consciousness arises from matter; but in fact it's the other way around. To the enlightened mind, though, all "data" is meaningless. After all, what good is analyzing illusions? Anyhow, if you really understood the nature of thought, you'd howl at the idea that brains can think. But even if they could, you'd still have to ask yourself, "Who is the one that's *aware* of these thoughts, these dreams, these experiences?" It's as plain as the puzzled look on your face that the ever-present observer must be *you*. So you have to get at the one who's *witnessing* the mind and its thoughts—the one who's *experiencing* the world and its activities. In short, you've got to identify the *dreamer* of the dream.

DK: *Sheesh*. You make Nietzsche seem like Psychology 101.

J: It all sounds more complicated than it is, and words only muddy the water. Just go inward and find the one who came to believe that he was a body-mind in the first place. After that, bodies and death will lose all meaning. You'll see for yourself that what you call "life" is just a stirring of consciousness and that, in reality, nothing has ever "happened."

DK: Dreamy philosophy aside, the fact remains that we all have to die. For me, that's a real downer.

J: Once you've realized the false nature of personality, you'll have "died" long before the moment of physical death. This is what I meant when I said, "He who *loses* his life…will *find* it." Die now, while you're still "alive," and you'll finally know life in its exalted splendor. You'll come to know your eternal nature and understand why nothing happens at death.

DK: That's a long day's walk from the teachings of religion, which has made quite a fuss about the implications of death. In Christianity, we're taught that our spirits go flying off to Purgatory to await the opening of the Book of Life. It's the grand finale— the dreaded Day of Judgment, when a hundred billion souls are gathered before God's throne to be condemned or redeemed.

J: You forgot the part about the magic dust, an evil witch, and the dance of the sugarplum fairies.

DK: Don't be so flippant. This stuff comes straight from the boys of the New Testament.

J: Then I'd say they were born about twenty centuries too soon, because they'd fit right in over at the studios of Disney. I'm telling you, your spirit isn't another thing among things. It's the *essence* of you—the essence of *God*. Spirit isn't affected by circumstance, and it certainly isn't contained by the body. You might say it's temporo- spacially inapposite.

DK: I'm not sure I *could* say that. In English, please.

J: Time and space don't affect it. If the soul were a *thing* with its own separate existence, and if it *were* being temporarily "housed" in the body, then obviously it *would* have to wind up *somewhere* after the body's death. But where would it go? Off to another part of the universe called "heaven"? If so, then why wait around? Why not build a spaceship to fly you there now?

DK: First of all, wise guy, because we don't know where it is. In case you haven't noticed, the universe covers a fairly large area. And secondly, maybe God created *multiple* universes or many *dimensions* of reality.

J: Then you'd have to conclude that God created *one* universe as a kind of proving ground to see if you're up to snuff, while dangling a *better* one before you like a spiritual carrot on a stick. Sounds kinda bizarre, no? Not to mention a little sadistic.

DK: Look, just spit it out: do we have souls, or not?

J: So what if you do? It still begs the question.

DK: What question?

J: Well, if you're making the claim, "I have a soul," then my challenge once again would be this: Who, what or where is this 'I' you're referring to? Who is the one claiming to possess a soul? Get what I'm saying? There must be something *apart from* or *prior to* the soul for it to declare, "I have a soul."

DK: I see what you mean. But still… call it a gut feeling or whatever… I have to conclude that a soul exists.

J: Alright, but even if it does, why did God bother cramming it into a physical body? If the soul is a separate and distinct *thing*— with shape, character and personal identity—then it's actually just another kind of *body*, right? So why the need for two bodies at once? As I suggested earlier, wouldn't it have been more sensible for God to create you as a perfect soul and then place you directly into heaven immediately?

DK: What about our free wi—

J: Hold it, hold it—stop *right there*. Lookie here, amigo… you can give me your tired, your poor, your huddled masses. You can give me liberty or give me death. Or give me a home where the buffalo roam. If you simply can't help yourself, you can even gimme some o' that old-time religion. But *please*... for *godsakes*, don't give me any more of that *free will* crap.

DK: I seem to have struck a nerve.

J: Listen... it's true that all power in heaven and earth is yours through God. But neither possesses powers that don't exist. So free will doesn't mean that you're free to destroy yourself or free to change what God created changeless. Spirit's very *nature* is to extend itself in freedom; therefore it can never create bondage. Free will, as most people think of it, applies only to the dream state: you're free to choose between illusions and truth. But don't waste time believing that you're free to make chaos of unity or free to separate yourself from the all-encompassing Source.

DK: Surely God doesn't want robots. Wouldn't He have to allow for rebellion?

J: If the Bible's creation mythology were literally true and God was bent on permitting his children to reject Him, He could simply place everyone in heaven with the option to leave at any time. Why send 'em on a perilous mission to a strange and confusing testing facility in an obscure little solar system at the dark edges of an infinite universe? Why the need for the circuitous detour into a different dimension of reality? I mean there's just no *sense* in it.

DK: Maybe you're right. In fact, I'm not at all happy about jumping through moral and theological hoops to prove myself worthy to my own creator. Forcing everyone to suffer life and death on earth before getting a shot at redemption in some unknown heaven makes God seem like a total blockhead. But what the hell can we do about it?

J: Go beyond death entirely by seeking the part of you that's eternal. Once you find it, you'll know with unshakable certainty that you and God are not what you've assumed. *A Course in Miracles* says, "When your body and your ego and your dreams are gone, you will know that you will last forever...The Holy Spirit guides you into life eternal, but you must relinquish your investment in death, or you will not see life though it is all around you."

DK: And how do we relinquish our "investment in death"?

J: Just disinvest in the evanescent.

DK: No one likes an omniscient show-off.

J: You relinquish your investment in death by refusing to invest in things that *die*. Each day, as often as you can, place your attention where moths don't destroy, rust doesn't consume and thieves can't break in and steal. That focal point, of course, is the self. To find it, proceed in the direction of I AM.

DK: If I don't need to save my soul, create converts for Christ, or waste energy on meaningless ego pursuits, then what the heck should I do?

J: Try to relax and heed some advice from Zen: Don't just *do* something—*sit* there!

DK: C'mon, I gotta fill the day *some*how. I mean I'm usually up well before eleven.

J: You can always take up the glockenspiel. Or try your hand at the bansuri or the shakuhachi.

DK: You should've been a lexicographer.

J: I couldn't bear the winters in Kentucky...

CHAPTER FORTY

DK: You look sleepy. Shall we take a break?

J: Well, engaging the body does take some adjusting. But the ground is muddy and I didn't bring a pillow—so, alas, the Son of Man has nowhere to lay his head.

DK: Hey, look, I don't wanna be known as the guy who blew the interview with God. Let's shift gears and get back to Christianity.

J: Alright, shift away...

DK: Well, earlier we talked about the Crucifixion. Now let's focus on the *other* side: the Resurrection. My own feeling is that the Resurrection is Christianity's keystone. After all, if the story had ended with you buried and forgotten, you'd have been lucky to make page twelve of the *Judean Times-Herald*. Probably nothing more than a quick human interest blurb with a catchy header.

J: "Crucified Messiah Still Dead."

DK: Yeah, precisely. The only reason you were headline material was due to the exceptional claim by your disciples that you sprang back to life. Scripture says you then appeared in the flesh to several hundred of your supporters in the days afterward. Now, I don't have to tell you that some people have a real problem with that story. They have no frame of reference for anyone resurrecting after death and entombment. Some even say your crucifixion didn't actually kill you.

J: Oh, really? On what theory?

DK: That you were taken from the cross, just barely alive, and then nursed back to health over the following days. There's speculation that the nurse may have been Joseph of Arimathea. Others say it was Mary Magdalene, who some people claim was also your wife or girlfriend. Adding to the mystery of it all, it turns out there's quite a volume of literature detailing claims that you later traveled to India, where you lived out the rest of your life, teaching and continuing your ministry. You've even got an official burial place on Khanyar Street in the Rozabal section of Srinigar.

J: I believe I have one in Shingo, Japan, as well.

DK: Yeah, but nobody takes that one seriously, because the claim is made without a speck of proof. It's just another tourist trap.

J: Well, as far as that goes, so are the two most revered burial sites claimed for me in the Holy Land: The Garden Tomb and the Church of the Holy Sepulchre. Scholars reject these, too, because there's no good evidence for either.

DK: Okay, but my point is that a lot of people, Christians included, have wondered why you didn't make the rounds after the Resurrection and show yourself to *everyone*. That certainly would've provided a lot more credibility. I mean why not, in true messianic fashion, hop right back on the donkey and go riding victoriously through Jerusalem, as you did just prior to your arrest? In fact, why not go knocking on the door of Pontius Pilate himself? Wouldn't you have loved to see the look on his face?

J: You should be writing spy novels.

DK: No, no—I can already see it on the silver screen. There you are, standing before the guy ultimately responsible for your death. Calmly and without flinching, you look him straight in the eye, slowly extending your upturned palms with their freshly healed wounds. Finally, with a condescending smirk, you speak: "Hi, remember *me*? We met a few days ago at the Praetorium." Now *that* would be the stuff of box office legends!

J: Good grief. Next you'll have me throwing roundhouse kicks at the high priest.

DK: Hey, not a bad idea.

J: *Aghhh.* You're so hopelessly… *Western.*

DK: But really, now—what about this Resurrection thing? Because without *that*, you'd have been just another disgruntled martyr with an attitude.

J: Let's clarify something. When we were discussing the "Great Commission," I suggested that we return later to the verse you alluded to from Luke—chapter 24, verse 46—because it's highly problematic. And here's why: the Resurrection has no foundation in ancient Judaism. The Israelites were never anticipating a Messiah who would be killed and then resurrected. So the Christian Resurrection was not a fulfillment of some revered Old Testament prophecy—because there *is* no such prophecy.

DK: Not so fast. The Luke passage says, "Then he opened their minds to understand the scriptures, and said to them, 'Thus it is written, that the Christ should suffer and on the third day rise from the dead…'" So, apparently the Resurrection *did* fulfill ancient prophecy.

J: You'd better re-examine the evidence, Holmes. There's not a single Old Testament passage predicting any messianic resurrection, and even in *my* day the notion would've been a joke. No serious Jew would've expected the Messiah to rise from the dead. Not after three days, not after three weeks—not even after three jugs of hooch. The Old Testament never calls for any resurrection of a coming savior-god. The gospel writer has me alluding to scripture that doesn't exist.

DK: I was always told that you were referring to Hosea 6:2, which says, "After two days he will revive us; on the third day he will raise us up."

J: Well, if that's what the writer of Luke was selling, then he was really stacking the deck. Start reading from the first verse of Hosea chapter four and you'll see that God was chiding his people for their faithlessness. The passage in question is the Lord's prediction of what his disobedient children will be saying when they realize the errors of their ways. They'll proclaim, "He'll revive us… He'll raise us up."

DK: Yeah, for some reason they're speaking in the plural.

J: Of course—because they're talking about *themselves*. There's not the slightest allusion to a future Christ or Messiah, much less to any miraculous resurrection from the dead.

DK: I'm embarrassed to admit it, but in all my years as a Christian, I never bothered to check it out for myself.

J: Don't feel too bad. Your ignorance qualifies you for membership in a pretty large club…

DK: Then let's tackle a question you posed earlier: what exactly was resurrected? Most Christians assume that the focus of the Resurrection was your *body*. But *you* say your body was no big deal.

J: It's the same error we discussed concerning the Crucifixion: the idea that my body was special. But even a *resurrected* body is still only a body. Eventually it stops functioning anyway, and then you're right back where you started.

DK: Not necessarily. Maybe God can create bodies that last forever.

J: Then why hasn't He done it?

DK: I dunno. Population control? Although come to think of it, you made the point earlier regarding Genesis 3:22 that, even from the beginning, God was never thrilled about the prospect of human immortality.

J: God has already assured your immortality—but immortality as *spirit,* not as flesh and blood. In the grand scheme of things, bodies are completely unnecessary; you don't need them for your existence. So the implication of the Apostles' Creed is dead wrong: resurrection of the body has *no relevance* to the life everlasting. And rising from the dead is improbable from the start, wouldn't you say?

DK: Yet there you sit!

J: Don't make the mistake of believing that you understand what's happening here. When I appear to people, which I do from time to time, they have no idea what they're witnessing. They can't really know who or what I am, where I came from or how I got here. Heck, they can't even answer those questions about *themselves.* Besides, my occasional appearance doesn't prove or confirm *any*thing about the Bible. Like I said, even in *my* day the concept of physical resurrection would've been a very tough sell. It's just not something the average citizen would've accepted. So no one really expected my reappearance after I was killed. Even my disciples didn't huddle with bated breath outside my tomb.

DK: No, in fact they all fled after your arrest. Although, scripture does indicate that those who saw you after your tomb was found empty were ultimately convinced of your bodily resurrection. It's an inspirational story, I suppose. But for those of us who weren't actually there, it's all pretty hard to accept. I guess it just requires a leap of faith.

J: Well, that's one *giant leap* for mankind. Fortunately, though, it's not a leap anyone's asking you to make. One of the earliest Christian writings, used as source material by the authors of Matthew and Luke, is a document called The Synoptic Sayings Source—also referred to by scholars simply as "Q." This document, along with The Gospel of Thomas, which has some parallel material, was written within the first two decades after my death. The four New Testament gospels, of course, were composed much later. This is critical, because neither "Q" nor The Gospel of Thomas consider my death an important facet of the Christian faith. Neither do they resort to any claims about resurrection. Their emphasis is on my *teachings.* New Testament accounts of the Crucifixion and the Resurrection didn't appear until *decades* after I was gone. That should tell you something.

DK: It tells me that our doctrines may need a little tweaking.

J: As far as I'm concerned, dogmatic adherence to doctrine is just close-minded conviction that won't be shaken by facts—and most religion is founded on this very basis. Religion plants the idea that unquestioning faith is *vital* to one's salvation, thereby discouraging critical inquiry. Anyhow, even if I say the Resurrection happened exactly as claimed, what difference would it make? I mean how would that help *you*? Would it bring you any closer to knowing yourself? In that sense, it can't help at all. So whether you take the gospel at face value doesn't matter in the least. God is neither impressed by your fervor nor offended by your doubt.

DK: The gospel says that even your friend Thomas was skeptical when he first saw you after the Resurrection. Apparently, the possibility of rising from the dead was completely foreign to his thought system. He didn't believe it was you until he touched the wounds on your palms.

J: Okay, but for *you* that's only a *story*. So you've got two choices: remain incredulous or accept it all on faith. Either way, it's got no connection with my message of spiritual liberation. *That* requires a very *different* kind of "hands-on" experience...

CHAPTER
FORTY ONE

DK: I suppose it's no surprise that New Testament accounts of your life would cause so much flak. First off, there's no biblical description of anyone actually confirming you dead. Also, there wasn't a single eyewitness to your Resurrection. We're told only that an obscure centurion informed Pilate that you had died and that Joseph of Arimathea removed you from the cross and took you to his own tomb site. So maybe the conspiracy folks are right. In theory, at least, it's possible that you hadn't really died.

J: Ah yes, the old trick of fooling the medical examiner by closing the eyes and going all day without breathing.

DK: But it's not just a question of vital signs. The story has *other* big problems, too. The author of Matthew says that an untimely darkness descended upon the earth for three hours prior to your death. Which kinda makes folks wonder what the hell happened to the sun. He also reports that when you died there was an earthquake. Unfortunately, neither of these mega-dramatic events has ever been substantiated by any *non-Christian* writings. And here's the *real* zinger: the gospel writer makes the remarkable claim—which, again, remains unverified—that when you breathed your last, lots of dead people rose from their graves and went to visit the townsfolk in Jerusalem.

J: Hmmnn. Evidently, resurrections that week were more common than sand flies...

DK: Finally, we're told that, several days after your death, you mysteriously began appearing to your friends. The book of 1 Corinthians says that you appeared first to Cephas, then to all twelve apostles, and ultimately to more than five hundred people at once. I can only imagine how much wine had to be conjured for *that* one.

J: If derision were a gift of the spirit, yours would've required delivery by freight.

DK: Listen, I'm willing to cut the scripture writer some slack and overlook the fact that you couldn't possibly have appeared to all twelve of your disciples after the Resurrection. Judas was already dead, so only eleven were left. But I'm definitely skeptical that you appeared to five hundred others. For starters, that's never mentioned in the four gospels. And suspiciously we've not found even one first-person account from that alleged crowd of five hundred witnesses. Even the gospel writers themselves are mysteriously silent on this issue insofar as any first-hand testimony. Not one of them says, "Oh, and by the way... I saw Jesus with my own two eyes a couple days after he was crucified, and the boy was livelier than a scalded cat."

J: No diaries stashed away in secret caves, eh?

DK: Not so far, at least. What's worse, not a single known historian of the day corroborates any of these epic events. Surely the era's most respected record-keepers would have made careful notes of the earthquake, the inexplicable three hours of darkness, and the stunning resurrections of people long deceased. I mean we have enough historical records from that era to fill a freakin' *library*, and yet *not one* of the writers talks about *you*. Instead, all we've got are some terribly biased Christian narratives, written no sooner than several decades after your death—and we don't even know for sure who *wrote* 'em. Now, truly I say unto thee: that's some pretty fishy journalism, dude!

J: Hey, gimme a break. Not one pen stroke of those writings was mine. I knew that future generations could never verify the events of my life. Do you think I'd allow your spiritual awakening to hinge on your willingness to accept, without a scrap of hard evidence, some of the most outrageous claims ever advanced?

DK: All I know for sure is that the Resurrection is Christianity's most imperative aspect: without it, the faith has no basis. And despite its scientific implausibility, the church says the Resurrection is critical to our salvation.

J: Nonsense. Again I ask: even if you embrace the Resurrection story exactly as recorded, what good does it do *you*? Does it merely give you hope that, despite your inevitable death, you might enjoy future glory in some faraway heaven? How in the world does that help you *now*?

DK: Well, like you said: at least it provides hope.

J: Hope is an item that's way overbought. If hope is the best that religion can offer, then it's time you went shopping somewhere else. Hope only covers your eyes with the blinding mud of anticipation. It sucks you into a black hole of needing reality to be different before you can be truly happy and really start living. It keeps you waiting for God to do something *tomorrow* that He damn well *should* be doing *today*.

DK: So hope is ultimately unhelpful.

J: In many ways, yes. But *faith*… now, *there's* an asset you can work with. If you can stop giving faith to your beliefs and instead bring that faith into every moment by not judging, clutching or resisting—well, *then* you've got something worth having. But living on *hope*? Forget about it.

DK: In that case, what good is resurrection of the body?

J: It's a useless idea. The only meaningful resurrection is the restoration to your awareness of your own divinity. And it either happens right now or not at all. So never mind this notion of bodily resurrection. The body is just one of the *myriad* forms in which you, as pure consciousness, experience and express yourself. Mine was no different.

DK: Then what's the connection between the Resurrection and salvation?

J: Physically, resurrection is irrelevant. Its *true* significance takes you *beyond* the idea that life is centered in the body. Learning this for yourself is the spiritual resurrection I allude to in the gospels. The *knowledge itself* is your salvation.

DK: But we're right back to the Christian dilemma. The church insists that the Resurrection has one main purpose: as the soul's only avenue for escape from hell.

J: How could *my body* possibly benefit *your soul*? Again: there *is* no hell, and your soul doesn't need salvaging. Salvation, which is *of* the mind and *in* the mind, is unrelated either to my body or to yours. In traditional Christianity, the Resurrection only serves to prove that I was special. Therefore, your own legitimacy as a child of God depends strictly upon your willingness to accept that baloney. Never let religion define your worthiness, because with God the issue was never in question.

DK: The church teaches that God does indeed love us. But it also warns us that our acceptance of you as his "only Son" is essential to our redemption.

J: So the church insists that you're either saved or condemned by your beliefs. But *how*? Beliefs are just thoughts, and the mind can focus on only one thought at a time. I mean you can't be thinking, "I believe in Jesus" at the same moment that you're thinking, "I'd better roll up the car windows before it rains."

DK: Whoa, there… hold up a sec. I'm about three steps behind.

J: In other words, you aren't Christian—or Muslim or Hindu or whatever—*by nature*. Because there's nothing about the self that could be located, identified or labeled. So it's pretty funny that a bunch of fraternity members, for example, would feel such strong affinity for a couple of random letters from the Greek alphabet. No part of their essence has even a slight connection with any of that silliness. People are convinced that they're one thing or another only when they're actually *thinking* about it. Catch my drift?

DK: Oh, I'm *drifting* alright.

J: Maybe another example will clear it up. Let's say you accidentally touch a red-hot stove and you're suddenly in excruciating pain. For all practical purposes, in that instant you're no longer Christian, male, Republican, zookeeper—or even a human being. Because in such moments you're not *aware* of yourself in those terms. In fact, when your attention is completely focused in the present moment, you essentially *become the experience*—in this case, extreme pain. Can you see that, in a given instant, you're nothing but your present-moment attention?

DK: So upon burning my finger at the stove, I wouldn't be aware of the notion "I'm a Christian"—at least not until the initial moment of distress had passed and I had opportunity to regain my senses. Only then could I resume my "Christian-ness" concept.

J: Or, for that matter, any *other* concept. But even so, every concept or memory you have is still only a thought or series of thoughts. Concepts have to be recalled and *thought* about before they have relevance. Take your most cherished beliefs, ideas, or self-definitions and see how meaningful they are the next time you're having an orgasm.

DK: I'll make a note…

J: This stuff may sound a little esoteric, but in fact you enter this selfless state every morning upon awakening. For a brief period during the initial state of grogginess, there's only pure awareness. It takes time before thought and the notion of "I" arises. So this "I'm a Christian" concept is, like any other idea, relevant only when you *think* about it. Your attention can be on only one thought in a given moment, so you're able to think only one thought at a time. It may not seem that way, because thoughts come at you so quickly and the gap between them is almost imperceptible. But the gap is always there, separating one thought from the next. Can you see the bizarre implications of this as it relates to Christian salvation?

DK: Well, if what you say is true, then our soul's redemption would essentially depend on the specific thoughts we happen to be thinking when our bodies stop functioning.

J: *Now* you're running at a gallop. So what happens if your dying thought is, "I should have taken that job in Seattle"?

DK: It does sound pretty crazy in those terms. On the other hand, I committed my life to God when I was a teenager. I imagine the church would say that an earnest declaration of faith makes an important shift in the *soul*, but not necessarily in the mind-body entity.

J: Thoughts don't alter your eternal reality, and that's where most religions crash and burn. The essence of Christian salvation is that God is ever changing his mind about his children and is continuously shifting his intentions about their destiny. And all of this based solely upon their *thoughts*!

DK: So if we believe the church and its salvation theology, God's judgment is determined entirely by what passes through our minds—by what we elect to think about and believe.

J: Right. Which basically means that *you* have become God and that ego has supplanted God's will and imposed its own instead. God is reduced to just another figure in the story and is fundamentally helpless to save his children with any degree of assurance. So biblically, something doesn't click. One minute, God's declaring that everything in the universe is "very good." Then, without explanation or notification, He's developing flammable water for his hellish lake of fire.

DK: Yeah, He's terribly upset by our inherited "evil" nature.

J: And yet the moment you profess *me* as your Lord and savior, God smiles once again and welcomes you back into the inner circle.

DK: I'm breathless with befuddlement.

J: Breathe a giant sigh of relief, my friend, because none of that ecclesiastical swill means a thing. God *never* changes his mind about you—and He hasn't since the moment of your creation.

DK: Shouldn't we at least allow that God *could* change his mind?

J: Only if we allow that his intentions can be foiled or that his initial assessments can be mistaken. In the case of humanity, either God has lousy foresight or He created you imperfect from the start. If the first is true, then He has no business issuing prophecy or chiding anyone else for *their* lack of vision. If the second is true, then He has no right to judge or condemn. And if *either* is true, then He's not the God the church would have you believe He is.

DK: You're obviously leading me *somewhere*, but I haven't a clue where it is. All this theological bantering is the intellectual equivalent of eating celery: it leaves me feeling as hungry as when I started.

J: Then let's cut off the fat and get to the roast: *who cares* what happened decades ago—or even yesterday? A past declaration of faith is meaningless. Because unless you're thinking of something *right now*, it's beyond your awareness and virtually lifeless. Take someone who's deathly afraid of heights. He may be the bravest guy in town, but put him on the ledge of a cliff and the poor guy's a basket case. He's consumed by fear. But place him in his favorite restaurant across the table from a stunning brunette, and suddenly his acrophobia's nowhere to be found. In that moment it doesn't exist.

DK: And your point is?

J: *So what* if you accepted me as your Lord and savior back in high school? Unless you're actually thinking about it *now*, it's just another dead thought, long vanished from consciousness.

DK: Certainly *God* remembers my profession of faith.

J: Ha! You think God is busy cluttering the great Universal Mind with the convoluted, strung-out dream sequences of everyone who's ever lived?

DK: Are you saying that God has no memory?

J: I'm explaining that God lives only in the present moment—because only the present moment *exists*. It's self-evident that reality can only be real *right now*. That's why the salvation peddled by religion is hogwash: it has you constantly *looking ahead* for your deliverance. It's a giant game of spiritual Three-card Monte, and *you're* the gullible dupe!

DK: Religion's methodology may be more bizarre than I imagined. I'm beginning to see that our souls don't need to be protected, redeemed or altered. But then, what exactly is salvation?

J: Well, if you accept that human ignorance has resulted in what sometimes amounts to a living hell, then it's obvious that the "good news" of salvation could mean only one thing: freedom from the suffering born of ignorance. Salvation is relevant only within the false state of separation and has no meaning in reality, where the knowledge of your eternal unity with God is heaven itself.

DK: Spirituality aside, sometimes we need saving from *material* circumstance.

J: Then what are you to conclude about a God whose saving grace is *withheld*? I mean the God of religion may work the occasional miracle, but He also allows wars, famines and pandemics to wipe out millions at a crack. If religion's God gets credit for saving you from periodic need or disaster, then He's gotta take the blame for the failings and tragedies as well. Given the often-cruel nature of worldly existence, how much concern could God really have for *bodies*?

DK: I suppose you're gonna say that it's all beside the point because it's all part of the dream.

J: Right on target, ace. No matter what your perception is showing you, you're never really in need of anything but awakening. That's the one need you have but consistently fail to recognize.

DK: So in reality there's nothing to save.

J: Nothing at all. It's ironic, but you could view salvation as liberation from the belief that you *need* saving.

DK: Then what is the purpose of the world?

J: The world has no high meaning or purpose. For the awakened ones, it's a temporary source of joy and amusement—a wondrous wandering through a fascinating playground of form. For those still asleep, however, the world can be hell itself and could have only one function—to serve in healing the separation. But make no mistake: although spirit *inspires,* it doesn't *participate*. How could it "do" anything in a world with no objective reality?

CHAPTER FORTY TWO

DK: So the man walks out of the woods after twenty centuries of strumming harps in heaven and immediately starts a campaign of philosophical carpet-bombing. No world, no bodies, no evil—and no material existence! Lawd o' mercy, you're stretching me too thin.

J: Well, all of it exists in the sense that it presently affects and influences you. But none of it is ultimately real. An important lesson from *A Course in Miracles* has a lot to say about what's real and what isn't. Referring to this very subject it says, "Belief is powerful indeed. The thoughts you hold are mighty, and illusions are as strong in their effects as is the truth. A madman thinks the world he sees is real, and does not doubt it. Nor can he be swayed by questioning his thoughts' *effects*. It is but when their *source* is raised to question that the hope of freedom comes to him at last. Yet is salvation easily achieved, for anyone is free to change his mind, and all his thoughts change with it…"

DK: So the "source," in this case, is a distorted thought system that sees things as separate, chaotic, or even threatening.

J: Right. And that's a key precept in the *Course*, so let's drill a bit deeper…

"There is no world! This is the central thought… Not everyone is ready to accept it, and each one must go as far as he can let himself be led along the road to truth. He will return and go still farther, or perhaps step back a while and then return again. But healing is the gift of those who are prepared to learn there is no world, and can accept the lesson now. Their readiness will bring the lesson to them in some form which they can understand and recognize. Some see it suddenly on point of death, and rise to teach it. Others find it in experience that is not of this world, which shows them that the world does not exist because what they behold must be the truth, and yet it clearly contradicts the world."

DK: Sounds like an experience I had many years ago during one of my life's more depressing periods. I was sitting at home one evening by myself, when out of nowhere came this astonishing wave of ecstasy and bliss. During those incredible minutes of revelation, or whatever it was, the world was suddenly inconsequential—it barely had a thread of reality. The central impression was the indescribable joy of existence.

J: And that's how it is in the original state of unity. Here's a bit more from the same lesson:

"…the world does not exist. And if it is indeed your own imagining, then you can loose it from all things you ever thought it was by merely changing all the thoughts that gave it these appearances… You are as God created you. There is no place where you can suffer, and no time that can bring change to your eternal state. How can a world of time and place exist, if you remain as God created you?"

DK: A challenging point. It would seem that suffering and divine perfection are polar opposites. But if the world is only an *idea*, as the *Course* says, then what of the vast millions who are counting on you to save them after they die? Scripture says you'll resurrect their lifeless corpses during the last days, at which time they'll join with you in floating off to heaven amidst the angels' chorus and the blaring horns.

J: Is the writer describing a theology or a Spielberg production?

DK: C'mon, we already talked about the script that calls for the trumpet to sound, the angels to appear, and for resurrected bodies to go flying into the clouds. It's salvation, Christian style—directly from the New Testament.

J: Which also states that "*Now* is the day of salvation." Again, future redemption is meaningless, and beliefs are just a lazy stand-in for thinking.

DK: Look, I apologize if I'm over-pulling the taffy, but I'm still compelled to press you about the Christian party line and the main events of your life. For example, the New Testament says that, after the Resurrection, you ascended to heaven. What about that?

J: You've got the same problem with the Ascension that you had with the Resurrection. If you assume that it applies only to me, then you've wandered way off the trail. Ascension is the lifting of the reawakened soul to its creation state of oneness with God—the leaving behind of the dream world. The opening of consciousness that I attained is available to everyone at any moment, and history is packed with real-life examples.

DK: Then we don't have to buy off on a physical Resurrection or Ascension?

J: Let's get something straight: I'm not asking you to believe *any*thing. All beliefs are based on uncertainty, and all uncertainty is just ignorance of the self. I'm urging you to make the journey inward to the place of true *knowing*. Once you've done *that*, you'll never again limp around on the crutches of belief or assumption.

DK: I'm beginning to think your agony on the cross was entirely unnecessary.

J: Well, unfortunately I wasn't given the option of retiring, and those who wanted me dead were in no mood for compromise. Besides, it would've really screwed up the cadence of the Apostles' Creed: "He suffered under Pontius Pilate, was defrocked, and went on to make a fortune in the wine business."

DK: *Heh heh.* Doesn't exactly flow trippingly off the tongue… But honestly—after all you've said today, do you still expect us to believe that you didn't die in vain?

J: I expect you to realize that *I did not die.*

DK: You mean because you were the Christ.

J: Not *the* Christ. An expression *of* the Christ—the complete embodiment of its holy, celestial nature. "Christ" is derived from the Greek CHRISTOS, meaning "the anointed." I became what you and all your brothers and sisters will also become: fully awakened children of God. Like me, each of you is divinely "anointed," a perfect and blessed reflection of the Cosmic Supreme. But it does you no good if you don't *know* it. Truth that isn't *your* truth is un-truth.

DK: Once more you're contradicting long-established biblical doctrine regarding your special nature. I'll refer again to the famous passage from Philippians, which declares that "at the name of Jesus every knee should bow" and that "every tongue should confess that Jesus Christ is Lord." The literalists say that anyone not submitting to you in this fashion will be damned to the fires of eternal hell along with Satan and his fiendish legions.

J: *Holy mother-of-pearl!* They really should ban those do-it-yourself home lobotomy kits...

CHAPTER
FORTY THREE

DK: By the way, you never elaborated on your possible connection to India. In addition to the camp that claims you traveled there after surviving the Crucifixion, other writers assert that you were there during your "lost" years, long before you began your public ministry in Palestine. Even Matthew says, "... and *coming to his own country* he taught them in their synagogue, so that they were astonished, and said, 'Where did this man get this wisdom and these mighty works? Is not this the carpenter's son? Is not his mother called Mary? And are not his brothers...and...all his sisters with us? Where then did this man get all this?'" So the passage doesn't leave much doubt that you'd been gone a long time and that people in your home region were impressed by the knowledge and power you had acquired.

J: Why should anyone doubt that I would travel far and wide to learn all I could about the mystery of life? As you said in your letter, the gospels fail to account for a pretty big chunk of my history. Let's just say that through travel, study, meditation, and tapping into the ancient wisdom of others, I finally saw that everything I was searching for had been tracking me like a shadow, and the treasure I sought had been with me from the start. Naturally, the same is true for you. So while my personal story may be interesting, it's no substitute for knowledge of self. And for *that* you needn't even leave your bedroom. You have everything you nee—

DK: I know, I know. We have everything we need *within*.

J: Well, Hallelujah, son! Whack you over the head with somethin' fifteen, twenty times and you're on top of it like a duck on a June bug!

DK: You're only as good as your teacher.

J: *Heh heh.* Joy on the day that your wisdom keeps pace with your wit…

DK: Evidently, Judaism wasn't your only "course of study," so to speak.

J: I honored the truth *wherever* I found it. In particular, I gained a lot of esoteric knowledge from the Essenes, and a good bit of my teaching came from my association with them. But I didn't subscribe to everything they proposed. For example, they were teetotalers, whereas I liked a good belt of wine now and then.

DK: I've heard a little about the Essenes. Weren't they considered a cult?

J: Hey, *there's* a winning strategy: discredit something by *labeling* it. When another group's ideology threatens your own, just call it a cult and you instantly remove all legitimacy. It's one of the oldest plays in the book. In fact, stop writing for a minute and pull out your dictionary.

DK: Got it right here…

J: Okay, now look up the definition of "cult."

DK: Let's see here… "A group of followers. A sect which adheres to a particular set of practices or rituals."

J: By *that* description, then, Christianity is the biggest cult on earth. My own disciples would easily have qualified as a cult in the eyes of both the Romans *and* the Jewish rabbinical authorities. In the years immediately following my death, if there was one group that could safely be called a cult, it was the Christians. After all, they were the new kids on the block. So it's a real joke for present-day Christians to legitimize themselves by speaking condescendingly of the Essenes, or of anyone else, as a cult.

DK: Frank Zappa said the only difference between a cult and a religion is the amount of real estate it owns.

J: Sure, it's mostly a matter of net worth and the number of assets on the balance sheet. And by the way, there were *several* major "cults" in my neck of the woods. Along with the Essenes, we also had the infamous Sadducees and Pharisees. The Zealots had a pretty good following too. And there were several others. Christians are pretty familiar with the Sadducees and Pharisees, since they're referred to several times in the gospels; but most believers have never even heard of the Essenes, because the New Testament never mentions them.

DK: Yeah, which is very strange, since the Dead Sea Scrolls, some of which pre-date your birth by more than two hundred years, show that somebody was practicing a kind of prototype Christianity *many generations* before your followers did. Most Scroll scholars seem to think it was the Essenes—although others argue the point. Some researchers have suggested that even John the Baptist, who evidently was a very learned man and quite spiritually advanced, may have been an Essene who grew up in Qumran.

J: And the Essenes, along with other non-traditional, pre-Christian Jewish groups, had quite a few rituals that Christians may find uncomfortably familiar. For example, the Essenes practiced baptism for the remission of sins and performed healing by the laying on of hands. They also had a communion consisting of bread and wine, and their internal structure was practically identical to church government as described in the Book of Acts. They even referred to themselves as "the meek," "the poor," "the New Covenanters," "the chosen ones" and "the elect."

DK: So these folks actually scooped the Christians.

J: Yes, and the timing wasn't even close. Essene teachings had been respected and revered for at least five hundred years before my birth. Evidence for some of their traditions dates back even as far as the Sumerian glyphs, around 4000 BCE. And the fingerprints of these early traditions appear not only in Christianity but in nearly *all* of the world's major religions. So the New Testament's failure to mention the Essenes is pretty darned suspicious.

DK: I know that some scholars believe the Essenes, or perhaps their offshoots, actually *were* the original Christians and that their writings may have comprised the earliest Christian scriptures. And apparently some of those first works did actually reference the Essenes. But church authorities gradually laundered them.

J: Bear in mind that most of the New Testament was written *outside Judea*, some of it a century or more after my death. So it's quite obvious that the books of the New Testament couldn't possibly have been the earliest Christian texts. In fact, you've got *several* problems during the decades between the Crucifixion and the scribing of the New Testament. Not only did the languages evolve, causing serious problems for interpreters and translators, but there was plenty of opportunity for distortion, embellishment or outright misrepresentation.

DK: Unless, of course, all the writing was done by God Himself.

J: In which case He's got a helluva lot of 'splainin' to do…

CHAPTER FORTY FOUR

DK: Hey, I've got a small gripe.

J: Go ahead.

DK: You won't get upset?

J: I've only been cross once.

DK: Christ the comedian—who woulda figured? So my problem is this: Your view of Christianity clearly challenges the respectability it enjoys across so much of the globe. Now, no one can deny that humanity's in bad shape and that Christianity certainly hasn't made our world into a paradise. And we're in full agreement that religions have been responsible for as much conflict and bloodshed over the centuries as just about anything one could name. Nearly *all* of 'em could use a good kick in the frock. But still, maybe we're not giving credit where it's due. Perhaps there's some merit to the church's claim that, despite its many failings, its influence on the world has been mostly positive—if not always on the *mundane* level, then possibly on the *spiritual*.

J: Listen, let's not beat around the burning bush. Historically there's not the slightest reason to believe that Christianity provides any large-scale solutions to *anything*. In fact, its polarizing dogmas have frequently added to the suffering. Bertrand Russell went so far as to compare literalist Christianity with Communism. He said their most dangerous features were frighteningly similar: "fanatical acceptance of doctrines embodied in a sacred book, unwillingness to examine these doctrines critically, and savage persecution of those who reject them." Russell's stance was clear: "The whole contention that Christianity has had an elevating moral influence can only be maintained by wholesale ignorance or falsification of the historical evidence."

DK: Okay, but you'd expect that from a guy who wrote *Why I am Not a Christian*.

J: But was he wrong? I mean *really*—what has Christendom given the world that the church considers so indispensable?

DK: Well, I won't try to argue that it helps relieve suffering by feeding the poor and caring for the sick and all that, because then you'll say that kindness certainly didn't originate with the church and that people don't need religion in order to show compassion. But what about all the great Christian architecture, literature, music, and art?

J: Kind of a lame offering, considering the church's many centuries of violence and oppression. If it meant avoiding their barbaric fate, I'd venture that all those ever tortured or killed as heretics or heathens would've happily deprived the world of the Sistine Chapel and Handel's *Messiah*.

DK: At least Christianity helped establish the calendar.

J: *Heh heh.* I was looking for something a bit more substantial...

DK: What about monotheism? Weren't Judaism and Christianity the first religions to recognize only one God?

J: Even though he couldn't make it stick, the father of the Egyptian boy-king Tutankhamun, Pharaoh Akhenaten, is generally credited as the first in recorded history to attempt establishing full-scale monotheism. The great Persian empire also had a one-god religion that could be argued to have preceded Judaism. These facts are probably moot, though, because it's well known among scholars that the Old Testament refers not just to *one* God, but to *many*. Bible translators nearly always use the word "god," in the singular, when in many, many instances the original text contains the word *"elohim,"* which is Hebrew for either *god*, in the singular, or *gods*, in the plural, depending on context and other factors. Many people have the false impression that the entire Old Testament refers to the words and actions of just one deity—but that's simply not true. Hebrew perspective on the subject was complex, and it varied significantly over the centuries. So Jewish scriptures may indeed *appear* to focus on just one god, but the early Israelites weren't always thinking in terms of monotheism, which is quite clear from their behavior. Even Yahweh Himself never tells the Israelites that other gods don't *exist*; He merely orders everyone not to pay them any *attention*. But never mind Judaism. I'm curious to know how you figure that Christianity is monotheistic.

DK: I already know where you're going. You're gonna say that Christianity actually has *three* deities: the Father, the Son, and the Holy Spirit. But the church says that's not polytheism because they're all part of the one God.

J: Alright, but how is that any different from, say, Hinduism? In the same way that a single ray of light splits into many colors by passing through a prism, the various Hindu gods and goddesses are considered manifestations of the one Supreme source, called Brahman. Christianity, with three distinct members in *its* Godhead, is essentially no different.

DK: I guess that's reasonable. I mean if we're gonna tolerate the argument with the one religion, then we have to accept it with the other.

J: And let's not disregard that the God of the Old Testament and the God of the New Testament have virtually nothing in common. They seem, in fact, to be two wholly different characters. So Hinduism and Christianity are both either monotheistic *or* polytheistic, depending on how you view it. But getting back to the main thrust, surely the Christian church offers something more innovative and significant than its somewhat dubious claim of only one God.

DK: I suppose the church would say that Christianity's chief contribution is that it gives humanity hope of salvation.

J: Well, there's certainly nothing original about *that*. Religion has proffered saving of the soul practically from its inception. Besides, it's a helluva strange salvation that leaves so much death and suffering in its wake. Going by the headlines, I'd say that Christianity and other religions are as likely to *destroy* the world as they are to *redeem* it.

DK: Much more talk like *this* and you'll get *me* crucified.

J: Relax, it only hurts for a while...

CHAPTER FORTY FIVE

DK: So the big lesson is that we don't need religion, because we're hooked at the hip with God even though most of don't know it. It's a nice idea—but it'll never fly with John Q. Public.

J: Hey, this ain't some warm and fuzzy New Age feel-good slant. The understanding of cosmic unity has been around for thousands of years and was an essential concept even in original Greco-Christian theology. Two of Christendom's most respected early theologians, Clement of Alexandria and Origen, were both revered teachers who understood well the principle of oneness within multiplicity and the inseparable connection of all things to what they called "First Cause."

DK: No doubt you've got quotes.

J: Clement wrote of being "brought together into one love, according to the union of the essential unity..." He urged his readers to "follow after union, seeking after the good Monad." He spoke of "the union of many in one" and "the production of divine harmony out of a medley of sounds and division." Origen asked of a particular passage, "...what can the meaning of Scripture be except the harmony and unity of the many?" It was Origen, incidentally, who referred to me as "the Sun of Righteousness" and declared that those who emulated my example would unite with me and would themselves become Christs. An early writing called "The Gospel of Philip" states the same thing regarding those who achieve "*gnosis*," which we'll discuss in more detail shortly. The main point is that *everyone* is potentially the Christ.

DK: I still insist that something sets you apart. The New Testament is jammed with so many stories of your godlike powers and your crowd-stirring charisma that I would think *some* of it must be accurate.

J: Even so, I wasn't the trailblazer most Christians seem to think I was. The average Christian has no idea that large chunks of his religion were "borrowed," shall we say, from other, far older traditions. Some had existed for centuries, or even millennia, when Christianity was still in diapers.

DK: What's the story?

J: It all begins with the ancient "Mystery" religions and the concept of a slain-and-resurrected godman whose mission is to save humanity from sin and death. The Mysteries flourished around the ancient Mediterranean, and each tradition had its own variations on the central deity figure. But in nearly every case, this divine or supernatural being was revered for wielding miraculous powers, unjustly suffering death at the hands of evil persecutors, and ultimately bringing salvation to the people by sacrificially atoning for their sins and delivering their souls from corruption and punishment.

DK: Who *was* this godman?

J: Well, he had lots of identities through the centuries, but he was essentially the same mythical being in different cultural guises. He arose first in ancient Egypt as the solar god Osiris, and his story appears in pyramid texts written at least twenty-five centuries before my birth. The *Book of the Dead* says that Osiris, also the god of resurrection and of the underworld, came to save the fallen, who now resided outside the Garden of Eden. In true godman fashion, Osiris is unjustly murdered by his brother Seth, and his body is then cut into fourteen pieces and scattered throughout the land. Afterward, he's magically reassembled by the goddess Isis. His body is then wrapped in linen and he's soon resurrected, thereafter granting rebirth and everlasting life to the faithful. Osiris had scores of names, but a few would be especially interesting to Christians: "King of Kings," "Lord of Lords," "the Resurrection and the Life," and "the Good Shepherd." Osiris was also said to cause people to be "born again."

DK: Sounds like you saviors follow some kind of script...

J: Later, in Greece, Osiris was fused with the popular wine god Dionysus, although he had other Greek names as well. And his legend steadily spread. In Persia he was called Mithras. In Italy he was Bacchus. In Asia Minor he was Attis, and so on. But their similarities are too consistent to be ignored. That's why, nearly three hundred years before me, this ubiquitous godman was already referred to by the combined name Osiris-Dionysus.

DK: So when *you* were born, other savior-gods were already being worshipped.

J: The deities of the Mysteries had been revered far and wide for centuries, and Palestine was swarming with followers of these various religions. Christianity arrived relatively late to the party and was started by people who were already comfortable with the concept of a world-saving godman. So even though Christianity's foundation was Judaism, many of its building blocks came from the assorted Osiris-Dionysus legends.

DK: I don't get it. What does the biblical Christ have in common with those mythical muckety-mucks of the Mysteries?

J: I'll give some examples and you can judge for yourself...

The varied pre-Christian myths of Osiris-Dionysus have him on earth as part god and part man. Born of a virgin, OD's birth date is often given as December 25th, and sometimes the event is even heralded by a star. Surrounded by twelve disciples, Osiris-Dionysus turns water into wine, helps fishermen fill their nets, exorcises demons, heals the incurably sick, calms raging waters and conjures miraculous meals for his followers.

DK: Man, you must feel like a Xerox copy.

J: There's more. Osiris-Dionysus rides triumphantly through town on a donkey and is later betrayed for thirty silver coins, a theme also associated with the death of Socrates some four hundred years before me. Ultimately Osiris-Dionysus is crucified in a sacrificial offering for the sins of the world. His mutilated corpse is wrapped in linen and anointed with myrrh.

DK: I'd say we're getting way beyond statistical coincidence.

J: But we're not finished. Osiris-Dionysus resurrects on the third day, reappears in the flesh to his followers and then ascends back to heaven, waiting to serve as divine judge at the end of time. In some versions of his mythology, he dies and resurrects on the exact days that some early Christians employed to mark my own death and resurrection: March 23rd and March 25th.

DK: Well, it's no great puzzle why the church sweeps its ancestry under the rug. Its storyline painfully parallels the old pagan motifs.

J: And we've barely scratched the surface. In some ways, Christianity and paganism were practically identical twins. Nearly three thousand years before my birth, the sun god Horus was a powerful figure among the Egyptians. Some ancient records establish him as the son of Osiris, who later inspired the godmen of the Mysteries. His mythologies are inconsistent and diffused among disparate sources, but they contain elements that should sound pretty familiar to Christians…

Horus was known as "the good shepherd," "the lamb," "the son of man," and "the word made flesh." He was also called "the anointed one," which, again, is the literal meaning of "Christ."

DK: Boy, the stuff they don't tell us in Sunday school!

J: Horus' mythology also has him struggling with his archrival Set, the Egyptian god of the desert and of chaos. I reportedly struggled in the desert with Satan—Christianity's ruler of *spiritual* chaos—where we, too, engaged in a cosmic scuffle of Good-versus-Evil. Horus was said to have resurrected after death and was believed to bring eternal life to his faithful followers. As you can see, Christianity was basically a cut-and-paste version of the religions of ancient Egypt and later traditions known as the Mysteries.

DK: The *biggest* mystery is why the gospel writers weren't sued for plagiarism!

J: You can bet your bottom shekel that these similarities are no coincidence. Christian literature contains loads of thematic elements lifted straight from the pages of ancient paganism. Believe me, Christianity isn't just *any* old religion: it's a genuine *Mystery*…

Chapter Forty Six

DK: I just got a call from your agent. He says crucifix sales are *plummeting.*

J: Look, I realize I'm rocking the boat here—but facts are facts. Christianity was strictly an offshoot of paganism, and the gospel version of my life is just a clever clerical clone job. That's why taking the Christian saga literally is loco. You might as well do the same with Aesop's fables.

DK: How did your life story become so distorted?

J: Once Christianity solidified into the rigid and powerful Church of Rome, all vestiges of the mystical forms that preceded it were pretty much eradicated. From there on, literalists controlled the presses, so to speak. They were then free to fashion their religion as they pleased.

DK: So Christianity was just a newer twist on a very old tale.

J: It was paganism with a new pair of shoes. And most early-Christian groups knew very well that gospel claims about me were just fresher variations of ancient pagan Mystery themes—themes that were clearly meant to be *symbolic*. One of the earliest and better-known groups with this view came to be called the Gnostics, a term that wasn't actually introduced until the eighteenth century. Not all Gnostics were Christian, though; some were Jewish or even pagan. And the groups that *could* be categorized as "Gnostic" were every bit as diversified in orientation and opinion as the countless sects of early- and modern-day Christians.

DK: What was their common thread?

J: In general, Gnostics were seeking what I referred to awhile ago: a state of GNOSIS, which is the Greek word for understanding or knowledge. In their case, it implied striving to attain a mystical, intuitive insight into the celestial mysteries, both spiritual and scientific. Most Gnostics understood that the revered godman stories of antiquity were supposed to lead initiates *beyond* the shallow waters of formal religion to an inner revelation of the divine. And this notion was very familiar even in the earliest days of the church. Just before Easter, during the vernal equinox and the festival of the "resurrected" sun, many Christians would conduct a baptism ceremony called PHOTISMOS, meaning "illumination." Now, this ain't exactly the behavior of fire-preaching, heaven-and-hell literalists.

DK: Yet during your ministry, you never said *anything* about GNOSIS.

J: I discussed it *frequently*. But remember: the New Testament comprises only a narrow sliver of the early-Christian literary universe, and it was heavily edited in an effort to purge any trace of Gnosticism. But because many of its censors didn't have noses for GNOSIS, some of the Gnostic thinking slipped through anyway. Most Christians don't realize it, but if they know what to look for, a lot of Gnostic influence is staring 'em in the face right there in the gospels. All they need is the "secret code."

DK: Which is what?

J: Nothing but a slightly different *perspective*. As made very clear in several of my gospel quotes, the kingdom of heaven lies "within." So what could it be? Only one thing: a transformed consciousness. And here's the key to breaking the code...

In most of the passages where I'm quoted referring to the "kingdom of heaven" or the "kingdom of God," just substitute the phrase "cosmic consciousness." Immediately some of these mysterious parables begin to make sense. In fact, in many instances they don't make sense *until* this understanding is applied. Once it is, you can begin deciphering some of the stories' hidden wisdom.

DK: A few examples would help.

J: Alright. I once told a group of my disciples that there were some present who would not "taste death" until they experienced the kingdom of God—that is, cosmic consciousness. Here's another: unless you become as little children, you cannot enter into the kingdom. And why not? Because "the kingdom," or the enlightenment of cosmic consciousness, generally comes to those who are unpretentious, simple and without guile. I was referring to humility as a condition for spiritual awakening.

DK: Ah, okay. Therefore, blessed are the meek and the poor in spirit.

J: Now you're catching on. Of course, not all of the "kingdom" parables are that simple. Some are considerably more complex and require a good bit of wisdom to interpret. But they're all pointing to the same thing: a radical rebirth of consciousness and the conditions most favorable for its emergence. You can uncover the concealed teachings of these stories once you've got the proper bearing. Even the apostle Paul's writings contain these same kinds of cloaked references to the new awareness, and in some instances Paul refers to anyone who has it as simply being "in Christ."

DK: For instance?

J: In 2 Corinthians 12, Paul speaks of an incident, years earlier, of having met a person who was "in Christ." But Paul knew *hundreds* of Christians. Why would he single out one man in this special way? Only one answer makes sense: Because of his powerful experience on his famous trip to Damascus, Paul understood enough about the cosmic state that he would have recognized it in another.

DK: And all of that relates to this thing called GNOSIS?

J: What else *could* it mean if "God's kingdom" lies "within you"? In the original Greek text, 1 Corinthians 12:8 has Paul, a sort of quasi-Gnostic and the earliest of the New Testament authors, referring specifically to GNOSIS as a spiritual gift.

DK: So the New Testament does indeed have serious Gnostic connections.

J: Yes, and in ways that most Christians would find shocking. In fact, much of the gospel of John is essentially a Gnostic composition, starting with its very introduction positioning *me* as the new LOGOS, a concept handed down from ancient paganism. These hints of Gnosticism are scattered throughout the New Testament. One example appears in Mark, the earliest of the New Testament gospels, and similarly in Luke, where I tell my disciples, "To you it has been given to know the secrets of the kingdom of God; but to others only in parables…" Now, *here's* the surprising part: in the earliest Greek text, the word translated as 'secrets' is MYSTERIA.

DK: The Mysteries!

J: Exactly. And that particular passage prompts an important question: If soul salvation through "acceptance of Jesus Christ" were all that anyone needed to know, then why would I have to explain anything to my disciples *in secret*?

DK: I can't imagine.

J: It was because I was feeding milk to a spiritually infantile public while covertly giving my closest students the meatier teaching of enlightenment. Paul occasionally mentions having the same frustration.

DK: Why all the cloak-and-dagger?

J: Well, most people consider enlightenment a radical notion. It makes their external gods and authorities obsolete and supersedes their treasured scriptures and belief structures. It implies that their understanding of reality is terribly warped and incomplete. Their egos, of course, perceive this to be quite threatening. Nevertheless, I had a job to do. But as you can see, much of it had to be done behind closed doors. And while I held great respect for the followers of Judaism, I ultimately told them, as a clever person once quipped, "You go Yahweh and I'll go mine."

DK: So even though it threatened certain religious groups, the concept of spiritual illumination was apparently old-hat material to students of the Mysteries.

J: Sure, because they appreciated the value of *symbolism*. That's why they rejected Christian literalism as kid's stuff. But even the Gnostics weren't sailing uncharted waters. Five hundred years before me, pagan philosophers were already scoffing at taking the godman stories literally.

DK: Did any influential early Christians hold that view?

J: Clement of Alexandria comes to mind. Although he was beatified by the Catholic Church and is traditionally thought of as a literalist, his thinking was far closer to Gnosticism. He said outright that my words were symbolic and were never intended literally. He called Gnostics the "true" Christians and fully embraced the process of *gnosis*. And other important figures in the church held similar views. They didn't appreciate the growing Christian tendency to historicize popular ancient legends. In fact, another beatified Catholic saint, Dionysius of Areopagite, said that apart from the wisdom of their *encoded* meanings, the Christian scriptures were nothing but childish myths.

DK: And they actually *sainted* this guy? I'm surprised they didn't hang him as a heretic. Who else didn't march lockstep with the establishment?

J: Clement's successor, Origen, certainly didn't. He's another highly respected early-Christian philosopher whose work is far more liberal than most traditionalists would care to believe. Although church apologists sometimes quote the works of Origen to bolster their cause, Origen's philosophical stance was miles from Christian orthodoxy. He wasn't Gnostic, however, and in fact wrote treatises refuting certain Gnostic tenets. But he did believe that *all* beings would eventually attain salvation, which to him was a purely intellectual realm where the soul would forever explore the great mysteries of the divine.

DK: Plainly no literalist.

J: Not in the least. He cleanly admitted that many gospel stories were obviously allegorical and that some were not only untrue but were "utterly impossible." He declared that even the writings of

302

the Apostles were not "purely historical" and contained "incidents that never occurred."

DK: Definitely not in the fundamentalist camp.

J: No, in fact Origen felt that literalist Christianity was strictly a product for the sophomoric mainstream. He said the subtlety and sophistication of certain pagan philosophy was like high cuisine, whereas literalist Christianity was nothing but unrefined fare for the masses. To use a present-day analogy, Origen viewed Christian literalism as a kind of fast-food religion for those who didn't want to do any real thinking. And despite being Christian, he fully realized, and thus taught his students, that a thorough comprehension of Christianity required solid historical understanding of the *pagan* world.

DK: I'm still grappling with the idea that Christianity's roots took hold in the soils of paganism.

J: Paganism suffers a lousy reputation that's mostly undeserved; and it's extremely hypocritical for Christians to belittle such a wide swath of ancient wisdom by maliciously calling it "pagan." I mean they'll jeer at the notion of worshipping the sun—which is at least something that can be seen and felt—and yet they don't hesitate to send *their own* prayers and reverence soaring into the vacuum of outer space. Nevertheless, they spit out the word "pagan" as if it's a curse. That's just pure ignorance, though, because Christianity itself is essentially a pagan religion.

DK: Alright, but you've got to admit that paganism contained elements that were certainly primitive and unenlightened.

J: Sure, but so does Christianity. Take the Eucharist, for example. I mean *eat my body* and *drink my blood*? Sounds kinda primitive to *me*.

DK: Some of us believe those words are symbolic.

J: And you're sure that all the pagan stuff *wasn't*?

DK: I concede the point.

J: Don't be so tough on paganism. It's not a synonym for ignorance, barbarism or witchcraft, you know.

DK: Weren't a lot of pagans atheists?

J: Some were—many weren't. But so what if they were? Paganism doesn't imply atheism, nor vice versa.

DK: But what do you say to someone who doesn't believe in God?

J: I'd say, "Which God is it that you don't believe in? Because *I* probably don't believe in that God, either."

DK: Then you're not down on atheists?

J: I'm not down on *anyone*. But I will say that I always had trouble understanding how the atheist can be so bloody *confident* about his denial. Usually he can't even allow for the *possibility* of a higher power. I mean is it really intelligent or objective to conclude unilaterally that the coordinated brilliance of creation is all completely *accidental*? For a being of such high consciousness to reject even the mere suggestion of a universal intelligence is almost comical. It's like a child in the womb eschewing the possibility of a mother.

DK: I've often considered that kind of unbending close-mindedness as an indication of something much more significant—an issue that goes far beyond intellectual theorizing. It seems to reflect something deeply and personally *threatening*. Maybe it has to do with your premise about ego and its inherent fear of God.

J: Motives are as varied as the minds that contain them, of course. But on the other hand, the atheist is sometimes the most intellectually honest person in the room. The various religions offer him a bizarre assortment of deities, all with their own strange and indecipherable penchants and eccentricities. Since he can't find any convincing evidence for the existence of these alleged beings, nor any sense to some of their purported words and behavior, he simply chooses to ignore them. There's nothing unreasonable about *that*. And actually, there's not much difference between the atheist and the Christian. The Christian has elected to deny all gods but one, while the atheist merely refuses to make that final exception.

DK: But even aside from its varied positions on the existence of God, there's still plenty not to like about paganism's dark history.

J: A good portion of pagan history is no darker than Christianity's—and some of it far *less* so. Lots of pagan societies were quite spiritually advanced, and the pagan world spawned some of the greatest cultural, intellectual and artistic accomplishments ever. Consider some of humanity's most brilliant minds: Socrates, Pythagoras, Hippocrates, Plato, Aristotle, Diogenes. All of these great thinkers were essentially what Christians would call "pagan."

DK: Okay, you win: paganism doesn't suck. But I don't see how it has much in common with the gospel accounts of *your* life.

J: C'mon, pilgrim, don't be obtuse. I already gave you a dozen examples of specific parallels between the stories of my life and those of Osiris-Dionysus. What more proof do you need, Señor Cynic?

DK: As much as you can muster, Master.

J: Alright, then, let's go back to the Eucharist. The concept of divine communion through consuming the god is older than heartburn. It's found even in the Egyptian *Book of the Dead*, which predates my birth by centuries. It was a common rite in the Mysteries, too. It gave the initiate a chance to unite symbolically with Osiris-Dionysus.

DK: I thought the bread and wine thing started with the Last Supper.

J: Don't confuse the Last Supper with the first communion. Long before Christianity, the Mysteries of Mithras utilized a "holy communion," and sometimes the bread wafers even bore the sign of a cross. And the similarity to Christianity didn't stop there. The Mithras cult had at least half a dozen sacraments that were later adopted completely unchanged by the Catholic Church. In fact, overt pagan symbology can be found throughout the Vatican— and don't think for a second that insiders aren't aware of what it all means. Even the pope's miter headgear recalls the ancient Babylonian fish god Dagon.

DK: What about the virgin birth? I figure *that's* gotta be strictly Christian.

J: You should spend more time at the library. Ancient religions are so pregnant with stories of virgin mothers that you'd think the Holy Spirit was hopped up on horny goat weed. In the pre-Christian Mysteries alone you've got Dionysus born of the virgin

Semele; Aion of the virgin Kore; Attis of the virgin Cybele; and
Adonis of the virgin Myrrh—to name just a few.

DK: *Godfrey Daniel!* There's more knocked-up virgins in the
Mysteries than hidden Twinkies in a teenage fat camp!

J: Heck, we haven't even warmed the engine. Virgin birth stories
are connected with names from Alexander to Zoroaster. Across
various legends, divine or supernatural conceptions are also
attributed to the mothers of Buddha, Krishna, Plato, Pythagoras,
Augustus Caesar and King Tut. In one account, even the mother of
Genghis Khan claims that her child is the son of the *sun*. Another
story claims he was the product of a mating between a grey wolf
and a white doe. Centuries of virgin mother lore has women
impregnated by everything from gods, spirits and animals to
planets, lotus flowers and mystical wisps of wind.

DK: Objectively, I guess you'd have to say the pagan stuff is no
more outrageous than the Christian story.

J: The simple truth is that claims about my mother's unbroken
sexual purity are nothing special. That idea's been around
since the Egyptians worshipped the virgin goddess Isis, whose
depictions frequently show her suckling the infant Horus.
Centuries later, this well-traveled iconography was directly
pilfered by Christians in their nearly identical portrayal of
"Madonna and Child."

DK: The Immaculate Conception is starting to sound more like an
immaculately conceived hoax.

J: *Oy vey...* you're so Protestant. Immaculate Conception isn't the
same as the Virgin Birth, my boy. The Immaculate Conception
doctrine holds that my mother, despite her own normal
conception, was nevertheless free from the stain of original sin.
And the claim is at least logical in one respect. Because if you're
gonna propose that some cat is the Divine Dude incarnate, then
you'd better make sure he comes from bloody good stock.

DK: So you paint his mother white as the driven snow and spin
her as a model of moral purity.

J: Exactly. That's why most "mother of God" legends depict the
woman as a perpetual virgin. God's mother has to be entirely

without the "urge to merge" in the bedroom. But religion hasn't done women a service by offering up the ideal woman as a "virgin mother." The very phrase is an absurd contradiction.

DK: Apparently this virgin mother theme has been around awhile.

J: As old as political corruption, I'd say. For a true godman, it's practically a required item on the résumé.

DK: Okay, what else you got?

J: What else do you want? I could ramble for hours about pagan elements that were melted in the fires of the church and then recast in the Christian mold. And it wasn't just the "son of God" idea; Christians were picking the pockets of pagans from the very start. They lifted nearly every fable, symbol, legend, myth and sacrament they could—pardon the pun—lay their hands on. From cradle to cross, New Testament accounts of my life are laced with concepts from ancient paganism.

DK: Oh yeah? What're some others?

J: Take your pick. Specially informed shepherds, the Nativity and its attendant wise men, water baptism, the Holy Ghost, the concept of Alpha and Omega, heaven and hell. Even the foundational Christian image of me as the LOGOS incarnate was a centuries-old pagan model, and the ancient Greeks directly referred to the god Hermes using this very title. Also inherited from pre-Christian traditions were the sign of the fish, salvation from sin, Easter time crucifixion and resurrection, three hours of darkness, a three-day descent to the underworld, and an Apocalypse with a corresponding Last Judgment.

DK: Then none of these elements originated with Christianity?

J: Nope, nor even with Judaism. In fact, the Jews had no predilection whatsoever for the notion of mystically uniting with any slain-and-resurrected savior-god. That part of the Christian motif came directly from the Greek Orphic traditions and, before that, the ancient religions of Egypt. So this stuff was pure "paganism"—if you're compelled to label it that way—and it all existed centuries before the Christian era.

DK: What about some of the *specific* stories? Water to wine, healing cripples, restoring sight.

J: Direct rip-offs from pre-Christian mythology.

DK: Walking on water and raising the dead?

J: Pagan from peeling to core.

DK: Well, shoot.... at least we've got Easter eggs.

J: Actually, that little ritual has its roots with the ancient goddess Ishtar, whose name was later morphed into the word Easter. One of her legends claims she traveled from the moon to the earth in an egg.

DK: Damn, another sacred holiday scrambled. You're raining all over the Christian parade.

J: I'm afraid so. Believe me, you put this stuff in print and you'll need riot gear...

CHAPTER FORTY SEVEN

DK: It appears I should've been more diligent researching my religion. For me, this heavy Christian-pagan connection is a real revelation.

J: Well, it's no revelation to scholars and theologians, my friend. Some of this knowledge has been around for centuries.

DK: Then why weren't more early Christian writers aware of it?

J: Are you kidding? Most of 'em knew all about it. But like a lot of religious faithful, they didn't let facts disrupt their agenda. On the contrary, they frequently went out of their way to obscure the truth.

DK: Evidence, please...

J: Okay, take the Christian historian Eusebius of Caesarea. He's considered one of early Christianity's most glowing apologists—some even call him the father of church history. But as a church father, he was a pretty dysfunctional parent and was hardly the pillar of objectivity you'd expect. At times, Eusebius was just an opportunistic propagandist. Before he attended the First Council of Nicaea, he was convicted as a heretic for supporting a guy named Arius, who was condemned at the Council of Antioch. But in Nicaea, Eusebius managed to win the favor of the infamous emperor Constantine by agreeing to renounce his support for Arius. Afterward, Constantine made Eusebius his official historian and biographer.

DK: Sounds like nothing more than a harmless case of political back-scratching. Is that a problem?

J: The problem is that Eusebius deviously concocted a fake chronology of the church, which others, including Augustine, later used as the basis for *their* writings. So anything centered on the work of Eusebius was built on a foundation of sand. Among serious academics, Eusebius is a well-known liar. One modern scholar called him "the first thoroughly dishonest historian of antiquity." In fact, it was Eusebius who magically produced a work attributed to Josephus that no one had seen before. Josephus, of course, is known by students of church history as one of the most prominent of the early Jewish historians.

DK: I've read a little about Josephus. He's one of our best sources of first-century background on the Jews. Some people use his writings to help prove up *your* existence.

J: Until Eusebius came along, though, early Christian writers didn't resort to the records of Josephus. There was nothing to say, because Josephus never talked about me. But then Eusebius shows up with a "new and improved" version. Suddenly the long-dead Josephus is declaring that I was the Messiah, while providing fresh details about my life—including my appearance before Pilate.

DK: Evidently it was good enough to fool the early church.

J: Yes, but it didn't fool modern-day scholars. Whoever embellished the writings of Josephus was a little too ambitious. In a real explosion of creativity, the mysterious editor has Josephus claiming that I miraculously cured Pilate's wife of an illness and that, consequently, Pilate decided to let me go. He says the Jewish priests then bribed Pilate to proceed with my execution anyway.

DK: A total contradiction of gospel accounts.

J: But that's not all. To refute the anti-Christian argument that my disciples removed my body from the tomb, the Eusebian version of Josephus makes another astonishing claim. It says thirty Roman centurions stood guard by the tomb along with *one thousand* Jews. Now, if all this stuff were true, you'd have to wonder why no biblical writers bothered to record it.

DK: Okay, it's pretty obvious that Eusebius was a true Christian patriot. But should finagling of the facts discredit the man completely?

J: Well, it should at least discredit him as an unbiased source of information. But no, Eusebius' heart wasn't made of granite. In some ways he proved to be quite brave, eventually standing up to the emperor regarding the fraudulent nature of the Nicene Creed. Despite his intimate involvement in the structuring of the Creed at the First Council of Nicaea, Eusebius later wrote to Constantine and confessed that he and his bishop buddies had committed a grave error by signing it. Basically, they considered the Creed a work of heresy. He later admitted to Constantine that he endorsed the Creed only because he was afraid of what might happen to him if he refused. As it turned out, his fears were well justified. Every bishop who rejected the Creed was eventually exiled as a criminal—by direct orders of the emperor.

DK: Then maybe Eusebius wasn't such a scoundrel after all. Maybe he was only demonstrating some political savvy.

J: No, I think Christendom has to wake up and smell the snake oil on this one. Eusebius once declared that it was an act of virtue to mislead people if it would further the cause of the church. In one of his works, he's got a chapter entitled, "How it may be Lawful and Fitting to use Falsehood as Medicine, and for the Benefit of those who Want to be Deceived." In other words, it's alright to lie when the truth won't suffice.

DK: I see what you mean. The man doesn't exactly inspire unwavering trust.

J: And Eusebius was no isolated case of some overzealous convert cooking the books. Other notable Christian defenders were every bit as dishonest and one-sided. Justin Martyr, another guy whose work the church looks to for its legitimacy, once made the absurd statement that anything noble or worthy that may have emerged from paganism was actually the rightful property of the church!

DK: A little over-the-top, perhaps.

J: Not to be outdone in Christian arrogance, Saint Augustine declared a couple hundred years later that if the followers of Plato and other pagan philosophers had said anything that was "in harmony with the faith," Christians were to resist the earlier teachings and then reclaim them from those who had "unlawful possession" of them. Now, let's not tiptoe through the tulips, bub. That's not just lame and contradictory—it's downright *stupid*.

DK: Hmmnn. I'm beginning to think some of these church fathers were the result of marriage between cousins…

CHAPTER FORTY EIGHT

DK: If it makes you feel any better, JC, I'm starting to see your point—that is, the need to distance yourself from some of this Christian craziness. I've witnessed some harebrained stuff from the church in my day, but I never knew there was so much humbuggery right off the blocks.

J: You haven't heard the *worst* of it.

DK: Hey, if you've got the dirt, I've got the shovel…

J: Okay, let's go back to Justin Martyr. He may be a respected church father, but the man is straight out of the cuckoo's nest. Martyr, among others, embraced an idea called "Diabolical Mimicry," a highly imaginative theory devised to explain why Christian doctrines and practices so closely resembled those of earlier pagan groups. The premise was that Satan plagiarized

Christianity *before* its arrival as a way to discredit it when it finally arrived.

DK: Oh, now *that's* priceless. The Greatest Story Ever Foretold.

J: C'mon, you're being too kind. The idea's kookier than a jump tester for bungee cords. And a lot of early Christians bought into that sixty-five I.Q. kind of thinking. What's crazier is that even in the twenty-first century, millions of believers are still just as gullible.

DK: I'm shocked there was so much philosophical flummoxing among purported Christian 'intellectuals.'

J: Early Christians were hardly one big, happy family of saints and martyrs. There were basically two camps. On one side were the literalists. They insisted that every detail of their particular godman story—featuring me in the starring role—was historical fact. On the other side were the symbolists, like the Gnostics, who understood that most of the elements in the Christian narratives were figurative and were based on familiar pagan legacies.

DK: How did the church come to adopt the literal view?

J: In a nutshell, the Christian and pagan Gnostics were gradually pummeled out of existence by the Roman establishment. This was accomplished systematically with the help of folks like Constantine and, a few decades later, Emperor Theodosius, who was responsible for making Christianity the official religion of the empire. The Gnostics were generally peaceful and were mostly content with striving to attain enlightenment. Being somewhat elitist in their thinking, they didn't do much evangelizing, so they weren't normally converting people or fighting to lay the groundwork for a powerful institution. But literalists, especially those with influence, were very much interested in establishing an imperial religion that would solidify their grip on power and strengthen their political control.

DK: So they happily encouraged a soul-threatening theology that would keep the sheeple docile and acquiescent.

J: Yes, and they were extremely aggressive in their efforts to eliminate any "competition." You hear lots of talk about Christians being persecuted, but they themselves did plenty of persecuting. By the time emperor Arcadius took the throne in 395, his Christian predecessors had run roughshod over prominent groups of pagans by saddling them with burdensome laws, inhibiting their social advancement, and disallowing their heirs any estate inheritance. At the extreme, Roman Christians often confiscated pagan holy grounds, looting and sacking their religious treasuries and sanctuaries. Under some of the harsher administrations, even members of the church weren't always safe from Rome's economic and political oppression. Those who didn't knuckle under to the emperor were killed, exiled, or excommunicated and driven underground. But after Constantine's imposition of literalism upon the empire, pagans and "fringe" sects—like the Gnostics—were especially vulnerable targets.

DK: *Sheesh*. What ever happened to Christian tolerance?

J: Don't be fooled: some of these rulers were Christian in name only. Constantine, who would more accurately be called a Christo-pagan ruler, was a virtual dictator. And even though he was Rome's first official Christian emperor, he would probably qualify as a member of history's Top 100 most savage tyrants. Like Theodosius after him, Constantine wanted a "catholic," or universal, religion for his empire, with him as the unquestioned leader. Literalist Christianity was just what the doctor ordered.

DK: So even under some of Rome's "Christian" regimes, Christians weren't necessarily spared from persecution.

J: Not always. But here's a bit of irony: historically, through wars and various other settings of intolerance, more Christians have perished at the hands of their fellow believers than were ever killed by any Christian-targeting government. And until about 250 CE, Roman persecution of Christians was generally isolated and sporadic. When Emperor Decius came along, however, Christian persecution began in earnest and lasted several decades.

DK: But Constantine's rule evidently changed all that.

J: Definitely. After being staunchly rejected by most Roman citizens for several centuries, Christianity at last began taking hold when Constantine formally adopted it himself. The religion finally was given the big boost it needed to eventually pervade the empire. And for some it was an easy transition, because Christianity was practically a carbon copy of the Mystery religions they already knew. But there *was* a critical difference: the newer, literalist version was authoritarian and left no room for dissent.

DK: I do know the New Testament is big on obedience. The faithful should submit to government, wives should submit to their husbands, children to their parents, and so forth.

J: It's no coincidence that some New Testament writers even go so far as to command slaves to obey their masters. To Christian literalists, the ideal believer is indeed a slave to the faith, and good stewardship essentially amounts to believing and doing as you're told. For a control freak like Constantine, encouraging a religion of subservience was an ideal political strategy, since it advocated unconditional loyalty. In contrast to the Mysteries, which were practiced by many of the day's most learned and respected philosophers, literalist Christianity quickly dispensed with those freethinking intellectuals who advocated individual autonomy. They were considered dangerous to the empire, as they tended to denounce the emperor's tactics of control through intimidation and terror.

DK: So like the powerful leaders who embraced it, the upstart Christian religion demanded unquestioning servility.

J: Yes, and because of rulers like Constantine, Christianity's historical shift from inner to outer authority had begun, tragically destroying in its path all emphasis on self-liberation.

DK: But you gotta hand it to the guy: Constantine had far more impact on humanity than he could ever have hoped. I mean who'd have thought this bloody villain would play such a huge role in shaping one of history's most influential religions?

J: A colorful character, for sure...

DK: There's another story about Constantine that's always had me curious. Long after his so-called "conversion" to Christianity, Constantine claimed that, years earlier, just before a significant battle, he and his troops had seen a cross in the noonday sky. He said that along with the cross in the sky were written the words, "By this conquer." He went to bed baffled by it all. He said you then came to him in his dreams and instructed him to wipe out his enemies by using the heavenly apparition as a symbol to adorn his warriors' shields. He later won the battle decisively.

J: So if we can believe Constantine, he dutifully murdered his fellow human beings under the instruction, guidance and protection of Christianity's lauded "Prince of Peace."

DK: I guess you could see it that way. Onward, Christian soldier and all.

J: It makes for a good story, maybe. But it's just another example of God-is-on-our-side kind of thinking. It's like declaring, "God helped me slaughter my brothers." You don't get much crazier than that.

DK: Even so, Constantine's war victory apparently gave him sufficient motivation to spread Christianity throughout the realm.

J: Well, his motivations were *suspect*, to say the least. But all things considered—during his lifetime, anyway—Constantine's plan to convert the empire was pretty much a bust. Even Eusebius, who died shortly after Constantine, could name only a few Christian townships in the entire Holy Land.

DK: Not exactly a rousing success, I suppose.

J: The main thing is that Constantine did whatever it took to enforce allegiance, brutally eliminating opposition—both politically and philosophically. He wanted a compliant citizenry, and literalist Christianity helped provide it.

DK: Hard to believe it was this same monster that presided over the creation of the Nicene Creed.

J: The Creed, like the young church itself, was every bit as political as it was religious. It was literalist by design and was directly intended to help Constantine and his bishops consolidate power and establish control. Essentially it was a work of fiction, and the bishops knew it. At the time it was ratified, only a very small percentage of Roman citizens gave the Creed any authority. Having been raised with the symbolism of the Mysteries, few Romans would've embraced a literal godman story—even if they didn't dare publicly condemn it. And even after its significant modifications during the First Council of Constantinople in 381, it would still be many generations before the Nicene Creed became widely accepted church doctrine. Now it's recited faithfully by millions of Christians every week. Ironically, to some degree they can credit a wickedly brutal Roman dictator for its introduction.

315

DK: Evidently Constantine was his era's version of the Christian right wing.

J: Except in his case there *was* no other wing: it was his way or the graveyard. To give you some idea what a sweetheart the guy was, after he was satisfied with the proceedings in Nicaea, he returned home to embark on a monstrous killing spree, wiping out a long list of old friends and associates. Incredibly, he even had his wife Fausta murdered, along with his son Cripus and his sister's son Licinius, who was just a young boy.

DK: Ah, the familiar conservative emphasis on family!

J: Thinking he'd found a loophole to avoid divine condemnation for his life of evil, Constantine intentionally avoided baptism until he was dying, having himself doused at the last minute by a distant relative, another fellow named Eusebius. This guy, Bishop Eusebius of Nicomedia, had been angrily exiled by Constantine many years earlier because of his vehement opposition to the Nicene Creed during its creation. He finally regained imperial favor, though, and the calculating Constantine asked him for an eleventh hour baptism, hoping to obtain God's forgiveness and thereby secure himself a place in heaven.

DK: Wow. With guys like Constantine on their backs, the poor Gnostics and pagans never had a chance.

J: Nope. And even though Gnostics were among the very earliest Christians, they were persecuted out of existence by literalists before they ever got their historical day in court. Even most of their writings were destroyed. And since history is written by the victors, it's no secret why you don't read much about the Gnostics. In fact, if Constantine and his successors had gotten their way, the world might never have even heard of them. But luckily for the Gnostics, a funny thing happened on the way to oblivion.

DK: And what was that?

J: In December 1945, some Egyptian peasants stumbled upon an archaeological bonanza. They found thirteen ancient papyrus codices buried across the river from Nag Hammadi, a town near the east bluff of the upper Nile River valley. Known now as the Nag Hammadi Library, the codices comprise about a thousand pages and represent more than fifty separate manuscripts. Many are Gnostic scriptures, and some were even brought into use by the early Christian community, which simply took the desired texts and substituted changes where appropriate. In any case, the writings provided important information about Gnosticism and its wide-ranging views on philosophy and religion.

DK: So the Gnostics finally had a confirmed place in the evolution of Christian history.

J: True—but as you might expect, their bearing was poles apart from the literalists. The Gnostics viewed literalists as the ones who were misguided, and they considered literalism to be highly superficial. They felt it fostered an "imitation" church that mistook symbolism for history and emphasized blind faith without imparting any real spiritual insight. So each group saw the other as heretics.

DK: Not much different from the sectarian feuding and backbiting going on today.

J: No, not really. And it oughtta be mentioned that "Gnostic" is simply a convenient umbrella term for a spiritually diverse bunch of sects with plenty of disagreement between them.

DK: Then the Gnostics had *their own* philosophical skirmishes.

J: Oh, absolutely. But generally, at least, they were on the right track. They sought an *inner* knowledge—a mystical joining with the divine—that could never be shaken or lost. The Gnostics were considered a threat because mostly they saw no need for an ecclesiastical hierarchy. They were seeking a spiritual kingdom *within*, while the literalists were busy building an *earthly* one.

DK: Hey, the literalists did a bang-up job, I can tell you that. A few years back, TIME magazine said the Catholic Church alone was generating several billion bucks a year in revenue. Running the Vatican is big business.

J: Well, imagine the fortune *you* could amass with centuries of diplomatic immunity and exemption from all world taxes. Did that article give a figure on court settlements?

DK: I know this much: Christian organizations have owned or held interest in everything from theme parks and golf courses to beachfront retreats and hotel chains. They're involved in TV, radio, merchandising, manufacturing—even international banking. There's no doubt about it: Christianity is a thriving enterprise.

J: I'm sure Constantine would be proud.

DK: And you?

J: I'm sitting here wondering where the hell I went wrong…

CHAPTER FORTY NINE

DK: So it's pretty clear that Gnosticism, along with other, more ancient and far-removed spiritual traditions, had a huge effect on the development of Christianity. The new religion wasn't just a branch pruned from the tree of Judaism.

J: No, and even the Jewish influence was a complex mix. Having been captive in Babylon, the early Jews were heavily affected by the great pagan cultures of Mesopotamia. The neighboring Egyptians across the Sinai obviously left their mark as well. And don't forget the Greeks: they too had a big impact on the Holy Land. By the time I was born, Galilee was so colored by Grecian culture that some Jews called it "the land of the Gentiles."

DK: That's interesting, because biblical Palestine is usually portrayed as an obscure, almost barren country with practically no connection to the outside world.

J: A lot of folks have that impression. But we weren't the isolated backwater hicks that most people imagine. Actually, Palestine was a cultural melting pot. For example, in Gadara there was a school of pagan philosophy. On Galilee's southern border, in the town of Scythopolis, there was a center for the Mysteries of Dionysus. Not far from the holy city of Jerusalem, the cities of Ascalon and Larissa produced pagan philosophers who were known as far away as Rome. But of course, having been a Christian for so long, you already knew this, right?

DK: My ignorance is surpassed only by my embarrassment.

J: Well, you're not alone. Few Christians go much beyond traditional Bible study. They memorize verses and learn a bit of historical background, but they seldom question how their religion *evolved*: they don't examine its *foundation*. They seem to think it popped up from nowhere, right in the middle of Judaism—as if created from thin air by God Himself.

DK: That's sort of how *I* viewed it.

J: But that's hardly realistic. Ideologies are a product not only of *their own* culture but also of the legacies of cultures that *preceded* them. My disciples and I were certainly not immune to those influences, and Christianity was never just a simple follow-on to Judaism. In addition to its Jewish connections, it was steeped in the powerful vestiges of myths, superstitions and beliefs of civilizations dating back many, many centuries.

DK: But even if Christianity was a blend of what appears to be a kind of Judeo-paganism, wasn't your personal message of salvation new and unique?

J: Far from it. Way before my time, the ancient Persian prophet Zoroaster proclaimed, "I am the Way, the Truth and the Light." Lao Tzu and the Buddha said nearly the same thing. And these influential teachers all existed long before the Christian era. Also worshipped many centuries before me was Mithras, the god of fire and light and the central figure of Mithraism. Mithras was widely revered by Romans and, as a result, his worship was spread by way of Roman soldiers to the farthest reaches of the conquered empire. He was known variously as "the Way," "the Truth," "the Light," "the Life," "the Word," "the Son of God," and "the Good Shepherd."

DK: Be careful, you may owe royalties.

J: Like me, Mithras is frequently depicted with a lamb, and his followers celebrated his birthday on December 25th. This period—when days are shortest, right around the winter solstice—also marked the anticipated return of *Sol Invictus*, the "Invincible Sun." Worshippers celebrated the occasion with gifts, candles, bells and hymns.

DK: Damned lucky for the church there's no copyright on pagan rituals and holidays.

J: Mithras' legend states that he was born from a rock and laid to rest in a rock tomb called "Petra," which of course was the same name I'm said to have given my disciple Peter when I told him, "And on this rock I will build my church." Furthermore, the most prominent image in the cave temples where Mithras was often worshipped is a *tauroctony*—a scene in which Mithras slays a sacrificial bull, thereby giving his followers eternal life. Importantly, both the Christian and Mithraic atonements carry profound cosmological symbolism involving astronomy and astrology. And not by coincidence, both "events" took place during the vernal equinox.

DK: So once again, Christianity and the Mysteries share common ground.

J: Yep. And much like Christians, Mithras' followers also believed in a final "day of judgment," when their savior would descend from heaven and condemn non-believers. Not surprisingly, the deceased faithful were to be resurrected and then delivered into "paradise," a word derived from the Persians. Had enough, or do you want more?

DK: Heck, no point in holding back now. You've already stirred the embers, so you may as well fan the flames. I mean what the hell—I've already lost the Catholic endorsement.

J: Think how I've saved you from those tedious book-signings…

CHAPTER FIFTY

DK: Well, congratulations. In only one afternoon, you've knocked about ninety percent off the value of your stock.

J: But it's time to get this stuff on the table. As long as the church keeps selling me as God's own Superman, my real message gets lost in the spectacle. Either I'm set up as an idol or written off as an irrelevant storybook figure who came to save a relatively small part of humanity from scorching in hell. I mean what a con game. And it wasn't even *original*.

DK: Let's run with this theme of Christianity's evolution. You've got me interested.

J: Well, as you can see, it's not uncommon for cultures to lay claim to various saviors, messiahs or "sons of God." A lot of these characters are said to have had miraculous births, performed marvelous wonders, arisen from the dead and all that. Some were strictly mythological, of course, but others were actual persons. And some of them beat me to the punch by hundreds or even thousands of years.

DK: It's becoming clear that similarities between you and your predecessors are more than just general in nature. Some of the stories are nearly identical.

J: No religion is an island, and it should be obvious that Christianity was intentionally constructed from legends that were much older and firmly established by the time of my birth. To complicate the issue further, not one statement about me in the New Testament gospels is provable historical fact.

DK: There's no arguing *that* point. Hell, we may have more convincing evidence for the Loch Ness monster. After centuries of archaeological and other scientific research, support for your very existence remains slim and theoretical at best. And even though the Romans typically kept meticulous records, we've yet to find documentation that you ever interacted with Pontius Pilate— much less that you were tried and executed by him. Actually, there's no good indication that you ever lived. We've got nearly thirty well-known, non-Christian writers who wrote either during your lifetime or within a hundred years afterward, and not one makes a single reference to *you*. Not even the great Jewish writer Philo. Almost fifty of his works still survive, but the guy never mentions your name.

J: Maybe I wasn't the big celebrity I've been made out to be.

DK: But that worries me. I mean you'd think the first earthly appearance of "God's only Son" would've garnered a little more coverage by the media. Excuse my blunt manner, but except for a few highly conflicting accounts by those said to be part of your inner circle, we know almost nothing substantial about you. This wholesale lack of independent confirmation is extremely suspect and frustrating. For example, what about the historical record penned by Justus of Tiberias? He was one of Philo's contemporaries and lived near Capernaum, a place you were said to have visited often. Justus composed a history dating back to the days of Moses and extending through to his own lifetime. So if anyone were likely to write about you, it would've been him. But in all of Justus' writings, your name never pops up. We could talk about Josephus, but you already explained that *his* passages about you were phony and were inserted by someone else.

J: It's true that Josephus never wrote about me. In fact, he believed the Roman Emperor Vespasian was actually the divinely prophesied world ruler. Even Origen admitted that Josephus would never have accepted the Christian claims about me, because Josephus sided with the Romans and completely rejected the notion of a Jewish messiah. And believe me, the Catholic Church was not amused by Origen's honesty.

DK: Why? What happened?

J: A couple centuries after his death, they condemned him as a heretic. Which is too bad, really, because Origen was about as sincere as they come. The poor guy actually emasculated himself to demonstrate his deep commitment.

DK: *Ouch.* Self-inflicted castration—the unkindest cut of all. That's what I call giving it all up for Jesus!

J: *Heh heh.* Nothing more devoted than a eunuch in a tunic… Ah, but we're burning daylight, my friend. What are we aiming for?

DK: I guess my point is that if you weren't sitting in front of me, I'd have serious doubts about you myself. I mean by comparison, we've got a trainload more information on the personal life of Islam's Muhammad than we do about you. As you say, there's not a *single detail* of your life as presented in scripture that can be irrefutably proven. Many Bible scholars assert that not one of the actual scripture writers even met you, which seems pretty obvious from the tone and structure of their work. New Testament expert Rudolf Bultmann once said that it's almost hopeless to know anything factual about you. He said the gospels are too patchy, inconsistent and legend-based to be a reliable source of

322

information. So historically speaking, you've hardly got a wave to walk on. Even the brilliant doctor Albert Schweitzer, a highly devoted Christian and a pretty competent theologian, called you an "ineffable mystery." He essentially felt that the Christ of the gospels is impossible to prove.

J: Well, he was right. The biblical Christ is a *composite* figure—a mythological fusion of pagan-based godmen from antiquity. I wasn't that man at all. I was just a humble teacher, traveling around Palestine preaching a simple message of love and unity while encouraging enlightenment for those who were ready. After I died, all kinds of wild claims sprang up as a result of my followers' passion and their eagerness to drum up new business. A few decades later, they turned me into a Jewified version of Osiris-Dionysus, the godman of the Mystery religions.

DK: Then you weren't the guy we read about in the four gospels?

J: How could I be? A combination of a dozen fictional characters rolled into one is... well, *nobody*.

DK: You're really trashing my comfort zone.

J: But what I'm giving you are the cold, hard facts. Myths that for centuries had been interpreted allegorically were suddenly made into "history" by Christian literalists. Thus was born the Christo-pagan Jesus of Greco-Roman creation.

DK: I think the world just lost a hero. Some of us took big consolation in a role model who could alter weather patterns and convert tap water to Shiraz.

J: The trouble with making me special is that it keeps you from questioning religion's version of reality, thereby retarding your spiritual awakening. *My* goal is to destroy your dependence on external authorities—human or otherwise—and urge you to begin looking to your own inner silence for answers. I hope to discourage you from seeking reality in a book, a philosophy, or a story. Reality merely *is*. And it *is* at every moment. Scriptures sometimes provide maps, but they're certainly not *the territory*.

DK: I'd like to believe that at least *some* of what we've read about you is factual.

J: But so much of what's written after a teacher departs is just hearsay that can't be verified or critically assessed. As the years roll by, claims of their supernatural powers tend to be hugely exaggerated. Eventually the stories lose credibility and the saints wind up sounding like comic strip characters.

DK: I guess every field has its spin doctors. But I still don't see how Christianity could be so wildly successful when its leading man is just a fictitious pagan knock-off.

J: But that's the fact, Mac. Nearly every important claim about me was also made in behalf of other revered teachers or deity figures long before my birth. And I'm not just talking about the Mystery religions. Stories of the Hindu god Krishna contain striking parallels to the gospel accounts of *my* life. And so do several other godman legends. Scientifically, the Christian story is no more defensible than most of the others, and nearly every major gospel theme can be found in mythical pre-Christian traditions—even specific elements such as heralding stars, angelic annunciations, and of course specially informed shepherds.

DK: Man, what would religion do without those ubiquitous shepherds? It's probably best there haven't been any *American*-born saviors. It just wouldn't sound the same: "And there were in that country cowboys keeping watch over their herds by night..." Crazy hicks prob'ly would've offered gifts of rope and chewing tobacco...

J: Why don't we conclude this "multiple messiahs" bit with a list of just *some* of the ancient figures who've been honored or worshipped as Christs, saviors or divine intermediaries, some of whom were even said to have been crucified...

Two of the best-known, of course, are India's Krishna and Buddha of Nepal. Then there's Osiris, Horus and Thulis of Egypt; Zoroaster and Mithra of Persia; Baal and Taut of Phoenecia; Indra of Tibet; Bali of Orissa; Thammuz of Mesopotamia and Attis of Phrygia.

DK: Ye gods!

J: There's also the sun goddess Amaterasu-Omikami of Japan; Hesus of the Celtic Druids; Quexalcote of Mexico; Alcestos of

Euripides; Quirinus of Rome; Crite of Chaldaea; Muhammad of Arabia; and Prometheus of Greece.

DK: Saints deceased! With so many saviors coming and going, you'd think there'd be nary a sinner in sight.

J: And that's just a few of the *hundreds* throughout history that various groups or cultures have considered special or divine. Even in recent times, you've had plenty of folks claiming divinity, including flakes like David Koresh, Jim Jones, Sun Myung Moon, and many others. I could go on, but you'd rack up a fortune in publishing costs.

DK: Yeah, you'd better stop there. You keep this up and you'll have fewer followers than a four-hundred-pound aerobics instructor…

CHAPTER
FIFTY ONE

DK: It seems you've spent most of the day draining your own well.

J: I've gotta strip away some of the age-old myths surrounding my life. An invisible wall has been erected between me and humanity because the church has wrapped me like a mummy in layers of specialness. But now you're discovering the truth: my world bore little resemblance to the quilted fabrications of the New Testament. To appreciate my life's higher meaning, folks need to dig beneath the surface. It's time to end all that "right hand of the throne" stuff and allow me into your moment-to-moment awareness where I can do some good.

DK: Why do we mortals so desperately desire deities and divine intercessors?

J: Fear, mostly. And maybe a little mental laziness. By designating only a few individuals as divine, people tend to view *themselves* as second-hand goods relegated to God's scratch-and-dent department. They avoid going inward by putting their "salvation" off on someone else. Without thinking it through, a lot of folks vaguely figure that since God created them defective, He can darned well take responsibility for *saving* them. It's a cop-out for those who want a drive-through religion. Sometimes a savior only saves you from *thinking*.

DK: Maybe we *need* a savior. The average person doesn't strike me as all that godly.

J: Well, how could they? Even from childhood, millions are taught that they're inherently shameful, unworthy and deficient. In the hallowed halls of Christendom, they're told of their creator's longstanding unhappiness with them due to a relatively harmless act of disobedience several thousand years ago by a naïve young couple in Mesopotamia.

DK: The doctrine of original sin.

J: Yeah, the church teaches that all children incur guilt immediately upon arrival—condemned from the start for committing the damnably presumptuous act of being born. Theologically, by the church's reasoning, this haphazard event makes them fully deserving of God's unmitigated wrath and its potentially dreadful consequences. Strangely, even eternity in the fires of penance isn't considered too severe for this heinous show of arrogance called birth.

DK: I'll bet you were hell on your high school debate team.

J: People usually live what they learn, so it's no surprise if they wind up acting out the negativity laid on them by the world and its religions of judgment. Now, I'll admit that with all the focus on sin and your allegedly defiled nature, it's easy to conclude that you're essentially flawed. But why are you so quick to *accept* the idea?

DK: Well, for the reason you just mentioned: because the scriptures *say* we're flawed. I'm a sinner, this I know—for the Bible *tells* me so.

J: Ah, so you believe that you're showing humility by denigrating yourself as sinful and evil. But *true* humility acknowledges the self's divine grandeur by affirming, "I am whole and perfect, just as God created me."

DK: I can see how that might apply to guys like *you*. But I don't see how you can argue that every human is "whole and perfect." I'm probably squeezing the life from the lemon by harping on this, but I still feel that somehow you must have been unique. Even your closest friends apparently thought so.

J: The enlightened always appear special to the ignorant. The caterpillar looks upon the butterfly and can't even imagine that he carries the same magnificent potential.

DK: Still, it's not every Tom, Dick or Harry who gets tagged with the title "son of God."

J: Actually, that term was fairly common. It was used for kings, pharaohs, great philosophers, national heroes, miracle workers, holy men and others. The "son of God" idea pops up even in the Old Testament. In the book of 2 Samuel, for instance, God says of David, "I will be his father, and he shall be my son."

DK: But at some point *you* were upgraded from coach to first class. What happened?

J: Again, the Nicene Creed had a lot to do with it. Once the Christian gospel started permeating the Roman Empire, that "son of God" label began to be taken literally. This was quite by design, of course, and eventually the concept became dogma. So my status as "divine" didn't really take hold until that First Council of Nicaea in 325 CE. But even that didn't settle the matter, because some people didn't accept the idea that God could be killed. So it took the church another hundred and fifty years and three more Ecumenical Councils before it finally hit upon an explanation that most believers could live with. It concluded that I must've had *two* aspects to my nature— one fully human and the other fully divine. Which is actually not far from the truth, except that it's also true of everyone else.

DK: Nevertheless, no one since you has been able to pull it off. In all of Christendom, not a single person—no matter how saintly— has commanded the church's reverence in quite the same way that you have.

J: The notion that I was God's only child was never suggested until well after my death. It's referenced only a few times in the entire New Testament, and most of those books weren't written until decades after I was gone.

DK: Let's delve a little deeper here. The New Testament's first "only Son" reference occurs in John 1:14. The writer says, "… we have beheld his glory, glory as of the only Son from the Father."

J: Okay, see there? Did you catch that? The phrase reads, "as *of* the only Son"—not "*as* the only Son." In other words, it was the kind of glory an only son might receive from his father. For all the church knows, the original document may even have said, "glory as of a father's only son." As it stands, though, the meaning is anything but clear.

DK: Further down, in verse eighteen, there's a second "only Son" reference that says, "No one has ever seen God; the only Son, who is in the bosom of the Father, he has made him known."

J: But what if the *original* text was slightly altered or misinterpreted? Try it this way: No one has ever seen God; only the Son, who is in the Father's bosom, has made him known. By switching "the only Son" to "only the Son," the sentence instantly becomes sensible and meaningful. *The invisible Absolute is made known, or manifest, only through the expression of Its relative creation, figuratively referred to as "the Son."* This notion of the shifting, relative world as merely a reflection of the unchanging Absolute is what enlightened people have been teaching for thousands of years.

DK: I have to confess that I've come to consider this "God's only Son" thing to be one of the screwiest concepts ever. Quite frankly, a lot of people find it insulting to human intelligence.

J: I said early on that God's offspring, or his "Son," is just a metaphor to describe creation. God creates only by extending Himself. So the "Son," by necessity, is always in the Father's "bosom," meaning *united* with Him. Why choose to ignore an interpretation that makes perfect sense in favor of one that makes no sense at all?

DK: Because the church doesn't give us the option: its doctrines aren't up for discussion. But who knows? Maybe this interview will finally move the church to relax its dogmatic stance.

J: I wouldn't wait by the pulpit…

CHAPTER FIFTY TWO

DK: By the way, we never discussed the New Testament's *most famous* verse referring to you as the "only Son": John 3:16.

J: Ah yes, the preferred passage of placard-bearing Christian sports fans everywhere: "For God so loved the world that he gave his only Son, that whoever believes in him should have eternal life."

DK: Right. Now, some Bible scholars believe those words are yours, while others say they're the words of the gospel writer. At this point I'll side with the second group, since you've made it clear that you weren't teaching a salvation that hinges on beliefs.

J: If I had embraced the idea *behind* those words, then why wouldn't I come right out and say, "For God so loved the world that he sent *me*"? I never encouraged dependence on the man Christianity calls "Jesus." In Matthew 23, I tell my disciples, "You have one master, the Christ." I *didn't* say, "You have one master—and it's *me*." So I was pointing to something *beyond* my transient human persona. I mean who the hell goes around speaking of himself in the third person?

DK: I could name about twenty celebrities…

J: Listen, the force behind creation is not an ego-personality, and the proposition that it has only a single child is absurd. It's theology for the mentally challenged.

DK: All the same, your status as God's one true child is biblically unequivocal.

J: What are you trying to do, get arrested for impersonating a journalist? The Bible's very first book, Genesis, refers to *all* men as "sons of God." And it does this not once, but twice.

DK: Well, alright… but that's *Old* Testament.

J: Are we not talking about the collection of works the Christian church refers to as the unchanging, inerrant and internally consistent Word of God?

DK: I should've anticipated that one.

J: Regrettably, the Genesis writer refers to women only as the "daughters of *men*," which just reflects the bigotry and male chauvinism of early Jewish culture. Anyhow, the "only Son" concept is flawed from the start, and it was *someone else's idea*, not mine. Incidentally, the Book of Job also makes several references to the many "sons of God." So does the first chapter in the book of Hosea. There the Bible states that "the number of the people of Israel shall be like the sand of the sea" and that they'll be called "Sons of the living God." In 1 Chronicles 22, God says of Solomon, "He shall be my son, and I will be his father…"

DK: It appears that God's immediate family is growing by leaps and bounds.

J: Okay, so it's time again for a little logic. If there's only one Father, and if all of the children are created in his "image and likeness"—that is, with the same nature as the Father—then they would all be *equal*, no?

DK: A touchy topic, to be sure. Even the Apostle Paul had problems with this baffling "only Son" concept. More than once he tries to *work around* the issue by suggesting that everyone except you is "adopted."

J: In other words, God first *created* you and then He *adopted* you. How sensible is *that*? And how is it any different from a mother giving birth to her child and then declaring that the kid was adopted!? *Adopted* sons—what a crock. Unbelievable how religion turns a perfectly good mind into mush.

DK: Maybe you could dip back into that cosmic databank once again and provide a little more scriptural backup on this idea that all humans are divine. Gotta cover my flank, you know—look out for number one and all that.

J: Spoken like a true American. Alright, open your Bible, follow along, and learn of your little-advertised divinity…

"You are gods, sons of the Most High, *all* of you."
Psalms 82:6

DK: Hey, that one all by itself is pretty compelling.

J: And check out these others…

"…Adam, the son of God."
Luke 3:38

"To all who received him…he gave power to become *sons of God*."
John 1:12

"…for all who are led by the Spirit of God *are sons of God*."
Romans 8:14

"…it is the Spirit himself bearing witness that we are *children of God*…"
Romans 8:16

"…to be conformed to the image of his Son, in order that he might be the first-born among *many* brethren."
Romans 8:29

"For the creation waits…for the revealing of the *sons of God*."
Romans 8:19

"…and to *them* belong the *sonship*…"
Romans 9:4

"…and I will be a father to you, and you shall be my sons and daughters, says the Lord Almighty."
2 Corinthians 6:18

"that you may be…*children of God*."
Philippians 2:15

"See what love the Father has given us, that we should be called *children of God*; and so we are."
1 John 3:1

"Beloved, we are *God's children*…"
1 John 3:2

DK: Okay, an impressive list. And in several passages where the phrase "children of God" appears, the footnotes say that some Bible scholars interpret the original text to read, "*sons of God*."

J: Translators frequently take the path of least resistance. Can't give the impression that Jesus is just like everyone else, right? I mean who'd pad the plate for a message like that?

DK: There's one other gospel passage specifically referring to you as "God's only Son." It's 1 John 4:9. Most Bible scholars attribute that letter to the same writer who's generally credited with writing the fourth gospel—although it's now been proven that the author of those books was *not* John the Apostle. But it makes sense that the writer would use the same "Son of God" phraseology in both works.

J: But a huge problem remains: you haven't got an original document backing a single book in the entire New Testament. So the whole thing is really a giant crapshoot. Every book has loads of scholastic and theological challenges, and any or all of them may have had unidentified "editors," completely unbeknownst to the original writers. And since we're talking about the book of John, I should mention that some Bible scholars have serious concerns with the authenticity and reliability of that gospel because it differs so radically from the other three. As with several other books of the New Testament, some early church officials didn't want John's gospel included in the Holy Scriptures.

DK: It's interesting to speculate on how Christianity might look if John's gospel had been omitted.

J: Kinda makes you wonder which verse they'd be using on those ballgame posters…

DK: I'll give 'em credit for one thing: they sure have gotten the word out. I doubt there's a sports fan anywhere who hasn't been exposed to John 3:16.

J: Despite its great popularity, though, that verse is actually just a lead-in to one of the most discouraging passages in the New Testament. The sentiment of John 3:16 may sound promising at first, but most Christians overlook the critical but less-promoted corollary statement, which is summed up two verses later: "… he who does *not* believe is *condemned already*…"

DK: You're right, we never really address that part.

J: Well, you might as well forget about Judgment Day. Because according to several New Testament writers, for those who can't bring themselves to embrace church doctrine, the judgment has already occurred. And you can see why the church might omit this concept from its marketing plan. According to scripture, God so *hated* the world that He set up a system whereby the vast majority of his children would damn themselves to eternal torment through their ignorance, honest skepticism or outright disbelief. Try using *that* as your poster-board slogan, see how many converts you get.

DK: Are you *sure* you wanna start a tent revival ministry?

J: Look, I know I'm giving out some off-the-wall stuff. But isn't it clear that your world is in dire need of something radical? *Your* way just isn't working. Your worn-out theologies are the *problem*, not the answer. When a guy's willing to ostracize, neglect, abuse or even murder his neighbor in the name of religion, something's gone terribly wrong. It's insane to believe that you can profit spiritually from someone else's suffering or loss. In their deluded state of separation, humans are the only creatures on the planet that actively work *against* their own best interests.

DK: No wonder Yahweh brought on the Great Flood. He must've figured the best solution was to drown the whole sorry pack and start over. Maybe we find it easy to believe in an angry God because we see the world's insanity and think, "Hey, if *I* were God, *I'd* be pretty pissed off, too." So we project our fear and frustration onto God, figuring that any forthcoming punishment is probably well deserved.

J: Yes, but like I said, a creator who grows piously angry and feigns astonishment when man screws up is unworthy of your defense. According to biblical literalists, the God of the Bible knows *all* things—future included. That means He has to know beforehand what's coming, right?

DK: If God is truly omniscient, then I don't see any way around it.

J: But the Bible God's reaction to evil is absurdly inconsistent with omniscience. When man soon indulges his destructive tendencies—something that would've been *foreseen* by an all-knowing deity—God quickly becomes indignant and begins spewing horrific threats and meting out cruel punishments. At first the penalties are restricted to *this* world. But later, via the New Testament, they're carried into perpetuity. Now tell me, old chum: is there even a thread of common sense sewn in among the lunacy? I mean here we have the Universal Lord of All cranking out defective merchandise and then having the chutzpah to bemoan the quality of the goods!

DK: Talk about refusing to assume product liability!

J: You ain't kiddin'. This has gotta be the most blatant case in history of the need for a manufacturer's recall. If God were incorporated, He'd face a string of lawsuits longer than Methuselah's memoirs.

DK: You know, when you look at things *that* way, the Bible God seems like nothing but a chronic whiner—a real titty-baby.

J: But things get crazier still. In several Bible passages, God is actually said to be the *cause* of man's downfall. In Exodus 14:4 God says, "I will harden Pharaoh's heart..." Verse eight then confirms the dirty deed: "And the Lord hardened the heart of Pharaoh king of Egypt..." Later in the chapter, God decides to make a name for Himself among the Egyptians by murdering Pharaoh's entire army. After formulating his genocidal brainstorm, God brags to Moses by declaring, "And I will harden the hearts of the Egyptians so that they shall go in after [the Israelites], and I will get glory over Pharaoh and all his host, his chariots, and his horsemen."

DK: So Moses waves his magic trick-a-stick, and the Lord parts the Red Sea, allowing the Israelites to pass through unscathed.

J: Yes, and then, with Egyptian forces in hot pursuit, God intervenes by clogging their chariot wheels with mud. Once the Israelites arrive safely on the other shore, God again commands Moses to stretch out his hand. This brings the great walls of seawater crashing back down like monstrous tidal waves upon the suckered Egyptians, and in a single fit of righteous anger, God drowns the whole unsuspecting bunch.

DK: And the rest, as they say, is history.

J: Actually, there's no proof that *any* of it is history—so maybe I'm a revisionist. Because here again we have scripture describing an egomaniacal God who takes the most shockingly cavalier attitude toward mass killing. Not even the poor *horses* were spared. And refusing to be upstaged, God wants to make damned sure that *He* gets full credit for this remarkable episode of murderous hatred.

DK: So even though it was *God* who caused the Egyptians' callousness, He chooses to kill them anyway.

J: That's what the scripture says.

DK: Is it possible that biblical writers were just speaking metaphorically when they said that God hardened someone's heart? Maybe they meant that He merely *allowed* their mental inflexibility, since He knew that He would eventually be victorious in his revenge.

J: Even at that, it's not a very *godly* choice. I mean does it ever occur to this noisome deity that instead of going around *hardening* people's hearts, He could occasionally *soften* them instead? If He can do the one, then He can certainly do the other.

DK: Maybe it was a special, one-time event, necessitated by the grave circumstance.

J: 'Fraid not. Once again, let's consult the scriptures. This time we'll take a look at Joshua, a book that generally describes a far-reaching campaign of terror and genocide. Starting at chapter eleven, verse nineteen, we read: "Except for the Hivites living in Gibeon, not one city made a treaty of peace with the Israelites, who took them all in battle. For it was *the LORD himself* who hardened their hearts to wage war against Israel, so that he might destroy them totally, exterminating them without mercy, as the LORD had commanded Moses."

DK: Yep, you're right. There's really no wiggle room. The great Heart Hardener is working overtime.

J: So again, God is clearly said to be the instigator of various wars against the Israelites' enemies. In fact, it sounds like He sets 'em up just so He can knock 'em down. And pay heed that God instructs Joshua to be *completely merciless* when slaughtering these people.

DK: And what, I hesitate to ask, was Joshua's dutiful response?

J: I'll quote: "At that time Joshua went and destroyed the Anakites from the hill country: from Hebron, Debir and Anab, from all the hill country of Judah, and from all the hill country of Israel. Joshua totally destroyed them and their towns. No Anakites were left in Israelite territory…"

DK: *Damn.* Evidently Joshua wasn't all that soft-hearted himself.

J: But consider the utter hypocrisy of these stories. Going back to the Exodus account, God first makes the Egyptians aggressive and unyielding by setting their resolve on pursuing the Israelites in

335

their famous escape from captivity. But even though it's God who puts the entire plan into motion, He suddenly grows offended when the Egyptians actually perform as programmed. Apparently outraged at the success of his own carefully formulated scheme, God murders every man in Pharaoh's army by drowning the full brigade in the Red Sea. I mean what the hell kind of half-cocked, psychoneurotic schizoid are we dealing with!?

DK: I'll tell ya what: if God's anything like that in heaven, I'd just as soon take my chances down south.

J: Maybe not a bad choice. Believe me, hell hath no fury like the heartless, heart-hardening God of the Bible. If you're gonna keep subjecting yourself to this character, you'd better book a visit with your cardiologist...

CHAPTER FIFTY THREE

DK: I'm beginning to realize how little I know about the Old Testament. Apart from some of the more famous stuff—the Garden of Eden, Noah's ark and such—I didn't spend much time on it because it seemed so dry and tedious.

J: No, no—it's *full* of great crime stories.

DK: Well, I was so confused over the *New* Testament that I pretty much ignored the Old. To me, a lot of it never made sense.

J: Now you can see why I was so amused by your cynical opening letter. As a follower of early Judaism, I had the same kinds of issues with the Books of Moses and the writings of the prophets that you have with the New Testament. Why do you think I was always breaking the rules? I wanted to show that a lot of that stuff is intellectually and morally offensive.

DK: To be truthful, that Red Sea story symbolizes everything I've grown to resent about religion's usual depiction of God. I just can't fathom the Almighty actually inducing men's ignorance or instigating their sinful demise.

J: But it's a fairly common theme in the scriptures. At one point, even Moses propagates this crazy logic. Growing exasperated with the Israelites, he tells them, "…to this day the Lord has not given you a mind to understand, or eyes to see, or ears to hear." Moses is angered by his people's wayward behavior, and yet he declares that *God* is the one preventing their understanding.

DK: That hardly seems fair.

J: Fair? You expect the God of the Bible to be *fair*? Oh, that's *rich*! In 1 Kings 22, God Himself is feeding faulty forecasts to the false prophets: "Now therefore behold, the Lord has put a lying spirit in the mouth of all these your prophets…"

DK: You mean God was directing certain prophets to *lie*? Man, how long could those fellas stay in business with a flawed data feed like *that*?

J: Well, it's not like they *wanted* to distribute bad info. But with *God* opposing 'em, the poor schmucks never stood a chance.

DK: At least now we know the false prophets were genuine.

J: But you've gotta wonder why the Bible God was handing out deceptive predictions in the first place. And it wasn't as though his *favored* prophets were the salt of the earth. In the second chapter of 2 Kings, the prophet Elisha becomes irate when a group of small boys pokes fun at his baldness. Scripture says he then "cursed them in the name of the Lord."

DK: A bit lacking in self-control, maybe—but it sounds harmless enough.

J: Unfortunately that's not where it ends. If a revered prophet cursing small children in God's name isn't sufficiently bizarre, the story turns downright macabre when God immediately *obliges* Elisha's request by sending two bears from the woods to thrash and tear forty-two of the boys to bloody pieces.

DK: You're not serious.

J: It's right there in the word of the Lord, my son.

DK: Looks like I should've joined those Old Testament study groups after all. I missed out on all the *good* stuff.

J: So now you've gotten a small taste of prophetic madness. But there's lots more. In Jeremiah 18, for example, the "godly" prophet is madder than a riled hornet.

DK: Aren't they always?

J: Well, in this case, Jeremiah's miffed because God's people are ignoring him and aren't showing enough gratitude for his previous intercessions. So he calls upon the Lord to inflict merciless revenge. He wants God to kill all the fathers and to starve and slaughter their children.

DK: *Sheesh.* Apparently ol' Jerry wasn't big on being led beside the still waters.

J: Still waters? You kiddin'? Some of these Bible prophets were more likely to be found near *raging rivers of blood.* And since you allude to the Psalms, let's examine a snippet from Psalm 137—another work that's often attributed to Jeremiah. In this piece, he lashes out against the Babylonians: "Happy shall he be who takes your little ones and dashes them against the rock!"

DK: Smashing the enemy's children against the rocks will bring *happiness*? What's this hothead got against kids?

J: Actually, gruesome biblical images of savagely murdered children aren't that exceptional; many other Old Testament passages use the same kinds of lethal language. The prophets—who, like their deity, usually felt unappreciated—really seemed to thrive on churning out ghastly predictions of grave violence. Interestingly, two of these kill-the-kids prophesies bear the same chapter number and verse. Isaiah 13:16 threatens the usual mutilation and killing of children—but with the additional promise that the women will be raped as well. Hosea 13:16 predicts the same brand of madness but goes a step further and warns that pregnant women will have their unborn children slashed from their bellies.

DK: Heavens to Hannibal! So much dashing, smashing and slashing! You're right, these touchy prophets are sounding dangerously similar to their God. And not only are they incredibly violent, but they all seem to need a helluva lot of attention.

J: Funny you should mention that. In Jeremiah 16, the Lord utters a diatribe of unrelenting anger against the people, and He leaves no threat or condemnation unspoken. They'll die and be left as dung on the earth, He says. They'll perish by famine and sword—two of Yahweh's more favored catastrophes. He angrily declares that His victims' corpses will lie rotting on the ground as food for worms.

DK: Boy, how did anyone put up with this character? I mean a fella can take only so much steadfast love.

J: But the really interesting thing is the *reason* for the Lord's upset. Start reading at verse ten...

DK: Lemme see here... "And when you tell this people all these words, and they say to you, 'Why has the Lord pronounced all this great evil against us? What is our iniquity? What is the sin that we have committed against the Lord our God?' then you shall say to them: 'Because your fathers have forsaken me, says the Lord, and have gone after other gods and have served and worshipped them, and have forsaken me and not kept my law, and because you have done worse than your fathers, for behold, every one of you follows his stubborn evil will, refusing to listen to me...'"

J: So the Lord is consumed with a venomous, deadly wrath against his people. And why? Because no one will *listen* to Him. And once again, his chronically disgruntled people are chasing after other gods—gods which monotheists keep swearing don't even *exist*. Now, this evokes some important questions. First, who *are* these other gods that constantly turn the Lord so green-eyed jealous that He's compelled to make the very first commandment a rule prohibiting their worship? Are they the same gods the Lord was addressing as peers in Genesis 3:22? If they do indeed exist, they may well deserve the same consideration as Yahweh. If they *don't* exist, then why is He constantly denouncing them and warning folks to keep their distance? And second, if the Bible God's nurturing leadership is so prone to make his people successful and content, then why the hell are they always wandering off in search of superior deities?

DK: Maybe prophets like Jeremiah were just using a God made in their image as a surrogate mouthpiece to project *their own* frustrations.

J: It sure looks that way. In fact, Jeremiah's anger was as likely to lead to his people's death as to their deliverance. He even takes shocking delight in calling down those violent curses on children.

DK: Sounds like Yahweh's kinda guy…

J: Ironically, biblical calls for vengeance against offenders' offspring stand in direct contradiction to many Old Testament mandates that children shall not pay for the sins of their fathers. Ezekiel chapter 18 covers this in quite some detail. But then, it's hard to give that stuff much credence when God personally proclaims in Exodus 20, "…for I the Lord thy God am a jealous God, visiting the iniquity of the fathers upon the children…"

DK: So Jeremiah's veins are running with the blood of murderous rage against his own friends and neighbors.

J: Yep, the man's raptly intent on carnage and death. Nowadays he'd be considered certifiably insane. And even though the Lord frequently denounces the attitudes and objectives of the so-called *"false"* prophets, He constantly picks guys like Jeremiah to be his messengers.

DK: Pretty crazy, alright. But I wonder why the Lord was so hard on the false prophets. From a business stance, instead of *attacking* the competition, it might've made more sense to *recruit* them. I mean if the Almighty had a specific agenda, why didn't He go straight to the oracles in person, so to speak, and tell 'em exactly what to say? Assuming He had proper I.D., I'm sure God could've spun the phony forecasters a hundred and eighty degrees.

J: He apparently had no intention of turning a prophet.

DK: Oh well, I guess if the dudes had *really* had talent, they would've seen it all coming. Anyhow, God evidently cleaned up his act by the time *you* came along. In the New Testament, He displays a little more sense and compassion.

J: Hey, don't think for a minute that the Bible God's spiteful behavior is confined to the Old Testament. Second Thessalonians 2:11 says, "Therefore God sends upon them a strong delusion, to make them believe what is false, so that all may be condemned who did not believe the truth…" So not only do we have God inspiring prophets to tell lies, but now He's causing certain people to *believe* them. To put the icing on the cake, He then takes smug satisfaction in condemning the whole group because of it.

DK: Why would He do that?

J: Twisted sense of humor, bad case of senility—who knows? Maybe He was desperate to fill a few vacancies in hell.

DK: This guy has to be found and stopped.

J: Heck, we've only touched the tip of the iceberg of divine psychosis. For those who care to dig through the records, there's lots more biblical chronicling of God's sanctimonious, sociopathic behavior.

DK: Such as?

J: Take the story of Jacob and Esau, for example. Genesis tells us that Esau, Isaac's firstborn son, is a hardworking, upstanding kind of guy—a truly solid citizen. He's constantly out hunting and gathering, providing food and clothing for his mother, father and brother.

DK: In other words, bringing home the bacon.

J: Or, in this case, the beef… His younger brother Jacob, on the other hand, likes to spend his time kicking back and lounging inside the tents. Now, what he's doing laying around the tents all day I have no idea.

DK: Probably hanging out with the concubines…

J: Anyhow, when it comes time to receive his father's blessing, Esau is told to go hunting and then prepare one of Isaac's favorite meals for him. After that, Isaac assures him, he'll receive the rightful blessing of the firstborn son.

DK: This is one of the few Old Testament stories I actually remember. To me it sounded like an ancient-day soap opera.

J: Well, in this episode, Esau hustles out to find game, eagerly anticipating the ritual for which he's waited *years*. In the meantime, Isaac's wife Rebekah secretly warns Jacob of Isaac's imminent plan to give his paternal blessing to Esau.

DK: If I'm not mistaken, scripture says that Rebekah loved Jacob more than she loved Esau.

J: Right. So she tells the favorite son Jacob to hurry in and steal his brother's blessing from their father Isaac, who's very old and practically blind. But Jacob is afraid to follow through with the scheme. He protests to his mother that Isaac will know he isn't dealing with Esau once he touches Jacob's skin, since Esau is quite hairy and Jacob's skin is soft and hairless. Take notice, however, that Jacob isn't concerned that the whole idea smacks of treachery and deceit. He's only worried that he might get *caught*.

DK: This guy could've made a *fortune* on Wall Street…

J: So the wily Rebekah dreams up a creative plan to fool her husband into giving Esau's blessing to Jacob. She instructs Jacob to bring in two young lambs, which she slaughters and then cooks in preparation for Isaac's requested meal. Next, she dresses Jacob in some of Esau's clothes and then straps the fresh lambskins around Jacob's arms and neck to give him the hairy feel of his brother.

DK: With a cockeyed plan like *that*, it's not surprising if Jacob had reservations. I mean you can't blame the guy for feeling a little sheepish.

J: The story ends, of course, with Isaac—who's not only old and blind but evidently a little gullible as well—falling completely for Rebekah's lambskin ploy and unknowingly giving Esau's merited blessing to the younger son Jacob.

DK: So with his clever wolf-in-sheep's-clothing routine, Jacob steals his brother's birthright.

J: Yep, the entire story's a confusing lesson in spiritual and moral corruption. I mean here we've got Esau living a humble life of integrity, serving as a strong, reliable provider and working hard to care for his family. Jacob, however, is just loafing around the tents, playing video games and watching reality TV. Yet it's the scoundrel Jacob who winds up with the big reward and the historical honor. He was lucky the Ten Commandments hadn't come around yet, because he broke at least *four* in the birthright drama by coveting something that wasn't his, bearing false witness, dishonoring his father, and stealing.

DK: Tell me *another* bedtime story, daddy.

J: I detect a hint of scorn.

DK: I'm just trying to ferret out the point.

J: Well, the point is this: in the Old Testament, God declares through his prophet Malachi, "I have loved Jacob but I have hated Esau." Now, tell me: what are we supposed to think of this crazy celestial coot? Why should He deserve our respect? He's a bigoted, emotionally juvenile hypocrite. He's fruitier than a peach daiquiri and more confounding than a vegan with a Big Mac. He's a giant version of Homer Simpson.

DK: Yeah, but not nearly as funny...

CHAPTER FIFTY FOUR

J: Let's follow just a bit further the high-level weirdness of the Bible God's outrageous declaration of hatred toward Esau. Many years after Jacob had fled the country in fear of Esau's revenge, the two brothers finally meet up again. But instead of *killing* Jacob, as he could easily have done with his army of four hundred, Esau is surprisingly forgiving. He even embraces his conniving brother with tears of joy.

DK: A pretty noble gesture.

J: Absolutely. So even if Esau did things that God disapproved of—and if he did, we're never told what they were—he should've received plenty of karma credits for his magnanimous dealings with his ungrateful, double-crossing family. I mean if the birthright deception had been Jacob's *only* transgression, I might cut the Bible God some slack and overlook his flakey favoritism. But not only did Jacob deceive his father and steal from his brother, he also showed serious sexual indiscretions by practicing bigamy with two of his cousins and committing fornication with two housemaids.

DK: So compared to Jacob, Esau was a veritable saint.

J: Which is why it's so befuddling for God to proclaim that He loved Jacob but *hated* Esau. Now, some will tell you that God was really referring to Esau's *descendants*, the Edomites, who became bitter enemies with the Israelites many centuries later. The Israelites, of course, were descendants of Esau's brother, Isaac. But once again you'd be on very dangerous ground trying to argue that God was only speaking symbolically—because if some Bible passages need to be *interpreted* and can't be taken at face value, then you've *really* opened a can of worms. So literalists can't even *begin* to allow for this kind of soft and mushy approach to the scriptures. If they ever admit that many Bible verses are subject to inference, opinion or deduction, then they'd also have to convince the world that *their* inferences, opinions and deductions are the *right* ones. They'd be skewered so fast it would make their heads spin.

DK: Well, it's bad enough that this Bible God is so spiritually immature that He harbors hatred for his own children and carries personal petty grievances. But why the need to *showcase* it all by immortalizing it in scripture? And how the heck does God *arrive* at these bizarre judgments?

J: Good question. It's like the Genesis story of the destruction of Sodom and Gomorrah. In that account, God decides to incinerate the two infamous cities because the inhabitants were of low moral character. But God inexplicably spares the life of a man named Lot, even though Lot had cowardly offered up his two virgin daughters to be gang-raped by the men of Sodom in order to save himself and two allegedly angelic houseguests from harm.

DK: On the other hand, if the menacing Sodomites *hadn't* been appeased, God mightn't have had a Lot to spare.

J: You're lucky there's no purgatory for pathetic punsters...

DK: I can't explain the strange partiality concerning Lot. But in the case of Jacob and Esau, God was probably making an example of Esau so that others would tow the line.

J: An *example*!? Are you kidding!? *Jacob's* the one who should've been made the example. I mean what did Esau do that was so bloody appalling? Scripture never says. No, in my opinion that whole Jacob/Esau disaster is one big, nasty contradiction. In fact, God's professed hatred for Esau is nearly as nutty and bewildering as his passionate affection for King David.

DK: In what respect?

J: Well, as you know, David is considered a genuine biblical hero. I'm not sure why, because the Old Testament depicts him as just another brutal, unscrupulous dictator. Prior to becoming Israel's ruler, David is a traitor who lives among his enemies the Philistines under protection of their king, all the while plundering and pillaging the local inhabitants with his army and then murdering them to cover his tracks. He continuously lies to the king to stay in his good graces and even offers to fight alongside the Philistines against his own countrymen!

DK: Sounds like the man could've taken up any number of thrones in the modern world and done pretty well.

J: In one character-revealing episode from 1 Samuel, David, who isn't yet monarch and is still relatively unknown, tries extorting a well-to-do livestock owner named Nabal into giving him certain gifts and provisions as repayment for David and his men not harming or stealing from Nabal's workers while they lived near David and his army. It was something of an ancient-day offering of Mafia-like "protection." But Nabal understandably refuses to be strong-armed through such intimidating tactics when he doesn't even know who David is. David turns furious and vows to take his army and kill Nabal and all the other males on the property. The farmer's wife, Abigail, hears of the plan, goes groveling to David with a mule train of gifts, and shamelessly begs David's forgiveness for her husband's behavior. David then relents and assures Abigail that he won't follow through with the slaughter of Old MacDonald and the others. Several days later, though, Nabal is mysteriously found dead. David quickly declares that Nabal was obviously "smote" by the Lord for his intolerable arrogance.

DK: I'll assume the story's ending contains some kind of moral lesson.

J: Not so much. The minute David hears that Nabal is dead—if indeed it was truly a surprise—he sends for the farmer's wife and sleeps with her, thereafter making her one of his many wives.

DK: *Crikey.* According to my Sunday school recollections, King David was practically Captain Marvel.

J: By scriptural accounts, though, he's a cold-blooded killer who sadistically slaughters thousands of innocent men, women and children. Vulgar in his treatment of his ladies, David is a sex-crazed polygamist with at least nine wives and a harem of concubines. One of them—princess Michal, daughter of King Saul—David secures by killing two hundred men and then delivering their foreskins back to the king.

DK: Whoa! Talk about knifing your way to the top!

J: David is also a drunkard who prances naked in front of his housemaids. He's an adulterer who steals the wife of one of his most faithful and honorable soldiers, gets her pregnant, and then has the husband, along with many of his comrades, intentionally killed in battle to conceal the illicit affair and thus protect *his own* hide.

DK: Well, I can see why they made him king. I mean who'd want the guy living next door?

J: Evidently, even Yahweh is a little put off by David's violent nature—and that's really *saying* something. In 1 Chronicles 22, David tells his son Solomon that the Lord has forbidden David to build a tabernacle for Him because David has shed too much blood.

DK: And this is the man the gospels proudly proclaim as the starting point of your family lineage!?

J: Yeah, the very same hero to whom the book of 2 Samuel assigns the title of "the sweet psalmist of Israel."

DK: Actually, I've heard that even some Jewish scholars have doubts that King David had anything to do with scribing the Psalms.

J: Well, let's take the traditional stance for the moment and assume that he did. To get a feel for the psalmist's "sweetness," read a few verses of Psalm 109 sometime. He calls on the Lord, prophet-like, to inflict one dreadful calamity after another onto his enemies. He wants their children to become fatherless and to go begging in the street.

DK: Boy, what is it about these Old Testament characters that they carry such mean-ass grudges against their enemies' kids?

J: They were a fierce bunch, alright. Even as he lay dying, King David is still full of hatred and vengeance. Instead of choosing the same forgiveness for which he himself often supplicated the Lord, with his last breaths David orders his son Solomon, heir to the crown, to carry out the murders of two old men. One of them was his nephew and faithful longtime military commander, Joab. Himself a bloodthirsty killer of thousands, Joab was largely responsible for helping David achieve greatness. In light of their history together, David's request for Joab's murder is one of the strangest incidents in the Old Testament. As David's top general, Joab, degenerately but nonetheless faithfully, had even carried out the king's cowardly order to have Bathsheba's husband, Uriah, killed on the front lines of combat. He also helped David regain his throne after losing it to his son Absalom in a coup. The other target of David's deathbed fury was Shimei, a man who had indeed treated David spitefully during the Absalom ordeal. However, demonstrating a rare level of tolerance—perhaps due to a guilty conscience brought on by forty years of serious *personal* moral failures—David had solemnly promised not to kill Shimei.

DK: So David technically kept his word to Shimei by not killing him, but still had the last-minute satisfaction of knowing that Solomon would find a reason to do the job instead.

J: Right. David probably figured that his son might as well get a taste for what life would be like as king. So Solomon faithfully carries out the orders—but not *personally*. Being a chip off the old block, he has his man Beniah perform the killings *for* him. As a point of interest, Shimei was ultimately killed not for his past behavior toward King David, but for violating Solomon's confinement order by chasing down a couple of runaway donkeys.

DK: It seems these biblical rulers were not always the towers of spiritual strength and moral integrity we've been told they were.

J: Well, in David's case, the man wouldn't have known an ethic if it slapped him in the face. And in fact many of Israel's kings and other leaders were guilty of commonly committing the so-called "works of the flesh" so strongly condemned by the Apostle Paul in the fifth chapter of Galatians: immorality, enmity, strife, jealousy, anger, selfishness, dissension, envy, drunkenness and carousing. And that was just the *small* stuff. Read the last part of verse

347

twenty-one to hear Paul's pronouncement regarding the fate of people whose lifestyles reflect these demon qualities.

DK: Okay... He says, "I warn you, as I warned you before, that those who do such things shall not inherit the kingdom of God."

J: But unbelievably, in the Book of 1 Samuel, God proudly declares that King David is a man after his own heart!

DK: Well, considering God's *own* alleged behavior, I can see where He might feel that way: the two had a lot in common. But to balance the ledger, I could argue that you've cited only a few examples from a book of a thousand pages.

J: Yes, but these aren't just isolated accounts. The Old Testament is *stuffed* with similar stories attributing to God the most outrageous displays of fear mongering, intolerance, double standards, and trifling mean-spiritedness. And here again, *that* was only jacks-for-openers. Plenty of passages detail divine outbursts that are far more serious, including a goodly number of episodes involving indiscriminate, large-scale human slaughter.

DK: My Sunday school teacher used to say that Yahweh's power knows no bounds.

J: Yeah? Well, neither does his destructive rage. It runs the gamut from continuously instigating war to cursing large populations with a cruel assortment of physical plagues and hardships. Sometimes his victims included the Israelites themselves. The Bible God seems to especially relish causing hunger and starvation. He frequently sends down plights of famine, years of drought, waves of crop-destroying insects, and a host of other societal disasters. As we've discussed, Yahweh is occasionally credited with the annihilation of *entire cultures*—and the biblical descriptions of these terrors sound eerily similar to the horrific "ethnic cleansing" episodes with which the world has become far too familiar.

DK: The Bible God certainly appears preoccupied with revenge. It's almost like that's what gets Him out of bed in the morning.

J: The irony is that He's constantly urging humanity to show compassion and forgiveness, while He personally maintains a zero-tolerance policy. His overriding attitude is basically, "That'll teach 'em to mess with *me*!"

WRESTLING with JESUS

DK: Well, He did warn us when He said, "Vengeance is mine." Apparently He damned well meant it.

J: Yeah, but who figured He would make it into his *life's work*!? And all of it to prove that *He's* the indisputable *Boss*. It's crazy, but this Bible God would just as soon fry their fat in the fire as to save anyone. He's perfectly happy with the reputation of Cosmic Hitman as long as they spell his name correctly in the shift report.

DK: But again, this is all *Old* Testament. His *New* Testament persona—theoretically expressed through *you*—seems to be far more centered on love.

J: How can you make that argument when Christianity's quintessential theology ends with most of humanity burning timelessly in hell!?? You call that *love*? Believe me, if the Bible can be taken at its word, the creator's most heinous behavior *still lies ahead*. Remember: if you don't make the final roster, then you're condemned to *eternal torture*. Behold, dear mortals, how thy biblical God doth *love* thee!

DK: Now, wait a minute. Paul says in the ninth chapter of Romans that we shouldn't even *question* God. In fact, he specifically mentions the Jacob/Esau story. Paul declares that God has every right to be inconsistent because...well, because He's *God*.

J: Oh, so if *Paul* says that God has the right to act like a blithering fool and hate his children just for the hell of it, then who are *you* to question it? Is that the argument?

DK: Fundamentally, at least.

J: Gosh, what a great way to kill discussion. Just include a Bible passage telling everyone that God's ways are unfathomable and above reproach—no matter how cruel, idiotic or hypocritical—and that settles it. What a beautiful strategy. And the best part of this "don't even ask" policy is that it discourages all intellectual discernment. It precludes any critical evaluation by implying that anyone who *does* question scriptural stupidity is subject to the knee-jerk wrath of the Almighty. As a result, most Christians decide just to look the other way and not let sleeping lies dog them.

DK: But Paul doesn't quit. In his justification of God's behavior, he writes, "What shall we say then? Is there injustice on God's part? By no means!" He then quotes God as proclaiming, "I will have mercy on whom I have mercy and I will have compassion on whom I will have compassion."

J: In other words, Paul argues that God's position is a perverted twist on the Golden Rule. In effect God declares, "Whatsoever I would that you should do unto *me*, you had better bloody well *do* it. And whatsoever I wish to do unto *you*, that will I damned well do!"

DK: Maybe I'm not doing Paul full justice. He further explains, "So it depends not upon man's will or exertion, but upon God's mercy… He has mercy upon whomever He wills, and He hardens the heart of whomever He wills. You will say to me then, 'Why does He still find fault? For who can resist his will?' But who are you, a man, to answer back to God?"

J: To which you might rightfully reply, "I'm a child of God's very own creation, *that's* who! And I damned sure recognize hypocrisy when I see it!"

DK: I doubt many people will take that approach. For a lot of us, the Bible has instilled a pretty healthy fear of God.

J: Despite what you read in the Bible, there's nothing healthy about fearing God. It's a good example of why people have got to stop viewing the world's religious books as the ultimate authority. Some of the writings exude a warmth and beauty you'd expect from sacred works, but others are so polluted with contradictions and fearful ego-projections that they wind up distancing people from God. They're used as a means to judge and create a sense of superiority. At the extreme, they're even used to justify murder.

DK: To a lot of believers, the Bible actually seems to *encourage* judgmental thinking. Or at least that's been the result.

J: I advised my disciples to *"judge not."* I don't see how that statement could possibly be misconstrued.

DK: Well, unfortunately those simple words get overpowered by hundreds of other passages describing a God of anger, vengeance and punishment. I think that's why so many believers operate from fear.

J: Not too surprising, I suppose. They've inherited a God who's a scary, schizophrenic psychopath. He uses double standards, plays favorites, and even predestines certain people to be evil—ultimately *judging and condemning* them for it! The Old Testament in particular portrays God as a mean and whimsical flake. Under *his* rule, it's quite possible, as with Esau, to live a reasonably sincere, honest and productive existence and still wind up on the "B" list.

DK: Yes, but didn't Christianity change all that?

J: I'm afraid it doesn't offer much relief. New Testament theology implies a policy of 'guilty by birth' and then *compounds* the guilt by making *you* responsible for *my death*. Then the church comes along, telling you to cut the power to your brain's analytical circuits and declaring that questioning divine idiocy is presumptuous and should be avoided. The implication, of course, is that anyone who does so could be subjected to God's fury. Now, level with me: does any of this sound reasonable? Or intelligent? Or *loving*?

DK: Not really.

J: And how *could* it? Anyone the least bit objective can see that biblical literalism is dangerous and leads to mindless absurdity. Nowhere does the New Testament extol the virtue of true intelligence or advocate critical thought regarding its theology. Blind adherence to the "inspired word of God" has inflicted centuries of cruelty and pain onto the world. Humanity has endured unspeakable suffering at the hands of religious believers—Christians and others—who were firmly convinced by ancient writings that they were doing God's bidding.

DK: I can't argue with history. Along with some other religions, Christianity has a pretty sorry record of human rights violations.

J: But what else would you expect? Christendom's entire belief paradigm comes directly from the pages of the Bible, and the Bible tends to confirm man's worst fears about the nature of the creator. It practically *sanctifies* intolerance. Too many believers figure that if God can treat *his* enemies like maggots, there's no reason *they* shouldn't do the same. They just assume that God shares their attitudes of righteous indignation toward those who disagree with them. And other religions' writings have produced similar results. So in effect, for millions of people around the world, scripture has become their war manual.

DK: I don't know about devotees of other religions, but I know from experience that the average Christian has practically no in-depth knowledge of how the Bible evolved. Even many who can quote it forward and backward act as though it was bequeathed to mankind directly from God.

J: It's the Ten Commandments syndrome. Some folks seem to believe the Bible was divinely compiled and then handed down straight from heaven, fully edited and ready to print. I remember one dear lady in particular—a sweet old widow with poor eyesight. She'd faithfully read fully through the four gospels every month. Once, during her nightly prayers, she thanked God for making things easier by highlighting *my* words in red…

Chapter Fifty Five

DK: You know, I probably shouldn't point fingers at the literalists. For about thirty years, I believed the Bible practically fell from the sky. After doing a little research, I discovered that its compilation actually dragged on for centuries.

J: Not one of my favorite topics. And you could fill a few train cars with books on the history and development of Jewish and Christian scripture. But maybe we should discuss it to clear the air.

DK: Well, considering the Bible's importance to both Judaism and Christianity, it's certainly worth some time. But the subject *is* a little bland. Maybe we could omit tedious details and just focus on highlights.

J: Ah, the *Reader's Digest* version.

DK: Exactly.

J: Okay, whatever turns your crank. You start, and we'll go from there…

DK: Well, my first surprise was learning that the Old Testament in its present form didn't even exist until at least fifty or sixty years after your death.

J: True. But the Hebrew Bible, from which the Old Testament books are taken, was around long before my birth. And even though Christians began referring to the Hebrew canon as the "Old Testament," for *non-Christian* Jews—the overwhelming majority—it was the *only* testament. They didn't accept the proposition that I was the Messiah.

DK: No, and they still don't.

J: Which is all a bit ironic, don't you think?

DK: How so?

J: Well, the whole of Christianity looks to Judaism for its validation, right? But the Jews don't acknowledge me as the Messiah, so they reject the entire New Testament as ill-founded and groundless—null and void. The irony is that Christians built their religion upon the historical and theological foundations of the very people who repudiate their claims.

DK: It is a little odd.

J: Odd? It's like a defense attorney in a murder trial arguing his client's innocence by producing witnesses who saw the guy pull the trigger!

DK: Okay, I stand corrected: it's *very* odd. Now that you mention it, I suppose the coupling of Jewish and Christian scripture is actually a pretty strange pairing.

J: From the standpoint of most Jews, it's totally senseless. They see no legitimate connection between the two religions, so the term "Judeo-Christian," like the term "Old Testament," is met with jeers by a lot of Jewish hardliners. They're useful labels only from the standpoint of Christians. I wouldn't go tossing them around in the local synagogue.

DK: Thanks for the tip. Always good to know what's politically correct…

J: Now, the Christian "Old Testament" was, as I said, derived from the ancient Hebrew Bible—so establishing its contents was fairly straightforward. But although the standard Old Testament contains 39 books, that arrangement is not universally agreed upon. The Orthodox communion, for instance, uses an Old Testament that contains 51 books. The same kinds of differences also apply to the New Testament. The Syrian Church, as an example, uses a New Testament that utilizes only 22 books instead of the usual 27. It almost goes without saying, of course, that even though Christians respect and employ the Old Testament as scripture, the Jews don't reciprocate with the New Testament. Within Judaism, the New Testament isn't used, nor is it regarded as divinely inspired. For them it's completely irrelevant—blatant heresy.

DK: I would imagine that during the early years of Christianity, Jewish leaders must have been appalled at what was developing.

J: Many were. And it didn't help that Christians, the newcomers in town, had begun using their own versions of various "Old Testament" books as a source of "proof" for the prophecy of *my* arrival. Christians were claiming that ancient Jewish scripture had predicted my advent as the Messiah, and they were hijacking some of the old, ambiguous Hebrew texts and presenting them as the under-structure of their new religion. One of the most important examples of this scriptural coercion involves the popular Christmas verse from Isaiah 7:14. Christians intentionally mistranslated the Semitic word *almah*, meaning "young woman," to the Greek word PARTHENOS, meaning "virgin." That little switcheroo allowed Christians to claim that Hebrew scripture called for the Messiah to be born of a virgin, a concept that was standard fare among the Mysteries but completely foreign to Judaism.

DK: Well, *that's* a fairly serious problem. I mean the virgin birth is the church's number one assertion in defense of your special nature—the very starting point of the Christ story. And I have to be frank: even a lot of Christians are quietly uncomfortable with the idea. Now, I'm told there's a phenomenon in nature known as "parthenogenesis," in which certain creatures can reproduce by the development of an unfertilized ovum. For most skeptics, however, that explanation just doesn't satisfy. In fact, there's not a single scientifically verified case of human partheno—

J: Excuse me for interrupting your fascinating little biology discourse, which has me just *riveted* to my seat with its rockets' red glare and bombs bursting in air—

DK: Go easy, now…

J: —but I'm compelled to point out that I never talked about my birth. As I've said, the virgin mother idea first took hold in the Mystery religions, and that's how it wound up in the gospels. But as any honest Bible scholar will tell you, original Hebrew scripture made no prediction of any coming Messiah's virgin birth. To most of my countrymen, the notion would've been absurd. Not once did I make the slightest allusion to the outrageous notion that my mother was still a virgin when I was born. Only two gospels— Matthew and Luke—actually include the virgin birth story, while no other New Testament writers even *mention* it.

DK: It *is* an interesting omission, considering the remarkable nature of the claim.

J: The gospel of Mark was the original document from which the other two "synoptic" gospels of Matthew and Luke were derived, but Mark doesn't include the virgin birth account. The story was added later by Christians trying to enroll new converts. They sought to build their new religion's legitimacy by pouring as much grain into the sack as possible. But there's not a single non-Christian report of any miraculous birth in Bethlehem from that period, and even Christian accounts of it weren't written until decades later.

DK: I do know that the Apostle Paul, fervent as he was about spreading his version of the Christian message, was never willing to resort to the virgin birth claim.

J: Paul's letters were written well before the gospels, and his writings show that he was unaware of the stories that wound up in Matthew, Mark, Luke and John. His letters contain no parallels to them. Besides, Paul had strong Gnostic tendencies and therefore viewed me more as a *mystical* figure. Have you noticed that he never really talks about my life? This should be especially puzzling to literalist Christians, since Paul does claim to know people who knew me. Strangely, though, he never refers to my parables, my run-in with the Romans, my sermon material, or anything else that would indicate he knew the so-called "historical" details of my life. He never utilizes my sayings in his letters, even when doing so would bolster his arguments. The only time he bothers quoting me is in the eleventh chapter of 1 Corinthians. Few Christians know it, but what he's actually citing is the ancient Mystery formula for the Eucharist!

DK: You mean Paul was familiar with the Mystery rites?

J: Intimately. In 1 Corinthians 2, he writes about imparting a "secret and hidden wisdom" to "initiates." This is definitely not the sort of talk you'd hear from someone who was a Christian literalist.

DK: Then it doesn't seem likely that Paul would've bought into the virgin birth story as literal fact.

J: Not a chance. Paul was fanatical in some ways and at times could be pretty unreasonable—but even Paul had his limits.

DK: You must realize that debunking the virgin birth claim is no small detail. I mean it's not like declaring that you were actually blond or something. We're talking major league revision here. Nearly every Christian church on earth teaches that God magically impregnated your mother and that you had no true earthly father. It's one of the main pillars supporting your divinity. A lot of Christians consider it *crucial* to believe that you were cosmically conceived; otherwise it could imply you were no different from the rest of us.

J: Gosh, now wouldn't *that* be awful.

DK: Then you're not concerned that people might come to see you as their equal?

J: *Au contraire, mon ami.* I'll sleep much better when they *do*…

CHAPTER FIFTY SIX

DK: Well, you've managed to demolish yet another sacred shrine. By disclaiming your mother's eternal virgin status, you instantly bring yourself down to the level of everyone else. Christendom puts you squarely on the pedestal of divinity—and you keep jumping off! I can see you won't be happy 'til you get yourself demoted.

J: Tell ya what… since we're examining the evolution of the Bible and Christianity's forced coupling of Old Testament and New, let's take a look at the famous Christmas passage in the first chapter of Matthew and see if there's any true scriptural compatibility. Matthew says, "All this took place to fulfill what the Lord had spoken by the prophet: 'Behold, a virgin shall conceive and bear a son, and his name shall be called Emmanuel.' " As I explained, the original Semitic word was actually *almah*, indicating only a young woman, not a virgin. Any Hebrew writer wanting to convey virginity would immediately have used the term *bethulah*.

DK: It's ironic that in the Revised Standard Version of the Bible, Matthew's quote from Isaiah cites the word "virgin." But when you look up the actual verse in Isaiah, the passage reads "young woman," as you say it should. Apparently, with the original passage, translators just couldn't bring themselves to use the word "virgin."

J: Of course not. They knew darned well what the writer meant.

DK: Even so, they did insert a footnote saying, "or 'virgin'."

J: Only because they were dealing with a political hot potato and were trying to appease the virgin birth proponents. By the way, that prophetic Old Testament passage that I just quoted from Matthew is taken from the seventh chapter of Isaiah. The words were written around 735 BCE and were intended to comfort King Ahaz, who was distraught about Syria threatening to attack Jerusalem. It was hoped that Isaiah's words would shore up the Hebrews' wavering courage.

DK: Yet the early Christians argued that Isaiah was heralding *your* nativity.

J: But the prophecy referred only to the *near-term* future, and even Isaiah's contemporaries never took his words to indicate the predicted birth of a god. Furthermore, nothing in the passage even remotely hints at my own arrival centuries down the road. I mean think about it: how in the world would Ahaz find reassurance in his hour of crisis by learning that a great redeemer would show up fifteen or twenty generations later?

DK: Not much consolation in *that*, I suppose.

J: No, it would be like Isaiah telling Ahaz, "Things may look bleak at the moment, your highness, but don't worry: a kid from Bethlehem's gonna set everything straight in about seven hundred years."

DK: *Heh heh*. Hardly cause for Ahaz to hover over his sundial.

J: The thing is, the Jews of Isaiah's time, like those of my day, were looking for an *earthly* rectifier, not a heavenly one. They desperately wanted a conqueror—someone to even the score with the enemy *du jour*. But they never thought in terms of any future *divine* leader. They wanted vengeance, and they wanted it *now*. In fact, one of the famous Dead Sea documents, the War Scroll, even lays out a battle plan for the expected clash, which was predicted to occur at Har Megiddo, now popularly known as Armageddon. Ironically, it was the site of one of the first recorded battles in history, and more than thirty conflicts have been fought there. Some Christians believe Armageddon will also be the location of history's *last* battle as well—the end-of-the-world scenario deduced from a painfully literal interpretation of the book of Revelation. But the War Scroll made clear that the prophesied confrontation was to be solely between humans, with no celestial implications whatsoever.

DK: So there's no mention in the War Scroll of a devil or of any spiritual struggle between heaven and earth?

J: No description at all of any cosmic battle between good and evil. The envisioned fray was to be strictly between the "Children of Light"—that is, the tribes of Israel—and the "Sons of Darkness," the Jews' derogatory name for the Romans and other antagonistic groups. The Jewish hope was that a great deliverer would arise from within their ranks and lead them on to military victory. The War Scroll specifically designates the expected Messiah to serve in the mighty battle as Israel's supreme martial commander. It was the kind of thing Isaiah had in mind when he made his prophecy to King Ahaz. But the Jews were still waiting for their savior more than seven centuries later when I showed up.

DK: A lot of 'em still are.

J: Well, I can tell you this: even if their anticipated Messiah does emerge, he won't have any connection with Isaiah's prophecy. That prediction was expected to materialize very soon after it was written.

DK: If Isaiah wasn't referring to *you*, then what's the bottom line on your mother's contentious pregnancy?

J: The bottom line is that my beginnings were no different from yours. There's no serious scholarly support—and *zero* hard evidence—for the gospel's virgin birth account. I never talked about it, the New Testament all but ignores it, and there was never any Old Testament prophecy predicting it. But like I've said, virgin birth was a pretty common theme among the Mysteries, so it's not unusual that Christianity adopted it—especially given the uncompromising commitment to it later on by various Roman authorities. The main point is that the gospels were written *evangelically*: they were meant to encourage new converts by creating an atmosphere of mystery and divine authority. They express the kind of fervor you'd expect from impassioned devotees.

DK: But if the virgin birth story was widely known and believed, it's mighty strange that the gospels of Mark and John would fail to use it. After all, it would've been some of their best material. I mean you don't just overlook a thing like that.

J: Don't lose perspective. The four New Testament gospels were written independently over several decades following my death. They were never intended to be affiliated pieces of a collective work, which is why they differ so radically in places and often conflict—the virgin birth story being a prime example.

DK: Yet here's the church, twenty centuries later, still talking about it like... well, like it's *gospel*.

J: Years after my death, things which in the beginning were only myth, symbol, opinion or interpretation ultimately became dogma. They were presented as "facts" by a young church eager to expand its influence and power.

DK: It sounds like the church has used the Bible to slip us a wooden nickel.

J: Well, there's no doubt that the Christian story of my life is a superficial hodgepodge—and plenty of scholars know it. The gospels were written and assembled a long time after I was gone, and they were continuously revised for centuries. Like the traditional Christmas narrative, the result isn't much more than a folk tale. Fragments of my life were strung together, embellished, commingled with ancient pagan themes and artificially linked with unrelated Old Testament verses. The entire assemblage was then glossed over and dispensed as a unified whole. For sheer honesty, it's right up there with the tooth fairy or a White House press conference.

DK: You're blasting some pretty big holes in mainstream beliefs.

J: Remember: beliefs don't *establish* facts; they usually *distort* them and render them invisible. As with the virgin birth, the church continues encouraging beliefs that should offend the sensibilities of thinking people everywhere. Using threats of divine punishment or eternal damnation as weapons, religion is still fearfully guarding access to the Tree of Knowledge.

DK: I guess you realize that you're absolutely *killing* my chances for an appearance with Oprah...

CHAPTER FIFTY SEVEN

DK: Wow, what a trip. Religion has flourished for centuries by selling sinners an irritated God who's never quite happy. Now *you* come along and destroy one temple after another by claiming there's no sin, no eternal punishment, everyone's divine, and reality's all berries and cream. You insist that you're just like the rest of us and that most of what's written about you is tripe. You say your mother conceived you in the normal fashion and that your crucifixion was actually unneeded. Next you'll be telling me that you were married—with three kids, two dogs and a full-time nanny.

J: I'm glad you brought that up.

DK: Uh-oh...

J: As you know, in the gospels I'm often addressed as "Rabbi," which means "teacher."

DK: Yeah, why do you mention it?

J: Most people don't realize it, but the gospels never claim that I was celibate or unmarried. And it *was* fairly unusual for a teacher to remain single. In some circles, getting married upon becoming an adult was viewed as one's moral duty—an important part of the divine plan for procreation and growing the "family of God." But I'll leave it at that. You've got plenty of trouble already.

DK: You're right, I'm not sure the world is ready for Jesus the family man.

J: Well, in that case, let's get back to your spellbinding exposition on the Bible. Go ahead and grind away.

DK: Ah, c'mon. Is it *that* painful?

J: About one notch above circumcision.

DK: I'll try to pick up the pace…

Around the third century, the most popular Greek translation of the Old Testament was known as the Septuagint. Supposedly it took 70 scholars nearly a century to translate it from Hebrew between the 3rd and 2nd centuries BCE. One can only imagine the errors involved with *that* logistical nightmare.

J: Unless, once again, you accept the possibility of divine intervention. And some would say that's exactly what happened. Regarding the Five Books of Moses, the Jewish Talmud states that Ptolemy II Philadelphus, king of Ptolemaic Egypt from 283 BCE to 246 BCE, gathered 72 elders and placed each one in a separate chamber, not telling any of them why they were there. The king then instructed each cloistered elder, "Write for me the Torah of Moshe, your teacher."

DK: "Moshe" meaning Moses.

J: Right. The Talmud then declares that the king's experiment resulted in something quite miraculous: "God put it in the heart of each one to translate *identically* as all the others did." The well-known philosopher Philo of Alexandria would later add that the process itself took exactly 72 days.

DK: So the claim is that all 72 elders came up, independently, with the *same, exact wording* for the entire Torah!?

J: That's what the Talmud says.

DK: Hmmm, very peculiar. This Bible translation stuff is a real shot in the dark, no?

J: It's tricky business, for sure, and language scholars have always struggled with its jots and tittles. In fact, the creation of the famous Vulgate Bible is one of the most striking examples of this built-in frustration factor. When Jerome was commissioned by Pope Damasus to produce a Bible in Vulgar Latin—that is, the form spoken by the common man—he essentially had to invent a new written language. Even though Vulgar Latin was the spoken language of the Roman middle class, nearly all writing was either Greek or Classical Latin, and the middle class couldn't *read* Classical Latin. Nor could they read Ecclesiastical Latin, which was the form invented by a fellow named Tertullian who, as a point of interest, was also the guy who claimed that the Apostle John was thrown into a vat of boiling oil by the Romans and escaped unharmed.

DK: *Heh heh.* A Kentucky fried miracle.

J: Well, anyhow, to create a Bible in the language of the masses, the Pope's man Jerome was forced to invent a written form of Vulgar Latin. The result was the Vulgate, a Bible composed in something of a makeshift language and based on previous versions that were filled with errors and compromises. And even the Vulgate underwent lots of revisions: they were changing it for centuries.

DK: Ha! Who would've figured that even God would have so much trouble with editors!

J: And don't forget that until Gutenberg showed up in the fifteenth century and cranked out the first mass-produced Bible with his newfangled printing press, compiling Bibles was highly labor-intensive. It was tedious, time-consuming business. That left even more room for distortion—accidental or otherwise.

DK: Well, there you go. You just proved the point.

J: Oh, good… I'd forgotten there *was* one.

DK: What I mean is, here we had lengthy ancient documents being reproduced by hand, converted from one difficult language to another by countless translators from diverse cultures over many hundreds of years. In other words, translations of translations and copies of copies. And since all of the original manuscripts from both Old and New Testaments are long gone, nobody knows *what* the original authors really said.

J: Not verbatim, anyway.

DK: Then it seems to me that we've taken a helluva lot for granted. After all, the church has led us to believe over the centuries that the Bible contains no errors and that every syllable was divinely inspired. As a practicing Christian, I never even suspected that certain groups or individuals had altered scripture to suit their own political or social ambitions. *Now* I learn that even church fathers were less than scrupulous about reporting the facts.

J: You're beginning to sound like a rebel with a newfound cause.

DK: Hey, after devoting the better part of my life to Christianity, I think I've got a right to feel somewhat hornswoggled. I mean a court of law wouldn't allow that kind of basic fact fudging on a small-time probate will!

J: But that's what I've been harping on all day: Christendom has built a global empire on a foundation of mud and with the very flimsiest of evidence.

DK: Well, excuse me, then, if I'm just a little damned upset. Dishonest scholars, power-mad dictators, and Councils with secret agenda. Hell, it's the kind of stuff you'd expect from a bloody mystery novel—not from a major religion. The whole sordid mess is beginning to sound like a huge game of politics and mind control!

J: Mellow out, McCarthy. You're bordering on subterfuge, and you don't need to stretch nearly that far. Sure, some of the key players in Christian history sought to mold the church into their own image—but not everyone involved was disingenuous. Some were merely over-zealous or just plain ignorant. Also, you've got to factor in the consciousness of the times. The entire Bible was written during eras of myth, superstition, religious misinformation and general spiritual ignorance. *You* know, sorta like today.

DK: *Criminy*. If there's an audience left, I'm not sure who it is…

J: The point is that you don't have to be a paranoid conspiracy nut to question the authenticity of the Bible. With or without any tampering, Bible translation is terribly difficult and imprecise under the *best* of circumstance. Take the Lamsa Bible, for example. It was the first English translation of the Bible from the fifth and sixth century Aramaic Peshitta texts. Dr. Lamsa, the project's director, said there were enormous differences between the Aramaic Peshitta manuscripts and the Hebrew and Greek texts. In fact, he estimated the number of discrepancies to be somewhere between ten and twelve *thousand*. In the New English Bible, Sir Godfrey Driver's introduction to the Old Testament speaks pretty well to the general endeavor of Bible translation. The British scholar comments that although the first five books, the Pentateuch, are translated fairly well, the rest of the Old Testament is pretty dicey and sometimes contains "sheer absurdities."

DK: So not exactly rocket science.

J: No, I s'pose not…

DK: [Jesus' tone had suddenly turned impassive and aloof. I looked up from my notes to catch him gazing glassy-eyed at a group of ducks swimming in the river.]

You seem distracted.

J: I'm trying to decide what's worse: discussing Bible history, or death by crucifixion.

DK: Sorry, I'll drone a little faster. Here's one of my main beefs:

The Old Testament's Hebrew scriptures were obviously the bedrock on which Christianity's foundation relied. But given our discussion so far, I think both groups may have been juggling the books. On the Jewish side, their scriptures are obviously not the straightforward, divinely inspired writings that many people assume they are. As for the Christians, it appears that certain factions did everything they could to "influence the election" by forcing their newer writings to synchronize with those of the ancient Israelites. But those earlier works, by all evidence, had nothing to do with you or any part of your life.

This seems hugely important, because creating an artificial Jewish/Christian connection gave the false impression that Judaism was merely intended as a steppingstone to Christianity. But that's a notion that even the Old Testament God Himself never mentions.

If I understand correctly, when Yahweh laid down the law, there was no suggestion that it would someday be rescinded. And if *that's* true, then we're *really* living in Whacko World. Because I don't see how God could expect the Jews to renounce their sacred traditions when He never forewarned them that every scrap of their legal and moral code—*their entire way of life*—was nothing but a precursor to something that would eventually render it all completely moot.

It seems outrageously unfair that Yahweh never once informed his "chosen" ones that He had an "only Son" who would later be taking over the enterprise and who could, if the Jews weren't careful, turn out to be the source of their condemnation!

J: Is this a summary or a filibuster?

DK: C'mon, I've got a truckload of serious questions here. Besides, more than *two billion people* claim to follow all or part of the Bible's teachings. So I figure it's worth a few minutes covering its basic history.

J: Alright, objection sustained. But let's move on or you'll be witnessing my Second *Going*...

CHAPTER FIFTY
EIGHT

DK: You seem a little edgy. Patience is a virtue, you know.

J: So is *brevity*.

DK: Don't worry, we've only got one Testament left...

Now, as for the *New* Testament, it presently contains twenty-seven books. But none of the churches I attended ever taught that these twenty-seven manuscripts were not the only ones considered for canonization.

J: No, in fact huge volumes of writings were generated by my followers during the first few centuries after my death. Only a small fraction ever made its way into the Bible, however, and even today the church can't identify the real authors of most of the books in the New Testament.

DK: Yeah, I've read that even the authorship of the four gospels remains a mystery, since scholars now know for certain that the apostles Matthew, Mark, Luke and John had nothing to do with writing the New Testament books that bear their names. Shockingly, some researchers contend that several of Paul's epistles—along with the letters ascribed to Peter, James and John— are outright counterfeits. They figure that since these documents were written by people claiming to be someone else, they aren't worth the papyrus they're forged on. And if their *very foundation* is a lie, then calling them holy or inspired is absurd.

J: Agreed. But it was pretty widely accepted that many Christian writings during the first two hundred years or so were anonymous. Either that or they were pseudonymous, meaning the work was *credited* to an important person, such as an Apostle, but was actually *written* by someone else.

DK: Kind of a sketchy system, though. To me, it doesn't justify the deceitful practice of writing fraudulent letters.

J: No, but at least it provides insight regarding the general methodology of the time.

DK: Okay, but there's no evidence that you ever instructed anyone to establish a new written code or authority. And even if one makes the case that you initiated a new spiritual orientation, there's certainly no indication that you were founding a new *religion*. So why the need for an official Christian holy book in the first place?

J: My followers wanted a record of my life and teachings to study and pass on to future generations. But there were other issues, too: continuity, control—that kind of thing. Unfortunately, designating something as "scripture" would nearly always generate conflict. Once Christian writings began proliferating, some sects started shaping them according to convenience, embracing some and rejecting others. There was lots of wrangling about the meaning and importance of the works that were circulating, and one cult's heresy was another cult's creed.

DK: The same kinds of disputes that are taking place today.

J: Yeah, pretty much. Eventually, church authorities—real pros at control, if you know what I mean—stepped in and established certain documents as "official" while discrediting those they didn't like.

DK: Canonization was obviously far more human than it was divine.

J: An entirely arbitrary affair from start to finish. No voices from heaven, no lightning bolts—not an ounce of divine intervention at any point. It was solely the discretion of various churchmen across several centuries that determined which books became scripture and which ones got thrown out.

DK: It seems the New Testament has been causing nonstop conflict since even before it was finalized, which was in 367 CE, I believe.

J: That year is sometimes used as the *unofficial* date for establishing the Christian canon, and that same list of "approved" Bible books was indeed adopted and affirmed at various synods and councils over the next ninety years or so. But widespread *official* acceptance didn't occur until many centuries later, in 1546.

That's when the Latin Vulgate Bible was printed. Some scholars defend the earlier date because in the fourth century Bishop Athanasius of Alexandria teamed up with a theologian and wrote an Easter letter to the churches under his jurisdiction. The two men proposed a limited canon of only twenty-seven books. They hoped the idea would curb expansion of the New Testament and that it would settle long-running disputes about what was official scripture and what wasn't.

DK: Then Athanasius was really just offering a New Testament based on compromise.

J: Yes, and part of his compromise suggested that the book of Revelation be included in the canon, even though he knew the Greek church flatly rejected Revelation as scripture. He also wanted the book of Hebrews included because it was thought at that time to have been written by the Apostle Paul. Of course, biblical scholarship has now shown that isn't true. The writer of Hebrews merely used Paul's name to make a bigger splash.

DK: Man, if those scripture writers were alive today, they'd be spending most of their time in court. But I didn't realize there were *multiple* versions of the New Testament.

J: Quite a few, actually. Scripture considered legitimate by one group was often repudiated as unworthy of canonization by opposing factions. Disputed works and collections included Codex Sinaiticus, Letter of Barnabas, Shepherd of Hermas, Codex Alexandrinus, Clement I, Clement II—and many others.

DK: So there was lots of cat fighting.

J: Enough to frustrate the average lion tamer, I'd say. And the chasm between opinions about scripture-worthiness was constantly widening. In the late second century, for instance, even while *scores* of gospels were circulating, church father Irenaeus insisted there should be only four. His logic was a little fuzzy, though. He said there should be only four gospels, just as the earth has only "four principal winds."

DK: Thank God he didn't base it on the number of lakes.

J: It was this kind of random justification by powerful churchmen that caused lots of popular, respected writings to be tossed out, even though many believers already considered them sacred.

DK: With the exception of the relatively recent news about the Gospel of Judas, we never hear much public discussion about other gospels.

J: Most Christians don't even know they exist. But there's lots of interesting stuff to be learned from some of the rejected works, which also include a lot of obscure gospels: Gospel of Thomas, Gospel of Peter, Gospel of the Hebrews, Gospel of the Egyptians, Gospel of James, Gospel of Mattheus, Gospel of Truth, and Gospel of Mary. Many of these writings were quite well known in their day, but determining which ones should be canonized was a real moose tussle. As an example, Irenaeus—a hard-liner who said there was no salvation outside the church—adamantly rejected the authority of 2 John, 3 John, James and 2 Peter. But all four were included in the New Testament *anyway*.

DK: Well, it's no surprise if folks were confused. The scripture selection process might as well have been conducted by Larry, Curly and Moe!

J: Things settled down a bit by the early third century as the church's list of official scripture grew more refined. Two especially popular books, Wisdom of Solomon and the Revelation of Peter, were finally excluded, as were the Secret Book of James and Dialogue of the Savior. At that time, the Letter to the Hebrews was accepted in the East but rejected by the West, whereas the Revelation of John was eagerly embraced by the West but resoundingly snubbed by the East.

DK: Never the twain shall meet…

J: In the fifth century, the Letters of Cyril, which were actually canonized as scripture by an official church body at the Fourth Ecumenical Council at Chalcedon in 431 CE, were nonetheless ultimately booted from the New Testament. The church decided that, for a document to qualify as scripture, it had to be either written by one of the original Apostles or, at the very least, sponsored by one of them. The Letters of Cyril didn't meet either requirement.

DK: Well, I guess if you're going to assemble an official Christian guidebook, those standards make as much sense as any.

J: Normally I might agree. But each of the New Testament gospels was written by *several* authors—all of whom remain unknown—using material from a wide distribution of sources.

DK: That might explain why the gospels contain such a strange mix of literalism and Gnosticism.

J: Sure. In the long years during the gospels' evolution, both groups opportunistically added their own editorial slants. And Christians need to know that not one of the four gospels was written or sponsored by an original Apostle. Nor, for that matter, were the letters of John, the book of Revelation, or the Letter to the Hebrews. And despite the fact that Paul is considered an Apostle, he really wasn't one in the sense of having known me "in the flesh." Technically, then, his letters wouldn't have qualified, either.

DK: So if the church had known centuries ago what it knows today, most of the current New Testament wouldn't even exist.

J: Precisely. Using the church's own "Apostle-related" criterion to determine scripture, only *three* of the New Testament's twenty-seven books would now make the cut: the two letters of Peter and the book of James. And as you said, even those three books are squarely spurned by some scholars as forgeries. Strangely, the Gospel of Thomas was rejected, even though scholarship attributes as many of my authentic sayings to that gospel as it does to any of the four gospels that were deemed Bible-worthy. Thomas was, after all, one of my original Apostles. His writings, by the way, never even mention my birth, my death, or any resurrection. This by itself was probably sufficient threat to motivate church authorities to omit the Gospel of Thomas from the official canon.

DK: But was he the document's true author?

J: What does it matter? Either way, it shouldn't detract from the book's comparative validity. After all, no one knows for sure who wrote the four gospels of the New Testament.

DK: It appears there were quite a few inconsistencies with the church's canonization scheme.

J: That's putting it mildly. Fifteen hundred years after my death, some in the church were still arguing over which documents should be included in its formally sanctioned Bible. Even as late as the Reformation in the sixteenth century, Martin Luther himself was disputing the scriptural worthiness of Hebrews, James, Jude and Revelation. Finally, after nearly sixteen centuries of hostile controversy, political gamesmanship, interpretation disputes and translation nightmares, the church cemented the Bible in its present form during the Reformation Council of Trent, from 1545 to 1563.

DK: So even *that* development took nearly twenty years!

J: Yep. But even though the church ultimately resigned itself to the Bible's current version, every Christian should understand that the final product was hardly a collection of universally approved "inspired" writings. Even now, some denominations around the world are using Bibles whose contents differ to one degree or another from the popular Western versions.

DK: I doubt most Christians realize that the scripture selection process was so haphazard. Using books of the Hebrew Bible for the Old Testament was certainly sensible enough. But evidently the church was purely arbitrary—and extremely *divided*, obviously—about what the New Testament should contain.

J: The process was anything but straightforward. In effect, the church fathers—no *mothers*, mind you—whimsically decided which documents they wanted as scripture and which ones they didn't. Anyhow, that's the nutshell evolutionary saga of what's sometimes called "the literal, inerrant and inspired word of God."

DK: Strange, but in all my years attending Bible study groups, no one ever mentioned that *none* of the New Testament books was selected because of "divine inspiration."

J: To avoid controversy, or threat to its power, the church silently encourages the notion that the Bible's authority stems from the Holy Spirit. But the books of the Christian Bible were chosen specifically to supply the perceived needs of a growing institution and were largely determined by influential forces *within* that institution. Unfortunately, some of these folks had highly questionable motives. And in every case, deciding on a particular document's "holiness" was really just a matter of opinion or even authoritarian insistence.

DK: So the whole enterprise of scripture-making was actually quite secular.

J: Well, lots of people *believed* some of the revered works to be inspired. But the church certainly didn't use "confirmed inspiration of the Holy Spirit" as the criterion to determine New Testament content. It's strictly a fact of history that, over a sixteen-hundred-year period, the church decided that scripture would consist solely of what various church bodies *said* was scripture.

DK: Quite a little cartel they created.

J: Indeed. And it established a dangerous precedent, which far too many Christians have either blithely accepted or willfully overlooked. By presenting itself as the ultimate authority on good and evil, on what's divine and what isn't, the church—implicitly, at least—has actually assumed the role of God, even usurping the function of its proclaimed Christ as the sanctified mediator between heaven and earth. In short, the church has positioned itself as the sole arbiter of righteousness.

DK: Pretty frustrating when you consider that the definition of goodness shifts between polar opposites from one age to the next.

J: The worst part may be that the church effectively institutionalized epiphany and inspiration. No longer was the Cosmos free to reveal Itself to *every*one. Only those consecrated by the church could safely claim heavenly contact. Anyone else would thereafter risk harassment, derision, ostracism—even torture and death. One minute you're tending the herb garden, and the next you're being torched as a witch in Town Square.

DK: I'd say the church has embarked on a real power trip.

J: In that respect, though, Christianity is hardly alone. Nor is the problem relegated only to history. In many parts of the world today, religious heresy can be fatal—just as it was for me twenty centuries ago.

DK: Well, at least Christians are no longer burning heretics at the stake.

J: No, but there are some who would if they could…

DK: Okay, I think I'm ready to move on.

J: Allah be praised!

DK: Oh, c'mon, it wasn't *that* grueling.

J: It's just that all this Bible stuff leaves me in a fog. In fact, here's some free advice: if you ever discover you've got only six months to live, spend as much time as possible reading Bible history. It'll *seem* like *eternity…*

CHAPTER
FIFTY NINE

DK: Our little scripture dialogue has been pretty enlightening. But I'm afraid you've gone and bled most of the mystique out of your number one bestseller.

J: Hey, don't put the Bible off on *me*: I had nothing to do with it. In fact, the term "Bible" wasn't used until well over a thousand years after my death. And by the way, calling it the "Holy Bible" was largely a political move. The church knew that very few people are willing to question anything "holy."

DK: But even in *your* day you had venerated scriptures.

J: All the books of the Tanakh were revered, of course. But the most sacred scripture was the Torah—the first five books of what Christians refer to as the "Old Testament." Keep in mind, however, that these Five Books of Moses—Genesis, Exodus, Leviticus, Numbers and Deuteronomy—were just a best-effort attempt to describe a fabled "history" as many as fifteen hundred years earlier. So when you consider how a story becomes utterly distorted after just a few days of being told and re-told, you can only speculate about the sweeping changes that take place over many *centuries*.

DK: Then the Books of Moses obviously weren't dictated by heaven.

J: Bible scholars can tell you that they weren't even dictated by Moses. This should be evident to anyone who's read Deuteronomy 34, where Moses allegedly writes of his own death and burial.

DK: Well, I suppose if you're the kind who really plans ahead…

J: The important thing is that our scriptures were based on *oral* traditions dating back many hundreds of years. Naturally, a lot of people considered them divinely inspired; but in fact they were no more inspired, consistent, or free of error than the New Testament books that followed centuries later. Incidentally, relatively little of our scripture referred to how one should live. It was mostly the storied history of a relationship with a personalized God as recorded from a very biased Hebrew perspective.

DK: I guess it's understandable that scriptures referring to the Israelites as God's "chosen" were composed by those very people.

J: Of course. Those documents were written *by* the Israelites *for* the Israelites. Christians simply commandeered ancient Hebrew writings and then retroactively claimed partial ownership of them by interpreting vague passages as prophesies about me and my life. So you can see why the Jews and others considered it pretty outrageous for hardline literalist Christians to declare their newly created religion relevant—and in fact *compulsory*—for everyone on the planet. Even the Israelites themselves never proposed anything so presumptuous. Their scriptures were directed specifically to the original twelve tribes, a people whose numbers, in comparison with the world's population, were, and still are, positively minuscule. And I'll tell ya straight: even from an early age, I had plenty of problems with *my* people's holy books, too.

DK: Oh yeah? Like what?

J: Some of it we've already covered. Mainly I never liked the fact that so little of our scripture was devoted to teaching peace. Way too much space was given to stories of personal and inter-tribal strife and violence. God is portrayed as a judgmental, intolerant, bloodthirsty oppressor who goes around stirring up conflict and slaughtering humans as though He's killing a mound of ants.

His hypocrisy is rampant. He commands the Israelites to do something, but then *He* does just the opposite. These writings even have God condoning slavery, murder, torture and rape. They depict Him as a villainous, barbaric despot who gives the impression that He's out *looking* for trouble.

DK: I assume you've got the goods?

J: Let's look at 1 Chronicles 21, where God becomes furious with David for ordering Joab to conduct a national census. After the census is taken, God decides to play mind games with David by engaging in a twisted and gruesome version of "Deal or No Deal." The Lord delivers his macabre offer through Gad, one of David's prophets, who gives David the good news: "Yo, Dave, thus saith the Lord: I'm going to *punish* you, old chap—but I'll let *you* pick your poison. You've got three choices."

"Let's hear 'em," says Dave.

"Well, first, I can smite your people with three years of famine."

"That one's overdone," Dave complains. "What else ya got?"

"I can let your people's enemies slaughter them for three months while I render them helpless."

David remains unimpressed: "Not very tempting. What's number three?"

"Well," Gad explains, "the Big Guy says that you can spend three days fighting with *Him personally*. But here's the catch: in the meantime He's going to kill your people, send pestilence through your land, and order his angel of destruction to wreak havoc across the entire country."

DK: You mean God challenges David to a one-on-one grudge match? What a rotten set of choices! I'll presume that having David offer a simple apology was never an option.

J: Nope. And don't forget that God declares elsewhere in the Bible that his love for David is never-ending.

DK: *Sheesh.* After Gad showed up, David was probably wondering when it ever *started*. So, what happened next?

J: Well, after mulling over God's latest offer of endless love, David says to the messenger Gad, "Okay, pal, I've given it some thought. Tell the Lord that I'll take my chances with *Him*. After all, God is *merciful*—and I'd rather scuffle with the Lord than suffer at the hands of a bunch of nutjob humans. There's no telling *what* kind of idiocy *they'll* instigate!" And with that unparalleled show of naïveté, David gives the go-ahead to his "merciful" God, who nonchalantly distorts the population count still further by causing the deaths of *seventy thousand* innocent Israelites through one of his notorious plagues. This, of course, left David's remaining subjects with a burning question: "When will Yahweh ever come to his census?"

DK: *Heh heh.* God blew a great comedic opportunity by having you killed.

J: Just to compound the bizarre nature of the census episode, the Bible God—whose ways, as we all know by now, are *very* damned mysterious—decides that the perpetrators of the whole fiasco, David and Joab, should themselves be spared from any harsh punishment!

DK: Must've been a no-fault state…

J: After the census debacle, David is understandably giddy. Having dodged death once again, he's feeling luckier than a condemned man whose executioner just got called for jury duty. With great relief and jubilation, David does what any normal man would do after ducking a divine bullet in such fashion: he throws together a makeshift altar and burns a few defenseless animals.

DK: I generally just have a beer.

J: But the guilt-wash apparently works. Smelling the sweet, smoky perfume of David's glorious ox-burning, the Bible God is finally mollified. He calls off the heavenly dogs just before his angel of death wipes Jerusalem off the map.

DK: Pretty clever of David, saving a few million Israelites just by charbroiling an unlucky ox or two. That's what I'd call some seriously holy smoke!

J: But c'mon... seventy thousand starvation-induced murders because a couple of guys took a friggin' *head count*!?

DK: Maybe the results showed a trend for overpopulation. Either way, though, a good stiff fine of gold and silver probably would've sufficed—maybe throw in a few days of sackcloth and ashes for good measure. But you're right: the Lord's response is completely unfathomable. I guess sometimes we just have to trust his judgment. We've got to believe He knows what He's doing and depend on his mercy.

J: Well, if He's anything like He was in those days, I wouldn't *count* on it, if you know what I mean...

CHAPTER SIXTY

DK: I don't mind telling you, that census story is downright scary. I mean with a divine protector like *that*, who the hell needs enemies?

J: Now you know why calling every scripture "holy" really wrinkles my robe. And you can scrap any ideas about the Bible's divine inerrancy or internal consistency. Even the story of David and the census is told completely differently in 2 Samuel 24 than it is in the account we just discussed from 1 Chronicles. The two versions are at odds in almost every respect, including the results of the census and the terms of God's unusual offer of punishment alternatives. The strangest difference is that in 2 Samuel it's *the Lord* who "incited" David to perform the census, even though He later kills the seventy thousand Israelites because of it. In 1 Chronicles, however, it's *Satan* who does the inciting. God on the one hand, the devil on the other.

DK: Quite a striking discrepancy.

J: There's one fact, though, about which the two books are in full agreement: God's inexplicable, indiscriminate killing of the seventy thousand "chosen" people, who were seemingly guilty of nothing more than having been subjected to David's census poll.

DK: That's gotta be one of the most bizarre stories ever.

J: Listen, I'm not kidding when I tell you that this Bible God can make Chairman Mao look like president of the Rotary Club. It's no wonder the Israelites preferred to keep Him at arm's length.

DK: In what way?

J: Well, even after the Lord had allegedly delivered them from Egypt, opened an escape path through the sea, liquidated their enemies, fed them with heaven-sent manna and offered them hope of a permanent home flowing with milk and honey, the Israelites *still* chose to worship a golden calf instead.

DK: Hey, who could blame 'em? With a metal cow, at least you don't have to sleep with one eye open.

J: The weirdest part is the story's ending: it makes the entire Exodus seem like a lesson in futility. After leading them safely out of Egypt amidst loads of dramatics and then testing them in the wilderness for a couple of years—even though the promised land Canaan lay within easy walking distance—God finally brings the Israelites to the edge of their anticipated paradise.

DK: Wasn't that the goal?

J: Sure. But unfortunately it turned into a giant human resources disaster. In the end, Yahweh is able to make only *two men*—no women, of course—fit for entry into the new territory. Apart from Caleb and Joshua, God decrees that everyone else, including Moses, will be barred from the promised land because of the people's faithlessness. So the Lord sends the peeps packing back to the desert and leaves them wandering there for the next *forty years*, until all those over the age of nineteen have died. No milk, no honey, no lovely parting gifts or discounts on future purchases.

DK: It appears the promised land was more like the land of broken promises. If I were one of the chosen chumps, I think I'd be longing for the waters of Babylon or the good old days of Egyptian slavery.

J: Some may see it as a victory, I suppose. Because eventually, after their forty-year penance in the desert, the Israelites—the ones who hadn't bitten the dust wandering, that is—finally take possession of their new homeland. But not much had changed. The Israelites have barely unloaded their trailers when God promptly initiates a new round of wholesale slaughter. He quickly orders his people to begin murdering most of the land's longtime occupants.

DK: Man, this dude needs serious sensitivity training. But hey, look at the bright side: at least He finally delivered his people and kept his promise of protection.

J: But was it truly protection? Or had the Israelites merely swapped one cruel overlord for another? I mean it's not like the Bible God made a habit of conducting opinion surveys. Like the Pharaohs of Egypt, Yahweh typically just went around issuing orders: everything was on *his* terms. And as Jonathan Swift observed, government without consent of the governed is the very definition of slavery.

DK: Any way you look at it, I guess, life in the promised land certainly hasn't been the bed of roses the Jews initially envisioned.

J: Hardly so. For nearly everyone involved, the Bible God's "protection" usually resulted in a virtual smorgasbord of pain. Despite his big-time promises to the Israelites, what they actually *got*, according to scripture, was a long and miserable litany of disappointment, hardship and suffering—including starvation, exile, enslavement, war and death.

DK: Picky, picky, picky…

J: As you can see, being numbered amongst the Lord's "chosen" was never any high privilege. Nor was it a day at the circus for many of the *non*-chosen peoples who crossed their path. All things considered, the history of the Jews has been one of chronic duress and continuous high-stakes drama. No doubt Tevye speaks for many Jews by suggesting to the Almighty in "Fiddler on the Roof" that perhaps He could choose *someone else* now and then.

DK: It seems there's a fine line between devotion and resentment…

J: Let's move on to some other intriguing Old Testament tales, like the one found in the thirty-first chapter of Numbers. Here's yet

379

another invigorating story highlighting the Bible God's wise and mysterious nature. In this account, the Lord commands Moses—and again, heaven forbid God should ever issue a simple *request*—to have twelve thousand troops slaughter all the people living under the five kingships of Midian. Incredibly, Moses considers this a perfectly reasonable demand, even though it's based solely on the very last motive one would expect of a loving deity: revenge. It seems Yahweh was terribly upset because the Israelites were once again finding reason to worship other gods—even though there aren't supposed to *be* any others.

DK: Perhaps God merely used the Midianites as scapegoats for other people's guilt.

J: Well, biblically He does have a penchant for that sort of thing...

DK: So God directs Big Mo to begin the latest round of massacres and eliminate all Midianites from the planet.

J: Yes, and without further ado, Moses instructs his army to wipe out their entire culture posthaste, thus vastly simplifying future genealogy research on the peoples of Midian.

DK: Five bucks says the soldiers celebrated by burning animals.

J: Nothing so mild, I'm afraid. After their little job of genocide is complete, the chosen people start doing a little choosing of their own. First, they choose to steal everything in sight, then they choose to burn every Midianite camp and city to the ground.

DK: It's a lucky thing the Israelites were chosen by God. I doubt anyone else would've *had* 'em.

J: But the fun didn't stop with the killing and looting. Later, on the outskirts of his peoples' encampment, Moses discovers that his soldiers have spared the lives of the Midianite women and children. Upon hearing this offensive news, Moses flies into a maniacal rage. He immediately tells his officers to get back to work: "Now therefore, kill every male among the little ones, and kill every woman who has known man by lying with him. But all the young girls who have not known man by lying with him, keep alive for yourselves."

DK: This is just too much. A long-venerated Bible figure orders his army to murder thousands of people because he believed that *God told him to*? Could such a thing even be possible? I mean these days we *lock away* any crank who claims he killed someone because of instructions from God. And yet, using that very justification, this biblical "hero" exterminates *five major populations*!!??

J: Except for the little girls and virgin women, of course. He has *other* plans for them. In the meantime, the young boys and their mothers, having just endured the bloody slaughter of their fathers and husbands, must now watch *one another* being butchered at the hands of his elect warriors.

DK: Holy Moses.

J: And here's the best part: once the gory decimation is finished, Moses tells his army officers to keep and divide amongst themselves and their families all the young Midianite virgins— *thirty-two thousand* or so—after they've just witnessed their loved ones murdered in cold blood. The same kind of thing is described in Judges 21. In this instance, God's people murder nearly everyone in the camp of the Benjamites—who, by the way, were fellow members of Israel's original twelve tribes—and then steal *hundreds* of Benjamite virgins for their own good pleasure.

DK: So in both episodes, the young girls are handed over to the brutal lusts of savage soldiers and other tribesmen.

J: Yep, a kind of victors' war spoils. Presumably they'd become concubines—basically sex slaves, forced maidservants, or lower-tiered housewives. Essentially, they were seen as nothing more than a useful commodity. Now, we could go on if you'd like, but I believe the unvarnished horror speaks for itself. And let's not forget that, in the case of Moses, the Bible God wasn't just a *passive observer* of this revolting terrorism. He didn't merely *allow* his people to engage in such bestial and ferocious violence. He was the one who *demanded* the initial carnage and then stood idly by while subsequent atrocities were executed. Adding insult to butchery, God actually *rewards* his people's sadistic madness by refusing to intervene when they divvy up the battle's plunder, with virgin young women serving as—dare I say it?—the most coveted booty.

DK: Wow, I'm not sure what to think. It's pretty hard to brush off an account like that. It makes me wonder about the implications of

God's words in Matthew 25:40: "Inasmuch as ye have done it unto one of the least of my brethren, ye have done it unto me."

J: Consider also that the "fruit of the spirit," described in Galatians 5, includes love, joy, peace, patience, kindness, goodness, faithfulness, gentleness and self-control. Ironically, Christians believe this list was inspired and itemized by the very same deity who ordered the holocaust at Midian.

DK: I get a sick feeling just *hearing* that story—it warps my whole perception of the Bible God. As for Moses… well, these days, guys like that are tried for war crimes. Strange how the most heinous acts of inhumanity are usually committed not by common criminals but by respected leaders of nations.

J: And Moses certainly wasn't the *only* Bible hero with a fondness for mayhem and blood. Other Old Testament leaders were equally sadistic and vicious during their own merciless reigns. Even by scriptural assessments, most of them were reprehensible. In one of the more infamous stories of imperial impiety, King Jehu has the evil Jezebel—queen to former King Ahab, a pretty nefarious fellow himself—thrown out a window to her death. With Jezebel's blood splattered over hell and creation, her body is then trampled by horses.

DK: Perfect material for a mini-series…

J: Now, in such a case, you might figure Jehu would show a little remorse—at least offer a prayer for the royally departed, or fire up the barbie for a burnt offering or two. Instead, Jehu's first move after watching Jezebel take a dive into the dirt is to sit down and enjoy a hearty meal with a good jug of wine. By the time he thinks to have Jezebel buried, her gory corpse has been eaten by dogs—right down to her skull. Presumably the episode was quite pleasing to the Lord, who allegedly had predicted it. Sordid stuff, this majestic madness… but hey, long live the king.

DK: Bloody hell! And Christendom has practically turned these shady characters into saints!

J: Well, believe me, nary a soul is safe when the *saints* go marching in.

DK: But okay, so Bible figures were human. I could argue that everyone's allowed an occasional bad hair day.

J: Try not to lose focus: these guys are viewed as *heroes*, and the writings are considered *sacred*. According to the church, this stuff is straight from heaven's PR department, thoroughly blessed with God's personal stamp of approval.

DK: Maybe so, but Judeo-Christian scriptures certainly haven't cornered the market on bloodshed. Even the Vedic scriptures—probably the world's oldest—contain stories of warring saints. Anyhow, the gruesome stuff doesn't comprise the entire Bible.

J: No, but the point is that the Bible leaves the impression that barbarity is part of God's nature, if not his most prominent characteristic. This stands in stark contradiction to many other Bible passages directing the gentle and compassionate treatment of *everyone*—including one's enemies. Yet somehow this book of totally oppositional teachings is marketed as the "internally consistent and inspired word of God."

DK: So its consistency is a bit—

J: Yeah, inconsistent. As a result, lots of believers have come to embrace a creator who readily approves of violence against those He doesn't like. We've only touched on a few examples, but there are hundreds of pages of stories of divine insanity and God-ordained murder—mine included—lurking within the pages of the church's "holy" scriptures.

DK: Fun for the entire family, eh?

J: *Oh* yeah. For education and amusement, the Bible's right up there with a day at the abattoir. I'm tellin' ya, the thing could just as easily have been titled "Divine Crimes Against Humanity." Or "Murderously Funny Tales of Yahweh." Or maybe "Inspirational Stories of Brutality and Death."

DK: You make the Bible God sound as though He can be downright evil. Is He?

J: Why don't we let *Him* answer that question…

In Jeremiah 18 God declares, "If that nation, against whom I have pronounced, turn from their evil, I will repent of *the evil that I thought to do unto them*." In verse eleven, He reiterates his capacity for wickedness and malevolence: "Thus saith the Lord: Behold, I frame evil against you, and devise a device against you."

DK: Hmmnn, devising a device. Sounds positively sinister.

J: In chapter thirty-one the Lord states, "…as I have watched over them to pluck up and break down, to overthrow, destroy and *bring evil*, so I will watch over them to build and to plant…"

DK: So the man readily admits to having a mean streak.

J: Yes, and when issuing threats, the Bible God isn't always so poetic. In the second chapter of Malachi, He rages against some disobedient priests for not giving glory to his name. He warns, "Behold, I will rebuke your offspring, and spread dung upon your faces…"

DK: Oooh, nasty.

J: In 1 Samuel 15 God directs King Saul to take up arms against the Amalekites. As usual, the motive is simple revenge, and no one is to be spared: not the young, not the innocent—and no, not even the animals. The Lord tells Saul, "Now go and smite Amalek, and utterly destroy all that they have; do not spare them, but kill both man and woman, infant and suckling, ox and sheep, camel and ass."

DK: Geez, this Bible God doesn't take pity on family, flora nor fauna.

J: He wasn't much of an animal lover. Once, He even ordered Joshua to cruelly slice the hamstrings of the enemy's horses—an excruciatingly painful procedure in which their leg tendons are severed by sharp knives. Obviously the miserable steeds would never walk again and would have to be killed. Evil enough?

DK: Man, this guy doesn't just clean house: He brings a bloody *wrecking ball*. He kills any creature in his path—and it doesn't seem to matter if it has two legs or four.

J: Just for kicks, here's a couple more examples of the Bible God's potential for malice...

Exodus 32 states, "And the Lord repented of the *evil* which he thought to do to his people." First Samuel 18 is even more direct: "… *an evil spirit from God* rushed upon Saul."

DK: There's no misunderstanding *that* one.

J: So now you've heard several passages of the Bible God openly admitting to harboring evil thoughts and intentions, and still other passages in which He actually carries them out. In fact, He's constantly planning, threatening and implementing horrific punishment upon his morally deficient creation. And even though He's handing down laws ordering folks to be kind to their neighbors and such, He's certainly not leading by example.

DK: You gotta give Him credit for one thing: when Yahweh makes a threat, He apparently means what He says.

J: There's no question about *that*. And for more proof, have a look at Numbers 11. The Bible God once again demonstrates his eternal love to his chosen people by literally incinerating a large group of them.

DK: What!?? You mean He *burns* them to death?

J: Torches 'em like a cheese fondue.

DK: Crikey, what'd they do *this* time? Mis-stack the firewood?

J: They complained.

DK: Well, *of course* they complained. Hell, *I'd* complain, too, if I was about to be burned alive!

J: No, I mean that's the *reason* he scorched 'em. They were complaining.

DK: You mean Yahweh charred "the chosen" just because they were doing a little whining? About *what*!??

J: You're stumbling over a feather, pilgrim. When the self-proclaimed Lord of mercy sets his children ablaze simply because they were grumbling, does it really matter what they were grumbling *about*?

DK: You're right, the man's completely over the edge. And yet we call Him a "God of love."

J: Actually, on the Bible God's list of priorities, judgment ranks far higher than love. Although I suppose you could make the case that He isn't always quite so *sadistic*. In Numbers 21, He kills off another unlucky throng of his cherished in a manner that could, if you're willing to distinguish cruelty by degrees, be considered slightly more humane. He merely has them attacked and bitten by lethally poisonous snakes.

DK: *Sanctified serpents*!! You know, until today, I thought I had a pretty good understanding of the Bible's nuts and bolts—but I never knew there were so many *nuts*. Hearing one biblical horror story after another, I have to conclude it's pretty darned strange that religion uses books like the Bible to teach its followers how to live.

J: And judging by world affairs, I'd say they're catching on pretty fast...

CHAPTER SIXTY ONE

DK: Well, you've proven one thing: it's no great challenge throwing rocks at religion. There's so much to ridicule, it's like being a political analyst. But in the end we have to believe in *someone*. I mean this Bible God may be a little fast on the trigger— but a flock still needs a shepherd.

J: Not when the shepherd's favorite meal is mutton. Besides, Christians may piously declare that the Lord is their shepherd, but the minute they enter the valley of the shadow, they're beating hell out of each other with their rods and staffs. Viewing revenge and aggression as viable alternatives, they shoot first and pray later. And why not? They figure that any behavior good enough for God is damned well good enough for them. And where did they *get* this dangerous idea? Why, straight from the pages of the "Good Book," of course.

DK: In *my* experience, a lot of mainstream Christians aren't all that familiar with the scriptures—especially not with the Old Testament. They probably don't realize how much divinely sanctioned brutality it contains. I know *I* sure didn't.

J: But the problem goes way beyond the violence. Apart from being *spiritually* incoherent, the scriptures are laced with serious *logical* discrepancies, too. As an example, the Genesis story says that God created all living things "after their kind." After *what* kind? If this was the original creation, then there *were* no "kinds" for God to use as models or prototypes. And what about stories that press the bounds of credibility? Did Jonah literally get swallowed and coughed up by a giant fish? Did Noah really build an ark and then populate it with two of every animal on the planet? Did he travel the earth for decades, collecting animal pairs from other continents? We're never given the answers. And this kind of craziness runs through nearly every book of the Bible.

DK: But I'm told that lots of Bible material has been proven historically accurate.

J: Sure, but plenty has been proven historically *in*accurate, too. It's the worst of logic to assume that, if *some* parts are true, then the *whole thing* is true.

DK: Okay, let's agree that it's unreasonable to believe every last word of the Bible. Nevertheless, some of it—even if not the literal truth—may be important *theologically*.

J: I'm afraid that dike won't hold—not if we're talking about intentional mass starvation, torture and various forms of genocide. Don't tell me that God killed seventy thousand people over David's census and then preach to me about the story's hidden *moral* value. I mean crazy is crazy. Declaring a pestilence-induced massacre justified because *God* happens to be the perpetrator… well, it just doesn't wash. The argument is morally repugnant. When some nut-case rapes an innocent young mother of three and then sends her off to her empyrean rewards by way of a twelve-gauge blast to the noodle, do you really wanna hear any moralizing psycho-babble about the dude's unfortunate childhood? Do you really care if his momma beat him with a wooden spoon and his daddy ran off with a stripper?

DK: I suppose you're right. God is the *last* one we should be making excuses for.

J: Listen, I don't give a friar's frock what deep and twisted philosophical or symbolic significance some of these screwball scriptures may have. If I'm the average human and religion tells me that God unleashed a murderous purge because a couple of mental scuds conducted a bloody census, then I don't want this deified dolt coming anywhere near me or my family.

DK: Well, hopefully *some* of that stuff is mere allegory or tribal legend.

J: The problem, though—and again, it's a problem only for the literalist—is that you can't say the Bible is the literal word of God and then call some of it legendary, mythological or symbolic. In creating an all-or-nothing proposition, the church has boxed itself in. By refusing to acknowledge the Bible's serious defects and claiming that every syllable is an utterance from beyond, it has to disparage or ignore the mountain of information that proves otherwise.

DK: It does make for an interesting debate. For example, did Moses really come down from Mount Sinai with a couple of stone tablets containing commandments issued by God? Or is the story merely good fiction? Either way, apparently *someone* believed it.

J: I'm glad you brought up the Ten Commandments—because I've got an axe to grind about *those*, too.

DK: I might've guessed.

J: You may be surprised to learn that the Torah contains not merely ten but more than *six hundred* separate commandments. Many, however, were relevant only to certain groups. In Christian circles, of course, the ten given to Moses have gotten most of the attention. Strictly speaking, though, they shouldn't even be called commandments—that's another mistranslation. The term would be more accurately rendered as the "Ten Statements." In fact, nowhere does the Old Testament refer to the "Ten Commandments." But *whatever* you call 'em, in the twentieth chapter of Exodus, God reportedly gives Moses his famous Top Ten. Actually, if you read 'em through carefully, you'll discover that you've got a few minor ones sprinkled in with the biggies. So technically they number more like fifteen or twenty. *Heh heh*— leave it to the Jews to negotiate a few extras.

DK: The Anti-Defamation League will be in stitches over that one…

J: So anyway, one of the decrees Moses brings down from the holy mountain is "Thou shalt not kill." But the implementation of this new policy gets off to a pretty shaky start. As soon as Moses returns from the mountain, he finds the Israelites worshipping the infamous golden calf, worked up at their request by Moses' brother, Aaron. As you can well imagine, Moses is not amused. And we already know that when Moses gets a bee in his bonnet, homicide is close at hand.

DK: I'll wager that Moses zeroes Aaron right on the spot.

J: Lucky for you I'm not a betting man, because Moses virtually ignores his sibling's central role in the debacle. He does conclude, however, that severe punishment is required and he wastes no time deciding on a strategy. Brushing aside Yahweh's freshly issued instruction not to kill, Moses quickly summons all those "on the side of the Lord" and orders these specially assembled ninjas to strap on their swords and go through the camp "from gate to gate" and begin killing indiscriminately their brothers, friends and neighbors. Naturally, Moses declares that this directive has come straight from the Lord. Later, with *three thousand* of his people barbarously murdered by his own decree, Moses tells his dutiful henchmen that their actions have "ordained" them "for the service of the Lord" and that the Lord will *bless* them for it.

DK: Gosh, who needs Rambo when we've got the Old Testament!

J: But never mind the vicious acts of inhumanity by Moses. God's warning to the Israelites not to kill was a fairly surprising edict in the first place when you consider his own long history of lethal behavior. But okay, let's give the Big Man a break: perhaps He finally realized that violence was no solution. However, in the two chapters *following* the public release of the Ten Statements, God pulls a strange and confusing turnabout by listing nearly a dozen offenses for which He actually *commands* the Israelites to *kill*. One of the explicit crimes is the relatively minor transgression of cursing one's parents.

DK: Wow. I'd have been dead by age five…

J: Next, after giving his divine blessing to human slavery, God lays out the following actions as deserving death: kidnapping; owning an ox that kills someone; engaging in sorcery; committing bestiality; and, of course, making sacrifices to those ever-pesky "other gods."

DK: So is that the extent of Yahweh's specified capital offenses?

J: Actually, there's one more—possibly the strangest of the bunch. The Lord lastly declares that *He personally* will kill anyone who wrongs strangers, orphans or widows. This, too, is a real paradox, since scripture asserts many times that Yahweh killed *thousands upon thousands* of strangers, thus filling entire territories with widows and orphans! In short, the Lord Himself is largely responsible for swelling the ranks of those He appears so eager to protect.

DK: I'm convinced: this guy needs full-time counseling and some industrial-strength Valium. Not to mention a serious course in anger management.

J: Want *more* Old Testament fodder? The Book of Leviticus informs us that insects have only four legs instead of the requisite six known to modern science. Chapter 11 declares that birds have four legs. Second Kings 8 says that King Ahaziah was twenty-two years old when he began his reign, whereas 2 Chronicles 22 states that he was *forty*-two. Then we've got the three well-known incongruities in the books of 1 and 2 Samuel regarding the death of King Saul. First Samuel 31 says that Saul committed suicide by falling on his sword. Second Samuel has two different accounts of Saul's death, neither of which corresponds to the suicide report. The first chapter of 2 Samuel claims that Saul was killed by an Amalekite, while chapter 21 declares that Saul was killed by the Philistines. The Old Testament also has what you might call a "giant" contradiction, as it leaves serious doubt about who really killed Goliath.

DK: What!? The fight between David and Goliath is one of the best-known tales of the Old Testament. The young David, future king of Israel, slays the supersize Philistine bully with nothing but precocious bravery and a slingshot.

J: Do the research and you'll discover all kinds of problems and contradictions with the 1 Samuel 17 story of David and Goliath. In the original Hebrew text of 2 Samuel 21, a member of one of David's elite fighting units, a man named Elhanan, is clearly said to have killed the famous Philistine giant. First Chronicles 20 compounds the confusion by declaring that Elhanan killed Goliath's *brother*. In another story involving David, 2 Samuel 8 states that when David defeated Hadadezer, he took seventeen hundred horsemen. But 1 Chronicles 18 says that David took *seven thousand* horsemen. Speaking of David, the Old Testament says in 1 Samuel 16 that David's father Jesse had eight sons. First Chronicles 2, however, states that Jesse had only seven sons.

DK: So we've got some accounting problems.

J: But it isn't just the Bible's *numbers* that don't add up: the *claims themselves* are flat-out extreme. In 2 Kings, the writer states with authority that Elijah was carried off to heaven by horses and chariots—made of *fire*! The book of Exodus says that all of Egypt's Nile River once turned to blood; that Moses lived forty days without food or water; and that placing striped sticks in the presence of breeding sheep produced striped offspring.

DK: Hmmmn. I wonder if placing an axe produced lamb chops…

J: Here's one that's always good for a chuckle. Judges 1:19 reads, "And the Lord was with Judah, and he took possession of the hill country, but he could not drive out the inhabitants of the plain, because they had chariots of iron."

So how 'bout *that*? The omnipotent God of the universe can't help Judah rid the land of its rightful owners because their bloody chariots are too sturdy!

DK: Must've been Japanese.

J: It's strange, though, because Yahweh had no problem disabling the chariots of the Egyptian army in Exodus 14. And here's another Old Testament oddity: in two unrelated chapters of the Bible—2 Kings 19 and Isaiah 37—we have God "inspiring" two different writers to say *exactly the same thing*.

DK: Well, at least God's inspiration was consistent. But I wonder which author owns the copyright…

J: Also, let's not overlook the biblical accounting of animals that *speak*. It's enough to start Dr. Doolittle turning summersaults. First, of course, is Eden's infamous slick-talking serpent, generally thought to have been a snake. It persuaded Eve to eat the forbidden fruit, thus becoming the most influential reptile in history. And what about *this* gem: in Numbers 22, Balaam's donkey lectures him on animal cruelty!

DK: Hey, it wouldn't be the *only* time a sermon's been delivered by an ass.

J: Here's another curiosity: according to Genesis, the whole, unfathomably vast universe was thrown together in only six days.

DK: Right, I believe that's a record.

J: So are we supposed to accept that a God of limitless power and intelligence used the revolution of an insignificant orb called "earth" as his timepiece during the course of creation? Did He really measure his work schedule by its rotations, starting in each morning like a common laborer? And why did He bother dividing the task into shifts? Did the Almighty Lord of creation just need an occasional *nap*?

DK: I know *I* damned sure would.

J: And what about Eve? Was she really created only as an afterthought because Adam was lonely? In the natural world, the *female* is the starting point of creation: life begins in the *womb*. But Genesis has a *man* at the center of the process. He essentially gives "birth" to the woman!

DK: Well, as you said, that's the kind of thinking you'd *expect* from a male-dominated society.

J: Of course. I'm only carping to emphasize that biblical writers were products of their environments. Their works reflect the same scientific ignorance, social inequities and myth-based theologies that pervaded their cultures. Taking every word literally is absurd.

DK: You're failing to account for divine inspiration. Surely God can circumvent worldly limitations.

J: Don't lean on the lazy belief that God whispered every word of scripture directly into the writers' ears. Here's a couple of scriptures whose claims differ by an *order of magnitude*: In 1 Kings 4, it's said that Solomon had forty thousand stalls for his horses; but 2 Chronicles 9 says that Solomon had only *four* thousand stalls. Did God get his figures confused?

DK: Alright, so there's a little discordance regarding Sol's stalls. Is that a problem?

J: Again, only for the literalists. They're forced to resort to the most ridiculous, convoluted explanations imaginable as they try to explain away obvious scriptural errors and discrepancies. The effort typically amounts to selling the idea that up is down and black is white, or that "x" doesn't really *mean* "x" but in fact means "y." These blatant scriptural irregularities put the church in a very uncomfortable position. For if it admits to *even one* biblical boo-boo, it can no longer claim the Bible to be "the inspired, inerrant word of God."

DK: Because that would bring into question every other passage in the Bible.

J: Right. Which means literalists are faced with defending stories that even the average ten-year-old would reject. So not only is the Bible indefensible as a history book, but it's packed with stories of a deity whose behavior is consistently base, illogical, and profane. This makes a terribly tough case for anyone taking the stance that *God* wrote it. Scientifically speaking, scripture is full of intellectual embarrassments, like the story of Lot's wife turning into a pillar of salt. In fact—*heh heh*—the Bible's *peppered* with 'em.

DK: I suppose when you think about it, very little of the Bible would strike an impartial reader as divinely inspired. And I'll bet that not a single biblical writer ever imagined that his work would someday be part of a revered holy book.

J: Old Testament authors would be especially shocked. Never in their wildest dreams would they have envisioned their writings being used to link Judaism with an upstart religion that directly and philosophically opposed it. I mean face it: the Bible was never intended to *be* a Bible. It's a thousand pages of mostly disconnected, meandering pseudo-history, some of which is downright silly. The Bible isn't without value, of course. But you can't flush common sense down the drain just because someone slaps an old manuscript between two covers and calls it "holy."

DK: Speaking of silly, I vaguely remember a funny scripture from my old Sunday school days. Something about guys with groin injuries being barred from the tabernacle?

J: The passage is from Deuteronomy. God declares that any man with crushed testicles should be disallowed from entering the assembly of the Lord.

DK: Yeah, that's the one—a pretty humiliating decree. I mean here's old Jacob workin' the stables one morning, when out of the blue he's whacked in the rack by a skittish horse. Suddenly he's *persona non grata* down at the temple.

J: Imagine the poor schmo running into a neighbor woman over at the well. "Haven't seen you in church for awhile, Jake. Been down with the flu?"

DK: *Heh heh.* Who could've known that crushed testicles would be so problematic back then? But maybe God had a darned good reason for that rule. A true Bible thumper would insist that no scripture is without spiritual significance.

J: What about Song of Solomon? That book never even *mentions* God.

DK: Some people say it's allegorical.

J: Oh, I see. Only certain *parts* of the Bible are the *literal* word of God, while other parts are to be interpreted *figuratively.*

DK: I should've kept my mouth shut.

J: Hey, don't mount the horse if you're not willing to ride it...

DK: Okay, then, any last bits of Bible-bashing before we move on?

J: Well, one of my all-time favorites is from Genesis 21, and it's a real doozy: "The Lord visited Sarah as he had said, and the Lord did to Sarah as he had promised. And Sarah conceived..."

DK: I can see where you'd get a chuckle out of the wording on that one. It's as if Sarah became pregnant directly by the... well, let's say *hand* of God.

J: Yeah, which would mean that her son Isaac's conception was every bit as miraculous as mine allegedly was. The accepted conclusion, of course, is that Sarah later conceived by way of her husband, Abraham, just as God had promised in Genesis 18. Everyone assumes that God "unlocked" Sarah's womb in the same way He did with the women of the house of Abimelech at the end of Genesis 20. But that's not what the passage *says.* It says the Lord *visited* Sarah. He didn't do that with Abimelech's women.

DK: The original writer probably meant something far different from a personal visit.

J: No doubt. And again, this stuff's problematic only if you're a literalist.

DK: The story is certainly intriguing, though. You gotta wonder why Sarah rated a special visit from God and exactly what transpired while He was there. Whatever it was, it clearly required a house call.

J: You can just imagine the neighborhood gossip *that* little episode must've generated: "You'll never guess who dropped by Sarah's house on Thursday…"

CHAPTER
SIXTY TWO

DK: I suppose this discussion of biblical bafflement could run on for days—but we've only got a couple more hours of sunlight. Anyway, I think you've made your point: we can't believe everything we read in the papers.

J: Well, why take your theology from people who believed the sun revolved around a flat earth?

DK: You know, I just realized something ironic: in several churches I've attended, they conclude scripture readings by proclaiming, "This is the word of the Lord."

J: They should probably tack on the phrase, "if you can believe *that*."

DK: On the other hand, a few religious groups *are* beginning to ask meaningful questions about their faith. Awhile back, the United Synagogue of Conservative Judaism even came out with a new Torah, called *Etz Hayim*.

J: Yeah, Hebrew for "Tree of Life."

DK: Apparently this new Torah takes into account the latest discoveries from anthropology, archaeology—and a few other "ologies" I can't even pronounce. Some of the scholarly writings included in *Etz Hayim* have created quite a stir. For example, they point to some pretty solid evidence that Abraham, the great biblical patriarch, may never have existed. The same may be true for Moses. In fact, they're suggesting the entire Exodus story may be grossly exaggerated, or possibly no more than a fable. So which is it, fact or fiction?

J: Frankly, I was never comfortable with that whole Israel-in-Egyptian-captivity thing. The focus was entirely misdirected. I always felt the most important question about it was the one that never gets asked: If the Bible God was so indignant about the notion of his people becoming enslaved, then why did He allow it in the first place? According to scripture, He invoked one miraculous power after another in getting the Israelites *extricated* from their captive misery. Why didn't He use those same powers to *prevent* it?

DK: Ah, c'mon, you've flittered around my question. Five percent of publishing royalties to your favorite charity if you'll give me an exclusive—a little something to hang my journalism degree on.

J: Fantastic!

DK: Then you'll do it?

J: No, I mean it's fantastic how you managed to dangle a *propo*sition and a *prepo*sition all in one sentence.

DK: You really know how to hurt a guy.

J: Listen, I said when you were hounding me about India that I'm not here to re-write history. I'm only hoping to discredit *certain versions* of it. My goal is to free my name from the clutches of religion; to squeeze through the prison bars of contentious, limiting beliefs; to clarify that no person or institution has control of the Christ and that each person potentially *is* the Christ.

DK: Okay, good enough. But have a heart and toss me a morsel or two. These new Bible discoveries are bigger than a Hollywood divorce scandal.

J: I'll give you this much: there's little or no direct evidence in Egyptian sources that a large population of subjugated Hebrews ever sojourned in that country. Even Moses, for all his *biblical* glory, never appears in Egyptian records of the period.

DK: Wait a minute—that makes no sense. Unless I'm mistaken, the Israelites were in captivity for, what, two or three hundred years? You can't have an entire nation enslaved for centuries to a string of monarchs on foreign soil without anyone in those various regimes documenting it. That's impossible.

J: But they didn't. There's no good evidence to support the story of Exodus, any more than there's evidence of the Nile river turning to blood. You'd think at least a handful of Egyptians living along the delta would've written a few lines about *that*, too. Same thing with Joseph. The Old Testament claims he was Pharaoh's right-hand man, the second most powerful guy in the land. Yet Egyptian records don't contain a word about either him *or* his famous coat with many collars.

DK: You mean coat of many *colors*.

J: *Whatever*. The point is that no Egyptian writing describes this stuff in any meaningful detail—not even the Sunday tabloids. If the Israelites truly lived in large numbers under the ancient Pharaohs, the Egyptians apparently didn't give an Aswan damn.

DK: Wow, things are really heating up; some time-honored Jewish history could be turned on its head. These new *Etz Hayim* writings even raise serious questions about the great King David. Some scholars say that he was probably only a small, provincial leader at most. In fact, large chunks of the Old Testament are now suspected by several academics to be complete fabrications. Even respected Jewish historians, such as Israeli professor Dr. Shlomo Sand and others, have solid research indicating that some of these stories may well have been only legendary or, at best, tremendously exaggerated.

J: Yes, but this isn't the big problem it may appear to be. There are plenty of Jews, just as there are large numbers of Christians, who don't read the Bible literally. Even some rabbis are self-proclaimed atheists. The simple truth is this: Honest academics know for a fact that the Jewish people never truly existed as a "nation-race." The entire saga presenting the Jews as a constantly oppressed, earth-wandering people of exile longing to return "home" to a land promised by God is actually a gigantic figment, carefully cultivated by Zionist ideologues in the 19th century. This even includes the popular "Diaspora" myth that sprang up following the destruction of the Second Temple. It's now a known fiction.

DK: So how'd the story get started?

J: Ironically, this part of the Jews' "history" was invented and perpetuated by *Christians*. They sold it as a story of divine punishment for the Jews' rejection of the gospel. But it never happened. The Romans didn't exile entire populations and didn't have the means to do so anyway.

DK: Then the Jews were never "scattered to the four winds," as we've always been told?

J: Nope. And most *non-Israeli* Jews are descendants of people who were *converted* to Judaism through aggressive proselytizing within their native lands. So not only is the Zionist mythos untrue, but for the vast majority of Jews around the planet, it's meaningless and irrelevant. For them, there was never any identification with Israel or with the concept of being a divinely "chosen" people or race.

DK: I do know that most of the world's Jews have never lived in, or even visited, Israel—and they seemingly have no desire to do so.

J: As I say, most Jews outside Israel don't feel any real kinship to the notion of a sovereign Jewish nation-state. They typically view themselves simply as legitimate citizens of their respective homelands. The average Zionist Christian would probably be astonished to learn that most present-day Jews— either in Israel or abroad—have no genealogical connection whatsoever with the biblical Kingdom of Judea. Ironically, these maverick Jewish scholars have shown that many *Palestinians* are much more likely than the average Jew to have ancient Semitic roots.

DK: Fascinating. And all the more compelling when you consider that it's the Jews themselves spreading the knowledge.

J: It shows courage. It proves that real spirituality doesn't need fairytales to keep it breathing. Religions the world over could use a good stiff dose of that same kind of honest self-examination; they should ask themselves what they're really accomplishing. I mean if saving souls is the best answer they've got, they may as well shut the doors and issue refunds—maybe do a little remodeling. *You* know, convert the joints into something useful: homeless shelters, hospitals...all-night taco stands.

DK: I think our misplaced faith is mostly just a product of ignorance. As you've said, we typically go through life without really examining our beliefs. I myself stumbled along unquestioning for more than thirty years.

J: That's a long time to wear a bucket on your head. Some of this stuff has been known for decades—even *centuries*. It would only surprise the uninformed or the super-credulous.

DK: Ooops… guilty on both counts, I'm afraid. For years, I actually thought of Eden as a literal garden. As a small child, I envisioned Adam and Eve hoeing and planting, just like my mother used to do in her little backyard vegetable plot. I wondered if they had sprinklers and if they also made *their* kids pull weeds.

J: Actually, that Garden of Paradise legend was around long before the Hebrews. Older variations are found in ancient mythology of the Greeks, Syrians, Egyptians, Sumerians and Ethiopians. One version has Cain and Abel with twin sisters—Luluwa and Aklemia. Another has Seth with a sister named Noraia. Still another account says that Adam had a lover named Lilith before he hooked up with Eve. It says she jilted Adam because he tried to dominate her.

DK: *Heh heh*. Some things *never* change.

J: It's all pretty simple, really. When dealing with scripture, learn some background info and use a little common sense. Don't be a jackass for Jesus.

DK: To me, it's mainly an issue of perceived authority. If someone we trust tells us that something came straight from the mouth of God, we tend not to question it—especially when we're young.

J: Well, let's be honest: most of religion's radical claims would never win credence beyond the pages of the "sacred" books that contain them. But why suspend critical thinking or your sense of disbelief for *God's* sake? I mean why employ intelligence and reason in every facet of life except religion? Besides, even if you turn a blind eye to the Bible's extraordinary *factual* claims, you've got serious trouble with Bible literalism just by virtue of its timeline. According to creationists, Adam and Eve showed up in the Garden somewhere around 4,000 BCE. But how could that be? By then, man was already using the plow and the wheel—even sailing the seven seas. It's scientific fact that humans have existed for hundreds of thousands of years.

DK: Then the Genesis story couldn't possibly be the literal truth.

J: And hence fundamentalist Christianity has *another* theological problem. Because if Adam and Eve were not the earth's first human inhabitants—and science knows for certain that they weren't—then Christianity's "original sin" account is null and void. Therefore there was no need fo—

DK: For *you!* Now I get it!

J: Well, I was going to say there was no need for the Christian Atonement. In other words, there was no reason for God to have me crucified on account of the alleged "first sin" in the Garden. But don't negate me entirely, because I still had my purpose. Only it wasn't what most people presume.

DK: I think you just removed about six notches from the Bible Belt. So where do we land after all this scriptural scrapping and scrubbing?

J: Right back where we started. After you stretched me on the rack with that bruising letter of yours, I explained that the Bible is just a collection of subjective documents written by men with highly colored viewpoints. Sometimes they were just recording ancient legends of their ancestors or reworking age-old mythology from other cultures. Eventually, the Church of Rome and other influential Christian groups intervened and arbitrarily assembled the parts they wanted while dispensing with any "inconvenient truths"—as we discussed in ever-so-painful detail.

DK: Have mercy on me, Son of David…

J: So the meat of the pie is that the Bible was written, edited, interpreted, assembled, canonized and ultimately proclaimed the literal and inspired word of God, with every little snippet done by *man and man alone.* All down the line, its contents were scribed, translated, copied, altered, doctored or even fabricated by men with heavily vested interests. The process wore on for centuries and involved a cast of thousands: thugs and theologians, fools and fanatics, popes and patsies, lackeys and laymen, schemers and scholars, friars and frauds. Selected words, lengthy passages—

even *entire books* were saved or deleted to suit the whims and predilections of those with influence or power.

DK: You know, in some ways your timing really stinks. You should've exposed this stuff a few centuries after your death, before things got so crazy. Now the church is dug in, and it won't surrender without a fight. On top of that, Christianity is splintering faster than a sheet of rotten plywood. Almost every protestant sect has bitter internal strife—and some are even splitting the sheets. Catholicism is holding up fairly well, I guess, but it's constantly plagued with scandal and haunted by its shady history. Now *you* come along and make Da Vinci's code seem like a twelve-dollar theft from the petty cash drawer.

J: I won't argue the point. If you think Christianity's in turmoil *now*, wait until *this* hits the papers.

DK: Not to spoil the party, but if you're hoping for a New Reformation, you probably shouldn't hold your breath. Even if some church leaders are learning the *real* Bible story, they certainly aren't tripping over themselves to spread the word.

J: Then I see two possibilities. One, they *want* you to know the facts but they aren't telling you. Or two, they *don't* want you to know and they *won't* tell you. Either way, you gotta wonder who's manning the lighthouse...

CHAPTER SIXTY THREE

DK: I can't speak for other religions, but I do know that Christianity is at least *supposed* to establish an environment of love. For all its faults, the Bible is, theoretically, a book of hope and redemption.

J: Alright, but your connection to God is *built-in*. Nothing outside you is indispensable when your hotline to heaven is hardwired. You can make the shift from polarity consciousness to unity consciousness without ever cracking a book or reciting a creed. So the Bible may or may not be helpful, but it certainly isn't essential to your spiritual growth.

DK: You've been walking on thin doctrinal ice for quite awhile—but I think you just busted through to the chilling waters below.

J: But the truth is, for many people the Bible has become spiritually counter-productive. Other revered writings have also led to some highly divisive brands of religion, and the results speak for themselves.

DK: Well, I'm the first to admit that it's sometimes difficult to read the Bible and avoid feeling that God is just a violent, self-serving bully who's not content until everyone else is miserable. He always seems to want us groveling prostrate in the dust. I mean when *God's* not happy, ain't *nobody* happy.

J: Scripture says that salvation is a gift of grace, offered by God in mercy and in love. At the same time, it declares that you should "work out your salvation with fear and trembling." Now, aside from the fact that your true self has never been in danger and doesn't need redeeming, any reasonable person knows that grace and love don't provoke "fear and trembling." That phrase, directly from the New Testament, is a good representation of the foreboding theology that so often pervades religion.

DK: Like I said in my opening letter, this whole notion of falling from grace and needing salvation from eternal fire is nutso. Frankly, I'm sick of hearing from religion that God is hovering over my shoulder, observing my every impure thought and recording every moral infraction. I suppose it just proves your point that the Bible God is often nothing but an imperious control freak with a bad case of OCD.

J: Yeah, He rules with a short temper and a clenched fist. Even worse, He's a deity of absurd contradiction. According to literalists, He can create an inconceivably vast universe in just six days, and yet He needs *thousands of years* to effect his convoluted plan of salvation, a bizarre scheme which teaches that only gross injustice and a barbaric murder can finally bring love to perfection.

DK: You do have a way with words.

J: And incidentally, where the heck has this mysterious Bible God *gone* to, anyway? What's up with his sudden disappearance right in the middle of a pivotal period in history? I mean first He's hawking his people's every move for generations on end and meddling in their personal affairs on a regular basis. He's hounding them like a nosy neighbor while cranking out reams of law directing even the most mundane aspects of their lives. Then, suddenly, the man's AWOL. Without so much as "Amen" or "goodbye," He goes several thousand years ruling *in absentia*. He installs Christianity and then doesn't even make the obligatory showings at Christmas and Easter. He's lost all semblance of presence and power. Heck, He couldn't even get Pat Buchanan elected.

DK: It would seem that *some* miracles even *God* can't manage.

J: Well, He should've done *something* over the last two thousand years to let folks know He's still kickin'.

DK: That's true. He could at least send down a plague onto the world's central bankers or rain a little fire over at Goldman Sachs.

J: Probably just as well He's been so reclusive. If He knew how things were progressing, He'd likely start another big flood.

DK: I guess the Bible God is kinda like an eccentric great uncle. He may be weird, crotchety and unreasonable—but we tolerate Him because he's *family*.

J: I'd advise to forget this spooky God of your imagination and offload the mysterious scoundrel at the first possible stop. Believe me, you don't want this guy hanging out in your head. If "perfect love casts out fear," as the New Testament declares, then by definition it must also cast out the *God* of fear. You were dead on in your letter when you questioned the sincerity of a man who needs the hell scared out of him before he converts. That's not faith, it's a precautionary measure. Salvation through slavery is a sham and isn't worth the name. True salvation is freedom *from* enslavement.

DK: I'm surprised humanity's been so tolerant of a fearsome, vengeful God who condemns his errant children to a burning hell. The concept would seem to be way beyond an educated man's credulity. Yet I myself embraced it for *years*.

J: Ironically, it's the very *threat* of eternal damnation that prevents people from questioning it. Fearing for their souls, they resign themselves to the concept of hell and then take out insurance policies with their local religion.

DK: Well, Christians certainly come by their resignation honestly. They've got hints of hellfire sprinkled from Matthew to Revelation—and some are attributed directly to *you*. The church implies that scripture is beyond question and that certain doctrines are *critical* to salvation. So I think folks have learned just to accept it all at face value, even if it doesn't make sense.

J: If the Bible were really needed for some kind of soul redemption, then what of the countless millions who lived before there was widespread access to it? Perhaps their tombstones should read, "Condemned to hell due to the late arrival of the printing press."

DK: Still, I'm not sure it makes sense to burn the cornfield just because it has a few bugs. Some scriptures can be highly inspirational.

J: Fine, but we're not talking about mere inspiration: we're talking about *salvation of the soul*. Trust me, I'm all for getting inspired. If certain words help you along your path to God-realization, that's terrific. But when they create conflict or fear, when they promote divisiveness and exclusion instead of cooperation and unity, then heed the inner voice of reason and walk away.

DK: Is all scripture ultimately dispensable?

J: Technically, yes… because truth is your very nature. But pragmatically speaking, not necessarily. Some scriptures can certainly be helpful and even spiritually enlivening—that's strictly an individual thing. But if you find no value there, you're none the worse. Everything you'll ever need was given you eternally at your creation. You don't have to go hunting or begging for salvation, and you certainly don't need to establish your worth in the eyes of God. God *knows* you're worthy.

DK: Well, that does it. This is the last day I gird up my loins.

J: While you're at it, you can extinguish the fires of your burnt offerings, rise up from the dust of repentance, throw out the sackcloth and rinse off the ashes.

DK: Jeepers, how's a martyr supposed to have any fun?

J: Look, if God were the dreadful deity so many people imagine, and if He were truly concerned with the saving of your endangered souls, then why doesn't He just show up tonight for a little bedside chat with every person on the globe? In one evening, He could remove all doubt about Himself and his intentions. You'd think that saving his children from everlasting torture is worth a little additional effort.

DK: A bit impractical, perhaps.

J: Why impractical? This is *God* we're discussing. Going by the story of Sarah's miraculous conception, He's apparently quite capable of putting in personal appearances. Does He figure it's just not worth the trouble? Or is He simply too preoccupied with schoolboys fantasizing over the Victoria's Secret girls?

DK: He's probably kept pretty busy scribbling notations in that famous Book of Life.

J: But really, now… a God who parts the ocean and resurrects the dead should be able to solve this little "salvation" dilemma, don't you think? So why all the needless hassling with rules, doctrines and beliefs? The system practically *guarantees* the condemnation of *billions*.

DK: It does seem like pretty poor planning by the boys at headquarters. Maybe it's time for us to re-think our cherished beliefs about God.

J: A better start would be examining your beliefs about *you*. Because once you fully understand *yourself*, you'll never again misunderstand God.

DK: I'm reminded of an old saying: I had a thousand questions about God, but when I met Him, all my questions disappeared.

J: That's how it works. Once you *know* your reality, questions become unnecessary and beliefs lose their meaning: you finally see them for the imposters they are. In a hyper-intelligent universe, it's no accident that "belief" contains the word "belie." Open your dictionary and read the meaning.

DK: "Belie: to lie or give false or misleading ideas about something; to disguise maliciously or misrepresent; to prove false."

J: So beliefs always "belie" your reality. They're false gods—the intellectual equivalent of the golden calf. At the feet of these idols, you've sacrificed all God-instilled reason, intelligence and spiritual discernment. So start using your head, and don't believe *anything* you have to *believe* in.

DK: You keep insisting that beliefs delay spiritual progress. But why didn't you give a little prophetic warning about that before you took off? You could've prevented a whole lot of disharmony, suffering, and bloodshed.

J: Time and again I chastised those who practiced the false religion of word worship. Even in the gospels, you'll see that I never emphasized documents, dogmas or doctrines. I taught a spirituality that completely transcends words and concepts. I knew that focusing on words always leads to a superficial devotion to *ideas*—the very cause of most of your suffering. Instead of pointing to anything external, I constantly urged people seeking answers to go inward.

DK: You're quoted telling your disciples just before you left, "These things have I spoken to you, while I am still with you. But the Counselor, the Holy Spirit...will teach you all things..."

J: *Sheesh*. The way these writers quote me, you'd think I was sitting at high tea, philosophizing with a bunch of brainiacs from Cambridge. But notice I didn't tell my disciples that spirit would teach them *some* things and that they would learn the rest from special church-endorsed documents. I said that spirit would teach them *everything*. I intentionally shunned doctrines and theologies because they're ultimately deceptive and self-defeating. They keep you stuck in the intellect.

DK: What's the solution?

J: Let all thoughts come and go—release every concept. Be still. Be open. Acknowledge your ignorance and stop playing to the notion of an irritated, dysfunctional God who's obsessed with human behavior. Admit that you don't really know the first thing about Him. Better to stay present, remain quiet and wait for guidance.

DK: Sometimes I ask for guidance and don't hear a thing.

J: Then follow Bucky Fuller's famous rule of thumb: When in doubt, *don't*.

CHAPTER
SIXTY FOUR

DK: Time's a tickin', so we'd better keep clickin'.

J: Alright, what's next?

DK: Just some final stuff about a few of Christianity's brass tacks. Let's start with the sacrament of holy communion. We touched on it earlier, but now I'd like to wade in past our ankles. The church says that something mystical takes place as we partake of the elements. Your thoughts?

J: In early Christianity, the sacrament of communion was basically a remaking of the familiar Jewish Passover meal. As I've said, combining bread with the fruit of the vine is a motif that dates back to ancient pagan ceremonies. The sacrament itself is beautiful; but it's certainly not *required*. I said that those who worship God must worship him in spirit and in truth—not with spirits of vermouth.

DK: Christian conservatives claim the Eucharist is the literal "body and blood of Christ."

J: Geez, throw an abstraction into a room full of literalists and they'll walk out with a block of concrete and a bagful of dogma. If you really believe that a morsel of bread magically becomes my body and a cup of grape juice turns into my blood, then ingesting them makes you a cannibal, does it not? So why should a concept otherwise so repugnant suddenly find appeal within religion? The Last Supper has gotten way too much attention. Read the story again and you'll see that I didn't instruct my disciples to make it a ritual. I only said that whenever they *did* assemble, they should remember me and my teachings. I never taught or implied that anything physical is needed to facilitate man's communion with God.

DK: But even in the synagogue at Capernaum you were quoted as saying, "Unless you eat the flesh of the Son of man and drink his blood, you have no life in you..."

J: Holy hyperbole! Listen, sonny boy, that's just another rip-off from the Mysteries. Long before my birth, the godman Mithras proclaimed, "He who will not eat of my body and drink of my blood… the same shall not know salvation."

DK: Wow, the older version is nearly identical.

J: And believe me, no one took it literally. So heed my warning, my brainwashed friend: the monster of Christian literalism is insatiable. Feed it a wafer and it quickly demands a hundred and seventy pounds of *my flesh*. Don't get me wrong, though. I'm as tickled as the next messiah with the zany interpretations of a good literalist. But do you honestly believe I was commanding people at Capernaum to eat my flesh and drink my blood? Wouldn't that statement merely be consistent with my tendency to use metaphors? I mean *Saints of Sister Agnes*, son—it's some of the most obvious symbolism in the entire Bible!

DK: Conservatives won't cotton to *that*.

J: Confront a biblical fundamentalist with abstraction and he'll deny it three times before the cock crows. By nightfall, he's crucified the life right out of it. Within days, it's resurrected as literalist dogma, then quickly granted eternal life. In the end, you're threatened with the fires of hell if you don't believe it. As for munching my body and guzzling my blood… well, all I can say is, don't swallow everything you're told.

DK: Always encouraging rebellion, eh?

J: If you don't rebel against absurdity, you'll never have a prayer.

DK: That reminds me: I've got a few questions about prayer, too. Now, it's obvious that prayer is how most of us communicate with God. But I often wonder if anything's happening at the other end.

J: Prayer may be the most misunderstood aspect of spiritual life. A lot of people view it as a way to get something they don't have—a way to prod the Almighty into doing something He evidently doesn't *want* to do or hasn't yet thought of on his own. They see prayer as a formal entreaty, hoping God will be moved to grant their requests. Some even try striking deals: you give me this and I'll give you that. They view God as a kind of cosmic flea market merchant or a heavenly bellhop.

DK: So we use prayer as a spiritual bargaining tool.

J: Well, most prayer is based on belief in scarcity and separation. It assumes the petitioner is split off from God and that he's lacking something that God either neglected to give or chose to withhold. You can see, then, that the nature of someone's prayer is a pretty accurate indicator of how he views himself, his God, and their relationship. *True* prayer reflects the recognition that *everything has already been given and received*. It recognizes that nothing is needed, because nothing was ever lacking.

DK: Now, hang on a sec. Your flowery words are stirring, I'm sure. But how can you say that nothing is lacking? Here in the *real* world, we've got plenty of lack, Jack.

J: You consider this world real and assume that solidity is reality because of your ongoing illusion that you are the body. It's a cosmic case of mistaken identity and the very foundation of the human problem. It's the only reason you could ever feel deprived.

DK: You and your philosophical paradise!

J: Don't misunderstand. Living in physicality, it's obvious that you do need things. But rather than *confirming* this world's "reality," your sense of lack is one of the most compelling reasons to *question* it. If God created you as a body-mind complex, then why doesn't He also provide you with everything you need to be comfortable, happy and secure in such an unstable state? Some people have lives of ease and abundance, of course—but most of humanity *doesn't*. As you said earlier, many don't even have the basics: food, clean water, adequate shelter and so forth. Must they be driven to pray before receiving such things?

DK: Maybe God desires prayer to encourage appreciation of our dependence on Him.

J: An egotistical approach, to say the least. Isn't everyone entitled to expect an all-wise, all-loving God to attend to the obvious and provide them with life's essentials? Should prayer for such things really be necessary? As an earthly parent, would you require your children to come begging or gushing with gratitude before supplying them with even the fundamental elements of survival?

DK: I suppose I dare not mention free will again.

J: Don't waste your time. Free will is just a theological band-aid over the gaping wound of the unspoken fear—based on countless centuries of dramatic evidence—that God is not deeply concerned with the preservation and protection of the average body-mind entity.

DK: One could make the case that some prayers are simply inappropriate. If God has already provided sufficient resources and moral instruction for us to live comfortably and securely, then it's not his fault if we live like fools and gum up the works. Who could blame Him for ignoring meaningless prayers of hypocrisy? Maybe God figures He already gave us everything we need, and now He expects us to use and distribute it with fairness, compassion and intelligence. He's simply taking the "hands-off" approach while He sits back and observes.

J: That would make the earth nothing but God's little ant farm. In that case, what would be the point of prayer? A God of *laissez faire* policy is as good as dead—more useless than a freshly re-elected congressman.

DK: Perhaps He wants to see how we'll handle things on our own.

J: So you're offering the possibility that God is *able* to relieve the world's suffering but chooses *not* to.

DK: Well, if I've learned *anything* today, I've learned that, with the God of religion, *all* things are possible.

J: Wouldn't that make Him heartless and wicked?

DK: Alright, maybe He *wants* to help but for some reason He *can't*.

J: Then He's weak and impotent, clearly contradicting religion's claims about the nature of God.

DK: Well, that leaves only one possibility: God neither *wants* to help the world, nor could He do so if He tried.

J: Making Him both cruel *and* powerless, again challenging the whole of biblical and ecclesiastical teaching. Under *those* conditions, why bother calling Him God?

DK: It seems I've painted myself into a corner. Are you just gonna leave me standing while the enamel dries?

J: But you're not cornered at all. There's another possibility you refuse to consider: that your experience of yourself as a body-mind isn't your ultimate reality and that you aren't the person you take yourself to be.

DK: O joy, we're back to the dream again. Look, I know you're the last guy in heaven I should be arguing with, but this "illusion" stuff is tougher to stomach than my ex-wife's lasagna. Spin your pretty dream-web as you will—but the upshot is that I have *needs*. I may not subscribe to every last tenet of Christianity, but I don't see any wrong in casting a little prayerful appeal heavenward now and then.

J: Most of your prayers are actually declarations of mistrust. To proclaim faith in God and then swamp Him with fearful or needy requests is to demonstrate the weakness of the faith. The typical prayer is nothing but a veiled request for idols or asking to have your dream rearranged. What if the experience you interpret as "dreadful" is all in keeping with God's plan? Do you have enough faith to trust that only God sees the big picture and that all things do indeed work together for good? Is it possible that you could even come to see all things *as* good? Because anything less is a statement that things shouldn't be as they are. And when you argue with reality, you always lose.

DK: Hold it, I've got a problem. You've spent all day talking about how the world's a frightful mess and that it has to change or we're all going down in flames. Yet *now* you tell me there's no sense *praying*, because nothing is wrong and all things are "in divine order."

J: But again, we're looking at things from *your* standpoint, not from mine. I don't take the world seriously, because I understand its ultimate non-reality. Since you and most of humanity *do* take it seriously, we have to discuss it from *that* angle. So it's tricky. The same words can be true or *not* true, depending on perspective. The view *I'm* describing at least gets your mind proceeding in new directions. And I'd say that's pretty important for someone asking a space-and-time-restricted deity to modify a world of illusion based entirely in his own consciousness.

DK: Then prayer's a *bad* thing?

J: Not *bad*, of course—but often self-deceiving. True prayer is a form of praise and reflects awareness that you don't need anything and that nothing has to change for you to be peaceful. True prayer understands that I and the Father are *already* one.

DK: What does it matter that we're one with God if we can't put food on our plates? The fact is that we all have problems.

J: There's a state of consciousness in which the empty plate is no worse than the full. But until you *know* this in the depths of your being, it's just a bunch of hooey—nothing but intellectual whitewash. Again, whatever is not *your* truth is *un*-truth. The real purpose of prayer is to reunite you with God, not to get you a full-color spread in *Forbes*.

DK: But life can be painful. Sometimes we pray because we're truly suffering.

J: Of course. But spirit wants to eliminate the *root* of your suffering, which is in the *mind*. Awhile back, you quoted the Buddha's declaration that life *is* suffering. But he also proclaimed, "Behold, I show you suffering—and the *end* of suffering." *That's* enlightenment...

CHAPTER SIXTY FIVE

DK: I've got a confession to make.

J: You're in luck, my son. The last of the sinners has just left for happy hour and my confessional is empty.

DK: Well, you've said that God and I are one and that our will is therefore united. In my unenlightened state, however, *my* will is the only one I'm aware of, while God's will seems to be forever a mystery. So to be honest, I'm not always sure that I *want* God's will. It worries me to think what He might be planning.

J: Nearly everyone has a problem praying for God's will if they believe it to be in opposition to their own. And the Bible is full of stories that give the reader good reason to fear the so-called "will of God." In fact, for sheer scare value, nothing beats the story of the Crucifixion. The idea that God actually *planned* my murder at Calvary is one of the most insane notions ever conceived. God gives only *life*—and He gives it *eternally*. It's the main lesson of the Resurrection.

DK: Pardon me if I seem half-hearted… but if we've gotta suffer crucifixion before resurrection, I'm not all that interested in signing up. On the whole, I'd rather be in Philadelphia.

J: Sacrifice is the keystone of almost every religion. It's also their essential flaw. Because God isn't *asking* for anything—*ever*. You've arbitrarily connected God's will with the concept of sacrifice, which arises from your own fearful thinking. In a way, you've voluntarily *crucified yourself*, believing that God is pleased by your suffering. But those who understand reality scoff at the notion of sacrifice. You and God are one, and God doesn't sacrifice Himself.

DK: If God and I are one, then what's the good of prayer?

J: The basest form of prayer is fairly pointless. I mean let's face it: if you really trusted God to care for you and to know best what you need, you'd offer only one prayer: "Father, into thy hands I commend my spirit."

DK: Then asking for specifics is essentially a show of mistrust.

J: Well, my own prayers were generally focused on the *spiritual* side. I never doubted that I would be well provided for, because I knew that everything I needed would show up at my doorstep.

DK: Easy for *you* to say. In the seventeenth chapter of Matthew, when the government boys came around to collect your half-shekel tax, you sent Peter fishing. You told him that the first fish he caught would have a shekel in its mouth—sufficient to cover the tax for you both. Sure enough, we're told the fish coughs up the cash as promised. What do you say about *that*?

J: I say it was the first time in history that a fish got a human being off the hook.

DK: You should be in television...

J: The moral of the exaggerated shekel-bearing fish story is that life can provide in the most unexpected and surprising ways. Sometimes, the best thing you can do when facing a problem is to "go fishing." You stay composed, you do what you can—then you relax and let go. In the same way that the body tends to heal itself, most situations will resolve without your interference.

DK: Don't we have the right to pray when we're worried or in need?

J: Sure, but you often create a *new* set of problems by assuming that *you* know best what you need. I can assure you that you don't. Prayer is usually just a restatement of belief in scarcity. It says to God, "I'm deficient and incomplete. I need something outside myself to change before I can feel happy or secure." That kind of prayer is based on identification with the body and the belief that you and creation are separate.

DK: You're reminding me of an early lesson from *A Course in Miracles*: "I do not perceive my own best interests."

J: Pull it out and read a few lines...

DK: "In no situation that arises do you realize the outcome that would make you happy. Therefore, you have no guide to appropriate action, and no way of judging the result. What you do is determined by your *perception* of the situation, and that perception is *wrong*. It is inevitable, then, that you will not serve your own best interests... If you realized that you do not perceive your own best interests, you could be taught what they are. But in the presence of your conviction that you *do* know what they are, you cannot learn."

J: Can you see how the lesson relates directly to prayer? It calls you to relinquish your ideas about God, how He should behave, what your needs are, and how your life should look. The *Course* also puts it this way: "Do not point the road to God by which He should appear to you." So here you have yet another source warning about the dangers of assumptions and expectations.

DK: You've said the goal is to release expectations by keeping our attention focused in the present moment and forgetting the imaginary future. Sometimes, though, I find myself mentally stuck in the *past*.

J: Heed some words from the book of Luke: "No one who puts his hand to the plow and looks back is fit for the kingdom of God." Translation: when your awareness is not in the present moment, you've lost all access to reality.

DK: Are we just supposed to fly by the seat of our pants? I'm not sure it's practical taking life tick-by-tick.

J: Why not? That's the only way it comes.

DK: Then how does prayer fit in?

J: In its most helpful form, prayer looks past your specific needs *as you see them* and surrenders them to God, whose answer to prayer is always some form of peace. But surrender's not easy. It takes the kind of faith that stares down disaster without flinching. Your best prayer is free of all resistance, all begging, all dictating of terms. It reflects the understanding that you aren't the body or the mind and that spiritual awakening is your most pressing need.

DK: Needs aside, there are things I'd simply like to *have*. The New Agers tell me that I'm the Managing Director of my own life and that I can manifest whatever I choose.

J: Well, you're certainly free to set your intentions. Whether they'll manifest is anyone's guess—but even if they do, it's missing the point. Manifesting doesn't free you from the belief that something outside of you will increase your value. It's easy to allow material wealth to cover over a feeling of inner lack.

DK: Then bring on the covers, baby—I'm willing to live shallow!

J: Honestly, you're no further ahead until you know that *to have* is *to be.*

DK: Then I think we're on the same page, brother J, because I'd like *to have* whatever I want and *to be* insanely rich!

J: C'mon, Rockefeller, try to get a sense of priority. Spiritual enlightenment is infinitely more important than material comfort. And far more *fulfilling.*

DK: For me, that just doesn't cut it. I need things I can hold in my hand.

J: Surely you wouldn't trade spiritual liberation for a few fleeting doo-dads and trinkets.

DK: Actually, if it's all the same to you...

J: Jeepers, man, you can't see past your *nose*!

DK: Oh, sure. Whenever *you* need something, you just conjure a few gallons of wine or send a guy to fish out a holy mackerel with a gullet full of gold. But the minute *someone else* has a problem—

J: C'mon, don't be a literalist boob. The answer to all your problems is closer than your five o'clock shadow. Save yourself the headache and quit asking for gewgaws, baubles and knickknacks. I wouldn't be helping you by catering to your false beliefs and foolish self-images.

DK: Alright then, Scrooge, tell me how I *should* pray.

J: The most honored prayer is, "Help me to understand what's *already true* and to accept what's *already given*." Stop begging and bartering, and pray instead to hear the ever-present, "still, small voice" of Love.

DK: The New Testament exhorts us to "pray without ceasing."

J: Well, that alone should prove that true prayer isn't a matter of supplicating God on your knees. Otherwise, how would you reasonably be expected to do it without ceasing?

DK: So the advice is bogus.

J: No, it's just misunderstood. In a sense, you *do* pray without ceasing. You continually tell the universe who you believe you are by the way you live. Your daily decisions demonstrate your values and reflect what you truly want. So *your life* is virtually a living prayer. And believe me, nothing goes unnoticed. There's nothing hidden that shall not be made known, and even your subtlest thoughts have creative power.

DK: Ideally, then, how should we live?

J: Above all, peacefully. Calmly do what needs doing, but be ever aware of the life force within—the energetic presence that's "doing" your life. Try not to lose sight of it, not even for an instant.

DK: A tough assignment.

J: In the beginning, yes, because your attention is so thoroughly focused on the material plane. People spend most of their lives acting out fantasies and pursuing their worldly "dreams." Only when death is visible on the horizon do they realize that nothing external can bring the permanent happiness they seek. The solution, while it isn't difficult, requires clear understanding of the problem and often creates temporary pain. Fortunately, there's help every step of the way. Just stay peaceful and remain vigilant.

DK: Aren't there any shortcuts?

J: Maybe a few. First, develop the habit of forgiving all grievances. That part is critical, and there are no exceptions. Once again, *A Course in Miracles* says it best: "Forgiveness is the great release from time... There *is* no other teacher and no other way."

DK: Such a high-minded state! Who but a saint could achieve it!?

J: It helps to remember that nothing eternal is changed or affected by anything happening in the world. Practicing forgiveness is crucial, because it leads to peace and thus opens the mind to revelation. A conflicted mind never perceives reality as it is— another reason why you *must* question the mind's thoughts and its endless judgments and conclusions. Ask yourself if you can know for sure that something's true. Very often the answer is no.

DK: Alright, what else?

J: When you catch yourself daydreaming, or when you realize you're caught up in thoughts of past or future, bring your attention back to the present moment. To do this, simply become aware of yourself and your surroundings—the feel of the air against your skin, your breathing, the colors and textures of objects around you, the beating of your heart and so forth.

DK: That part doesn't sound difficult.

J: The process itself is pretty simple: just become the impartial observer while paying careful attention to what's happening within. When the mind presents a stressful thought, *question it*. The mere *acts* of self-inquiry and self-observation can bring amazing results. But always maintain an uncompromising commitment to peace, because without peace you can never know God, who is the Author of peace.

DK: Evidently, true prayer eliminates requests entirely.

J: That's the goal, yes. But there are lots of steps to the top of the "prayer ladder." So start where you are. If asking for specifics seems important, then ask. But don't assume you're being deprived when a prayer isn't answered according to your expectations. Spirit may be protecting you or helping you grow in ways you could never imagine.

DK: I remember hearing stories from 9/11 of people who couldn't make it to work that morning. Some folks were running late, some missed their trains, others had sick children—random stuff like that. At the time, they were cursing their bad luck. Later on, they discovered their misfortunes were actually blessings in disguise.

J: Yep, you'd be surprised how many people cuss heaven for something they'd be giving thanks for if only they had all the facts. Remember that, next time you're stuck in traffic.

DK: You appear to address this issue of detail-oriented prayer in Luke 11. You're quoted saying, "What father among you, if his son asks for bread, will give him a stone; or if he asks for a fish, will instead give him a scorpion?"

J: Yes, but the irony of most prayer is that folks *assume* they're asking for bread when they're unwittingly asking for the damned scorpion!

DK: What about praying for things like patience, kindness, wisdom, and compassion?

J: A waste of time. Those qualities are *developed*, not granted.

DK: Got any other prayer-related rules-of-the-road?

J: The chief thing is that ownership and need are dangerous ideas in the hands of ego. Spirit will never answer prayer in ways that would harm anyone or stifle your willingness to question this world's ultimate value. Whatever comes to you from spirit comes gently and easily, with the emphasis always on the real goal: the re-emergence of the true self.

DK: Okay, but you've gotta be realistic. I mean everyone has desires. So how do we distinguish the good from the bad?

J: As a rule, whatever you call with love is worthy and will come to you. Conversely, you're held back by nearly everything requested from greed, neediness or fear. It's crucial to ask spirit for guidance, because your twisted sense of self is a particularly poor counselor.

DK: Damn. Seems like there'd be *some* kind of *formula*.

J: Ah, c'mon. Try to muster enough faith to believe that the intelligence keeping the planets on course can also help you pay the rent. Admit it: on a cosmic scale, your life challenges are only momentary blips of consciousness. Pray without ceasing by not resisting what *is*. Just stay focused on the very next step and forget the rest. Realize that the answer to your prayer may not coincide with your preconceived notions of what's best, either for you or for anyone else. Eventually you'll realize that you have no problems at all—and that you never did.

DK: Again I protest. It's easy for you to spit out platitudes and theories. *You* don't have a mortgage, utility bills, or a crushing bar tab at the track. With all due respect, I need *real-world* advice, not metaphysical psycho-babble!

J: Calm down there, Willis. I'm not discounting the pressures of daily life. But living involves *choices*. There's an ocean of difference between what you need and what you want. Understand that praying to *get* something usually involves feelings of weakness and limitation. But those who know themselves have no reason to go begging for handouts.

DK: Some say that unless we tell the universe what we want, it doesn't have a clue. They say that if you just drift through life, then you're nothing but driftwood. The old maxim is that if you don't know where you're going, you'll probably end up *somewhere else*.

J: Does the oak tree supplicate the heavens for sunshine or rain? Must the sparrow plan for its future and remind the earth to provide straw for its nest? Does a car salesman *really* need his manager's permission to knock off another two hundred bucks?

DK: Huh? What the heck does that have to do wi—

J: Okay, that last one might've been a little off-track. The point is that you're making life a lot harder than it has to be. Trust God by trusting *yourself*, and show some real, down-home faith by refusing to manipulate or exploit, defend or attack, deny or deceive, contrive or connive, insist or resist. Stop "pushing the river," and allow things to unfold naturally.

DK: Well, isn't this just *perfect*. I luck into an interview with one of history's great spiritual Kahunas, and the best advice he can give me is "Let it be" and "Go with the flow."

J: Cheer up. I could've said life is a bowl of cherries.

DK: But c'mon, man. If you're gonna throw pearls to pigs here, at least make sure you've got some decent-size gems!

J: Oy, I might've expected this. A prophet is not without honor, except to a journalist...

CHAPTER SIXTY SIX

DK: I get the impression that you basically have no use for prayer.

J: Well, I mean think about it. Are you hoping your prayer will compel God to change his mind—as if *you* know best what the situation requires? Are you striving to help Him see a solution that He somehow overlooked? Or do you believe He's *withholding* assistance until you've sufficiently pleaded? Poor mortal sap to be saddled with a God so dim!

DK: I suppose most prayers do fall into one of those groups. I can see now that prayer is usually just a request that things be different than they are.

J: Not only that, but what happens when *you* pray for one outcome and *someone else* prays for another? One of you is bound to be disappointed. You're both acting as though God was uninvolved—or was powerless to influence—how things came to be the way they are. Either situation creates big theological trouble.

DK: So the implication is that if God was unwilling to take action in the first place, then why would He intervene simply because we pray? On the other hand, if God was truly *helpless* to affect how things developed, then a prayer to Him now is just wasted breath.

J: Hold yer tickets, folks! We have a winnahhh!

DK: But c'mon, there's certainly no comfort in the idea that God may be incapable of changing anything. Neither is it helpful to believe that He has some grand purpose behind a dreadful pandemic or a devastating flood. After all, He might just as well have good reason for giving me cancer!

J: That's true, He just might!

DK: Sorry, but I'd like to believe that I have at least *some* control of my destiny.

J: Man, you're a tough nut to crack. Still wanting to be in control, eh?

DK: Henley said, "I am the master of my fate: I am the captain of my soul."

J: Look here, Long John, you've gotta give up this control thing. Henley forgot to mention that every captain eventually goes down with the ship. Worry less about prayer and more about developing a little trust. Have faith that spirit will fill your needs without giving them unjustified weight. Surrender ideas about "happiness," and examine your constant need to acquire. It's said that as your consciousness grows lighter, so does your suitcase.

DK: Okay, I can maybe see the selfishness that usually infects the average *personal* prayer. But surely there's a difference between praying for myself and praying for others.

J: Ultimately, all prayer is for the One Self. Still, in praying for others, you at least begin to understand unity. By praying for someone else, you mentally make him part of you. That's how the healing of others leads to *your own* healing and why "praying for your enemies" is a contradiction in terms. To pray for your enemies means realizing that you *have* no enemies. To put it simply, you'll be healed as you let spirit teach you to heal others.

DK: By praying for others, then, we're actually helping to heal ourselves.

J: Of course. In this world, you've been taught that to give something away leaves you with less. It's typical egoic thinking, which is always upside-down and backwards. In the world of spirit, the way to *keep* something is to *give* it. Do you want to experience love? Then extend it to everyone. Do you want peace? Then offer only peace to others. In the spiritual realm, sharing something always *multiplies* it: both receiver and giver end up with more. It's the same reason God created *you*. Ya follow?

DK: It's funny... I used to view prayer almost like placing an order with room service. But I never knew if anyone would deliver—or if the message was even received.

J: Every prayer is heard and responded to appropriately. You don't often hear the answer because it's not what you're *expecting*. When you're compelled to pray for something specific, try to conclude with the thought, "not as *I* will, but as *Thou* wilt." This at least acknowledges that your present understanding is limited and that what's truly required may be something far different from your request. When operating from ego, your interpretation of what's needed is usually mistaken. If spirit's answers seem irrelevant, it's because the wrong "judge" is doing the evaluating.

DK: Should we repeat our prayers until they're answered?

J: Only if you believe that God is deaf or dense. The gospel quotes me as follows: "Do not be anxious, saying, 'What shall we eat?' or 'What shall we drink?' or 'What shall we wear?' For...your heavenly Father knows that you need them all." In other words, God is *God*—He knows perfectly well what you need. Why pester the man?

DK: Sometimes I remind God what I want because... well, frankly, He doesn't appear all that trustworthy. It seems He frequently overlooks our earthly concerns. Once again I'll refer to those hungry hordes. What more proof do you need? I mean they're *starving*, for God's sake.

J: Wrong! They're starving for *man's* sake! The fact that humans allow their neighbors to go hungry is certainly not God's fault. Should the universe suspend its laws each time something undesirable is pending? Imagine the chaos! Anyhow, there's no cosmic puppeteer pulling the strings; and if there were, the only thing you could safely conclude is that God is cruel, weak-minded, or incompetent.

DK: Goodbye, Rock of Ages.

J: C'mon, you have more than enough experience to know that the God of your religion doesn't exist as advertised—and He never did. You can change your mind about this now, or you can wait another thousand years. Either way, only the truth is true, and nothing else ever *was* true. Your task is to begin the conceptual demolition.

DK: But the fact that I exist at all makes me believe there's *something* beyond me.

J: You're half right. That "something" does exist. But it isn't *beyond* you—it *is* you. The belief that it's outside you is the root error.

DK: I'll give you this much: there's something lurking about that's incredibly intelligent and apparently wants to express itself. But who or what the heck is it?

J: Now, *that's* ironic. You're *aware* of this unseen force, but you automatically assume that it's something *apart* from you. We've discussed in quite some detail the impossibility of separation, and yet you still can't accept it. Why is that?

DK: I guess you could blame religion. It externalized the force by referring to it as God—so I took the bait. But who could blame me? I mean they've got Him living in another dimension where He's sitting on a throne surrounded by seraphim, cherubim, and other imported furnishings, just waiting for us to drop dead while He makes careful notes in our permanent records and gears up for the big Pink Slip Party. Sure sounds like an outsider God to *me*.

J: Concede that "God" is just a convenient term for something your intellect can't possibly grasp. I'm not judging, because *I* used the word, too. But in *naming* the power, we give it the feel of something external. It becomes just another thing among things— the biggest and most powerful thing, perhaps, but a *separate* thing nonetheless.

DK: Then you sympathize with our confusion.

J: I couldn't help you if I didn't. I was born with the same misunderstandings that have plagued humanity since time began. But somehow I questioned it all, even as a child. Eventually I discovered that I was part of all creation—or to be more accurate, that all creation was part of *me*. That's how I could declare with certainty, "I and the Father are one." The ancient Vedic writings put it this way: "*I* am that; *you* are that; and *all this* is that." Understand?

DK: Let's just say I'm a little confused about this and that.

J: Well, believe it or not, what I found to be true for myself is just as true for you. Your confusion may *delay* your awakening, but it can't prevent it.

DK: If the unity argument is correct, then your position on prayer makes sense and there's no need to ask for *anything*.

J: If you *really* trusted, you'd never have to say a word. When you read the prayers of the world's great sages and saints, they aren't asking for a house in the hills or a mountain of money. They're asking for more understanding—*more light*.

DK: Still, I don't see any harm putting a gentle elbow in God's rib now and then.

J: Must a child continuously remind her parents that she needs to be fed, clothed, sheltered and loved?

DK: Okay, but again you have to be *practical*. Sometimes we pray because situations need changing.

J: Do they? Hard as it is to believe, someday you may see it differently. In any case, trying to alter circumstance is taking the long way around the barn. Find the place of perfection *within* and you may find your world reflecting that same perfection. Prayers, rituals and incantations may foster a state of reverence or wonderment, but they're a pretty roundabout way of doing things.

DK: It sounds as though you're simply telling us to have faith.

J: That's true—but I would hardly call it simple. Rare is the person who lives by unquestioning faith. And I'm not referring to faith in doctrines or creeds. I'm talking all-out reliance on the unfailing power of love. O, for a child's trust! A mere mustard seed's worth is scarcer than a "Sell" recommendation on Wall Street.

DK: Personally, I find it's easier to trust when I have more of what I want.

J: But having faith when things are going your way is nothing special. Let me share an old story about the difficulty of maintaining faith when it counts...

A large ocean liner is sailing from New York to England. The ship is halfway across the Atlantic when a fierce storm develops and begins tossing the vessel violently in its massive waves. Naturally, the passengers are quite concerned.

Finally, a woman nearly hysterical with worry insists on speaking with the captain. Reluctantly, a crewman acquiesces and takes the woman to the ship's bridge, where she begins pounding on the door. The captain himself answers and invites the woman in.

"What may I do for you, madam?" the rugged mariner inquires. "Captain," the woman says in an unreasonable tone, "I demand to know how you intend to guarantee the safety of this ship's passengers!"

The captain maintains his composure and replies calmly, "Madam, I assure you that my crew and I have done everything possible to keep you and the other voyagers out of harm's way. All we can do now is place our trust in the merciful, almighty God."

"*Good heavens*," the woman shrieks in panic, "has it come down to *that*!!!??"

DK: *Heh heh*. There's a little bit of us all in that story...

J: What I'm telling you, I guess, is that your faith is never really tested until your situation has "come down to *that*."

DK: You know, I think you've got a knack for this stuff.

J: A fella gets pretty smooth with twenty centuries to practice...

CHAPTER
SIXTY SEVEN

DK: Well, twilight's closing in and I still have loads of material.

J: Better whittle it down to the vitals. I've got prayers for specifics pouring in by the *millions*.

DK: Alright, then, where'd you get the name "Jesus"? It's neither Aramaic nor Hebrew.

J: More residue from paganism. It's the result of Christians jamming as much meaning as possible into their godman story. Some of the earliest Christian authors employed what's now called gematria—from GEOMETRIA, the Greek word for geometry. It's a system of encoding certain words with meaningful numerical values using the words' constituent letters. Gematria was commonly used in other languages too, such as Arabic, Hebrew and Sanskrit. Christian writers took my original Aramaic name, Yeshua, which means "salvation," and created an artificially transliterated Greek version, IESOUS, later Westernized as "Jesus." Neither of these two names has any intrinsic meaning. However, IESOUS was created because it contains high mathematical and symbolic significance: in gematria, IESOUS computes to exactly 888.

DK: Sounds similar to the book of Revelation, where John assigns the number 666 to the antichrist, or what he calls "the beast." How did scripture writers come up with numbers like 666 and 888?

J: As with several ancient cultures, the Greeks placed big emphasis on the arts and sciences. In Pythagorean music theory, 666 is the string ratio of the perfect fifth, the interval of C to G. It's one of the two most powerful harmonic intervals—the other being the perfect fourth, or the interval of C to F. In early cosmology, 666 was also a significant solar number and was connected with a square—comprised of six rows and six columns—known as the "magic square of the sun." The square contains the numbers 1 through 36, arranged so that the addition of the numbers in every row or column, and even diagonally from corner to corner, would always total 111. Obviously, the total of all six rows or all six columns would yield 666. The number 111, then, was yet another solar number and, like 666, was relevant even to early Christian mystics. The number 666 is also important in the mystical Jewish Kabbalah, where it equates to "the spirit of the sun," or "Sorath," again reflecting the metaphysical importance of the solar connection.

DK: Then it wasn't just lucky coincidence that Revelation's "beast" had a name or title that calculated to 666.

J: Certainly not. And it allowed John to identify his loathed antichrist in a way that was far safer than giving an actual name. In the end, though, it was a pretty mysterious strategy—especially if John's vision was truly divine. After all, if God believed it was critical to reveal the beast's identity to his church, why would He encode the name in a way that made it practically impossible to know for sure who John was referring to? The other side of it is this: if John's contemporaries *did* decipher the name of his antichrist, then it had to be someone of *that* day and age.

DK: But that would cast doubt on the very legitimacy of a modern-day Rapture.

J: It would negate the entire prophecy, since it obviously never occurred as predicted. And even now, two thousand years on, the church *still* doesn't know the identity of John's "beast." Or if it does, it isn't letting anyone in on the secret.

DK: Alright, so that explains the importance of 666. But why was the special number 888 used to identify *you*?

J: It, too, was a key pagan solar number. For many early Christians, I was the new personification of the "*Solar* LOGOS." Like certain pagan divinities, I was known as "the Spiritual Sun" which, in ancient cosmology, was symbolized by the number 888. And don't assume that this designation of me as the new sun god was some radical notion espoused by a few obscure factions of heretics. Amongst many of the early Christian communities, I was known by such solar titles as "the only True Helios," "Sun of the Resurrection," the "true Apollo," the "Sun of Righteousness," and others.

DK: Well, Sun of the Biggest Gun! Now you've *really* got my attention! But don't stop here. This information all by itself should be worth a few late-night TV bookings.

J: Well, I already noted that my irregularly transliterated Greek name, IESOUS, was deliberately manufactured to total 888, symbolizing the *Solar* LOGOS. If we examine the Greek word for Christ, CHRISTOS, we find that *its* gematria value is 1480, representing *Illuminating Knowledge*. Along with 666, the numbers 888 and 1480 are both evenly divisible by 74. Adding together the two numbers for IESOUS CHRISTOS—888 plus 1480—results in 2368, which is the pinnacle of the solar hierarchy of the multiples of 74. To those who had the proper understanding, combining the two concepts completed the powerful revelation: *The Illuminating Knowledge of the Solar* LOGOS.

DK: My childhood Sunday school teacher must be writhing in her grave.

J: Ah, but there's more. In music, 888 is the string ratio of the whole tone, the step from C to D. Harmonically, then, the ratio of the numbers 666 and 888 constitutes the relationship of the perfect fourth, one of the two dominant harmonic intervals. The numbers 666 and 888 also have a significant *mathematical* relationship: their geometric mean is 769, which is the gematria value of the word PYTHIOS—another name for the god Apollo. This is important, because it was Apollo who preceded me as the personification of the *Solar* LOGOS and whose mythology served as the inspiration for some specially encrypted stories that were "reinvented" and incorporated into the gospels as "Christ" episodes.

DK: I definitely should've paid more attention in Greek mythology class.

J: Incidentally, the 8-8-8 pattern would also have been immediately recognized by those familiar with the Ionic Greek alphabet. Its three mathematical levels—monads, decads and hecatads—each had eight elements and thus, taken together, symbolized the comprehensive nature of totality, or "the all." And not by mere happenstance, 888 was also the number of the bard Olen who, according to legend, helped establish the oracle of Apollo at Delphi. So 888 was significant because it was considered to represent completeness, power, harmony, light and perfection.

DK: A number packed with meaning, eh?

J: Utterly. Early Christian Gnostics even designated my name as "the Plenitude of Ogdoads"—meaning "the Fullness of Eights"—and many actually referred to me as "the Ogdoad." The New Testament writers knew all this, of course, and in Philippians 2:9 the Apostle Paul declares that I possess "a name which is above every name." Now you know what he meant.

DK: Well, it doesn't take a genius to realize these numbers aren't coincidental. It seems the Greco-pagan influence on Christianity is really adding up.

J: Geometry and math were sacred science to the Greeks, and they're used throughout the gospels to reveal secret teachings to those initiated in the Mysteries. For instance, in John 1:42 the writer has me giving Simon Peter the name *Cephas*. In gematria, *Cephas* computes to 729, a pagan solar number representing the 365 days and 364 nights in a year. This was reminiscent of the solar god Mithras, whose name computes to 365. Mithras' mythology has him born from a rock, and thus he was called PETROGENES—the "rock-born" god. Likewise, Peter is called the "rock" upon which the formal Christian church was birthed.

DK: So Peter's absorption of these hidden pagan themes was intentionally engineered by the gospel writers.

J: Calculatingly so. Peter was also assigned some of the features formerly attributed to yet another of the solar deities: the Roman god Janus, for whom the month of January is named. Like Mithras and Peter, Janus, too, is connected with the solar earth year and is sometimes shown in statues symbolically forming the number 365 with his hands. As the sun god, Janus was considered the heavenly gatekeeper, and his main emblem was a key. In Christianity, these two pagan symbols were incorporated by way of Peter, who holds the symbolic key to heaven's "pearly gates."

DK: This gospelized gematria stuff is downright fascinating.

J: You like that? Here's more: the gospel account of the feeding of the five thousand is actually a mathematical "story problem," similar to one you'd see in a high school textbook. It entails a "hidden" scheme of encoded instructions involving the various numbers cited in the account: two fishes, five loaves, five thousand men seated in groups of hundreds and fifties, and so on. When properly understood and applied, the numbers produce an elaborate geometrical figure in which I'm represented by a twelve-petaled "flower" design. The number twelve, of course, is obtained by the twelve baskets of leftovers, symbolizing one for each disciple. Furthermore, each of the flower's individual arcs measures exactly 74 units, again referring to the solar hierarchy. Multiply 12 times 74 and—*voilà*—once more you've got precisely 888.

DK: This is bloody *astounding*. I never dreamed the gospels contained so many connections to paganism. Is there anything Christianity can call its own?

J: The Inquisition, maybe. Even Christianity's cherished fish motif had well-established pagan origins—so it wasn't by chance that it came to be adopted by the church. During *my* era, the fish symbology represented the approaching "new age" of Pisces.

DK: And you, evidently, were designated as the new avatar who would usher it in.

J: Exactly. In some respects, I was drawn up to be a newer version of Orpheus the Fisher, the ancient Greek god who inspired the Orphic cults. Another Christian fish-related item involves the famous "Star of Bethlehem" which allegedly heralded my birth. As you probably know, modern scholars have placed my birth between the years 8 and 6 BCE, right near the close of the passing age of Aries the ram. So the timing of my birth was perfectly in sync with the subsequent Christian theme of the "slaying of the Lamb." It was a time when even pagan circles were expecting the emergence of a new world teacher: a new godman or savior to lead them into the long-anticipated "Golden Age." Finally, in the year 7 BCE, they got the "sign" they were looking for—something so extraordinary that it takes place just once every nine hundred years or so.

DK: A politician kept a campaign pledge?

J: It was the fact that Jupiter and Saturn came into conjunction in the constellation Pisces three times in the same year. It happened in May, October and December. Each time, the two planets were within about one degree of each other, practically appearing to touch. Astrologers and astronomers alike took this to be extremely auspicious. In the symbolism of astrology, the fish sign Pisces—the final sign of the zodiac—is considered to represent the "last days." For the Jews, the combination of these two powerful planets was especially important. Jupiter was viewed as the "messianic" planet because it symbolizes royalty or kingship, whereas Saturn was associated with Israel and its deity, Yahweh. And it all came together with the dawning of the Age of the Fish.

DK: You're a walking, talking search engine! So now that I'm hooked, got any other fish on the stringer?

J: Well, early Christians used the Greek word for "fish"—ICTHYS—as a code word for my name and an acronym meaning, "Jesus Christ, Son of God, Savior." But these devotees, along with the gospel writers themselves, were well aware that, for many centuries prior, ICTHYS was the Greek name for the Syrian Mystery godman Adonis.

DK: Holy halibut! Seems there's quite a netful of Christian/pagan fishiness!

J: Let me school you just a little more on this fish thing, because it's pretty important to Christian symbology. In pagan sacred geometry, when two equal circles overlap so that each intersects the exact center of the other, they produce a fish-shaped figure known in pre-Christian times as *vesica piscis*. It's that simple line drawing of a fish so proudly displayed on Christian bumper stickers. When a rhombus shape is drawn inside this figure, it's found to have a height-to-width ratio of approximately 153-to-265. More than two hundred years before my birth, Archimedes was already referring to this geometric ratio as "the measure of the fish."

DK: What's the significance?

J: Dividing 265 by 153 yields a result of roughly 1.732, which is mathematically important because it's the approximate square root of three and the controlling ratio of the perfect equilateral triangle. It's also one of the root ratios at the very core of the natural world. Like the ancient Greeks and others before them, the earliest Christian writers understood that the universe is based and deployed in *Number*: ratios, proportions and so forth. So some of the New Testament writers purposely constructed certain stories to reflect these rudiments of ancient pagan wisdom. In fact, the

Orphic canon of number underpins several of the "miracle" stories found in the gospels.

DK: I swear to Poseidon, I had no idea.

J: But you may recognize the *vesica piscis* number 153 from the John 21 account of the fishes in the unbroken net. This story, when interpreted by those "with ears to hear," reveals a detailed geometric design with several meaningful elements conscripted *directly* from pre-Christian cosmological science. The resulting diagram, by the way, prominently features Root 2 and Root 3— that is, the square root of 2 and the square root of 3—both key numbers in pagan sacred science. All of this ancient wisdom long predates Christianity, of course, and its gospel appearance was hardly accidental.

DK: This is nothing less than Christianized paganism!

J: Yes, and academics have written entire books on the subject. So when you encounter these hidden New Testament mysteries, you can be sure that it was all quite by design. Root three was especially important to the Greeks because it's the foundational link in a precise geometric and algebraic relationship—also reflected in the "Christian" fish symbol—between the carefully formulated gematria names of the gods Hermes, Zeus and Apollo.

DK: I never realized Christianity was so strongly influenced by the Greeks. I thought it was mostly a spin-off from Judaism.

J: A common fallacy. The Greeks had at least as much to do with the construction of Christianity as the Jews did. After all, the entire New Testament was composed in Greek. And it makes sense that the Jews wouldn't be the main torch-carriers for a new religion centered on a man they viewed as a disgraced failure.

DK: Maybe that's why Paul had so little success preaching among the Jews.

J: Yes, but the Greeks, on the other hand, were ripe for the picking. Their long-established Orphic mystery teachings of the slain-and-resurrected Dionysus had paved the way. And while Jewish and Greek thought both had a clear influence on Christianity— Matthew, for example, presents me as a kind of reinvented Moses even as John depicts me as the new LOGOS—at its core, Christianity is a *Hellenistic* religion. Greek thought and cosmology are apparent throughout the New Testament, and in fact the Greeks deserve most of the credit for the birth of Western spirituality. So in many ways, Yahweh had far less impact on Christianity than did the gods of Olympus.

DK: Well, I couldn't help but notice that Apollo keeps popping up.

J: And with good reason. For the Greeks, Apollo was one of the most powerful and respected of the Olympian deities. In fact, the gematria numbers of Apollo and his "little brother" Hermes are directly involved in the gospel story of the 153 fishes in the unbroken net. Even the net itself originally symbolized Apollo's net-wrapped OMPHALOS stone at Delphi. In addition to being the legendary tomb site of Dionysus—one of the many slain-and-resurrected gods of antiquity—the stone primarily symbolized the starting point, or center, of the universe. As I mentioned regarding Mithras, Christians later transferred this well-established rock symbolism to Simon Peter, or *Cephas*, the central "rock" upon which I'm said to have founded my church. And not only is Peter the "foundation stone" of the church and the symbolic key-holder to heaven's gate, but Peter himself is the key to some pretty compelling esoterica.

DK: I'm an empty vessel…

J: Well, as the Christian OMPHALOS—Greek for "navel," thus signifying a birth or beginning—Peter is literally laden, as *I* was, with symbolism injected into his persona by gospel writers who were quite learned in Greek mythology. Just as Apollo's OMPHALOS stone at Delphi marked the center point of the Greek KOSMOS, so too was Peter made to represent the cornerstone of the Christian EKKLESIA—the assembly of Christ. And Peter's status as the bedrock of the new Christian theosophy wasn't merely superficial; the gospel writers took great pains to make sure it was "solid as a stone." You ready for this? 'Cause it's gonna hitcha right between the eyes.

DK: No problem, Son of David. Fill that slingshot and rock on.

J: The name "Peter" in Greek is PETROS, which means "rock," just as the name *Cephas* is derived from the Aramaic word for rock. As I've said, *Cephas* in gematria computes to 729, a solar number that was meaningful even to the likes of Plato and Socrates centuries earlier. It was also the number of DELPHINION, a temple of Apollo Delphinios. In one of his writings, the Apollonic priest Plutarch mentions that 729 is the number which symbolizes the sun. Geometrically, 729 gives rise not only to another impressive "magic square," measuring 27 by 27 units, but also to a three-dimensional cube, measuring 9 by 9 by 9 units. In other words, 27 squared—or 9 cubed—both result in 729. So if you thought you knew Peter before, now you've *really* got his number.

DK: Startling stuff. I mean results like that can't possibly be aimless or random.

J: Not in the least. Peter's gematrial gospel grooming directly mirrors his cosmological significance to the early Christians, a community well schooled in these ancient "pagan" themes. In an obscure work called *Clementine Homilies*, Peter himself teaches that God, though shapeless, can be represented by the six-sided cube, because He radiates out into the six directions of space: north, south, east, west, up, and down.

DK: Riveting! Although it sure doesn't "square" with my old Sunday school learning.

J: And the secrets of Peter don't stop there. If you take "The Cube of *Cephas*"—constructed of 729 separate mini-cubes, with 81 cubes per side—you obtain a total surface area consisting of 486 individual segments. Now consider that the gematria value of the Greek word PETRA, or "stone," is exactly 486 and you can see just how much meaning gospel writers designed into the literary "building blocks" of one of their main characters.

DK: Wow. Pagan mysteries hidden right there in the Christian gospels. Who woulda figured?

J: Church father Irenaeus, for one. Even that literalist rascal knew about this stuff—so it's no breaking news flash. Scholars have known for decades that certain Christian writers were incorporating into their work secret numeric and cosmological codes brought forth from earlier traditions. But don't expect the church to advertise it. Widespread knowledge of these coerced, pagan-inspired gospel elements might lead folks to wonder if the entire Christian tragedy isn't equally contrived...

Chapter Sixty Eight

DK: As long as we're discussing the New Testament's occult aspects, let's examine the Rapture in a bit more detail. We already know that, in the book of Revelation, Saint John assigns the number 666 to "the beast." And it seems that every generation tries to impose this "devil's number" onto someone living. Yet no one has proven conclusively who John was indicating. Some scholars believe it was the first-century ruler Caesar Nero.

J: It's true that Nero's name in Greek is an exact match for the number 666. And he was indeed widely despised by the Jews for his ruthlessness. He was also especially cruel toward Christians, so John would certainly have shared the general Christian bitterness toward Rome.

DK: But again, if John was secretly identifying one of his contemporaries—in this case, Nero—then that would destroy the entire foundation for a present-day Rapture.

J: Yes, but Nero couldn't have been "the beast," since he had already committed suicide when John was exiled to the island of Patmos by the new emperor, Domitian. That, of course, gives free rein to the imaginations of present-day fundamentalists, who seem ever anxious to bring on the devil in his full demonic glory. Wanting an easy escape from a troublesome world, some Christians are gleefully seeking their antichrist, hard at work ushering in the day of holocaust in hope that I'll take them floating off to paradise. It'd be funny if it weren't so dangerously dumb.

DK: Even so, a lot of Christians—literalist or otherwise—believe the beast is someone alive right now.

J: Heck, that's nothing new. Revelation's puzzle has allowed people to connect the number of the beast with presidents, popes and other political or religious figures for the last two thousand years.

DK: Some people claim that 666 could even implicate the Church of Rome itself—although the fundies insist that the beast is a specific person. They point to the King James Version of John's statement in Revelation 13:18 that reads, "… it is the number of a man." On the other hand, the Revised Standard Version is much more vague and says only that "it is a *human* number." Obviously some ambiguity.

J: You could even make the case scripturally that the antichrist isn't just one person. In the first letter of John, the writer says that already *"many* antichrists have come" and that the antichrist is *anyone* "who denies the Father and the Son." Seemingly, that would mean anyone who isn't Christian. In fact, the writer states forcefully that the spirit of antichrist "is in the world *already,*" and he boldly declares, "Children, it is the last hour." This resonates well with Revelation 3:11, where God assures the church, "I am coming *soon.*"

DK: So these letters were clearly addressing readers of *that* era, not this one.

J: Sure, the writers were addressing their *peers* and spoke of a redemption expected to occur *promptly.* John and his fellow Christians would've had absolutely no use for revelatory warnings of an apocalypse of terror some twenty centuries later.

DK: So c'mon, then, spill the beans. Who is John's antichrist? It's a question almost every Christian would like answered—especially those revving up for the Rapture.

J: Let's rectify a couple of misconceptions. First, there's no such thing as an "antichrist." God is everything, and everything has no opposite. Second, the Bible never uses the term "Rapture," and it was never part of traditional Christianity. The modern vision of the Rapture didn't really take hold until it was energized by a couple of extremist preachers in the 1800s.

DK: Still, it does seem to have a solid biblical basis.

J: So does killing psychics and gays. Besides, the Rapture is problematic from the start. How could God predict a great tribulation more than two thousand years in advance when, in certain Old Testament stories, He's not even sure what's happening *right now*? But apart from all that, the Rapture has a far more serious implication. For if the prophecy is truly inspired and set in stone, wouldn't it indicate that God knew all along that his suicide mission to save humanity from hell would ultimately fail?

DK: Hmmm, another angle I hadn't considered. God obviously didn't have much confidence in your chance of success…

Chapter Sixty Nine

J: As you're beginning to see, you've got some real challenges interpreting Revelation literally, as you'd *have* to do if the Rapture has any validity. For instance, why would God wait six thousand years after the storied "fall of man" to finally destroy his archenemy Satan? Doesn't God understand that by the time He gets around to responding, billions of his children are already condemned to eternal anguish through the wiles of the devil and his legion of fallen angels?

DK: Yeah, very strange behavior from the Almighty. How would such bizarre conduct be justified?

J: The answer, O ye of childish faith, is as simple as it is irrefutable: *"It's the inscrutable mystery of God!"*

DK: *Heh heh.* Yes, I've certainly heard that one a few times.

J: Here's more food for thought: According to John's vision, for those who manage to survive Armageddon, the earth will be a smoking badland of burned-out rubble. Yet John declares that he sees "a new earth." So how is God going to repair the place? How will He make it comfortable again for my scheduled thousand-year reign of peace? Can He instantly make paradise of a scarred and war-torn planet? Will He hastily beautify an earthquake-, famine-, drought- and plague-ridden wasteland from hell?

DK: Well, I suppose if He could create the entire cosmos in only six days, He can easily refurbish a relatively small planet in between hymns. For Him, it's just a quick remodeling job.

J: But if God has *that* kind of unmitigated power, then why hasn't He used it before now? Instead of waiting 'til the last minute to destroy the world in a devilish onslaught of war and deadly plagues, why doesn't He descend immediately and direct all that energy toward *healing* it? And again, why has God so long delayed his victory over Satan? Why has He permitted billions to suffer a temporary hell on earth, only to be condemned to another *perpetual* one in the afterlife? Has God dallied just to ensure that his eschatological timeline will coincide with the ancient scribbles of an angry old man hiding in a dank cave off the coast of Turkey? Quick! For a chance to win a lovely, one-size-fits-all, white ascension robe, how do you explain this stunning display of divine lunacy?

DK: Okay, I'll play along: *It's the inscrutable mystery of God!*

J: And if, as Revelation proclaims, there will be no spiritual corruption in God's unsullied heaven, then what happens to humanity's highly vaunted free will? How can God ensure that no one inside the pearly gates will ever sin? Residing in heaven didn't stop Satan and his angels from rebelling! In that same vein, why should God's coming Golden Age *earthly* paradise be any better than his *first* one back in the Garden? And speaking of Eden, if the serpent in the Garden was actually Lucifer in disguise, as many Christians postulate, then who placed him there? And *why*!? There's only one explanation for these severe tests of intellectual credulity, my trusting companion. *Shout it from the pews!*

DK: *It's the inscrutable mystery of God!*

J: Furthermore, if God is the only creator, then who made all the strange and evil life forms described in John's horrific vision? Who created the human-faced locusts, the six-winged monsters and the seven-headed red dragon? Who gave them their magically menacing demonic powers? Does Satan have the same omnipotent, life-giving potential as the supreme and immortal Lord of creation? If so, who granted the devil these magnificent talents—and for what purpose? Can this freaky, madcap prophecy really be the *literal truth*? Or is it possible that John had been watching too many cheesy, low-budget science fiction films? Don't bother mulling it over, my uncritical correspondent. Only one answer will burn away the fog, and it's right on the tip of your tongue! *Say it with me!*

DK: *It's the inscrutable mystery of God!*

J: Next, please tell me how stars a million-fold larger than your own planet—and light years away!—could instantly reverse the laws of physics and begin falling to earth, as described in John's "inspired" utterances. Wouldn't gravitational attraction work exactly the other way around? And how, in the midst of unleashing the most horrendous punishment the earth has ever known, does God justify engaging in still more absurd and needless drama by turning a third of the oceans' waters into blood? And why only a third, and not three-fifths or five-eighths!? Also explain, if you will, why it is that God's angels of destruction are always impelled to blow trumpets before starting into their work! And finally, if God is so adamant that humanity be fully prepared for the onset of his Great Tribulation, then why doesn't He just give 'em the *exact freakin' date*!!???

But never mind the rhetorical questions, O ingenuous devotee. *Praise to the power of demagoguery, and glory to the Gaaawwwd of the church-centric cosmos!!!*

[Laughing heartily, I applauded with gusto.]

DK: Bravo! Bravo!

[Beaming from ear to ear, Jesus stood up and gave an exaggerated stage bow.]

J: Thank you, one and all…

DK: Wow. Just as we're winding down, you go and get all wound up. But I think I've got the picture. When Revelation is interpreted literally, God becomes a cruel and insensible nutcase.

J: So it's easy to see why some early church leaders didn't want John's "holy" vision included in the official canon. Personally, though, my biggest problem with Revelation is totally unrelated to its *enigmatic* passages. What bothers me most are the parts that are clearly spelled out. For starters, Revelation's focus is strictly on the future, thereby disregarding the only moment that ever counts: the *now*. Revelation's cast-iron predictions leave no room for human ingenuity, social progress, or general spiritual advancement. In fact, its prophecies could rightly be viewed as God's very own prediction regarding his gross failure to triumph over Satan before most of the damage is done—a personal admission of his staggeringly blundering inability to save his fallen world.

But the literalist remains unfazed. To him, any suggestion of world peace prior to apocalyptic catastrophe would border on heresy. Peaceful, pre-Rapturous resolutions to earthly problems are out of the question, and Revelation's advocates have no use for the *present* except to make fearful preparation for an ominous, doom-filled *future*.

DK: How disheartening.

J: Not for the literalists it isn't. They don't view this dismal prophecy with the slightest degree of dejection or grief. On the contrary, they seem to *relish* the prospect of world destruction and can't wait for the gruesome games to begin!

DK: I've heard it said that, for those who have their spiritual houses in order, Revelation offers hope of redemption and everlasting joy.

J: Boy, when life gives lemons to a literalist, he doesn't just make lemonade—he starts a full-blown *orchard*. Look, there's nothing hopeful about a scenario that brings peace and salvation to a relative few while nearly everyone else is flung to the wolves. First they endure dreadful *earthly* annihilation and then, after the Judgment, ghastly *eternal* torture. Of course, it's only natural that a literalist doesn't fear the Rapture, since he smugly assumes that he's *special* and will therefore go soaring off the planet before incurring any harm. The only ones in distress will be the poor schmucks who didn't listen to his sanctimonious ranting about God's precious "elect."

DK: So the literalist figures the first trumpet will give him the last laugh.

J: Yeah, but verily I'll tell ya this: anyone who would take delight in the sufferings of another is as far from the Christ spirit as you could possibly wander. He wouldn't know me if I showed up in his living room with a six-pack and three cherubs.

DK: It seems that Saint John's vision of vengeance violates nearly every high moral principle that Jews and Christians ever embraced. In fact, by the time Revelation rolls around, the Almighty has done a complete U-turn from the first chapter of Genesis: And God saw everything that He had made, and behold… it sucked.

J: Unfortunately so. The God of John's notorious vision suddenly renounces the theme of forgiveness advanced in the gospels and inexplicably reverts to his Old Testament persona. Once again He resorts to addressing problems through violence and bloodshed. But aside from making a total nincompoop of creation's Uber-Genius, the entire Tribulation forecast is also a giant contradiction *theologically*—that is, if you put any faith in 1 John 2:16.

DK: You'll have to spell it out. I'm a little groggy.

J: In that passage the writer declares, "For all that is in the world… is not of the Father… And the world passes away." So the author of 1 John is clearly stating that the world has no ultimate validity and isn't a product of God's creation.

DK: Exactly what *you've* been saying all day long! *Sheesh*, I've read the New Testament twenty times over—but I never caught *that* before.

J: So now, literalist Christianity has another quandary on its hands. Because if the world is indeed a passing illusion, as scripture says, then why would God bother waging a long-publicized battle there? I mean what kind of jug head declares war on something that isn't real? In fact, why would God be the least bit concerned with *anything* "happening" in a world of dreams? But that's not the end of it. Another problem with this bleak vision is its total shredding of *my own* moral fiber. By way of John the Divine, I become history's greatest hypocrite.

DK: What's your reasoning?

J: Well, throughout Christendom I'm portrayed as the ultimate embodiment of compassion. For centuries, the church has presented me as the presumed Prince of Peace, the gentle Lamb of God—the great reconciler and redeemer of humanity. In the gospels, I consistently urge my disciples to practice unconditional forgiveness and to be loving and non-violent. How is it, then, that in the last days I suddenly change character entirely and return to earth as a vengeful, bloodthirsty warrior? In John's not-so-ecstatic vision, I'm inexplicably morphed into a death-crazed cosmic samurai. No longer intent on *saving* the world, I now return to utterly *destroy* it. I descend from heaven to inflict on the world a bitter and perverted "justice" consisting of Revelation's prophesied holy hell. In short, Hebrews 13:8 apparently has it all wrong: Jesus Christ may be the same yesterday and today—but not necessarily forever.

DK: Well, thank heaven. At least now I know I'm not crazy. For a long time, I questioned myself for refusing to join ranks with fellow Christians who were eager for the world's destruction. I always got the feeling that if the nukes weren't flying soon, these folks would be clinically depressed.

J: One of the laws of Mind is that whatever you focus on expands: you tend to create what you visualize and hold in your thoughts. So the most ironic part of this pathetic "end times" schlock is that John's wild prophecy could well become a self-fulfilling one. When millions of people hold fast to a vision, no matter how insane or destructive, they drastically increase its likelihood of manifesting. Remember: at some level, every thought creates. And the *collective* mind is *especially* powerful. If hell on earth is what people envision, that's what they're likely to get.

DK: Then what of your promise never to leave us or forsake us?

J: It's true that I'm with you always, even in devastation. But your choices remain your own responsibility. The *spirit* is never in danger—but nothing can stop you from blasting the *body* to kingdom come. Neither I nor anyone else can save humanity from self-inflicted stupidity. So consider this fair warning: if the warheads start falling, don't be gazing skyward expecting me to appear with a band of horn-blowing angels. We won't be arriving like the cavalry to levitate every harebrained fanatic with a death wish and take them hovering off to heaven.

DK: I imagine you could go hours picking Revelation to pieces.

J: Well, only its *literal* interpretation. For those with the ability to decipher it, the book is packed with hidden wisdom and prophecy, and the world will very soon begin to understand its true significance. For those who still insist on taking Revelation at face value, however, the main question they should be asking is this: Could God really be so brainless, warped and sadistic—or did John of Patmos merely ingest bad mushrooms?

CHAPTER SEVENTY

DK: As we head toward the home stretch, I don't think an interview with you would be complete without a serious discussion of miracles. Water to wine, casting out devils, instantaneous healings—it's all very inspiring. But calming a raging storm and walking on waves? Raising a man from the *dead*!? That's quite a bag of tricks. Compared with you, the average faith healer on TV is just a clever showman with a sponsor.

J: I said before that spirit is focused on *content*, not on form. Miracles are simply expressions of love, so they, too, are centered in content. Now, every thought is creative and there's no doubt that when the mind is changed, outer forms will frequently respond. But miracles aren't meant to *impress*: they're meant to *heal*.

DK: Heal what?

J: The only thing that's really sick: the separated mind. The mind that believes the universe is fragmentary and chaotic—the mind that sees everything as disconnected parts of a random collection. Miracles are reparative in the sense that they restore wholeness where there was separation, and peace where there was conflict. This unification occurs not in the *world* but in the *mind*. That's where the real healing is needed.

DK: Is anything beyond a miracle's power?

J: No, because nothing is beyond the influence of love. From hangovers to hangnails; from stormy seas to stormy relations; from outlaws to in-laws; from asteroids to hemorrhoids—miracles can change them all. But a miracle's *form* is relatively insignificant. It's the power *behind* the miracle that's important.

DK: How exactly do miracles heal?

J: By reminding those who witness them that their reality is far beyond the limitations of the body or the material world. The miracle heals by helping you remember who you really are.

DK: Speaking of miraculous healings, I've watched many a preacher lay hands on some trusting soul with an affliction, illness or disability. The preacher spouts off a prayer, invokes "the name of JAY-sus"—and then smacks the guy on the noggin. Next thing you know, the dude's falling backward into someone's arms and claiming to be healed while the ushers pass the collection. Is that a miracle?

J: It's a miracle no one's arrested.

DK: C'mon, I'm serious.

J: Maybe it's a miracle, maybe not. Healing and physical changes aren't the same thing: they occur on two different levels. A physical alteration doesn't always mean someone's healed. But then, nothing related to the body has much to do with genuine healing in the first place. This should be obvious, given the brief nature of any "cure." Despite all rituals or remediation, the body inevitably stops functioning anyway.

DK: Then some things that *appear* miraculous really aren't.

J: While some things that seem ordinary are actually quite miraculous. Most miracles can't be observed, because true miracles imply true healing, which is always of the mind. Miracles *must* focus on content instead of on form, since sickness originates not in the body but in the mind that holds the belief in separation.

DK: Do you still heal people?

J: I don't do anything else.

DK: How is that possible when you aren't here in the flesh?

J: Only my *spiritual* presence is required. I heal people the same way I urged *you* to do it early in the interview: by remembering their unity with God *for* them until they remember it for themselves. This practice works because it engenders peace, the number one prerequisite for real healing. You could even say that true health is nothing more than inner peace. But neither is it anything *less*.

DK: We've known for years that physical sickness is often psychosomatic. But do you mean to say that *all* sickness originates in the mind?

J: The entire *universe* originates there! Now, in a material world, bodies are naturally affected by elements and conditions. But consider someone whose body is ailing or diseased. If he's living from the peaceful center of his being, which is unaffected by circumstance, then is he truly sick? On the other hand, someone who's been "cured" of cancer may still be filled with anger, hatred, resentment, or some other form of fear. Is that person truly healed?

DK: So *real* healing comes from spiritual insight.

J: Right. Healing is merely the removal of all that stands in the way of knowledge. That's why a miracle's *form* doesn't matter. What matters is its *source*: the omnipotent love of God.

DK: What exactly constitutes a miracle?

J: A miracle is a change in *perception*—an inner shift from darkness to light. It may or may not involve the material world. Miracles supply a perceived lack until those they touch come to realize their wholeness. Miracles are miraculous because they bring more love and strength both to the receiver *and* to the giver. Therefore they seem to reverse the laws of time and space, which are always irrelevant to spirit.

DK: Let's talk about your own miracles. If the gospels have it straight, your various on-demand healings must've had folks rushing the stage. And what a great way to stuff rags in the mouths of your critics!

J: It's a mistake to think that I used miracles as spectacles to induce faith. Miracles are intended not to foster *new* beliefs but to shatter *old* ones. They help liberate you from your ideas of what's possible. After all, you can't think outside the box until you first realize that you're *in* it. And here's something else: if I were the only one capable of miracles, they'd be almost worthless. Miracles demonstrate that all of God's children are equal, both in power and in standing.

DK: It all *sounds* good. But personally, I need stuff I can see and touch... *you* know, some honest-to-goodness, crowd-pleasing displays of material manifestation and divine wonderment. Or at least something I can show off in Valet Parking.

J: *Oy.* Here I am, offering the keys to the universe, and you're wheedling for Cadillacs in the driveway!

DK: Hey, at least I'm *clear* in my depravity.

J: Look, miracles are *thoughts*, not *things*. The only ones worth having are those that reawaken you to your reality in God. Everything else is just a temporary fix. Even if you could do it—which you could, with the right understanding—changing water to wine wouldn't help you much. But offering love instead of hatred, forgiveness instead of condemnation, compassion instead of judgment—now, *those* are miracles that can transform your life! They can practically create heaven on earth. Believe me, you have no appreciation for the amazing power of love. One small change of heart. One harsh word withheld. One small act of kindness or a gentle smile at just the right moment, and you can literally change the world.

DK: Do miracles happen only to those who are spiritually worthy?

J: Realize that love is most needed when it seems least deserved. One reason you don't experience more miracles is because of your idea that some people are unworthy of your unconditional love.

DK: On the other hand—and pardon me for being so blunt—why would I bless someone who's a jerk?

J: The fact that a miracle may benefit *someone else* should never be your concern: the miracle always blesses *you*. The law of creation is that everything emanates *from* the self *to* the self. So a miracle withheld from your brother is a healing denied to *yourself*. Whenever you offer a miracle of forgiveness or love, everyone gains. Especially you.

DK: Noble spiritual ideals, of course. But how do love and forgiveness relate to things like walking on water?

J: Forget about walking on water. Concentrate instead on not walking over your brothers. Miracles are about *service*, not Nielsen ratings. Miracles are the greatest service you can render, both to others *and* to yourself. By offering miracles—that is, aligning your thoughts with spirit instead of with ego—you constantly affirm that you and your brothers are one. This simple process simultaneously re-awakens love in *your* mind *and* in theirs.

DK: So miracles are about shifts in *thinking*.

J: Only that. If conditions shift too… well, that's gravy.

DK: Then miracles have nothing to do with healing cripples, restoring sight to the blind, or raising the dead.

J: Nothing's impossible, of course—and miraculous healings occur every day. But the Bible stories detailing my miracles have much deeper significance than generally supposed. Miracles dissolve sick *thought patterns*. So metaphysically, they do indeed bring sight to the spiritually blind, movement to the spiritually paralyzed, and life to the spiritually dead. For those affected, being lifted out of such a state is nothing short of resurrection.

DK: You say nothing's impossible, but I would think that some things are simply beyond hope or healing. Some damage is beyond repair.

J: Miracles don't differentiate between big and small. That's part of what makes them miraculous. Since all effects are mind-made illusions, there's no situation the miracle can't heal. It can even undo the past in the present by showing you that your reality was never subject to temporal laws. The miracle is the most powerful tool for healing at your disposal, and its power is without limit.

DK: When is a miracle appropriate?

J: Whenever pain appears real. When suffering of any kind rises to blind you, turn within. Knowing you can never have peace for yourself alone, ask for peace for everyone concerned—no exceptions—then give the situation to the Holy Spirit. If you're tuned in, you'll know if there's anything more to do.

DK: It seems too easy.

J: Your contribution is small, yes—but it's *spirit* that works the miracle, not you. All that's required from you is a little willingness to see things differently. This subtle shift in thinking is what *A Course in Miracles* calls the "holy instant," of which it says, "You prepare your mind for it only to the extent of recognizing that you want it above all else. It is not necessary that you do more; indeed, it is necessary that you realize that you *cannot* do more. Do not attempt to give the Holy Spirit what He does not ask, or you will add the ego to Him and confuse the two. He asks but little. It is He Who adds the greatness and the might. He joins with you to make the holy instant far greater than you can understand. It is your realization that you need do so little that enables Him to give so much…"

DK: Then it's not *our* responsibility to decide what miracles are needed.

J: Definitely not. Miracles are natural and should be involuntary, like the beating of your heart. They arise without the least effort when you step aside and allow them to manifest. Simply inject a quiet, peaceful knowingness into any situation that seems to require healing. Call down peace for all involved, and then step back.

DK: But sometimes a *physical* response is needed.

J: If action is required, then act. In time, you'll learn to recognize when to get involved and when to refrain. Quite frequently, your best move is to heed the following *Course* reminder: "I need do nothing except not to interfere." Stop shouldering the heavy burden that you've got to save the world or figure out the answers. You can be the *agent* of miracles, but you're never the source.

DK: Isn't it presumptuous to be anticipating miracles?

J: Miracles are your natural reality. You can be sure that when they *aren't* occurring, something has gone terribly wrong. Here's a good motto: "Be realistic. Expect a miracle."

DK: Does that apply to any situation that causes concern?

J: Without question. The real power of miracles lies in their indiscriminating nature. Spirit doesn't distinguish between difficult and easy, so no circumstance is beyond transformation. But again, refuse to decide when and where miracles should arise, or what form they should take. You can't rely on physical appearances to evaluate a miracle's necessity—or even its effectiveness. Your field of vision is far too limited for you to know what's truly needed or what's happening at the deepest levels of consciousness. And don't forget: there's divine perfection inherent in every moment, if only you have "eyes to see." So quit trying to run the show. Just walk your journey, stay centered in the *now*, and let life handle the details…

CHAPTER
SEVENTY ONE

DK: Okay, one final topic. I recently read the fascinating story of an American woman, now deceased, who said that she was boarding a bus in Paris one day when her personality just instantly vanished. She said her sense of individuality was there one second and gone the next and that she suddenly realized, all in a moment, the delusion of the ego-based "self." She quickly lost all identification with the body, and in a flash her historical self-images faded into nothingness. As a Westerner unfamiliar with this "selfless" state, and with no teachers to guide her, the woman struggled for years trying to integrate her new perspective. Finally she did, and her life became a beautiful moment-by-moment experience of oneness, just as you've described.

J: Awakening does tend to happen abruptly. It's just a rapid, unexpected recollection of something you've always known. It's like trying to recall where you left your car keys: you can give it a lot of thought and still not remember. But then you're making a peanut butter sandwich and *wham*—suddenly it hits you. That's how it is with enlightenment. Depending on your resistance, though, it can take a long time before the revelation bubbles to the surface. In this case, the woman's experience on the bus was preceded by years of inner searching, most of which was happening far beneath awareness, in the deep, dark waters of the subconscious.

DK: I know that Buddhists are pretty big on this "no-self" concept—but they aren't the only ones. Over the years, I've read books, heard stories and watched videos about some of the great spiritual beacons of history. People like Saint John of the Cross,

Sri Nisargadatta Maharaj, Meister Eckhart, Ramana Maharshi and others. Like you, they all talk about the illusory nature of worldly existence.

J: As I've said, even across centuries, cultures and religions, enlightened individuals say pretty much the same things. They talk about the deception of the personality, or what you normally refer to as "I."

DK: Okay, so here's my question: did your own teachings touch on any of this stuff? And if so, how can you help us better understand it now?

J: The concept of "no-self" is pretty well known around India and in some of the Asian cultures. Their saints, sages and mystics have expounded on it for thousands of years, and even as a young man, I was profoundly influenced by these traditions. When I finally experienced this knowingness myself, I assimilated some of the ancient mystical teachings into my own. I alluded to the awakened, ego-less state by using terms such as "poor in spirit," "meek," "merciful" and "pure in heart." I talked about dying daily and losing your life in order to find it—that is, relinquishing your false sense of self to find the *true* self.

DK: Wouldn't it have been more helpful to have spoken of these things openly?

J: Not amongst Jews in ancient Palestine. Many would've considered it threatening—and I had enough trouble as it was. So I used parables and other coded messages to communicate with those who had been privately instructed in the cosmic mysteries. It was these people I referred to when I directed my teachings to those who had "ears to hear." Like many of my countrymen back then, modern Westerners find the concept of an impersonal "self" to be strange and incomprehensible.

DK: Well, it's hostile to our entire social structure.

J: Sure, because it threatens everything you're taught from childhood about the importance of the individual—the I, me and mine of your existence. You *glorify* this egoic sense of self, and you identify with it intimately.

DK: Maybe that's why so many of us feel compelled to make some kind of splash in the world.

J: Of course. You spend your whole lives literally "making a name"—that is, an identity—for yourselves. But in the blink of eye, all your self-images will vanish like snowflakes on red-hot coals.

DK: Ah, once again we're back to death—the conversational favorite of messiahs everywhere.

J: It's just that you've got to learn *balance*. In the West, you've focused on the body and largely ignored the spirit. In the East, they've done just the opposite. Neither path is correct, because both of them create a split in the mind. So it's important to understand that spirit and flesh are *both* expressions of the Absolute—one eternal and the other quite fleeting. Concentrating only on spirit creates animosity toward the physical, while becoming mesmerized by the physical tends to cause neglect of the spirit and makes you forget the very short-lived nature of the earthly journey.

DK: I'm not so sure. It could be that, somewhere deep within us, we *do* realize our mortality. That could explain why we spend so much time and effort establishing identities and building monuments to ourselves.

J: But the strategy of enduring through achievement has one small hitch: you're working to immortalize a self that doesn't exist.

DK: Well, that certainly seems to be the consensus of the Society for Gurus, Saints and Spiritual Know-it-Alls. But it sounds pretty crazy to those of us who still need a course on Enlightenment for Dummies.

J: The notion of a limitless, impersonal self contradicts all your cherished learning and challenges everything you believe about reality. It even threatens your social hierarchies, because it implies that, at the level of spirit, everyone is equal. To most Westerners, that kind of talk is okay for dinner parties and church socials—

DK: —but let's not get carried away and change the zoning codes, is that it?

J: Exactly. For many Westerners, the thought of real equality is revolting—especially for Americans, many of whom would rather be caught stealing cookies from girl scouts. After all, they've been raised in a culture that exalts "rugged individualism," embraces "manifest destiny," and venerates personal accomplishment. Americans wear their specialness like a badge of honor. Confronted with the prospect of being ordinary, some would almost prefer death.

DK: Hey, we Americans pride ourselves on standing out from the crowd.

J: Now, *there's* a piece of irony: I describe the ugly symptoms of a spiritual disease, and you brag that it's a national epidemic!

DK: I'm just having trouble with this "no-self" thing. I mean *everyone* has a unique sense of identity, right?

J: Yes, but it's generally based on the belief in separation. The belief in a personal self is strictly a delusion of the mind, caused by your identification with the body and the related thinking that centers on it—your continuous thoughts about "me and my story."

DK: Isn't that fairly normal?

J: It's normal—but it isn't *natural*. Many centuries before my birth, the Upanishads declared, "As a lump of salt dissolves in water and cannot be removed... even so, beloved, the separate self dissolves in the sea of pure consciousness, infinite and immortal. Separateness arises from identifying the self with the body, which is made up of the elements. But when this physical identification dissolves, there can be no more separate self."

DK: Alright, but if I lost my personal sense of identity, wouldn't I also lose motivation for living and accomplishing?

J: The only motive in the selfless state is love; any other motive can only lead to trouble. You'll find that the farther you travel along the spiritual path, the less you'll feel driven to *do* things or to make yourself extraordinary. You'll have no desire to feel special. It's not that you lose zest for life; in fact, you may go on to achieve things you never thought possible. But you'll no longer feel *compelled* or *obsessed* by doing or accomplishing.

DK: Okay, what else?

J: Well, in the early phase, when the old has fallen away but the new hasn't yet taken hold, you may feel like you've lost all ambition. You may sense that life has nothing to offer, that you no longer have any passion or special abilities and that there's nothing left to contribute. That's when you consider running for office.

DK: A comic to the very end!

J: Just keepin' things bubbly...

DK: Say, if it's that doggoned chirpy, why do so few people experience this "selfless" state?

J: Mostly because they don't *know* about it. I mean if you aren't *searching* for something, then you aren't likely to *find* it, right? Folks generally aren't aware that there's an escape from the tyranny of the mind's incessant demands and insecurities. Also, they see their problems as *external*—so they're constantly looking in the wrong direction for solutions. Knowing the selfless state is an indescribable blessing; but rare is the one who desires it wholeheartedly. Most people won't release their hold on the illusory self until it seriously fails them. Suddenly they realize the sham of its existence.

DK: Can anything be done to speed our awakening?

J: I know it's a paradox, but really there's nothing to do. There's only something to *see*. Just recognize your enslavement to thought, and identify the true motivating factors in your life: ask yourself what you're really serving. Watch the obsessive, contradictory, non-stop commentary occurring inside your head. Notice how ego has practically no use for the present moment, but instead uses the present only as a means for arriving at some moment in the future. Do these things consistently and you'll soon understand the acute need for change. To see your condition for what it is, simply become aware of your thoughts. Then question them to find out if they're really true. Observe how you're driven by the endless dictates of the mind, which is constantly seeking after pleasure and defending against pain.

DK: Should we meditate?

J: Meditation is really just an intentional abiding in silence. So even if you don't formally meditate, at least make time daily to get quiet and pay attention to the eternal stillness that dwells deep within. Also, catch yourself when you're daydreaming or lost in reverie. Remind yourself, a hundred times a day if necessary, to bring your awareness back to the present moment—the *now*.

DK: What's so important about awareness?

J: Awareness is crucial, because most thoughts aren't worth thinking, and in fact many are quite destructive and self-defeating. When you're captivated by the voices, conclusions and pictures in the head, you're at the mercy of the mind and its endless ruminations: the *mind* is using *you*. Awareness enables you to *consciously direct* the focus of your attention and to stand apart from your thoughts. Inquiry then allows you to determine if they're true and to consider what effect they have upon your life.

DK: Keep talkin', I'm all ears…

J: Another secret of the masters is to stop resisting life and trying to steer everything to your own advantage. Watch how the mind insists that every situation render it some sort of profit or pleasure. Notice how it operates from fear and how it compels you to manipulate, attack or withdraw in aloofness when it doesn't get its way. Observe how even slight disagreements result in greater feelings of separation.

DK: It's true. The mind can be wickedly vicious.

J: Yes, but be careful not to label or judge what you observe. Just watch the mind's continual machinations and ignore the compulsion to act on its every conclusion. The mere process of observing and questioning the mind will slow it down and help produce the transformation you're seeking. The healing is in the seeing.

DK: Anything else?

J: Practice patience and acceptance. When you find yourself stubbornly insisting or trying to manipulate, remember that although ego wants control, what *you* really want is *peace*. Very often, the result you're trying to force will ultimately cause you pain.

DK: But if we don't make things happen, then nothing gets done.

J: The *Tao Te Ching* speaks of "letting events take their course." It urges having without possessing, acting without expecting, and leading without controlling. These, it says, are the supreme virtues. So it's not just the action that's important, but the wisdom *behind* the action. For that, you need plenty of introspection.

DK: Then we're not talking about apathy or inertia.

J: Not at all. But realizing that you can't possibly know what's best, you cease trying to arrange things in ways you believe would benefit you most. From your limited vantage point, you're in no position to see what you truly need, and your attempts to control can only cause sorrow and needless delay. Remain peaceful, and tune into the natural flow and harmony of life. Whatever you do, stay firmly centered in the *now*. Live each moment as if it's the only time that exists—because in reality *it is*.

DK: It would seem that, in the end, spirituality is the only important aspect of our nature.

J: Try a little experiment. Sometime when you've got a few minutes and things are quiet, close your eyes and become aware of your energetic presence. Not the mind and its thoughts, but the very *essence* of yourself. Without resorting to old ideas or beliefs, ponder a few questions about this essence within. Is it spiritual, non-spiritual—or neither? Is it good, evil—or neither? Is it religious, non-religious—or neither? Is it human, non-human—or neither?

DK: What's the point?

J: If you're honest, you'll discover that none of these definitions applies to the infinite, indefinable self. Even the term "spiritual" is just another concept, and it's ultimately as useless as dirty bathwater. You *are* what you *are*. Why label it?

DK: You advise to seek the true self, but how can we find it if we don't know what it is?

J: *What you're seeking is seeking you.* It can't be difficult to find what you already have or to be what you already are. Your awakening is inevitable, and the joy you so badly desire is already yours. The main task is to see the false and let it go. Maintain a one-minded devotion to removing the barriers, and the real will come flooding into awareness. That's the secret of the saying, "…therefore when thine eye is single, thy whole body also is full of light…"

DK: So persistence is the key.

J: Yes, but it's a persistence without "doing." You just gently look past everything that floats across the mind until—one day, perhaps—you suddenly see something you recognize as the real you. Be like the man who's digging for gold. He simply scraps everything that *isn't* gold until he hits the mother lode. And don't settle for the emptiness of paralyzing *beliefs*, which are "fool's gold." Have the courage to forget all ideas you ever held, and keep questioning until you know and you *know* that you know.

DK: Sounds rather draining.

J: Not nearly as draining as trying to preserve an insane persona with no basis in reality. Take refuge in the fact that, with the universe working in your behalf, you can't fail to realize the truth of your being. When confused or discouraged, just ask for help and remain open.

DK: Open to what?

J: The unexpected…

Conclusion

DK: Wow, what a day. Considering the two thousand year layoff, I'd say you've done pretty well.

J: Like fallin' off a cloud. So is it time for my big monologue?

DK: Yep, the floor... uh, that is, the ground's all yours. You talk and I'll write. But do me a favor and try to finish strong: the publishing business is *brutal*.

J: Don't worry, I've always had a flair for dramatic endings.

DK: I'm a captive audience...

J: Well, the very first thing you've got to understand, if you *really* wanna change your life, is that you have an almost paranoid *resistance* to change. You think you want change? Come off it! Stop kidding yourself! You don't really *want* to wake up—you much prefer sleep. One of religion's most appealing qualities is that it tends to keep you gazing comfortably *outward*. You're all the time talking about God and how He'll make everything wonderful after you die. The last thing you're interested in is shining the light on *yourself, right this minute*. Instead, you deal with externals. You focus on the world as primary cause and then formulate all kinds of wild theories about reality. It never occurs to you to ask if *you* had anything to do with it.

To realize any meaningful change in the way you experience life, you'd have to start by examining what you think you already know. If you're not willing to do *that*, then you may as well quit now. You won't take a single step forward until you're ready to question your sacred beliefs and your philosophical foundations—because *those* are the things causing you to perceive the universe as you do.

In the case of Christianity, you have to begin distinguishing between a religion *about* Christ and the wisdom teachings *of* Christ. The first is mostly contrived and all about *effects*; the second is entirely centered on *Cause*. That means *you*. You've got to start looking at *yourself* as the cause of your own worldly predicament. It's all about making conscious that which is presently *un*conscious. Who is the "you" that seems to be experiencing this strange, dreamlike world of fear and separation? Can you see that your unquestioned thoughts are controlling how you perceive your 'reality'? And how did it all come about? Could it be that *you* had a hand in your arrival here?

If you can't even begin to engage that line of thinking, to consider that your mind is that powerful, then once again you're stuck. No progress is possible until you accept some responsibility for your own experience.

And here's where you've got to ask how your religion fits in. Has it really served you? Has it ever once urged you to ruthlessly and dispassionately question your hallowed beliefs? Even your beliefs about God? Not likely. Most of the church's energy is spent expounding upon *my* name, upon *my* experiences—upon *my* significance.

Not only have they missed the point, but their approach is simply not viable. Because if you're gonna present someone as a heaven-sent soul saver, then you'd better have rock-solid proof about two things: that the soul is actually endangered and that said godman is capable of saving it. I mean you don't just create a new line of dogma, call it religion, and then threaten or censure anyone who doesn't bow in homage. While religion has for centuries put skeptics on the defensive, the skeptics are under no obligation whatsoever to disprove religion's outlandish claims.

Just as with science, the burden of proof for important assertions must always fall to *believers*, not to the dubious. And when it comes to backing Christianity's sweeping and stupendous declarations, the church plainly doesn't have the goods. *And they know it.* All the major tenets of Christianity were stolen from much older traditions, and only the most highly uninformed could fail to know this. So the church's position is flat-out untenable, and every facet of its bizarre godman story, with its ages-old theology of soul corruption and potential damnation, can be thoroughly dismantled—completely and forever demolished—by way of two simple words: "Prove it."

I suppose some will say that it just takes faith. But faith in *what*, I ask? Faith in a God who sits ready to torture billions of his own children for all eternity, simply because they were *human*? Faith that the God of the Bible, the harsh character who reportedly committed all those savage acts of insanity, is somehow worthy of your devotion? Faith that He'll show mercy and benevolence if only you'll profess *me* as your Lord and savior? Because if you can force yourself into believing *all that*, then I'd say you damned sure *do* have an ocean of faith.

But there's a wide gulf between childlike faith and childish credulity. As a rational being, you have to determine if your faith is *intelligent*. Can it bear the light of reason? Or do you fear using reason to examine your faith? If so, then you actually fear the power of your own mind. And if you fear your mind, then you must believe it's at the mercy of something *beyond* it. So what is it that you fear? Is it the phantom demon you refer to as Satan? And is his influence on your mind stronger than God's? If you're afraid to scrutinize your ideas about God by subjecting them to reason, then you must fear that your God is literally *un-reasonable*. And if *that's* true… well, then you've *really* got something to fear.

As you've discovered today, very little of Christianity can withstand careful inspection. So why, despite its pitifully shallow body of "evidence" and the extreme nature of its claims, does the church continue to attack its critics? Why does it threaten the very souls of those who question or disbelieve its story?

Consider this: how much confidence would you have in a scientist who made fantastic claims of some tremendous new discovery and yet became angry and resentful—even hostile—when his claims were questioned? What if he insisted that everyone should simply take him at his word? What would be your impression if he disparaged anyone who disputed his findings even though, when pressed, he couldn't actually prove them? With the possible exception of politics, where except religion does the world so meekly accept the dismissal of critical thinking and objective inquiry?

Perhaps we can agree, then, that with religion, as with any other subject of importance, some level of impartial assessment is paramount. Let's take as an example one of Christianity's foundation stones: the Crucifixion. Unlike the Resurrection, whose acceptance requires high levels of faith, the Crucifixion is an event that even a skeptic can entertain as at least an historical possibility. That is, no one could deny that a little-known religious reformer in ancient Palestine may have been unjustly killed. The problem lies in the church's *explanation* of these events: namely, that God drew up a plan several thousand years ago to incarnate on a suicide mission wherein He allows Himself—in the form of his alleged "only Son"—to be unfairly murdered in order to give Himself permission to absolve mankind's moral defects. And let us not forget that human beings' "sinful" nature was, by way of free will, a possibility incorporated into their design by this very same deity!

But even if you manage to conquer the mountain of intellectual challenges presented by this spectacular saga, and even if it *had* transpired exactly as claimed, who did it *benefit*? Certainly not the murdered man himself. Nor can we find any reasonable argument that the Crucifixion was of any real use to God, who can easily forgive his children without spilling anyone's blood. So the only answer that *might* make sense is that the Crucifixion somehow helped humanity. But again we've got to ask, "How?" How did my death benefit mankind in a way that the average person would find sensible and needn't take anyone's word for?

Do you see my point? Christianity simply asks too much. I mean it's one thing to talk about a whale swallowing a man. But now, to qualify for entrance to heaven, man is expected to swallow the whale!

And not only does the Christian story fail to pass any reasonable standard of scrutiny—or even the simple benchmark of common sense—but neither does it lend itself to any sort of *internal* verification: the Crucifixion as a response to human frailty is not an intuitively natural or intelligent solution to *anyone*. Thus, why should any greater credence be afforded the Christian view of salvation than is given to those of the Hindus, Muslims or Buddhists?

In the end, of course, it doesn't matter what arguments you employ, what info you dig up on the Bible, or what facts you may gather about its contents. All your scholarly research, your archaeological endeavors, your fancy syllogisms and your highbrow theories are ultimately useless. Because sooner or later you've got to confront one question: Do you really believe in the irrational, violent, impetuous and judgmental God of the Bible? Is this *really* the deity you worship? If it is, then you're only embracing his purported doctrines out of fear—you're just covering the bases. There's no way on earth you could truly *love* this frightening character, because there's nothing remotely lovable *about* Him.

So even if Bible literalists, using convoluted arguments and plenty of smoke and mirrors, can circumvent or rationalize all biblical errors and contradictions, they still have the impossible task of explaining how a "God of love" could also be a God of murder, injustice and so on. But since literalists are forced to continue trying to justify the unjustifiable, then justify they will. If you're taken in by those arguments, you're doomed: you'll never move beyond mere *beliefs*. And that's why Bible literalism is a problem. If you can't get past its surface, then you're stuck with an intellectually stifling thought system and a deity who's often evil, sadistic, hypocritical—and sometimes just plain dumb.

But okay. Perhaps you still insist on labeling yourself, on calling yourself a Christian—on assigning personal qualities to the miraculous, self-aware field of pure consciousness that's really you. Alright, fair enough. That's your prerogative. But if you *are* going to follow the Christian path, then at least do a little internal digging: determine *why* you're committed—and what exactly you're committed *to*. Don't be like Augustine, who admitted outright that he would never have believed the Christian story but for the fact that the "authority" of the Church *compelled* him to do so.

Far too many religious devotees have never really bothered examining the basis of their convictions. Perhaps they fear they'll wind up like Mother Teresa, who spent the last fifty years of her life tormented and secretly fighting waves of depression about her faltering faith. Her experience just didn't sync in any significant way with the church's claims regarding the nature of God and reality. While millions looked on in admiration, Teresa was filled with dark despair. "If only they knew," she confessed in her diary. The poor woman's belief system had completely collapsed—she questioned God's very existence. "Heaven means nothing," she declared hopelessly. Other Christian saints have struggled with the same doubts. Even the respected church father Tertullian could justify his Christian faith only by resorting to a kind of desperate reverse rationalization: "I believe it *because* it is absurd." Absurd indeed. I mean with *that* kind of reasoning, why rule out an Easter Bunny?

But let's suppose that you can indeed accept it all without question. Still, as a Christian, you've got to know that any meaningful practice of your religion would have to entail some soul-level, Christ-like *understanding*. Some real, spiritual maturity. Some genuine tolerance, forgiveness and compassion. Even Buddha, Confucius and Lord Krishna required the same. So your *thinking*, which is only the first step on the long journey of spiritual awakening, must eventually blossom into *wisdom*. And there's no wisdom in maintaining a set of dogmatic beliefs that pits you or God against your brothers and sisters. That kind of thinking doesn't benefit *anyone*.

My call to my disciples was always to seek the kingdom within. This has nothing to do with changing the world or anyone in it, and the farther you progress, the more you'll realize that proselytizing is a total waste of energy. Because other people are not the big problem. *Your thinking* is the big problem. So quit using your theology as a nightstick. When you allow religion to convince you that God kills in order to save, and that He condemns because He loves, you've gone way past devotion and become insane.

Life is short, my friend. It's like a carnival: a little cotton candy, a few cheap thrills… and suddenly it's time to go home. So now, using the words of scripture, you've got to "put off childish things"—things like searching outside yourself for love, security and a sense of worth. The mature of spirit know that these blessings, to be authentic and lasting, can only be found within.

It's time to wake up, pilgrim. Time to see the suffering caused by the mind's neurotic grasping, conditioned thinking, and habitual need for control. Time to end the incessant compulsion to fulfill every desire in hope that doing so will finally bring you the peace you seek. That peace is yours already, and the way to have it—the golden path back to heaven—is simply to become aware that you *want* it. Then, make the *choice* for peace. *In this moment.*

Each choice for peaceful awareness is essentially a decision to heal. And because all things are connected, whenever you make this choice, you make it not for yourself alone but for *everyone,* across all dimensions of time and space. For when you choose peace over conflict, and awareness over mindless identification with thought, you transform the universe in ways you can't possibly imagine. In the beautiful words from *A Course in Miracles,* you influence a constellation larger than anything of which you ever dreamed…

EPILOGUE

I awoke that evening to a million chirping crickets and the incessant rattle of cicadas across the countryside. I was sitting alone in my chair by the river—the second chair now empty, just as it had been in my pre-visit dreams. Still groggy, I checked my watch. A little after ten. I was filled with an eerie sense of expansiveness, unconfined by the usual constraints of time or perception.

What had happened? I was confused, to be sure. But I remembered—and quite clearly—that I *seemed* to have spent the entire day conversing with Jesus. I recalled that during our last thirty minutes together, I had asked Jesus if he would be willing to guide me in a short meditation. He agreed and suggested that I close my eyes. A few minutes into the exercise, I apparently lost conscious focus, and I simply do not recollect anything beyond that point.

As full awareness returned, I noticed there was a beautiful full moon gracefully providing sufficient light for me to gather my belongings, load up the truck and head back to the small town where I had rented a motel room the night before. The long day had caught up with me and I was dead tired. Despite my tremendous fatigue, however, I did not sleep well.

∾

I arrived home two days later, on Tuesday, around eight in the evening. I was road weary and mentally exhausted. I had tried almost continuously during the drive back to understand what had taken place there at the river. Was I delusional? Had I really had an all-day conversation with Jesus?

Unable to reach any conclusions, I decided just to forget it and focus on unpacking my bags, taking a relaxing bath, and then getting an early start on the sandman back in the familiar comfort of my own bed.

After hauling my things inside, I grabbed the small duffel I had used to store the few hundred pages of my handwritten notes taken during that long, mysterious day in the country. If nothing else, I thought, at least I have the notes to provide consolation that my experience had borne *some* kind of reality.

I pulled out the ream-size cardboard box into which I had hastily thrown the thick stack of handwritten pages after waking up by the river that night. Until this moment, I hadn't given them any thought; but now I was driven to have a quick, reassuring look, hoping to glean one last bit of emotional comfort from them before getting ready for bed. The notes, after all, were the one solid piece of "evidence" that I wasn't going nuts.

Placing the box on the kitchen table, I removed its lid. Suddenly I froze, barely able to move or think. There before me was the full conversation, word for word—but gone were the scores of personal jottings, along with the entire shorthand transcription of the day's lengthy dialogue. Not a single line of my own handwriting remained. Instead, the pages were fully typed-out in the favored font that I routinely use when composing at my computer. From all appearances, they might have been freshly coughed from my printer just a few minutes prior.

So upsetting and confusing was this development that what little energy I had left seemed to drain right out the bottoms of my feet, as if someone had pulled the plug on my body's electrical circuits. Nearly incapacitated with disbelief, I felt the immediate need to lie down and shuffled, stupefied, to the nearby sofa, practically collapsing into its cushions.

The rest of the evening is a complete blank, and I did not stir until sometime around two the following afternoon, having slept more soundly, and awoken more peacefully, than I had in many years.

Over the following months, as this manuscript began circulating, I was often asked, sometimes with hostility, how I could justify my story's mind-blowing claims. At first, I would dive into lengthy descriptions of the events leading up to my experience, trying hard to convince the skeptics of my earnestness and integrity. Most were left unimpressed. Finally, I gave up and began offering a far simpler response, the one I should have been using all along: "It's the inscrutable mystery of God," I would tell them.

And who can argue with a statement like that?

◌

ACKNOWLEDGEMENTS AND RESOURCE MATERIALS

'There is nothing new under the sun," says the writer of Ecclesiastes. Likewise, a great deal in this book has been conceived, spoken or written about by others across the last two millennia. The vast portion of the interview is original—but some is not, and after more than fifty years of living I cannot always recollect the sources for a given line or concept. I do forthrightly admit, however, that I have borrowed, and quite freely, from the works of many, and even when I have not quoted directly I have often paraphrased. Naturally, any errors are strictly my own responsibility.

Though countless books and other writings were utilized in creating this manuscript, the following have been especially helpful or influential and are recommended:

- *A Course in Miracles*, published by the Foundation For Inner Peace. This is doubtless the most life-changing book I have ever read. Especially useful—and challenging—for those who operate primarily from the intellect.

- *The Jesus Mysteries* by Timothy Freke and Peter Gandy. This was *The Daily Telegraph's* Book of the Year in 1999. The footnotes section alone is an education in itself, and the book should be required reading for every serious Christian.

- *Jesus Christ, Sun of God* by David Fideler. An academic masterpiece, this book, too, should be on most Christians' reading list. Packed with fascinating, in-depth information on the symbol-rich "paganism" that came to form so much of the Christian religion.

- *I AM THAT* (Talks with Sri Nisargadatta Maharaj). This Indian saint, like Sri Ramana Maharshi and others, is considered by many of his devotees to have been a pure embodiment of the enlightened soul. In these marvelously transcribed interviews, his words are as powerful, cutting and transformative as any I have encountered. A spiritual classic for the serious seeker.

- *The Power of Now* by Eckhart Tolle. This book is no secret among the metaphysical crowd, having now sold several million copies worldwide. Helped by his extended appearances on "Oprah," Tolle has become a true world teacher and has led countless humans to their first real understanding and experience of the power of "presence." A beautiful, long-needed blending of East and West, this is, at last, accessible spirituality for everyone.

Thanks are due as well to Byron Katie, the late Anthony De Mello, the late Malachi Martin, and to Dr. L. David Moore, himself a devout Christian and the brave author of *The Christian Conspiracy*. I also thank the Truth Seeker Company for their generous allowance of the use (and merciless mangling) of their materials, especially the "Open Letter to Jesus Christ" by D.M. Bennet, founder and first editor of Truth Seeker. Through their books and writings, many, many others have unknowingly contributed to the development of "Wrestling," and if I have failed to give credit where it is due, please feel free to contact the publisher and we will try to correct legitimate oversights in any future editions.

On a final note, I am wholeheartedly grateful to friends Alison, Brian, Cal, Pam and Patricia for their unflagging encouragement and support over the nine long, difficult and doubt-filled years during which this book evolved. Perhaps I am living proof of the following words: "Whatever you can do or dream you can, begin it. Boldness has genius, power and magic in it."

D.K. Maylor

44888271R00268

Made in the USA
Charleston, SC
06 August 2015